MY LIFE FOR YOURS

Frederick Borsch

ISBN: 1500179299
ISBN 13: 9781500179298

1

June 23 1994

Manslaughter has always sounded like a terrible word to me—worse than homicide. Whatever crime has been committed, I have to believe I am responsible. I am beginning to think there are ways in which two people have died—or are dying.

I have done a fair amount of writing in my life but have never kept a journal. I am starting this to try to stay a little sane and so there might be a record of some sort. Maybe it will help keep part of me—and maybe in some sense both of us—alive.

Yesterday I went to the gym at about four in the afternoon. That was twenty-four hours ago, but it seems my lifetime. I was going through my usual routine of pushing and pulling on the various exercise machines, somewhat bored but giving thanks for my relative pain-free health and likely feeling smug to be around younger men and women at my sixty-eight years. It was just like I often did—perfectly normal, before my half-hour on the treadmill reading the paper or the latest New Yorker, and then, pray God . . . dear God, I pray now, heading home to my house and to Susan and a shower, giving Barney a good tummy rub, maybe the evening news and a Scotch or two. Probably there would be a ballgame on TV. I would give anything to be able to do that now.

I was on that machine where you reach back and pull pads to your chest, facing across where there was a young man pulling up on a biceps strengthener. (I never learned the names of all these muscle-building contraptions.) I had noticed him before, but now he was right in front of me. I swear to God I was not staring at him. I was not fantasizing anything. He seemed relatively handsome though with a baseball cap turned backwards on his head, and a bit unkempt, needing a shave. But it was his body that was difficult not to notice— probably a good six feet tall, hard-muscled though still lithe-looking with a kind of olive-shaded skin. And he was pulling a ton of weight, exuding youth and strength. I was not trying to play some imaginary games. I was just wondering what it might be like to be young with a body like that—how it might feel.

Then he looked up at me. I started to look away. I swear that was all. His mouth seemed to open as though he might be going to say something, but it was more like his eyes locked on mine. I may have felt a moment of dizziness, but it was all so quick.

Next thing I am looking at me crumpled on the floor beside that chest-pulling machine, though otherwise I had not felt anything. Nothing hurt, but I could not help seeing it was me in the gray UCLA shirt, blue shorts, my gym shoes— my own face, mouth sagging, eyes staring vacantly.

I shook my head. Maybe this was some out-of-the-body experience. But how could it be if I was still breathing— could shake my head? I drew in a deep breath to prove it. I held up my arm. What in God's blessed name?

Someone yelled. I do not remember what. Someone shouted, "Get a doctor!" and then there were other gym guys between me and . . . me.

"No. He's not breathing," it was a woman's voice, and then I could see that big Russian man—must have been twice my size—was laying on top of me trying to give mouth-to-mouth, until an even bigger guy shoved him to the side and started rapidly pushing up and down on my chest. "Still not breathing." "C'mon. C'mon."

"Anybody know who it is?" I could tell them but kept staring stupefied, beginning to have trouble breathing, too, and chilled, trembling in the legs.

"They've called an ambulance," which makes sense I thought—realizing I was trying to distance myself at least a little. I should try to be objective and then to insist that this could not be really happening. It is a dream. It is a bad dream. I will wake up.

How many times I have told myself that since—squeezing my eyes and then popping them. Even slapping my face. "Wake up, idiot! Wake up."

"Oh, God," muttered the skinny older woman with the frizzy red hair, probably as old as I am. "I've seen him here lots of times. He looks dead. I don't know his name."

The Russian guy gave up and stood. He must have weighted two-forty at least. The other guy kept pumping on my chest. If my sternum was not broken yet, it was close. A couple people walked away, shaking their heads. A siren wailed in the distance.

Of course, I could tell them his name, but could not think what to say or how to say it. I could even take them to his locker and open it with my combination 10-34-24. "There. That's who he is. There is his wallet. There are the keys to my practically new SUV."

Maybe they would then think I had something to do with it—at best involuntary manslaughter of somebody.

3

"He's probably dead," a teen-ager said matter-of-factly to my chest pumper. He stopped and looked up for a second, but then insisted, "No. I thought his eyes maybe fluttered. They're not brain dead until four or five minutes if only I can get him going again."

The siren hee-hawed several times closer and stopped. In seconds the EMTs in their baggy yellow clothes were wheeling in their gurney. The bigger one shoved the chest pumper off me and was checking for a heart beat—any vital signs. It looked like he gave me a shot of some kind.

He stood up. "Any one know who this old guy is?"

I had been coming to this same gym for eight, maybe ten years and no one knows who I am. I recognized three or four of the people standing around whom I talked to now and then but did not know their names either.

That's when I threw up the first time. It was almost projectile vomiting. I do not know if he had even felt sick. It just happened. People backed off—started to scatter.

"Let's get him out of here to the hospital," the head medic said to the others and then looked at me. "You gonna be all right, kid. You look kind of pale." I put my head down on the bar of the biceps machine. The back of my throat burned. "What?" I got out. Everyone was now looking at me. "I mean . . . I mean. . ." *What could I mean?* "I think that's me", I wanted to say. "I mean that is me—Harold Barnes." Instead I said, "Yeh," wiping my mouth and then the front of my shirt with my gym towel.

They loaded me on to the gurney and in doing so uncovered my New Yorker lying under me. "Here, look," the chest thumper held it up. "If this is his, it's got his name and address on it."

"Great," the head medic grabbed it. "Let's get him out of here." And like that I was gone.

A slight Asian woman and a pale, skinny kid with glasses began swabbing at my mess. It looked like half of the gym had bailed out, but there were still several jogging away on their treadmills and a beefy, brunette, showing a lot of skin, was assiduously pushing her knees and thighs out and in, out and in.

Life goes on, I told myself, numbly aware that I did not know what that meant for me and that no one was paying attention anyway.

I tried to think . . . to imagine: I should go to the hospital. I should tell them who I was and claim my body. Get back into me. Encino Hospital would be the nearest. Maybe I could first get my wallet and keys out of my locker: 10-34-24.

Both the kid and the woman with their buckets and mops were eyeing me. "You going to be OK, young man?" she asked. "You don't look so hot."

"I am fine," I replied as normally as I could. The words were mine, but the voice was a pitch or so higher without the huskiness I had developed.

Traces of vomit yet burned in the back of my throat—even into my nasal passages. I felt like I could throw up again.

"You sure," she asked. "We could get those doctor fellows back again. Don't want two of you."

"No. No. No." I stood up. "I am OK." And it did feel better to stand, but now I also saw the cop. I suppose he had shown up just to be sure . . . what do they say? That there had been no foul play.

"God, officer," I would explain to him after I went to my locker. "I just wanted my keys. I just wanted to get into my car and drive to my house and tell my wife . . ." What would I tell Susan? "Look, honey. It is me. It really is me inside this guy's body. I know the hospital may have called. I am so sorry if I scared you. But it is going to be fine. All right?"

She would scream. "Don't you like me like this?" I would try to joke—try to hug her. She would scream more loudly. Alicia would come running over from across the street. She had probably been watching anyway. Maybe she had already called the police.

And if I dialed 10-34-24 on my blue lock, grabbed my keys at least, what if the cop looked me over. "Are those yours, young fella? Do you have any I.D. on you?" Maybe they'd think I had something to do with this, and, if I did get in my car, what if someone spotted me. Sooner or later it would be reported as stolen. Then what? Me with his car and his wallet shouting it was not who I looked like and I was really him . . . I mean, me? Even if I ditched my car somewhere, maybe his fingerprints would be the ones on it.

I was still standing in place. The woman had put the mop in her rolling pail and now leaned on it, watching me. The sweet-sick smell of vomit had not been entirely covered over by the Pine-Sol or whatever they used.

I tried walking. It felt a bit awkward, but I could do it. Everyone knows how to walk. These were strong legs, and I was a half a foot taller. I listed and righted myself. "Thanks," I said to the cleaning woman. "See you later."

I could feel something in my right pocket against my leg. It was a set of keys—what looked like a couple of house keys and a car key. I glanced around. There were still people working out, but less than there would usually be at this time in the afternoon. The wall clock read quarter-to-five. I had been working out for ten or fifteen minutes before it happened. Not more than a half-hour had gone by since . . . whatever happened.

The policeman was at the check-in counter with the large, red Bally's sign behind it. It was just like always except for the cop chatting away with a pretty blond girl not much out of high school. She might have been going through some records for him. She looked up, smiling: "Hope you enjoyed your work out." She had nice teeth. The cop did not even glance at me. He said something to the girl. She laughed.

I was then outside, taking a half-flight up to the parking lot which seemed less full than usual for this time of day. There was my two month old SUV—pearl white, they called the color. I had just had it washed yesterday. I did not have the keys. I wished I knew how to hot wire a car. I always locked my cars. On the back seat were the trousers and a sweater of Susan's I had picked up at the cleaners. "Where should I hang this for you?" I would ask as I crossed through the kitchen. "Here I'll take it, honey," she would start to kiss me if she had not already heard from the hospital. She would get Alicia to drive her down perhaps already having heard I was dead. "Can't you please do something? Get him breathing again. Please. Please."

And maybe, when she took my hand, I did suddenly draw a breath. My heart started beating again. I was a medical marvel. But who or what would be in my head now?

I had to throw up again. I made it to the bushes. Not much to heave up this time. Mostly the dry heaves, but I felt a little better if weak.

The young guy's car key had Toyota stamped on it. Just in the row ahead I could see four or five of them—two newer looking ones. He probably would not have a new car, I reasoned. An older looking, blue Corolla had a good-sized dent in the driver's side back door. No one was around. No one was paying any attention to me. But no luck with the key. Still no one was paying any attention.

I peered into the Corolla in the next aisle. It looked like it might have been cared for. No obvious dents. Probably it had had a paint job—a soft silver with a red racing stripe. There was a small pile of clothes on the passenger's side seat. The key worked in the door.

I sat in the driver's seat. I shut the door, shaking some, gripping the steering wheel. To anyone looking it would appear to be my car, my steering wheel and my saint's medal dangling from the rearview mirror.

The sun was yet several hours to setting. It was a lovely late summer afternoon here in sunny Southern California— the light only beginning to slant, shadows to lengthen. But I have to stop . . . probably to throw up again in this crummy apartment of his. I feel awful.

Friday 24th

It seems strange that I slept through the night. It was at least eleven hours straight through after a miserable night before—so sick of stomach and heart. One good thing is that this kid's body must have a young prostate. I had gotten to the point where I had to get up to pee at least once and sometimes twice during the night.

Then I was hungry. I found some cereal but the milk smelled like it might be going sour. I ate a handful of dry raisin bran and then a couple slices of toast with strawberry jelly that was too sweet and topped that off with a peanut butter and jelly sandwich and some old orange juice. And it stayed down. I shaved with his razor and, holding his toothbrush under about two minutes of hot water gave his teeth a hard brushing.

Following a soapy shower and toweling, I could not help taking a look, first in the bathroom mirror, then moving to a full length mirror—with a crack in it—on his closet door.

I suppose I could have found something to critique, but not much. The guy was hard-muscled almost everywhere, with a flat stomach and mere touches of love handles. When I held up my arms and flexed, the biceps and pecs stood out. When I turned sideways and flexed again, the triceps ridged, almost bulged. According to the driver's license, he was six inches taller than I am at six foot two. The shoulders and neck muscles looked strong with a muscular upper back.

I felt like a voyeur, and, while genitals are never handsome, his penis looked good-sized to me. He was circumcised like I was. It began to lengthen just in my looking at it. I kind of danced on his good legs. I could make it all work. His dick flapped up and down. Everything felt so young and strong.

It was hard to tell about his hair. He had shaved it. Maybe he was balding, but, on a closer look, I do not think so.

I examined his teeth. Not bad. One of the cuspids was slightly turned. I guessed he had never had orthodontia, and maybe they were yellowing a tad. But it was a nice smile, maybe a little rakish because of the cuspid. I would not say he was all that handsome. The nose was kind of hawkish, and the eyes maybe too close together. But over all, it was a damn sight better than the semi-balding, somewhat portly guy I had become. I could imagine that he would be able to look a little sly, perhaps shy and cute while still very masculine.

I found myself staring into his eyes. They were a kind of gray-blue hazel, not unlike mine. They say that eyes are windows to the soul. I leaned closer trying to peer in to see . . . to see myself. I could see only eyes.

I stepped back. I flexed again. Fine muscles rippled on his chest wall. I could actually see and feel abs. His dick began to lift again. Maybe this made me a homosexual.

I found a reasonably clean tee shirt that had MASTERS OF THE WORLD stenciled on the back and a fading motorcycle over the chest. He apparently wore briefs, and I had worn boxers for years. I got on dark chinos and running shoes. They all looked too big but fit fine.

Now what? I do not know, and that is only part of my problems. It is just after eight. I read over what I wrote yesterday until I felt too sick to go on. Certainly it sounds agonized enough. I do not know how long I had sat there that late afternoon in his silver, maybe ten year old Corolla with my nearly new SUV only across the aisle and a few spaces away. I finally noticed that I had on those partial gloves worn by weight-lifters with my fingers poking through—gripping and ungripping the steering wheel.

I tried to concentrate. Maybe he kept his car insurance card in the glove compartment: flashlight, papers, the insurance card, two maps, and, underneath them, there was his wallet. I drew a deep breath and blew it out: not much, twenty-two bucks, but an ATM card, his credit card and his driver's license: Marcus D. Zito. 06-18-1968. His birthday was just a few days ago. He was twenty-six years old.

I turned the key. The engine coughed but then came on full-throat. He had a stick-shift, but I could manage that. The most natural thing in the world now would be to drive home—up the big hill to 1848 Colina where we had lived for almost seventeen years. By the time I got there this crazy dream would end as weirdly as it began. My garage opener would be on the visor. The door would lift to expose the innards I had recently straightened up at least a fair amount. "Honey, it is me. I am home."

But when I did finally shift my way up the hill in this at times complaining car of his, it did not look like anyone was home. Susan's Volvo, which she often left in the front of the garage, was not there. In his Toyota I drove slowly past, conscious of how tall I felt behind the wheel. I did a U-turn at the corner and came back. I noticed how the palm tree out front needed trimming. The beard hanging down could become a fire hazard. If only I could, I would call Juan about that tomorrow. If only I could, I would promise to get everything right. I would give up Scotch. I would give up . . . I did not have that much to give up. I would be a lot nicer to people, I would be more generous and give more money to charities.

Maybe Susan had forgotten something for our dinner and was down at Ralph's or Gelson's. Or—and I swallowed in a half-moan—she was at the hospital crying, "Hal, I love you so. Don't leave me like this. I love you." How could I tell her that this could be in some way my fault? After all our years together?

Or maybe I was suddenly reviving and coming around now: "What's going on? But might it be him rather than me in me? "Who are you, lady?" This was insane.

I did another U and parked in front of the Barrington's, hoping old Barry would not come out to check on this stranger casing our neighborhood. I tried to be rational. There has do be some way out of this. There had to be someway I could come home even if I was in another man's body. Were I able to sneak into the backyard, surely Barney would know who I was. Or my daughter Shelley lives only a couple miles away. I could go to her house and explain.

But then Shelley drove up and pulled into the space in front of the garage. In a hurry, she was still careful with little George and Katie, helping Kate out of her car seat and talking to them both before using her key to open the gate and the front door. George and Katie trotted behind, perhaps thinking they would be able to get into the pool.

It must have been another five minutes—probably more. I sat there in a state of paralysis, alternating between a terrible sadness and a kind of panic, over and again telling myself to be calm—to use my head—everything I had told my children and students for years. It may look bad now, but . . . I may have even tried to pray, but for what?

Susan drove up as our garage door rose on the side where I usually parked my car. I could see her get out. Was she wiping at her eyes? The door swung shut.

I could only think that I must have died. And they were inside crying. Maybe even George was sobbing, if nothing else in sympathy with his mom and grandmommy, with Katie wide-eyed, trying to figure out why all the crying. And tears were dripping down his cheeks, coming from my eyes on my cheeks, salty. This was all my fault. It did not have to happen. My dad and Uncle Ron had both died of heart attacks, and Dr. Leonard said he might have to start treating my blood pressure, but that otherwise I was in good health for my age.

I was blubbering—my nose beginning to run. I felt so sorry for them and for myself because I was dead . . . and was not. Nobody should have to go through this. "I love you. I love you so much," I sobbed. There had to be some way to fix this . . . to put a note under the door . . . to ring the door bell and quietly tell them things that only I could know so that they would have to know it was me . . . like this. Or would they only be terrified . . . call the police?

I drove away slowly, starting to go round the block, but then kept on down the hill, faster—then too fast—braking too hard. I could just ramp on to the freeway and plow into a semi or a bridge column so I would not kill anyone else—any one more.

I felt like I would be sick again. I needed to be inside somewhere and the only thing I could think of was his place—on Britton according to his license which should not be too far off Ventura. It was apartment 3-G on the insurance card.

It took a while to find a parking place. If the three story apartment building had a garage of some kind, I would not know how to get into it. But I had keys which were likely to an outer door and 3-G. The clothes on the passenger seat were probably headed for a laundromat. I left them but took a file with papers half-falling out of it from under them. I hoped I would not vomit again before I made it inside.

I could not make either key work in the door inside the little foyer, and, after, three or four tries, stupidly pushed the button for 3-G—almost immediately wishing I had not. What if he had a roommate . . . a him or her? I knew nothing about him.

What sounded like a woman's voice, but low and gruff came out of the intercom. "Who is it?"

"I'm looking for Marcus Zito," I spoke into the intercom as calmly as I could.

"You and everyone else," she said so sarcastically I could not guess what she meant. "What?" I replied in a strangled voice.

"He hasn't been here for two months," she went on. Then, I think, "Why doesn't Mark tell anyone?" though it was not easy to hear through the intercom. Next, in what seemed a sudden change of tone, "You wait there, honey."

I thought of beating it out of the cramped foyer and racing down the street to his car, but just stood, facing the heavy, probably reinforced door. It opened and there was a woman as big as I as Marcus or Mark was. She was rather heavily made-up, though in her way not all that unattractive—long blondish hair. It occurred to me that she could be a man dressed up as a woman—maybe a transvestite.

She showed me a lot of teeth and said, "Well, lookee here. You do look a little lost. You a friend of his?"

"Yes," I replied, "But I don't know him very well."

"Neither do I, but I'll tell you one thing; you're good-looking enough to be his brother. A cousin?"

"We are not related," I told her.

"Here's his new address." She gave me a slip of paper. It's only a few blocks away. Unless you want to come up and freshen up, lamby."

"I cannot thank you enough. But thanks, thanks very much. I'm not feeling so hot." I turned to get out of the little vestibule and on to the street. "You take care of yourself, honey," she called to my fleeing backside.

It took less than ten minutes to find the older looking building. I again did not know how to get into the basement garage, but this time the keys worked easily, and I began my first unhappy night in this two-room apartment. I left on his television for a kind of company, but was unable to take much of it in. There was nothing in the news about an old guy falling over dead in a gym nor about the strange disappearance of Marcus or Mark Zito except for his body.

That was two days ago. Now it is almost ten on Friday morning. With the curtains pulled all the way back, there is quite a bit of sunlight in what I guess you would call his living room. Somebody needs to straighten his place up. But I am restless. I am also hungry again.

Almost by default I drove to the nearby Ralph's and parked about where I usually parked. Although they occasionally would fool me by changing things around a bit, I knew every aisle and where most of the produce, cans and jars I wanted were. I recognized the faces of two of the check out women and a slightly retarded guy who bagged.

I stuck an L.A. Times under my arm and ordered corn beef on rye at the deli counter—with lettuce and tomato, light on the mayo but a good bit of country mustard. I found a cold diet coke and, prepared to surrender half of the twenty-two dollars, headed to check out.

But his credit card worked without a hitch, and I scribbled a signature. For all I knew he had a load of debt on it, but, hey! for the nonce I had the power of purchase.

I brought my goodies to one of the wrought-iron tables next to the fumes from the passing cars. I unfolded two of their skimpy paper napkins to make a little place mat and another for my lap, knowing I might well get some of the mustard on me anyway. I admired the stack of corned beef and the way the red of the tomato and the green of the lettuce contrasted with the umber of the bread. I sipped at the coke and took a bite of the sandwich, enjoying the different flavors and textures as I chewed.

There was nothing startling or particularly new on the front page of the Times: something about post-apartheid South Africa, more on the crazy O.J. Simpson murders. A B-52 crashed up near Spokane—apparently without nuclear bombs or else the whole state of Washington might be gone.

I pulled out the B-section, complimenting myself on how calmly I was acting. As though I were watching myself, I turned one page, another, a third, and there I was: "Local Educator," with a picture of me, smiling in an academic gown. I recognized the photo from a graduation ceremony several years ago. A couple of faculty members were in the background though one could not tell who they were in the picture. I appeared affable, even kindly—not too old-looking given my age. "Harold D. Barnes, a former Master Teacher and for ten years Head of Westview Academy, died on Wednesday of a heart attack while exercising at an Encino gym."

I could feel my heart beating, but again told myself that I was acting calmly, even rather coolly under the circumstances. No one watching would know that I was reading my obituary. A deep breath was all that it took. So I was officially dead. "Local Educator" did not sound all that significant, but, *fair enough*, after all.

I remember old Bill Barrington joking about how he checked the obituaries every day just to be sure he was not in them. I guess most people wonder what their obituary will read like. I heard about a college teacher who had people write their hypothetical obituaries to prod them into thinking about their lives and what they wanted to be remembered for.

Mine went on matter-of-factly. Nothing was misspelled or in error. I liked the stress on my earlier career as a teacher of literature and composition and that I had been given the designation "Master Teacher as a teacher of teachers." What I did not like was the reference to "the scandal of the student sex club." That was more than nine years ago, and I thought the school under my leadership handled it as well as could have been expected. No, even better. But one could not tell that from the brief reference, almost as though it had somehow marred my tenure.

A newspaper editor I knew once told me how reporters go to what he called the paper's "morgue" to mine information from old stories and articles when writing a story or obituary. The Times had loved that sex club story when it first broke and would not let go of it for several weeks. Now I felt like writing a letter to the editor setting the record straight. It would have to be from "anonymous" or else I would sign it "Harold D. Barnes, deceased," and the L.A. Times could have its first ever letter from the dead.

They got in the expansion of the student body and the building of the new science center and sports facility; then there was my education: both masters degrees; my parents were named, followed by "born and schooled in Pittsburgh," and my wife, children, two grandchildren, brother. And that was it. Period. Life summarized. Life over.

I took a long sip from the Coke, followed by another bite of sandwich. I was no longer hungry—no longer feeling so strong of body.

I tried to be philosophical. *Who else gets to read their obit? Not everyone gets to have their obituary in the Times with a picture no less.* "Local Educator." I could have supplied them with as many as a hundred letters from former students along with my encomium from the trustees on my retirement. They left out the teacher of the year award from USC, and there was nothing about our efforts toward at least some diversity in the student body and faculty.

I could not believe it. It was over. Susan would make copies. And do what with them? Even I did not want one.

I was drumming my fingers so hard on the table an older gent looked up at me from two tables away.

I had another thought and looked for the personal obituaries. There I was again—Harold David Barnes, February 2, 1926 – June 22, 1996—this time beloved husband, father and grandfather. Even George and Katherine were listed. Memorial gifts and donations could be sent to the scholarship fund at Westview Academy. "Memorial service, Wednesday June 30. Valley Presbyterian Church. 3 p.m."

I would have liked it better at the Academy. It seems a little quick too—maybe because the 4th of July weekend was coming up. And of course, the school year was over. Some of my old faculty colleagues were already off to vacation somewhere. Almost all the students who were there when I was Head had graduated. "Life goes on," I announced only to myself.

No philosophy or religion for that matter—that I knew of—had anything to say about my situation . . . condition.

I thought about driving up to the house again. Instead I wrapped up what was left of my sandwich and drove to Bally's. Sure enough, my SUV was gone from the parking lot. Maybe Shelley—or more likely Steve—had taken the extra key down and driven it back to good old 1848 Colina. Or they had had the lock snapped in the gym and taken my wallet too.

I drove back to the Ralph's and went in pushing a cart. I was efficient—foods that I liked. But healthy: broccoli, bananas, oranges, some apricots and blueberries just coming into season. Also tomatoes, pasta, a half pound of salmon; then fresh milk, a loaf of 7-grain bread, some nuts, mint chocolate ice cream, a bottle of Scotch. I was about to check out when I went back and got a packet of sponges, paper towels and spray cleaner.

Back here in the apartment I put the food away and then took everything out of the refrigerator to try to clean it. I swept the kitchen and on my hands and knees mopped the floor with paper towels and then began working on the bathroom. It was all I could think of to do. I was not exactly a neatnik, but I never could stand dirty and messy.

Part way into it, I realized I did not have enough of the right cleaning supplies. Armed with his trusty credit card, I headed back to Ralph's. There I saw Ruth Shaw and David Allenby from our neighborhood, but they, of course, had no idea who I was.

I began to realize this was more than a one day job. It was not that it was all so dirty; it needed rearranging—reorganizing. He did not have a lot of stuff—clothes, two boxes of papers, some books that needed shelving. I became aware that I was half-singing over and over again, "Ding dong the old man is dead. Ding, dong, ding. The old man is dead." I was trying to . . . I do not know what I was trying.

After a while the Dodgers would be on TV—probably at 7 unless they were playing in the East. I half-laughed to think that I had gone two whole days without thinking of the those Brooklyn Bums come West to Los Angeles—having another so-so season.

Feeling exhausted, mentally but not physically, I sat down. I finished the corn beef sandwich and had some ice cream. The phone rang. I did not pick it up, but then heard, "Hey, Mark. Where are you? This is your friend. I hope I'm still your friend: Bill baby. Aren't you getting your messages? or did you let your machine fill up again? Anyway—what do you say? A ride tomorrow? or some beer and dogs? Call me." Then a pause and a lilting "bye-bye."

I had no idea who Bill was—or what I could say or fake if I did respond to him. Or what he would do if I did not.

How could I in any way be Marcus Zito? Probably there were other calls waiting on the answering machine? I read over what I had written of this day. *Fini*, I thought. This could be the shortest journal on record. I am dead. Mark Zito has a well-muscled young physique. But I am not him. I do not want to be him.

One thing I forgot to put down about yesterday was my desperate attempt to make contact with Shelley. If I could get anyone to understand, I hoped it might be my daughter.

I tried to plan carefully—even wrote myself a little text: "Shelley darling. Please do not hang up until you hear me. You may even want to sit down. I know this may be hard to take in. It is me. It is your Dad. I can prove to you it is me. I am not dead. Remember how in the doll house I built for you, there was that secret room where you could hide the little baby to be safe." I got that far, and I could hear her crying. "Don't cry," I told her. "Somehow this is going to be all right, and your mother…"

Shelley broke in her voice rising, "You listen to me," she said, her tone just short of hysterical. "I don't know who you are or how you know this or what kind of a scam you're into. You're not my father. My father is dead and we all have to live with that. You're not even his voice. Not even close. If you call back again…" "Shelley, dear Shelley," I tried to interrupt. "…and I'll call the police. I may anyway, you creep." And she hung up.

I listened for maybe ten seconds to the *da-da-da-da-* of the broken connection and had to check myself from throwing the telephone across the room.

25th

In a nightmare I had last night—somewhat screwed up like most dreams are—it is me in an open box and it is me watching and yelling. It is very dark and the box is being pulled closer and closer to a fire. I am trying to get out of the box and shouting, "I am not dead. Don't. I am not dead." Now there is a top on the box becoming tighter and tighter. I am pounding on it. I cannot breathe. The fire is hotter.

I woke up in a clammy sweat and tried to walk it off. It was something like 3:30 in the bleak morning. I turned on the television. I tried to talk myself down. I tried some Scotch, but it did not taste right at all. It made me feel strange rather than relaxed—unsettled in the head and stomach. Marcus may not have been a drinker—at least not of Scotch.

Maybe I had already been cremated or maybe the dream was somehow getting me ready for it. I shuddered. Susan and I had agreed on cremation years ago—over Scotch—talking like realistic grownups. Since everyone died someday, that is what we preferred—for whoever went first. It was also better for the environment. That was, I assumed, why there would be a memorial service rather than a funeral on Wednesday. Just like my parents. I would be reduced to a little urn of ashes. Ashes to ashes, if not dust to dust. There would be no body ever to get back into if ever I could have.

Even before that they may have *harvested* my good organs. I had filled out a form. Maybe it was Susan's last gift of me. I could not help but imagining it . . . what? Cutting out my eyes. Maybe someone else was seeing through them now. I did not need them. I had Marcus' eyes. I shut them.

Or kidneys. But not the heart; that suffered an attack. But other things if they could get them fast enough: some ligaments, skin, blood vessels. Not the brain. Hell that left first—or my mind or whatever. You tell me.

Then what was left for the incinerator. My teeth. I still had them all. They worked. They had worked. Did some ghoul yank my gold fillings? Gone my graying hair, my hands. I once heard that fingernails kept growing after death.

And my flabby penis with which as a phallus I had made love to Susan—had two kids—that had died too—useless. Burnt up. The almost oval birthmark on my right thigh— the knees that still worked pretty well. The ankles, my feet— my toes—at least *fini* for any athlete's foot. "'Why? Why? Why?'

Maybe it was now 4 a.m., and I warmed some milk and lay down on his couch where I had watched the Dodgers get pounded 16-4 by the Astros last night. I felt cold and went back to his bed that really needed a new mattress. I fell asleep—surprised that I did after I awoke and remembered where I was and who maybe I was. For better or worse. I seemed to be having my own dreams and not his. I did not need his, too, though it might help me to figure him out—wherever he was—dead too?

I cleaned up some more—straightened; moved two lamps to where I wanted them. I looked at his little library: some mysteries and pulpy-looking stuff, but a couple of Elmore Leonard's and books on weight-lifting and training, and *Tess of the d'Urbervilles*, of all things, and, Conrad's *Heart of Darkness* bound together with *The Secret Sharer*. There was a stack of *Cycle Worlds* and *Penthouse*, and another of *Men's Health and Muscle Fitness* underneath which there was a hefty anthology of poetry that looked like it had been bought used and under it what appeared to be a text book entitled succinctly *American History*. I started leafing through the top *Penthouse* and almost immediately began to get a hard-on. I guess that meant Marcus was a heterosexual. Also that I still was. They say that our mind is really our main sex organ. But it takes mind and body to tango. I also wonder if underneath my mind might be his reptilian brain, mostly controlling the breathing, the pituitary, erections, et cetera. Who knows?

Especially in the living room, but also in the bedroom, little kitchen and even the bathroom one can see zigzagged cracks running down the walls—several of them almost horizontal. They must be the scars from the Northridge earthquake in January which did something of the same to our house. One could ask how safe this building was. It may be why he moved here—to get a cheaper rent.

And what about money?—practical stuff. I had a pretty good retirement income and investments. I had not been paid like some heads of schools were. I did not want to; having been a teacher so long, I did not believe it was good for the overall morale or values of Westview to have the Head making two or three or four times as much as my colleagues. I know some of the trustees wanted to match some of the other schools—said they thought it would be good for fund-raising and wanted me to be even more aggressive doing that. That may be why, when I told them of my retirement plans, no one tried that hard to talk me out of it. All of which was fine. With the house almost paid for, and my investments in a joint trust, we must be worth nearly a million and a half—and a pension on top of that.

By *we*, though, I guess I must now mean Susan, and my estate—or is it her estate? If not already, soon. I should not be surprised if someone has already called Maxwell Righter, our lawyer—what a name for a lawyer—who was also one of the trustees of the school. Max might already be putting the legal pieces to work. Financially, I will have ceased to exist. I will be broke—dead broke. If I still had my ATM card, I would try to use it. Pin is 7227. That might prove to someone I am still alive and kicking or at least get their attention.

Marcus has an ATM card. Of course, I do not know the pin. I found his checkbook too—still with the old address on the checks. But, although he scribbled out what a few of the checks were for and how much, he did not keep a running balance. That could be in a bank statement—maybe in one of those file boxes. My guess and my fear is that there will not be much in his account.

I do have the credit card but there is likely a balance due. Pray not huge.

But he must have some income. Not much, I wouldn't think. Two of his stored calls were from the Bally's where he evidently was a trainer. Whoever Randy was he sounded more than a little pissed. Apparently Mark had missed one appointment on Thursday and four on Friday: "If you're sick you could at least let us know." Randy listed three scheduled appointments on Monday along with a kind of warning: "Better be here, Mark." I have no idea what I am going to do about that.

But mostly this morning I am mourning Susan—missing her, feeling sorry for her, feeling sorry for myself. We met at Penn, married before we were both 25, two wonderful kids, so many memories: apartments, houses, illnesses—the time all four of us had the flu at once and could barely get up to eat, our 40th anniversary party, her parents dying, and mine, her sister. The trip we had planned to Italy in the fall. I was crying. I am crying to think of her crying. Who does one have to share the memories with now? to laugh and cry over? to look at the pictures? There was no chance even to say goodbye. To say "I love you so." "I love you Susan, darling." Maybe somehow…somewhere, someday I will still get back to her. That is all that makes me want to live.

I kissed the back of Marcus' big Italian hand and used it to wipe my eyes.

Another of the missed messages was from Gaby—who must be Mark's sister. Several times she mentioned "Daddy," whom I gather she adores, and I apparently do not—or something. Nothing about Mommy. She also seems to love me but is worried about me, and is going to come over if I do not call her back soon. I have not figured out how I can fake the brother business or if I should try.

Then my buddy Bill-Baby-Bill called back and I answered. By this time I had seen the biker's helmet in the closet and realized what he had meant by a bike ride. I headed him off on that one. I had begged and ordered both Stephen and Shelley: "No drugs, no motorcycles." In college I had a friend who ended up brain-dead from a motorcycle accident. I was afraid of motorcycles.

But I did agree to meet Bill later this afternoon at a bar or beer joint named Dirk's Place. I still have to figure out where it is. Marcus had several bottles of Coors Lite in his refrigerator, so I am guessing he drinks at least that—that and what looks like a lot of protein supplement in powder form. I also reasoned that I might be able to learn something more about Marcus if I was careful and mostly listened to Bill. I mentally rehearsed what I would tell him: first the shock of the older man dying right across from me in the gym, which was true enough. Then I was dizzy and sick to my stomach part of the night. The whole thing had left me kind of disoriented with a bit of a brain freeze and forgetful. "You will have to forgive me if I do not quite seem myself" or something like that.

But now I am again restless—even agitated, legs moving up and down. This body I have inherited—at least temporarily—wants movement. I am going to have to give it some exercise—a lot of it, if I want to keep it in anything like its present shape.

The Dodgers are winning in Houston this evening, which is some consolation. Piazza and Brett Butler have hit home runs and Astacio is pitching a strong game. I was almost late for my drinking session with Bill—who turned out to be a quieter and more thoughtful young man than I imagined he would be—only about half my size. No, of course, more than that—but maybe only 5'6" or so and on the skinny side. I felt really big when he came up to hug me like a long-lost friend. So I need not have worried about recognizing him and he did most of the talking—sort of eager, wanting to please. It would be hard not to like him.

Earlier I had put on what I decided to refer to as "our running shoes" and gone out for what I intended to be a reasonably brisk walk. Before a block was out I was beginning to run, a bit awkwardly at first. I had trouble with the stride, almost tripped. His legs were certainly longer than mine, but I soon got it. It was still a day of "June gloom" with the cooler air and cloud cover coming off the Pacific—almost a mist in my face as I picked up the pace.

I had so much wind—I headed deeper into the valley, then east to Balboa Park where I had not been for years. I do not know how long I ran. It helped me not to think too much.

I know it was miles—resting only a couple of times when I found a water fountain—then faster for a while. I wondered what sports Marcus had played—imagining what a strong body this would be to play tennis in. I could play more singles again.

I felt even better when I got back—kind of tired but a good tired—and adventurous, like somehow I could make this work. I had to hurry the shower but noticing for the first time the small tattoo of an eagle on the outside of the right leg just above the ankle and then a bluish dove on the back of my left shoulder. I wondered what if anything he meant by that.

Bill (he once also referred to himself as "good old Billy") had two beers to my one, and we then ordered big burgers with fries with enough extra lettuce, tomato, and onions to make a side salad. He seemed surprised when I ordered another burger and finished off his fries. "When did you start putting catsup on your fries?" he asked.

I did not learn as much about Marcus as I had hoped to, though I tried to be subtle in asking some leading questions. Bill and I had apparently been friends for a while, meeting, I gather, at LA Valley Community College before he went on to UCLA. What had happened then to Mark was unclear. I think I was the one who got Bill riding motorcycles. We had been on trips together—up as far as Big Sur on the PCH, to Vegas and once as far as Salt Lake City. We must be close in age, but he seemed to look up to me as though I was older or he admired me. I was puzzled but tried to respond to his friendship—almost affection.

Somebody named Kevin—somebody Mark must have known—had lost his job and his girlfriend. I did, indeed, work as a trainer in a gym and did not seem to have any close woman friend for now. Bill had a job doing something in the film industry. It did not seem very high-up or all that interesting to him. Or at least he did not want to talk about it. I certainly recognized the smell of marijuana when he lit up a half-smoked joint he had kept in a Marlboro cigarette box. As he did not offer me any or invite me to join him, I deduced Mark probably did not do marijuana.

When I told him that I did not feel like taking a ride with him tomorrow—that I still was not feeling myself, he may have been a tad disappointed, but said he understood. "Maybe you're working out too much," he suggested. "Wished I worked as hard as you do."

He got up as if to go, but then said he had better finish his beer, which looked to me like it only had a half-swallow left. "Did you ask your sister if she'd ever want to go out with me?" He forced a handsome but still a shy smile. I could see how young women would find him attractive—"cute" they would probably say.

I kind of half-chuckled back—yet trying to look sincere while realizing I would need to spend some time looking in the mirror to check out Mark's facial expressions. I stalled. "She's great, isn't she?"

"You bet," he replied, and then sat back down, frustrated, perhaps a bit sullen.

"Have you seen her recently?" I tried.

"What do you mean?" He looked up. "I see her all the time."

"I mean to talk to?" I tried to recover.

Bill gave me a quizzical glance and then tilted his empty bottle back and forth, apparently thinking about my question.

"She only works across the hall. I try not to bother her, but she even sat with me while I was having lunch a couple of days ago. She mostly asks about you . . . worries about you. She really loves you, you know"

"Sweet" I responded.

"But I think she has another guy right now, doesn't she?" He again looked up at me.

"I really do not know" I told him. "But when it seems O.K. to ask, I will ask her about you—if she would like to date."

"That'd be great." He stood up and tilted the bottle for a last, non-existent swig. "But don't say 'date'—just to go out with me."

"Good." I stood up too.

"Thanks, Mark. You're a terrific friend," and he gave me a full hug—his head barely up to my shoulder. His slender body was warm. It had been a long time since I had been gripped by another man like that—if ever.

So I had learned some things: Gaby was, indeed, Mark's sister. That was likely a knick-name or shortening of her real name. She worked across the hall from Bill—maybe in the film or TV business too, in some way. She must not be too tall—if Bill wanted to date her. I had better call her soon—to let her know I was all right—that I loved her too

Now sitting here in his apartment, the legs feel sore from all the running. I burped from the beer and food. Then I belched. I am sad—and very alone. It is not yet all that late. I fear the night will be long.

Sunday June 26 1994

First thing this morning I masturbated. Staring at a strange pillow, I became aware of what felt like a very large hard-on sticking into the mattress and then, as I rolled over, up under the sheet. I remembered that young men could have erections while they were sleeping—sometimes several times a night. It was nature's way of keeping the organ limber. Now it felt rather urgent that either he or I or both of us do something about it.

It was quick but with maybe four ejaculations and an alarming amount of sperm and fluid. I could not help grunting with the satisfying release as I came.

I lay there becoming limp. Now what? I thought. It was a lot of wasted sperm, but then that was always true. One way or another I had ejaculated possibly several million sperm in my lifetime. Only two had struck home. But two great kids. *Home*, I thought; Stephen and Shelley. My son and daughter. Our son and daughter.

I remembered one early morning when we had taken the kids on a vacation to a cabin with a loft for them above our bed. Susan and I thought we could get away with a furtive quick one, which we believed we did until Stevie's head popped up above us, asking "Mommy, Mommy, are you all right? Is something hurting?"

I recreated Susan's lovely young body in my memory, and then when we became middle-aged and older. Certainly our sex had become less frequent, slower, but it was not over. In some ways it had become better—alone in the house and more time to ourselves—less inhibited, knowing each others' bodies and responses. After we were married, I never much thought about sex with anyone else—anyone other than the mother of my children. I would not know how. Right then, I missed her so. We would, I guess, never make love again.

What if, I thought again, I showed up to Susan like this— in this body? Too strange by far! for her, I should hope. I tried to laugh. Certainly for me. I was never very good at conjuring up sexual fantasies. I only wanted Susan. I only wanted to be me with her—in our bed—not this one in this apartment with the cracks down the walls.

Post-coital tristesse? Or the "little death" the sex act was sometimes called. How about the big death? That was more like what I was experiencing. There was a gap between what had gone on with him down there and me in his head.

A deeper shade of sadness slid over me as though the room were darkening. It was a sadness for myself past and present and whatever future there was to be—with or without masturbation, much less trying to have sex with another woman—much less making love to her. At the same time, I became aware that if I lay there just a little longer, Mark's groin could possibly be ready to do it again. I got up quickly— feeling embarrassed, as though somebody might be watching—possibly that I was watching him and me or maybe that I feel the need to record this.

I succeeded in brewing some coffee with his old Mr. Coffee. It was O.K. with milk in it and, though still feeling somewhat bloated from last night, I took pleasure in cutting up a banana and strawberries and having it with granola and peach yogurt like I often did at home.

"Now what?" I ask myself again. It's not yet 9 o'clock. I have a whole day in front of me. It is also the Sabbath. I am not going to church on the Sabbath. Except for special occasions, I have not gone to church in quite a while. Perhaps my death would make today a special occasion for Susan and the family, especially since my upcoming memorial service is on Wednesday. I could go this morning too, and make a miserable fool of myself.

Giving up church-going was not some major decision in my life. Susan and I had often gone together, particularly when Shelley and Steve were youngsters. It seemed to mean more to her than to me. I realize that I have sometimes written the word "God" over the last several days and may even have sounded like I was sending up a prayer. And maybe I was. There is always that foxhole religion when the soldier prays with the shells landing all about. I once did that. Then there is the category of "Prayers for the Dying." I do not know of any "Prayers for the Already Dead."

I guess I do not want completely to give up hope that my reincarnation—or whatever this is—could all be for some reason and that God's mysterious hand could be dealing these cards. "Here, Mark. Here Hal. Try this wild card—this joker." But God's mysterious ways have long been too mysterious for me. I would be glad to get just a few hints. I think most of us would.

No doubt, I was influenced by some of my colleagues, too—their occasional jokes about fundamentalist religion or literalist believers and generally going along with the secular views of life. It was not kosher, if that is the right word, to be against religion at Westview, but it became more and more acceptable not to pay much attention. Christianity had had its day and left a heritage of stories and music that should not be lost or forgotten. One could also be spiritual and believe that there was more to life than materialism and scientific reductionism, but as a formal religion Christianity just could not make enough sense of life.

As Westview's Head I felt it my duty and was pleased to continue the school prayer at graduation—to bow my head while wondering what was going through the heads of others. And we sang "America the Beautiful" with its "God shed His grace on Thee" and that interesting, "May God thy gold refine."

Which leads me to wonder if Mark has any religion, other than that saint's medallion dangling from his rear view mirror. So far I had seen no prayer books, Bibles, rosaries. Chances are he is Roman Catholic—perhaps mostly lapsed. At least we would be alike in that way, though maybe one ought to think of muscle building and exercise as his religion. I am into exercise, good nutrition and being in good shape, too, but I also staunchly believe in moderation. I will never be able to match him.

But if I do not, what will happen to this body? I am now still sitting here in his blue and white striped pajamas that probably need to go to the laundromat—unless there are laundry machines in the basement. The pajama shirt feels a little tight on me, especially when I flex. I also cannot believe how tight I can make his abs. I never had a stomach like this one.

So I should probably get some exercise, though not another run until at least tomorrow. And I do not like the idea of showing up at Bally's—not until I have had some time to think about it. Probably I would see people I am supposed to know there. Maybe then a nice walk—just like good old Hal used to do, and where I can think about what I should be doing—what I will do tomorrow.

This writing is helping, too, even if rambling. How does the saying go? "How do I know what I think until I see what I have to say?" I won't claim that I am doing much hard thinking here, but the process of writing gives me some conceit—maybe illusion—that there is the possibility of making a sliver of sense of it all. I guess there is also an awareness that someone might be reading this one day. Then I do not feel quite so alone.

I had to stop to go pee. Boy, that is another way his anatomy is high fantasy. I had not urinated this freely in years.

While standing there enjoying the flow, I could think of only one biblical story for this Sabbath on which I masturbated that might be slightly relevant to the day though also wildly inappropriate. I had now been dead for four days by biblical count just like Lazarus. I needed Jesus to come along and raise up my body too.

I cannot forget as a young man being asked to read this long and strange story from a large lectern Bible in the fine old King James Version. When I got to the part where Martha warns Jesus, "Lord, by this time he stinketh," some pious soul had carefully crossed out "stinketh" and written "smelleth" above it.

All flesh suffereth corruption. I hope my mortal coil no longer smelleth or stinketh, but it would be nice if Jesus could come by on this Sunday and raise it up so I could have some chance of reclaiming it.

But this will be a tougher one, Jesus. In a fumbled memory I realized that I had another version of my nightmare last night: with the box I could not get out of and the intense fire. I did not stinketh because I was already incinerateth to ashes. If Jesus could recreate from that, it would make the raising of Lazarus sound like a Sunday School story—which it is.

Time to get dressed—past time. I have never been a quitter, though I have never faced odds like this. Who has? I will go for the walk. I will think about tomorrow. I will maybe call his sister. I will maybe go to the laundromat. Maybe I will drive by home.

Marcus did not have a lot of clothes: one dark suit in the back of the closet and a blue blazer that looked like it might not fit over all his muscles. There were chinos, tee and polo shirts, a couple pairs of blue jeans, gym shorts, a leather jacket, several sweaters, several pairs of gym shoes, a set of cowboy boots, in which he and I would look even taller, and a half drawer full of socks and his jockey shorts. If this was going to go on, I would need to get myself some boxers. The jockeys felt too tight for me.

Of course, I still had a drawer full of boxers at home. Most of them could even fit on him—several of them a bit outlandish for a "Local Educator"—one from Valentine's Day with lots of red hearts.

Susan and Shelley would not have given these away yet. But sooner or later they would feel they had to. Some could go to Steve—some, I suppose, to Goodwill. God, it is hard to think about my clothes—many of which were mine for years: handkerchiefs neatly folded in the top drawer, my suits and sports coats I had worn at work, some old and some really nice shirts, maybe fifty years of ties—some skinny, some fat—most I would never wear again anyway. There were my slacks, a half-closet full of shoes well-cared for, sweaters—two new, and at least a couple of them presents—still in their boxes, my pajamas—everything. Little of it would fit the new me. I would give anything and everything to be able to wear them again. What happens to one's pajamas?

Monday June 27th 1994

I should give myself some credit: at least for effort, and I hope a passing grade for performance. I am a smart guy, I told myself: someone who has worked through not a few difficult problems in life and solved tough ones when necessary. A man who has taught others how to learn ought to be able to teach himself. With the Dodgers again winning in the Astrodome as my Sunday afternoon background entertainment, I read through several of his trainer's manuals: one called *The Art of Fitness* from which I learned that there is an International Fitness Association. *The Fine Art of Training* had useful illustrations. In addition, I remembered my own trainer that I had had for almost two months a year or so ago. I gave him up when I realized I was sometimes straining too hard while trying to please him. But I learned some basics and a few helpful exercises and techniques—a stress on not hurrying the reps, full range of motion and, particularly at my age, warming up and stretching.

I have no idea how long I am going to have to act the part of Marcus D. Zito, but I figure that he and I have to make at least some money if I am to go on living.

For last night's healthy dinner I cooked myself spinach, cauliflower with a tomato sauce and a turkey burger and then became aware that it was not enough and topped it off with a peanut butter and jelly sandwich, followed by a banana.

Pretty soon I would be ordering out for pizza too. Marcus probably filled himself up with a protein drink made with that powder stuff, but I doubt if I will ever get there.

I did not sleep well at first. I got up and tried some Scotch to see if it would help, but it did not taste right again. On the second sip I almost gagged. At home I have some sleeping pills, which I take in a situation like this. Ha! Ha! Ha! I would like to laugh hysterically. Whoever has situations like this? It does make me wonder, however, if Marcus has a doctor who could make prescriptions. Probably not at his age.

But afterward I must have fallen into a deep sleep. His radio alarm had to mount into a loud buzzing before I finally opened my eyes and again thought I had been dreaming this bizarre life—shutting and opening my eyes only to see all the cracks in the walls and then rubbing my hands over my flat abs and ignoring my semi-erection.

I showered and shaved, trying not to get into admiring our physique again. I cut up an orange and a banana and had a big bowl of raisin bran. I would have been glad to have a cup of tea with just a bit of milk and sugar, but first I will have to buy some tea.

I dressed in a pair of dark chinos and a black shirt with a Bally's logo. I checked in the mirror, decided that I at least looked like a fit trainer, and added a baseball cap that also said Bally's. I went over my little speech for dear Randy and anyone else about the shock I had experienced, not being myself and forgetting things, and took off in the silver Corolla with the racing stripe, intending to arrive at least 45 minutes early.

It was lucky I did. Wrong Bally's. They did not understand what I was doing there, and I could not understand what they did not understand. It turns out that almost all Mark's clients are in the Bally's further west in the Valley. Fortunately I had a good idea where that was and, with Bally's of Encino shaking their heads at me, took the freeway to the Topanga Canyon exit, parked in the Bally's lot, put his wallet back in the glove compartment and grabbed a gym bag (with another Bally's logo) off the floor of the passenger side, and strode in with my head high, just in time for my first appointment.

Clearly Randy did not find that good enough. Though built like a bull, he was a half foot shorter than Mark Zito, and I gave him a brief and less apologetic version of my speech while trying to tower over him. He only grunted something in reply and gave me a clipboard that fortunately had the names as well as the appointment times of my four clients. I recalled that folder with several sheets of paper in it which I had picked up from his car seat that first dreadful evening. I had lost it somewhere—maybe as I fled the foyer in his previous apartment building.

Amanda Smith turned out to be a matronly woman who must have a bit of a thing for Marcus. "Oh, do call me Mandy, Mark." She gave me a coy smile and seemed puzzled that I did not remember more about her, her sore hip, and the usual opening routine. I told her I had been studying some new exercises for her and tried to be both professional and friendly, frequently asking her how she was doing and about any pain she was feeling. She soon was thanking me for my "strong but gentle spirit today" and left with a "ta, ta, Mark" after soliciting my promise to be "right on time" on Thursday and have some more new exercises just for her.

I ended up with a total of six appointments—one a walk-in looking for a new trainer and another subbing for a trainer who had double-booked. Three were middle-aged or older men with whose physical condition and concerns I did not have much difficulty connecting. I practiced what

37

they call "attentive listening," made mental notes and kept offering positive feedback. When I could, I gave them a few extra minutes of my attention. The session with a brute of a guy near Mark's age did not go nearly as well. Several times he became disgruntled and incommunicative after I failed to satisfy his requests for specific information about the value of more repetitions versus adding weight. He walked off with a glare I interpreted as dismissive and no word about a next appointment.

In between several of the sessions I was in and out of the training room, mostly listening until I could pick up the names of other trainers (a Stephanie, two Jims, and one I did not get) and being non-committal but as friendly as I could in response to their comments. I did not get the impression that anyone knew anyone else all that well, or cared very much for that matter.

I also had some time to work out. I did not use weights like Mark must have done, but my usual routine felt so easy that I was able to more than double the pounds on the machines and speed on the treadmill before I felt I was pushing it.

I went to see Randy twice—the first time after I figured out that Mark had a locker but with a lock on it. When I informed him that, among other things, I had forgotten the combination and needed it broken off, he told me "That's your funeral" and that I would be responsible for any new lock. Turned out that the locker held only another Bally's cap and a crumpled towel, but I now had a future repository for the wallet and keys and perhaps a clean shirt.

The second conversation began with my asking when I got my money. "You know the rules," he answered. I tried to look like I both did and did not. "You weren't here Friday. It holds over 'til next Friday. Them are the rules."

When I did not object and sat down on the other side of his desk, he looked up and asked "What?" Trying a different tack I apologized for missing the sessions last week and for not being myself recently.

"This is different." He squinted his eyes at me.

"I do not want to be the cause of any trouble" I told him.

"No problems then. You do good stuff Mark, even if you have to fight your depression or whatever it is once in a while. I understand that."

"Thanks, Randy." I stood up to go.

"No, thank you, bud, and your check will be here on Friday. Minus my cut, of course," he chuckled with a half-smile. And that, I reflected, was about as much emotion as the two of us were going to be able to share with one another. But it felt like progress.

So Marcus Zito has had at least bouts of depression. That would explain several things. I wondered if he got any help for it. I doubt it. He probably could not afford it. Nor had I seen any medications or the like in his bathroom or elsewhere. Maybe he just called it the "blahs."

Funny thing though—as Marcus I am feeling rather good about myself this evening. For the most part I pulled it off today. With the one exception, my clients seemed to like me, and Randy and I at least got along. I know I am going to get some money, and I had had to pay such attention to my work that for stretches of time I forgot that I was dead and all the loved ones I was losing.

There were two hang-ups on the answering machine and an overly friendly call from Bill wondering if we could get together again soon and then asking if I had talked to Gaby. I guess I must call her one of these days.

June 28th Tuesday

I had only two appointments today at what I have decided to call "Bally's in the Valley" because I like the sound of it. The first was a rather heavy-set middle-aged woman who, I soon realized, had a lot of muscle to her. She kept up a steady line of chatter about her daughter, ne'er-do-well son-in-law, and her granddaughter as if I knew them all. If I was slow to suggest a next routine, she told me what she wanted. Very business-like.

An hour later came a gent who must have informed me four or five times that he was 81 and would not stop working out until they "carry me out feet first—and maybe not after that." I told him I hoped to do the same. He had had a mild stroke from which he was trying to rehabilitate. I was gentle with him, while he seemed to know how to pace himself.

In between one of the Jims asked me "how you doing these days?" He was a well-muscled young African American with a terrific smile. When I smiled in return and responded "not so bad; how is it with you?" he followed me into the trainer's room and, after a little banter, gently told me the young guy I worked with yesterday had announced to anyone in earshot that he was going to find a new trainer and that I could not train myself out of a paper bag.

I tried to look like I did not care. "The guy's an asshole." Jim offered me in consolation. "Man, up 'til yesterday you were doing great with him."

I fumbled a response, and he went on to share about one of his "problem children" and offered to give me a demonstration of several new routines he was working on. Realizing I could use a friend here, I tried to perk up, whereupon he started in almost lecturing me on the importance of having training gigs at one or two more gyms if I wanted to keep body and soul together like he did. And, indeed, Randy informed me that, while I had appointments scheduled on Thursday and Friday, there were none for tomorrow.

I drove home—if you can call it that—on Ventura Boulevard, feeling down and aware that I had reason to feel depressed for two lives. I tried to give myself a little talking-to—not sure who I was doing it to or for.

I continued on through Sherman Oaks, and into Studio City as far as the Tennis Center where I used to play once a week. I could find some old friends there, I told myself, wondering if Marcus had played tennis. I doubted it; there are no racquets or balls to be seen in this apartment with the cracked walls.

I looked around. The apartment was cleaner and neater. I had rearranged the kitchen and his small supply of dishes. I would not call it a dump, but it is far from Shangri-la. The view out the living room window was across to another apartment building.

On the way back from the Tennis Center I pumped some gas at an Arco but, without a pin, could not use his debit card to get the 10 cents a gallon off. Mine would have worked just fine—7227. With the high price of California gas, summer coming on and more games being played by the refineries, it was $3.18 a gallon. I stopped at the Gelson's in Van Nuys, where it was unlikely that I would see anyone who knew either of us. I bought myself some more salmon, spinach, and peppermint ice cream that had just come in. I got him a six-pack of Coors Lite and some potato salad in case he would still be hungry. I picked up the L.A. Times, though it would never have anything about me again. There was more on the Simpson murder case; "Shuffle at the White House May Not Save Clinton Losing Streak" and "US Weapon-grade Uranium Production Tops Estimates." The Dodgers were starting a three game series with the Giants who were apparently making another effort to rehabilitate Darrell Strawberry. None of this seemed to matter.

I badly needed someone to talk with: possibly Bill, I thought, as I pulled into the basement garage I had finally figured out how to get into, and parked the Corolla next to what I had also deduced was his Suzuki motorcycle. I had talked to sister Gaby last night. I screwed up my courage, trying to think ahead about what I would say if she asked me questions to which I had no clue. She, however, was effusive in thanking me for calling and in apologizing for not getting a hold of me over the weekend. But she did not have much time to talk since she was going out with friends soon. Most of the conversation consisted in filling me in on what Daddy was doing: that he was going out on a date next weekend, that business was great and, she assured me several times, she really missed seeing me.

From this I inferred that our parents were divorced or something had happened to our mother, but decided not to press my luck with that one. Instead, I asked her how Bill was.

"Bill?" she asked.

"You know, Bill at work."

There was a hesitation. "Oh, you mean Billy. He seems fine, but you must see him as often as I do."

"Yeah," I admitted and went on rather ineptly: "He seems really friendly?"

"Always," she replied. "He's really nice."

"Maybe he would like to be even more friendly."

There was a longer pause. "What do you mean, Markie?"

"I think he would like to date you."

"Date?"

"I mean go out with you to the movies or something."

"Well, sure. Maybe sometime. Tell him to ask me himself. I won't bite," she laughed.

I laughed too, and with more thanks for my calling, she told me she had to run.

I tried calling Bill, but no answer. I went down to the garage determined that I would at least drive by my house, and, if I did not see anyone there, maybe to go over to Shelley's and George and Katie's. There had to be something I could do.

But I just sat in his car, for I do not know how long, again gripping and ungripping the wheel.

When I got back upstairs Bill's voice was coming over the answering machine. I picked up and told him I had called because I wanted to see if he would like a beer and a brat or another hamburger. "I'm sorry. I can't," he replied. "But did you ask Gaby about me?"

"I did, Bill," trying to sound a mite mysterious.

"And?"

"And I think she really likes you as a friend."

"But would she like to go out with me?"

"I think maybe."

"Maybe? How maybe?"

"Well, it could be a little complicated."

There was a pause on his end. "But, Bill," I went on, "you should feel good about it. We can talk more when we get together next time."

"OK," he offered back a little disconsolately. "Gotta go. Thanks, Mark. Thanks a lot."

I sat there thinking my life had been reduced to a dating service and not a very good one at that. And tomorrow was my funeral.

Wednesday June 29th 1994

If I was not going to attend my own memorial service, there had to be something else I could do. What I thought up might be dangerous, but I liked that. One way or another it could put an end to this charade—or whatever it was—that I was living.

Almost precisely at 3 p.m. I pulled up in front of 1848 Colina, knowing everyone—even our neighbors—would be at the memorial service. I parked on the other side of the street to be a little less obvious, but stepped out confidently, found the key under the rock by the side gate and opened it quietly. The walkway by the side of the house needed my good broom work.

"Barney, Barney, Barney," I began quietly, and then a little louder. "Barney, Barney, Barney; Sweet Barney, Barney, Barney." He barked once, not all that loudly, crouched a bit, and looked quizzical before wagging his tail and back half vigorously. "Barney, Barney, Barney." He tried to jump up on me and again when I let him off the tether. "Down, Barney, you old ruffian," as I ruffled his neck fur and ears and put my face down where he could lick it. "God, Barney. I love you, Barney." My dog knew who I was. Barney knew. Admittedly he was a friendly beast and not the best watchdog in the world, but dogs know what people do not. I believe that.

I remembered that bumper sticker that I always thought was right on the mark: "Please, God, make me the person my dog thinks I am." I would get one that read: "Thank God my dog knows who I really am."

I located an old tennis ball and gave him four or five short tosses. Had we time, I could take him up on to a trail in the Santa Monicas and give him some long heaves to chase. We walked together around the pool and I inspected my tomatoes. "Coming along," I told him, "but could use some water."

Why not? That will give them something to think about! I unwound and stretched out my hose with Barney staying right on my heels and gave them just the needed amount. I recoiled the hose more tightly: *Something else for them to think about.*

I sat on the deck in the wicker chair as I so often did. It was a lovely afternoon. I examined the palm tree above the hedge in the Halladay's yard. It needed trimming to keep it from being a fire hazard. "Oh, Barney," I told him. "Just like always. Just like always." *Somehow, somehow, somehow it ought to be . . . had to become the same.*

I looked at my arm. It was Mark's big hairy arm and hand. I looked at his watch. It was not yet 3:30. "All the time in the world," I lied to Barney, and then began weeping.

What were they? Half way through the service: some prayers, probably a hymn or two. There would be a Bible reading. I hoped not that business about "in my house are many mansions." Hard to believe that.

People would be saying nice things about me. Steve? Maybe Shelley too. "Great father and grandfather." Susan trying to look stoic, but dabbing at her eyes.

I continued to shed some big salty tears of my own and then almost gagged. This was precisely why I had not gone to the church. "Who is that young man in the back sobbing so uncontrollably?" somebody would ask.

Barney was watching me closely—ready to jump up, to lick my tears if that would be helpful. "Barney, I will just stay here. And, when they come back, you will tell them who I really am, won't you? They will have to believe you." In fact, it would possibly scare the stuffing out of them before they called the police. Susan might have a heart attack.

"Just let me live here," I would beg—"off in the guest room. I won't be any trouble. I will help out and maybe slowly, slowly . . . you will come to realize who I am."

45

"Closure." That was what they were supposed to get from the memorial service. "What a bunch of psychobabble," Dave Trumble said after we held a memorial service at Westview for a parent who had died. Then there was that poor senior girl killed in an auto crash three weeks before commencement.

"I am the one who needs closure," I said aloud. *Hal Barnes has to die. He has died. I have to let go of him.* "But that's who I am," I muttered and pulled Barney close to me. He began licking my face—probably liking the salt of the tears.

I could think about suicide, but did not believe that would help anything. Maybe I could at least take Barney with me when I left. Then I would have something. Best I could tell, Barney thought that was a great idea.

That would be more sadness for Susan, and even George and Katie, I realized. And maybe they would then call the police to investigate a stolen dog. And maybe I had left Mark's fingerprints in various places. I stood and looked into my house—into our family room, the living room, our kitchen just beyond. I could see the charcoal and water color portrait of me that Susan had done. The key was in the pool closet. I would have to go around to the front door and then turn off the alarm, if Susan had even bothered to set it. "Piece of cake," I told Barney, who liked that idea too.

Then I could check out that large bouquet of flowers on the table in the living room: "In loving memory," from someone. It was ten to four. I did not know how long the service would be. For their sakes, I hoped not too long. There might be a reception at the church—or maybe back here. Or at Shelley and Rob's bigger house. I did not like the idea of my fine-young-man son-in-law presiding—graciously, I am sure, and with careful attention to detail, I am sure.

Several neighbors would be coming back first. They might spot this strange, young man coming out of the back yard.

"Closure," I gritted. I was not able to play out the scene where I stayed until they returned. I looked around my little garden area and the deck. "Maybe one last swim," I told Barney sarcastically, putting him back on his tether. I am sure it was sadness on his face.

Bravely, I told myself, until I have figured something else out. *Bravely*, as I shut the gate, fixed the lock, and put the key back under the rock. *Bravely*, as I drove off without looking back.

Using mostly the winding streets of hilly Encino I slowly drove the three or so miles to Shelley's house. No one was there, "but nice neighborhood," I told myself.

Then downhill, still more slowly, out onto the familiar traffic of Ventura Boulevard and then back up and past the church. For all the world, it looked like nothing had happened at Valley Presbyterian that afternoon. Marks' watch read almost quarter to five. I had not realized that much time had gone by, but knew I had not wanted to see anyone at the church. Still, I wondered who all was there: quite a few colleagues from the school, some students and former students, school parents? Other friends. Bet the place was jammed, I thought, not unreasonably.

But now it was a large empty hall of a church—some lovely blues and reds through stained-glass windows falling on the front pews. No one. Silent. "Deadly silent," I said almost aloud.

I probably should say a prayer, I considered. If not for Harold Barnes then for comfort and strength for his family:

"and may they continue to live and serve in the same spirit of love that was his, dear Lord. Amen"

I wandered about, perhaps looking for something from the service. The flowers were already gone, but suddenly the noise of a vacuum cleaner startled me. A spare, elderly man looked toward me, perhaps to see if the noise would be bothering me.

I smiled to him, and he went on for a minute or so, but then stopped and came toward me, inquiring if he could help me.

"I wanted to come to the memorial service earlier this afternoon," I fibbed, "but I was not able to." That last part was true.

"Would you like one of the bulletins for the service?" he asked in a quiet voice.

"That would be nice." I kept my voice hushed as well.

After what seemed four or five minutes (perhaps he had to go through the trash), he returned with a small stack.

"One would be fine," I told him.

"No, take them," he said. "There are always plenty left. You can send some to other friends who were not able to make the liturgy."

"Thanks," I was able to mumble.

"No, thank you for making the effort. I know the family would appreciate it," he replied as he headed back to his vacuuming. The old guy, despite his age, would make a good clergyman in training. Who knows? Maybe he is one of the clergy in a church trying to make ends meet.

I considered sitting there and going through what he called the bulletin. I had already glimpsed myself wryly smiling from the back cover—smiling good-bye.

But I did not want to try to relive my memorial there. Instead I walked back to Mark's car and sat behind the steering wheel going over my last service. I recognized the picture, taken by Rob, I think, a couple years back. Susan liked it and had it framed. I liked it because she liked it, though it did not make me look any younger. The smile was, indeed wry, but perhaps made old Harold appear knowing— as though I had been well aware of human finitude.

Places for several prayers were noted—including the Lord's Prayer. Shelley had chosen Donne's "Death Be Not Proud," and I could imagine her reading so well: "One short sleep past, we wake eternally / And death shall be no more; death, thou shalt die." Alison Denver, "President of Westview Senior Class of 1994" had read I Corinthians 13 about love being the one quality that never ends. Even better than faith and hope. And then, sure enough, there was "O God, Our Help in Ages Past," uncorrected for gender inclusiveness with that stanza you always hope will be sung for others: "Time like an ever rolling stream / Bears all its sons away / They fly, forgotten, as a dream / Dies at the opening day." This was reason enough to choose the music for one's final service, but how many people can really bear to do that?

Steve, God bless him, had spoken first. And then brother Bob. Of course he would come, all the way from Pittsburgh with his own health problems, and "Surely Shirley" as we used to kid her, and maybe Scott and Kelly and Terry who lived in Irvine. He might also tell them something about our parents and family life, and I felt the tears coming again. "Man up," I ordered myself to no purpose, wondering how it felt to him to lose his younger brother so suddenly. I had not cried like this since . . . I have no idea when. The last time I can even remember crying was when the previous Barney died.

The last speaker was Harold Campbell—the "other Harold" as we often referred to each other. I could not think of a better choice. There were times when we could argue it

out at faculty retreats, and I had to wonder if he was not envi-
ous when I was chosen as Head and then named President.
But who knew me and my values better and could be clever
in only alluding to my foibles and eccentricities? There
would have been some laughter, but he would have stressed
my dedication and creativity as a teacher—maybe even extolling what it meant to be a Master Teacher. And then, he
would have gone on to my accomplishments as Head—my
good relations with faculty colleagues and care for students:
"always an educator, always a teacher," he might have concluded. "Harold David Barnes, our Master Teacher."

I had at least stopped crying, aware that I had participated
in my own encomium. Or more simply, "Local Educator,"
I said aloud to the windshield. I was an educator first and
foremost. That was my profession in the best sense of that
word. I like to think that was the main reason they asked me
to be Head. I was not bad at all the administrative planning
and hassles, the public relations, and even the fundraising. I
learned to be a good salesman—helping identify what people
would care about and for which they would feel good about
giving their chunks of money, sometimes with their name on
it. Some of that wealth, I knew, was inherited and came from
avoiding or even evading taxes, cornering markets, driving
down the cost of labor. Then there was the always interesting
TV and Hollywood set and their producers, lawyers, agents,
and technical people. But to hell with it, I say. I liked most of
them. They were in many ways generous people; most of their
children were good youngsters and the world ain't perfect.
And so: "Local Educator." "Master Teacher." Harold Barnes
had many friends, and I was loved by my family and my dog.

As I drove to this apartment with the cracked walls,
crummy mattress, and Scotch I cannot drink, I asked again
why it all had to go so quickly: obituary, cremation, memorial

service—after dying about this time of day just a week ago. But then what would be the point of prolonging it?

Bill had left a message, which I am not returning this evening. This is enough for one day—for a day in my life and death. And I have to think about getting Marcus to work and his food and exercise for tomorrow.

July 1st Friday
Thursday was a crappy day and today was not much better. I could use a dirtier word but I have schooled myself (ha! ha!) not to use bad language lest I slip up in front of students or in my role as Head. Some of my colleagues had begun to think it was trendy to employ stronger language but I stayed old school (ha!).

The only good news was that Amanda brought a friend to see if she would like me as a trainer. Unlike Amanda, who had muscle under her upholstery, Carol Anne was truly out of shape and needed to lose considerable poundage. But she was cheerful and said that was why she had come. We started out gently, talked some about diet, and I gave her an exercise routine that she could follow on her own, interspersed with pep talks and as much encouragement as I could offer. She went away red of face, but I thought with a lilt to her step.

Earlier I told Amanda that I had had a rough day the day before. She wanted to know about it, but I responded in generalities and that I was still trying to understand what had happened. I had worried on Monday that her fondness for me might have sexual dimensions to it, but today at least it seemed maternal. Again, she did most of the talking. I think I exercised almost as much as she did while showing her how I wanted her to perform the routines and reps.

1994

This afternoon I got my check: $382.50 for two weeks. Quick calculation told me there was no way Mark and I could survive on that. It would barely pay the rent. Maybe it had been a slow two weeks. Maybe he was being cheated a little, but I did not know enough to ask how. Next thing I had to figure out was how to cash or deposit it.

Bill and I are going out for "eats" and maybe a movie in a few minutes. As far as I can tell, I do not think Mark has many other friends, if any. I am really stuck.

Saturday July 2

Today I determined would be finances day. Only ten days ago I had been on easy street: the house nearly paid for, our investments, two cars, my pension, plus social security, medicare, Susan's modest social security. Zero of that now. Nada. Zilch. As Marcus D. Zito I was broke. Worse than that I was almost surely in debt. A good looker perhaps, and with these muscles I could flex, and I could starve to death.

"No," I told myself aloud. I also had my brains and experience and a work ethic I could get going again. First thing was to figure out where we really were.

Except for his checkbook, in which the register had no real record for several months and no running balance, there were no papers lying around: no bills, no rent receipts, no Visa statements. The kid was a curious mixture of messy (the kitchen and bathroom that I pretty much had clean by now, and his closet) versus his bookshelves—spare as they were—and a desk with several writing pads, an expensive if unused fountain pen, a mug with mostly sharpened pencils. There were no pictures on the walls or anywhere else. One had the sense that he had not quite moved into 3-A. There might, it occurred to me, be more boxes or things of his in a storage locker in the basement.

But there were the two file boxes. "Box 2," as I decided to call it was by far the heavier—about half books and half files that at least at one time had been arranged with some care.

The books were again a surprise. In addition to his *Heart of Darkness*, which I regularly introduced students to in my senior course, and *Tess of the d'Urbervilles* on his shelf, here was Conrad's *Lord Jim*, Dickens' *Bleak House*, *Huckleberry Finn*, *Middlemarch*, *The Sun Also Rises*, *Absalom, Absalom*, a motley collection if ever there was one, but interesting. I found it a challenge to accept that Mark had actually read them. They might, after all, have had a previous owner. Whoever read them had marked them up with one of those yellow highlighters that I forbade my students to use on any book. Perhaps my friend, whose body was now mine, may have had a double life of some kind or, at least, at one time interests other than body building and motorcycles. It was hard to put together, though not as hard as putting me together with him.

The neatly arranged files held what seemed to be old school papers, short essays, maybe some letters and reports. My best guess was that he had not been into Box 2 for quite a while.

Box 1 gave evidence of earlier attempts to keep financial records in file folders, but now was mostly a mélange of unsorted paper that gave the impression of having been tossed in before the lid closed on them—maybe even to hide them from his daily sight. But it was what I was looking for.

I sorted it into piles. His bank account was with Bank of America and at the end of May he had an actual balance of $707.76. along with three cancelled checks—one for his rent of $550, which seemed like a lot to me, though I knew renting in much of LA—not to speak of here in the valley—could be expensive. The other two checks were for payments for the Toyota and the Suzuki.

He had rent receipts up through May. He may have paid for June, but I might still have to do that. There were back rent receipts for his previous apartment—almost $200 more. He probably had been trying to reduce expenses.

He had fairly regular check deposits from work. They varied—some weeks better than other, but usually around $250, only one for $325. In March there was a deposit for $1,000. That was probably what kept him going. I needed to find out where that came from—hoping it was not illegal in some way. There were a number of small cash withdrawals, mostly only $20—a couple $40s.

As of June 20th he owed almost the same on his Visa card—$718.82—as he had in his bank account. He had evidently been making minimum payments for some months, racking up hefty interest charges, which I hated paying. That would be the first thing I would try to get rid of. He did not, however, use his credit card that often, perhaps trying to live more with cash. I had used it more often during the past week than he did.

He was living hand to mouth, but I could do that at least for a while—maybe slowly make things better. I needed to figure out how to start using his checking account. With the cancelled checks I ought to be able to learn to forge his signature. I should be able to deposit his check at the teller's window. Maybe then I could write a check for cash as, without his pin, I could not use the ATM. That might be a tough nut to crack unless he had written it down somewhere.

There was, I realized, no sign of any health insurance. I had had good insurance for so long that it felt . . . what?—it felt precarious. Sure he was young and did not seem to have any major problems. Pray God, no AIDS. But who knows? *Memento Mori.* Look what had happened to Harold Barnes, though he, of course, did not need his health insurance in the end, while I will bet they ran a good tab just for my last trip through the hospital.

Then, I remembered, I had never gotten back to his dentist's office. I clacked up and down on our teeth. No pain. Strong jaw. I had had good teeth for my age: maybe a half-dozen crowns over the last 25 years. But Ronald Sinclair, D.D.S., had told me they were good for another 20—not knowing about the fires of cremation.

I had what I look back on as a reasonably good time with Bill last night. It is a challenge to share interests with someone almost young enough to be a grandson, and he was disappointed that I was so emphatic about not wanting to take a motorcycle trip sometime over the weekend. But his spirit of friendship and the way he looks up to Mark are hard to resist and made me realize that, whatever Mark's problems and issues, Bill must have seen some admirable qualities in him.

I did my best to respond in kind and enjoyed the two large chili dogs with onions and one beer to his two without any after burn, though I delivered myself of several good belches, over which we both got a laugh. I tried to keep the farts to myself at my age or any age.

I gave Bill several openings to talk about me but without much luck—learning only that we had shared several community college classes together in some form of math or engineering, and that I had evidently been gone for several years before we got back together again. Also my father was in the construction or contracting business. He mostly wanted to talk about his life, which was fair enough since most people do. He made it sound like he had a half-dozen lady friends, but none that "really inspired me"—or perhaps vice versa.

He maneuvered around to Gaby. I gave him a reasonable facsimile of my conversation with her, which clearly did not satisfy.

"But will she say 'yes' if I ask her to go out?" he almost whined.

I tried several tacks to encourage him to find out for himself, but he still wanted me to find out for him. At one point I would have liked to reach over and shake him, but instead found myself advising him in what seemed to me like father to son conversation.

"Women are flattered when a guy shows interest in them, Bill. You really cannot lose, even if she has another fellow right now or something else. She will remember. Right now she probably thinks you just want to be a nice friend. She will respect you for telling her you would really like to date her."

"Should I use that word—date?"

"The actual words do not make that much difference. The first time I asked Susan out she said she could not do it right then. Three weeks later she asked me out."

"Who's Susan?"

"That was a long time ago, but the point is to do it like a man—with confidence."

"Yeh, yeh; that's really good advice," he replied without a lot of confidence.

The movie afterward was unredeemable—some action flick so full of explosions, staccato gunfire, and mayhem, Bill could not believe I could fall asleep. Several times he elbowed my arm and reminded me that the action figure was Arnold Schwarzenegger.

"Why could they not give him a smidgen of decent dialogue?" I wanted to complain, while resolving next time to pick the movie and so try to find some common ground with Bill and for my own sanity.

4th of July

"We are free! We are independent! Rid of those Brits!" as I was wont to announce to young Shelley and Steve before taking the family down to Santa Monica and the pier for popcorn and rides, and then the fireworks. In the car on the way down the 405 I would make them listen to the 1812 Overture, and then remind them that on July 4th 1826 the main author of the Declaration of Independence and 3rd President of the United States and his sometimes colleague and sometime adversary, the second president, died within five hours of each other.

I saw my own stars and bright lights this morning when I whacked his head—which was quickly also my head—on a ceiling beam in the storage area of the garage level. I have probably bumped this head a half dozen times since becoming Mark—getting in and out of the car and once at the gym—but this time almost knocked me out. There was some blood too. It is a good thing I am letting our hair grow out. My bump won't show quite so much.

Whatever happened between my mind and Mark's, I still find myself surprised in the both simple and complex actions like running, reading and writing this, eating, chewing and swallowing, taking a dump, talking, reacting to pain. My mind and his body, with its lower brain functions and nerves and muscles and all, seem to have fitted together in ways I would have found hard to imagine. Ha! Try to imagine any of this! Someday I will have to turn myself in to the psychologists and neuroscientists who do all those brain and body studies.

The queasy stomach and vomiting throughout the first day or so may have been due to shock, but were perhaps also physical while adjustments were taking place. Maybe there was some imbalance in the inner ear.

There can yet be an awkwardness in adjusting to his stride and (I gently pat my scalp) remembering to duck the head. Then there are his erections. Otherwise it is a series of adjustments. Although I occasionally overreach when trying to pick up or take hold of something, it would seem we are both right handed with, no doubt, some of that activity embedded in his lower brain. The hearing is noticeably better than mine was. I am occasionally startled by the loudness of street noises and want to tell people to lower their voices. I can hear the TV in 3-B nearly 24/7 and the occasional argument.

Every once in a while I catch myself reaching for my reading glasses, but now I read with ease; nor do I have any need of glasses to drive or watch television. And what happens to them now? Likely they will sit around for a while. Then Susan will to put them in a drawer. There is a charity, I think I remember, that sends used glasses to Africa.

As far as food and drink are concerned, I am looking for compromises. Mark has a bigger appetite and can tolerate foods I had learned to avoid over the years. I can teach him to eat a bit less though with the occasional beer. I miss the Scotch but realize that I was probably more dependent on it than I was willing to admit. Susan was too kind to bring it up unless something happened to make her worry about me. On the other hand, we are going to have more fish, broccoli, spinach, kale, and chard than he was likely used to—more fruit, and little or none of his powdered protein drinks. I will make up for that by having a second dish of ice cream.

Gaby called to wish me a happy 4th of July. She reminisced about a time we all went to the Santa Monica beach and pier too—with Mom and Daddy. Did I remember when we got stuck at the top of the Ferris wheel with Mom, and Mother went on and on, pointing out how wonderful the view was to keep us from getting scared, but that my dear sister wet her panties anyway.

I asked if she was going out again this evening with her friends. She said she was thinking about it. There was no mention of my coming along.

Nor was there mention of Bill, and I thought it best to let that sit for a while. But she did want to tell me that "Daddy" might be getting serious about a woman he was dating.

"Have you met her?" I played along.

"She's not at all like Mom. Younger, of course. I'm sure she's a peroxide. But funny. You'd like her."

"How is she not like Mom?"

"You know: Mom was quieter and more into family when she wasn't busy with her teaching. Dolly's divorced, I think, but she doesn't have any kids."

"Dolly?" I laughed, but had the clue I was looking for. Pretty clearly our mother was no longer with us.

"It's her nickname. Sort of suits her. You'd like her O.K. Daddy thinks she's sweet."

I let Gaby go on for a while and, wanting to learn more about "us," dared to ask her if she would like to have dinner sometime next week.

There was a definite pause. "So what's up with you?" she replied.

"Not much. Nothing really. Just I have not seen you for a while."

"Well!" she responded half-mockingly. "Wouldn't that be nice? Do you want me to bring someone for you?"

"No. Just us."

Another pause. "Are you O.K., Marcus? You sound different."

"I have been feeling different. Maybe even want to be a little different."

One more pause—then kind of a low "huh-huh-huh" that sounded both noncommittal and not displeased, which was followed by what I found to be a frustrating negotiation about when she could fit me into her schedule, resulting in maybe either Saturday or Sunday night "depending." "Busy gal," I said to myself with a new appreciation of Bill's hesitation in asking her out.

Mark's storage area had a combination lock on it, but I was able to see through the fencing that the space did not contain much. There was a recliner chair that looked like it was mildewing and best left there, a desk lamp, a foot locker, and another file box. The file box had "pictures" scrawled twice on it, which could, I reasoned, be quite helpful—especially if there was a picture of Gaby and perhaps "Daddy" as well and Mom. Probably a younger Marcus. Who else?

The foot locker was padlocked with another of his combination locks. I would have to buy or rent a tool to snap it off too—which would make three so far. Even more intriguing were the stickers I could see on the trunk—one for Fort Hood and another Fort Benning.

Back in 3-A I opened up box 1 again and dug around. A manila folder marked "Military" had only one item but it was his army discharge papers. "Honorably discharged... Marcus

Ditmar Zito." He had been in the army from September 6, 1988 until June 10, 1992, three months short of 4 years.

"Well, well, well" I announced to the doors and windows. As Marcus Zito I had been a soldier boy. Surely that was to his credit.

Maybe he had had a couple of so-so years of community college, ran out of money or gumption or both and decided to try the military. But why not then finish college afterwards? Or might he have stayed with the army?—maybe gotten a technical training of some kind? Maybe he did, though now it did not seem to be doing him much good.

So we are both soldier boys and veterans on the 4th of July, for I had also done my patriotic duty, all right. I had also been at Fort Benning many years ago. And then there had been more training, waiting—even an eagerness for action with the 101st Airborne, before we were parachuted in behind Utah Beach, with my getting separated from the others. I could hear the Kraut voices before linking up and, killing or being killed. We lost maybe fifty in that first assault. Then there was more waiting, now scared of war when we were rushed in as reinforcements in the Battle of the Bulge under "Nuts!" to any surrender General McAullife, as we nearly froze to death with shells whining and exploding behind us. Then came the Panzers grinding past only yards away and a shrapnel wound bad enough to earn me a purple heart and a pass out of the rest of the war.

Maybe Steve gets my medals now. Or they will be passed on to George and to his son if he has one until someone cannot remember whose they were and certainly not why.

What I mostly remember from that week in Belgium was how frightened I was and how many buddies I lost. It all made me hate war and want to erase those days and nights from my memory. I will claim to be as patriotic as any American.

I love to sing "My country tis of thee/sweet land of liberty" and salute our flag. I look forward to the 4th of July, but not when it gets militarized and a bunch of politicos and TV pundits and all—most of whom had never been near shooting or been shot at—begin God-blessing the soldiers, and their bravery and sacrifice and glorifying war.

I am surprised how worked up I can still get thinking about it, though I guess it cannot matter any more. Now I wonder what retired Corporal Marcus Ditmar Zito thought or would think or should think about war.

He might possibly have been deployed as part of Desert Storm. I tried to keep my mouth shut when President Bush sent us into Bahrain against Iraq. I did quote Martin Luther King in one of my last school assemblies about how returning violence for violence multiplies violence and hinted at the possibility that there could be better ways to project the best of American values in the world.

That was enough for a couple of parents to write to me firmly if not sternly: we were only fighting in the Middle East to defend an innocent people from a dictator and aggressor, they wrote. One asked me to remember that Westview graduates could well be among those fighting for freedom and democracy and that I should say nothing that did not support them.

I resisted writing back and noting how historically one war has laid the seeds for another. Moreover, I would bet the number of Westview grads serving in our "fighting forces"— much less in harm's way—could be counted on the fingers of one hand—if that. Our involvement in the Middle East was for a whole set of reasons—some of which we could not even admit to ourselves. Instead I did what I had learned worked well. I called the parents and assured them that neither the school nor I was teaching anything other than the support of the best of our country's values and ideals. I was prepared to trot out my military service if necessary.

Douglas Bartlett McCutchen III and Andrew Greene, Esq., whose father was a retired admiral, seemed mollified, assuring me that they just wanted to know where the school stood at a time when the United States of America itself was standing up for what was right in the world. "Thank you for calling, Barnes. I appreciate it, and please know that Mary Alice and I are grateful to you and Westview for the education Douglas and Meredith are receiving there."

So happy 4th of July, Hal and Mark. Maybe George and Katie do not feel like going to Santa Monica without their grandpa today, but I hope they will. Maybe they will see Mark's sister there. I hope they will listen to the 1812 Overture on the ride down and remember that we do "hold these truths to be self-evident, that all men are created equal."

Meanwhile, I have a goose egg on the head of this one, if not two, lonely ex-soldiers. The Dodgers are getting goose-egged by the Expos. Perhaps there will be some fireworks after the game.

July 6 1994

"Must have been some 4th of July," Jim greeted me. "You might want to wear your cap for a day or two."

I tried to explain how I had bumped my head in the storage area of the garage. He gave me a sympathetic smile and looked a touch dubious at the same time. "How about that. Sorry."

Amanda was immediately concerned and suggested I might want to have a doctor look at it. "You could have a concussion, you know. That must have really hurt."

When I made the mistake of telling her the bump was the least of my problems, it took me a few minutes to get her focused on her exercises and stretching, and soon she was telling me about her daughter's marriage and gynecological issues in some detail. She was disappointed when I had to end the session exactly on the hour but departed with a kindly "You take care now, Marcus. Remember how tall you are."

I actually had five more sessions yesterday—an hour with a middle-aged couple with several ailments who had made a resolution to support each other in "getting back into shape." I think Mrs. Farnsworth was more serious about the effort than her husband, but they both paid attention and were careful to tell me what was difficult and what hurt—sometimes on behalf of their spouse. I put a lot of effort into being supportive and encouraging, but heard enough "ooohhs" and groaning toward the end of our time that I was not sure if either or both of them would be returning.

My big success yesterday was at the bank. First, however, I stopped at the CVS and bought some antibiotic cream, came back here, showered, and gently applied the ointment to the spot where I could feel I had broken the skin. Mark had one blue dress shirt hanging up in its cleaner bag. I was determined not to look apprehensive at the bank. I had, after all, his driver's license, his credit and ATM cards, and check book. I could even bring in his discharge papers, if necessary.

There were few people at the Bank of America branch, which felt a lot bigger than it needed to be for the business they were doing. Only a few years ago they had swallowed up my Pacific Security Bank.

The teller took the check and deposited it for me easily. "Anything else today, Mr. Zito? Here's your deposit record."

"Yes." I looked down on him. "I wonder if I could write a small check for cash?"

"Sure," he said, "though I'll need to see some I.D., but you can also use your ATM card if you'd prefer."

I had not planned this out, but tried, "Would you believe I cannot remember my pin number? Maybe it was this knock on my head. I keep forgetting things."

"Shouldn't be a problem," he smiled. "Just give me your driver's license and the ATM card if you have it with you or another form of identification."

I handed them to him and he began fussing with the computer. A minute went by. Then another.

"Any problem?" I asked, followed by my nervous cough.

"No, no," he said, still plugging away at the keys. "Either the computer's slow today or I am," he laughed. Another 15 seconds. "And can you tell me your mother's maiden name?"

"Hope I have not forgotten it too. Ditmar?" I failed to keep the question mark out of my voice. Ten more seconds.

"Bingo," he said.

"Double bingo," I thought while keeping my mouth shut.

"Here's your new number." He slid me a piece of paper. "I'll need you to punch it in twice on that pad to your left unless you want to change it.

"Maybe that would be a good idea," I responded, only to wish I had not.

I put it the oh-so-familiar number 7227 from my joint account with Susan. I would never forget that, I reasoned, but then began worrying whether the same number would be reported as a duplicate. And maybe 7227 could have someday been a way of proving that I was Harold Barnes. Now it would just be another coincidence in our lives.

But, hey, I have come back to our apartment with 40 bucks in the wallet and a working checking account and ATM card. This was progress, I complimented myself, realizing that it would be good not only to keep Marcus Zito alive and functioning in one form or another, but that we could accomplish some things together. Moreover, if I ever was to somehow reconnect with my former life, I needed a healthy Mark to do so.

Thursday July 7

This morning my 81 year-old duffer who had the stroke brought a friend, probably 15 years his junior, who, he told me, "really needed to get a workout again. Don't let up on him." He winked at me.

I had four sessions in all, along with some minutes to chat with Jim. He had been in the army, too, although, *perforce,* our conversation turned up far more about his time in the service than mine.

"I like my work here," he went on in a quieter voice. "But I'd like more responsibility—some more dough, too. I'd like to get married one day—have some kids."

"First you have to find a girl," I kidded him.

"No problem there," he swung his body back and forth, almost giggling. "You're the one who could use some help with that."

I let that go, realizing Jim probably knew more about Mark's love life—or lack thereof—than I did. Of course, he could be faking it some too.

I stopped by the Encino Bally's and did many of my old routines with Mark's strong body. I started to avoid, but then deliberately sat in the machine where I had died. They should put a memorial plaque on it.

I looked across to where I had become Mark and he had . . . or one of us had died. Or might his mind have gone into another body? That seemed too much like musical chairs for minds. I wondered if anything like this had ever happened before . . . some weird reincarnation. "Unbelievable," I repeated half aloud—if it were not so real right down . . . or rather up to the bump on my head.

I started on the tread mill without anything to read, and recalled how I had liked running last week. Running—or at least jogging—was what I liked to do when I was younger.

Then how nice it was to be outdoors—with little smog today, especially after I reached Balboa Park. There I alternated bursts of speed with fast walking and began thinking about playing tennis again. In latter years I played mostly doubles with colleagues from Westview, but now I might return to playing singles. I wondered again if Mark had ever played tennis, and then found myself remembering playing with Steve. Even before he was 12 we would hit the ball together and sometimes play a set. Several years we were a doubles team in father-son tournaments. He was on the tennis team at Westview and soon could beat me. After UC Berkeley and now his teaching position in San Francisco, we have hardly played at all. And now there were tears cooling on my cheeks as I ran. I was running and crying, thinking about how much my son missed his dad and how much I missed him.

There was no phone message from Gaby or Bill. I returned the call from the dentist's office and confirmed the appointment they had made for next week. It sounded like only a routine cleaning. I hope he does not have any cavities or other problems. Then I would have to figure out how to pay for it.

Friday July 8

"Have you been hiding from me, young Mark?" The tall, somewhat bent and slightly balding woman obviously enjoyed startling me when she snapped open the door to apartment 3-C as I was coming down the hall on the way home from work.

"I . . .uh. I . . . uh," I tried to reply until I realized she had meant her question as a friendly greeting. "I have been kind of busy. A lot has been happening."

"Oh good. You must tell me. I've missed our little conversations."

"Well, really not that much. Busy at work, you know." I was grateful I had kept on my cap and that she was not tall enough to see my head bump anyway.

"Well, come in for just a minute. An old lady can use a scrap of conversation."

I did not see that there was much chance to refuse and wondered if "young Mark" did this very often.

"Let me get something for the working man. Your glass of cold water or I could make you some tea, or," she tried to look conspiratorial, "something stronger."

"Water would be fine."

"Then rest your handsome bones, and I'll get you some."

With her in the kitchen struggling with the ice tray, I had a chance to look around and try to guess something about her. The basic apartment was laid out like mine: living room, in which she had a small dining table, the little kitchen and probably down the hall her bedroom and bathroom. There was a lot of furniture—two winged chairs with a red and green floral design, facing each other with a coffee table between and in front of a sofa for two—but bigger than what I would have called a love seat. End tables with substantial lamps framed the sofa. There were two sideboards against the walls, their surfaces covered with what appeared to be family photographs, all in frames. It felt homey and stuffy at the same time. The drapes and four or five paintings (one I recognized as a Cezanne reproduction) could not hide all the cracks in the walls. Presumably Mark knew her name, although he had only been in this building for a couple of months.

My guess was a widow without a lot of means, who then called out, "Mark, could you help me get the ice out of this damn tray?"

I did, and we had a conversation that did not last as long as I thought it would. I had hoped I might learn more about Mark from her, but realized she probably knew less than I did.

She wanted to tell me that she had been again on the phone to the "super" for our building who had been no more convincing in his reassurances that there were plans for repairs and painting. In the meantime we were all to know that the structure was sound and had been inspected and certified for occupancy.

I realized that she had probably been here on that Martin Luther King Day when the Northridge earthquake struck at 4:30 in the morning.

"Sure as hell was. I already told you that. Scared the living bejesus out of me. I'd been through earthquakes before, but none like that one. It's buildings like this with their basement garages that pancaked, you know. Where were you?"

I could not tell her that I was in bed with Susan. "In bed," I replied. "I did not get out until it stopped shaking. Must have lasted almost a minute."

"Thank God only a few people died—that policeman who drove right off of the freeway bridge."

It dawned on me that she was not far from me in age, and I smiled as shyly as I could: "I'm really sorry, but I cannot remember your name."

"Ha," she laughed. "I thought you'd never ask. I like politeness in a man. Eleanor—Eleanor Hubbard, but lots of people call me Ellie."

"Now let me ask you," she went on. "Do you know the names of that couple between us?"

"I am afraid I do not."

"But I'll bet you can hear them. Dagwood and Blondie—that's what I call them."

"I can hear their TV."

"And?"

"Once in a while their voices."

She widened her eyes. "Voices? Come on, admit it. You can hear them arguing plenty."

"Well," I shrugged.

"You know what they argue about—mostly money, just like you'd expect. Big time—even nasty with each other. But you know what's even louder?"

"No, I…"

"You probably can't hear it like I can. Their bedroom's on my side. I don't mean to embarrass you, but then it sounds like the furniture's being moved around and they're shouting different things to each other. And you know what? I think Blondie and her Dagwood are going to make it just fine. Couples can fight about money and things, but if they know how to bury the hatchet," Ellie guffawed, "they'll end up just fine." She looked at me for agreement.

"I guess . . . I am sure you are right," I did my best to say so.

"Voice of experience," she told me. "But now you've finished your water, and I know you're a busy young man. You ought to be married yourself by now. Go on down the hall and call up some nice young gal who's probably dying to go out with you. Just don't hide yourself from me again."

I told her I surely would not and sat down here bemused and confused by my double life. The only woman I wanted to talk with I could not That is also about the only thing of interest that has happened today. The Dodgers, who lost to the Expos again yesterday, are up against the Mets tonight, but I sometimes think I am beginning to lose my enthusiasm for them—or at least not to care the way I once did. Maybe I should try to go to Chavez Ravine one night and see if I can get some Dodger devotion going again. But that would also take money.

What I really would like this evening are some of my books. Maybe I'll get this "nice young man" a library card. Meanwhile I can always listen more attentively to what is going on in 3-B.

Saturday July 9 1994

"Looking up," Jim gave me a thumb up and that bright smile of his. "Haven't seen you here on a Saturday for a looong time." I had two scheduled sessions. The second of them was cancelled but Jim gave me one of his when an older man came in at the wrong time. On my way back here I stopped by the Sherman Oaks library branch. I had a card there for longer than I can remember, though I had not used it much in recent years. When I had the opportunity I preferred to go to the Central Library and often just browse around. They had done such a good restoration and fixing up since the fire and all the water damage—one of the better jobs of civic enterprise in Los Angeles. I even sent them a few dollars by way of encouragement and as one of the beneficiaries.

At one time I had thought of requiring my students to be public library users, but instead tried to entice and cajole them—usually without much success. So I was surprised when the woman who must have been at the Sherman Oaks branch for at least 15 years looked up and said "You already have a membership, Mr. Zito, though I do not think you have used it for some time. Would you like a new card?"

Pleased with the effect my youth and manners seemed to have on an older women, I thanked her and thought about what I might check out quickly that they would have on their shelves. In my mind's eyes I could see my rows of books— semi-arranged—in our library at home—including books I had not yet read or wanted one day to reread. I confess I am among those who never finished *Anna Karenina* and had hoped to rekindle an interest in Hardy—despite the bleakness of his overall view of life.

What I checked out was Roth's *Zuckerman Bound* Trilogy— another book—or set of books—I had never finished, though asking myself if Zuckerman would be all that salutary for me in my present predicament. I think the librarian thought somewhat less of me for my choice.

It looked like it could be a long weekend with me and Nathan Zuckerman. Bill had called back late yesterday afternoon and apologized profusely for not being able to keep our dinner and perhaps movies "gig," but, with high expectation in his voice, told me "I have a date" and hung up. I was wondering if my encouragement of his confidence in asking girls out had paid off with another woman and what if anything I should then tell Gaby. Then Bill called back and asked if I wanted him to see if Terry had a friend. When I told him "I am really not ready for that," he wanted to know, "why not?" but quickly let it go when I said I could not tell him right then.

But now my phone is hard at work. Gaby just called. I am guessing that her plans or hopes for this evening fell through, so she had better go out with her brother. In any case, we are to meet at the California Kitchen on Ventura, and I am going to take the lock-buster I borrowed from Bally's and look in that box of pictures in the garage locker. It will surely help if I have some idea what my sister looks like.

July 10ᵗʰ – Sunday
It is always interesting to discover the different shapes and sizes family members come in. The file box marked "pictures" had a dozen or so mostly family photographs—all of them in frames, of one kind or another. (The foot locker was a disappointment—only a few books and several thin files from what must have been Marcus' community college years.) What was probably the latest of the family pictures is of Mark (or I have now seen he sometimes signed himself "Marc") as a late teenager—already at least six feet tall. The man who I assume is his father is nearly as tall, with carefully combed dark hair receding from the front, glasses, and a wide smile. He has one arm over Marcus' shoulders and the other over a teenaged girl who was no more than five foot-two with long blondish hair and, frankly, a little lumpy looking. Next to them is a pleasant looking brunette woman, just a shade taller than her daughter, but quite thin in a print dress that appears a size too big for her. Only the dad is smiling his big smile. The other faces look more dutiful.

The other photos go back perhaps as far as ten years earlier with Marcus and Gaby as children, and their parents looking younger—Mr. Zito without glasses, but always the smile and a more attractive—really quite beautiful wife, somewhat fuller of figure. Several of the pictures have other people in them—possibly a grandmother. Maybe other relatives or neighbors?

Most of the pictures were taken in front of the same white-stucco ranch house, likely built in the 50s, and then added to, that are found in many places in the towns and

73

cities of the San Fernando Valley. I particularly noted that in two of the pictures there was a boy, then a young teenager, who looked enough like him to be Marcus' older brother, but perhaps a neighbor or a friend.

I considered taking one or two of the photographs to dinner with me, perhaps including the odd one out—a young woman whom I take to be Chinese—gazing rather dreamy-eyed from out of what could have been a studio portrait and was signed "Love, Cindy." I could tell Gaby I wanted to reminisce, but decided it might be too obvious or could wait for another time.

I need not have worried about identifying Gaby, who quickly told me she wants to be called "Gabrie," but is, indeed, Gabriella. She came charging out of the doorway and gave me a full frontal hug and two kisses that left no doubt who she was. Now about five-five she was somewhat full of figure, but moved and dressed so well it made quite a package. During the course of our time together I noticed other men and women glancing at her and found myself feeling proud that she was having dinner with me, even paying loving attention to me, not infrequently reaching across to pat my hand or arm, once even my knee. I had to remind myself that she was my sister. It occurred to me that she was the kind of girl who many years ago my buddies and I would have called "a barrel of fun" and meant it very much as a compliment.

Nor need I have been concerned about keeping up my end of the conversation. She did notice the bump on my head and that I was letting my hair grow out "some." I used it as an excuse to also tell her about the trauma of the old man dying in the gym right in front of me, complete with the detail of my throwing up. Both, I informed her, had "thrown me a little off course" and that I was even having trouble remembering some things.

That earned me two sympathetic pats on the arm. But she clearly felt that I was going to be just fine and knew that I wanted to hear about Daddy, which before long, came to be about Daddy and Dolly.

I listened with close attention and tried to make use of my "attentive listening" skills by offering short responses that, after a while, she seemed to find disconcerting. "You O.K., Markie? You have a funny look in your eyes."

I thought of giving her a pat on the hand but instead let her rest her hand—which must have had at least three rings and several bracelets on the wrist—on mine. It felt so warm, and I realized I was perspiring lightly.

I learned that Daddy must be an affectionate, even doting father—at least to his daughter. He was a contractor of some kind. In fact, he owned a not insignificant contracting and construction business and also either owned or managed apartment buildings. He evidently worked long hours, "even harder after Mommy died." I got the distinct impression that there was a time when he very much wanted me to go in into the business with him.

She interrupted herself to ask, "Why did you want to have dinner with me, Mark? You know I love it. I love seeing you, but we thought—I don't know—that you didn't even want to see us that much anymore."

"Don't be silly. I love you. I love my family. But I guess I've been through some tough personal times—the army and all that."

"What's the army got to do with it?" She asked with a note of suspicion in her voice.

"I mean that's just a part of it. I know I've screwed up some things."

"Oh, Mark," she patted my hand and frustrated me by sidetracking the conversation into a lengthy reminiscence of a family vacation up in Lake Arrowhead.

I could see that the waiter was wishing we would move on. I ordered two more coffees and put two twenties on the table, trying to assure "Ryan, our server," that he might get a decent tip.

"Let me pay," she started to reach for her purse.

"Not this time. But can we get together again—maybe in a week or so?"

"Sure. Really? Sure. I'd love that." She looked at me as if she were trying to figure me out. "You really are kind of different tonight."

I pulled in my breath and took this as my opportunity.

"Yeh. I guess I'd kind of like things to be different. Maybe with Daddy too."

She put her hand up to her mouth and pressed on it.

"I mean I first need to better understand what the problems are."

"Oh boy," she responded, resting her chin on her hand and looking away. "As if you didn't know."

And then it all—or at least a good part of it—came pouring out. Daddy had put a lot of money into my education, and I had ended up messing around and never shown any interest in going back to school. They had hardly heard from me during the years I was in the army. I had spurned his efforts to get hold of me when I moved back. I had not been with my mother when she was dying in the hospital and did not dress properly for the funeral or even come to the reception afterwards. "And then having to pay all that money when you got that girl pregnant."

"What girl?"

She laughed sarcastically.

"I mean...I mean. You mean Cindy?"

"Of course, Cindy. Like you don't remember that."

Ryan almost slapped the folder with the check down in front of us.

There was silence. I tried to look sad and contrite. Actually I felt awful. I felt awful for Mark and as Mark and as myself being Mark.

"I do, I do," I murmured. "Still I would like to see Dad one of these days. See if we could talk things over."

Gaby or Gabrie or Gabriella brightened. "Oh, that would be wonderful, Mark. I'll tell him."

"Not right away," I backed off. "You have given me so much to think about."

"O.K., but don't forget. Promise?"

We parted with another big hug and three of her kisses and promises to stay in touch—soon.

My Sunday excursion was to drive up past Shelley's house and park the car several blocks away. Then I was a nicely dressed young man out for a walk in the neighborhood who happened twice to pass by 2816 White Oak.

Being the Sabbath, I had even thought about going to church. Shelley and Rob and George and Katie would be there—probably even Susan now that I was not there not to go with her. But I was not ready for that. Maybe I never would be.

Instead I made myself a promise. I called it a solemn vow. Every week—at least once a week—I would walk past the home of my daughter and grandchildren. Not today, but some days I might at least catch sight of them. Maybe I would even see Susan visiting them.

July 17

Grind it out. Day by day. That is what I have come to think I am doing as Mark Zito—keeping his job, keeping him exercised and fed. The trip to the dentist went all right. Our teeth were cleaned and there were no cavities. Bad news was that Dr. Levinson tells me that he has been watching my wisdom teeth and recommends extraction of two of them. Susan had her wisdom teeth yanked after we had been married a couple of years. She looked so bruised and swollen. I did not want any of our friends to see her for fear they would think I was abusing her. No kisses for a couple of weeks either.

But I never even knew if I had wisdom teeth. Nor, at least up until now, have Stephen or Shelley had any problems.

Nor could I imagine how I would pay for it unless and until I could get dental insurance.

When I went to pay the bill, the perky blond gal smiled charmingly and said, "Hello Mark. Can we again send this bill to Mr. Victorino Zito at the same Woodland Hills address?"

That seemed an easy way out, but "Twenty-six years old," I thought, and "Daddy is still paying my dental bills."

"How much is it?"

"Seventy-five dollars," she smiled yet more sweetly.

I wrote her a check realizing that was more than I sometimes make in a day.

But Mark and I are actually doing better at work. I have obtained several more clients recommended by the people with whom I have been working. Handing me my check Friday, Randy commented, "You seem to have developed some chemistry with the geriatric crowd."

When I objected to "geriatric," he changed it to "midage plus" and, looked at me more appreciatively. "It's a good thing for all of us Mark, and for them. If you're good at it, go for it. Maybe we can send some others your way."

Those sessions can get boring, but I still have to pay attention and be in relationship with my clients. Several of them now seem almost like friends. But especially in the evenings and now on another Sunday, I have to admit that I am pretty far down in the dumps if not depressed. It is so hard to acknowledge that my life is really over. I mean, all my family, all my friends, all my former colleagues—everyone thinks I am dead and gone from this world. I have no more connection to my life. "I have no one to talk to," I announce in Mark's voice, full of self-pity.

There is my new buddy Jim at work, and on Friday, without asking me, Bill brought Chelsea along with his Terry. Chelsea was, at probably five-foot ten, all woman—attractive and also thoughtful and kindly. She would think things over in a meditative way before responding. Yet—at 23—she seemed like a daughter—or even younger. When the subject was music or films, I often did not know what they were talking about.

I was not past imagining what it might be like to take our clothes off and make use of this young body with her, and I could tell she felt some attraction to me. But then what? What did I say then?

As we broke up for the evening, I could tell all three of them were disappointed in me—perhaps Terry the most. Bill had likely given me a big build-up.

I keep telling myself there has to be some purpose for what has happened—even in an irrational world. Every once in a while I do get the strange sensation that someone is watching, but that goes away too.

The one person I do enjoy talking with is Ellie. She sees my car pulling into the garage or hears me on the stairs (the elevator in this building takes forever), or has some kind of sixth sense. But she knows I like seeing her and never has me stay for long. At her 71 we are not far apart in age. Her Bernie died as much as ten years ago. She has a daughter and three grandchildren in Idaho, but "I don't want to live in Idaho." And she was "a book keeper" for at least part of her life.

The other day I slipped up. She somehow got going about Tricky Dick Nixon and Watergate, and I started filling in some details about Haldeman and John Dean and the tapes when she pulled up in her chair and peered at me over her half-glasses.

"My, you must have been a very good student, Mark. Did you major in history?"

"I have read a lot of history," I responded, which is true.

Speaking of the car, the Corolla is making strange sounds, and there is slippage in second gear. I have never had much auto expertise but enough to know that it could be the transmission. *Oh boy!* I am making some more money, but a major repair or another car could set us back quite a bit. *Grind on, Toyota. Grind on, Marcus Zito.*

Wednesday July 20

Thank God for KUSC. I will forever miss my own tape and CD library, but, while I do not always agree with his taste in music, Jim Svejda seems like an old friend this evening. I may never know about Mark's taste in music, but I'm glad to have his boom-box on which I am listening to the Third Brandenburg Concerto, whose familiarity both soothes and lightens my spirits. It is better for me tonight than my barely so-so Dodgers who have already lost to the Mets again in New York anyway.

With the half-dozen CDs Mark has, however, I think we may be able to find a few inches of common ground. I cannot claim to have been an aficionado of Country music but—particularly if it is Willie Nelson or sometimes Johnny Cash—I know I like that. Ellie says Nelson is her favorite along with Dolly Parton.

For the moment I have kind of had it with Nathan Zuckerman. His combination of self-criticism and pity causes me to think too much about my past life that is past.

Gym work is O.K. For the last few days I have been less apprehensive, and it is nice to feel appreciated for what I am doing. I try to think of it as helping people, and it is income of a kind. I should worry more about that, but not tonight.

July 24—another Sunday

"Alas! That all we loved of him should be / but for our grief, as if it had not yet been," wrote Percy Bysshe Shelley when John Keats died. Today Harold David Barnes has been deceased for a month and two days. Four and a half weeks. On this date one month ago my obituary appeared in the Los Angeles Times.

A month and two days ago I became Marcus Ditmar Zito, prodigal son of Victorino Zito, contractor and rental tycoon. Yesterday I had coffee with Gabriella, formerly Gaby, now Gabrie Zito, my sister. She said she really needed to see me but coffee was evidently all she had time for.

She drove out to my Bally's and we had our coffee in one of those new Starbuck's. I was not sure what all the hype was about except for the price, but she insisted on paying.

Nor did I fully understand why she needed to see me. I got another big hug and kisses. Several times she ran her fingers through my new hair and told me how handsome I looked. I gathered that she was no longer so sure that Dolly was good for Daddy—that maybe she was after his money—even while claiming that "Daddy knows what he's doing." I calculated that Victorino (or quite likely Victor or even Vic) was in his mid-fifties and had been widowed for something like eight years. He probably knew what he was doing.

And then, "You really must see Daddy soon. I told him you wanted to."

I said that I would—that I wanted to. "But I am really trying to change some things, Gabrie. I want to be a different person—a different son first."

"That's wonderful, Markie. I'll always love whoever you are," followed by another full hug, kisses, and a rumpling of my hair. She bustled off in her shorts and tank top. I decided that I was beginning to love my new sister back.

Yesterday I did my walk by Shelley's (not named after Percy Bysshe) house but again did not see anyone. They could be away on vacation. About this time last year they were all up at Lake Tahoe together with grandpa.

After work on Thursday I bought a pair of tennis shoes at Shoes-for-Less (12 ½ and I am not sure they are big enough) and borrowed a used racquet at the Tennis Center, telling Florence (who had told me to call her Flo at least a dozen times before) that I was thinking of buying a new one just like it.

I had not banged the ball off a backboard in years, and it was not a great success. I am guessing that he rarely played tennis. We had a hard time with our footwork and getting an even stride. A few times he completely fanned on the ball. But, my, we are strong, and I do think I can make something of him.

August 14 1994

I cannot believe the baseball season is over. How dumb can a bunch of millionaire players and multi-million dollar owners be? Meanwhile, screw the fans and the little guys who sell the popcorn and hotdogs, and the parking attendants and ushers and people who work in restaurants nearby, and everyone else while they fight over the money from the TV contracts and ticket prices and parking passes they keep raising.

Meanwhile, the Dodgers were leading the NL West even though barely over .500, and, to tantalize us, they won their last two games in Cincy—the last one with a Ramon Martinez shutout. But now we will never know what they might have done. *Thanks, guys.*

And what else in my circumscribed life? Work is a little slow. Jim encourages me. "You're doing a great job with those elders, man. Things always slow about now. People go on vacation. It's hot. But, wait 'til we get into September. Always picks up."

Bill broke up with Terry. Apparently she wanted him to go disco dancing with her more often, and he thought that was "old-time," though there was likely more to it than that.

"Do not worry," I consoled him. "My dad always said, 'girls are like streetcars. There's another comin' along every five minutes'"

"Your dad must be crazy, Mark. There haven't been streetcars around here for fifty years."

"It's just a figure of speech, like, "Hey, man, there are plenty of fish in the sea."

"My pole ain't catching anything." He looked down dejectedly. "Besides, you're talking funny."

We sat in silence. I wondered why he would want to talk with Mark anyway after Mark's performance with Chelsea. What had Bill seen in him in the past, and, in any case, what could a 68 year-old man tell him? I could, however, listen. "You have had some nice women friends before, Bill."

So I heard about Sara and Emily and a couple of others. I heard that he wished he were taller and had a better job. I heard that he would like to get his rocks off, but mostly he wanted "someone I can get along with who won't be a lot of trouble."

We talked for a while about what that could mean until he looked at me, bobbing his head back and forth.

"But you haven't had a girl for a long time. Maybe you're still getting over her?"

I made my face sad.

"It'll happen again," he consoled me. "I don't think she was right for you anyway."

"Maybe not," I mumbled.

"What finally did happen anyway? You know it was right in here you first met her."

"What are you asking?"

"I mean, I know she got pregnant, wasn't that it?"

"Well," I put in.

"Then with her being Vietnamese."

"Yeh."

But he didn't go on until I said, "It was a mess."

"Cindy was really stuck on you, Mark. I think she wanted to marry you. Maybe that's why she got pregnant."

"Oh, wow," I groaned.

"It was her family, wasn't it? And then they went to your dad."

"Boy. Oh, boy."

"I never did hear whether she had the baby or an abortion."
When I did not respond, he asked again. "Don't you know?"
"Not for certain."

Now whenever Gabrie calls she keeps wanting to know if
I am ready to get together with Daddy.

I believe it is going to happen. Maybe I believe that I
am supposed to make it happen. Maybe, I ask myself, this is
somehow in some way part of what this all may be about. But
I know that I am nervous—even scared: with the Cindy story
and what Gabriella told me came before and just knowing all
the complexities that go into father/son relationships. And
surely it will be complicated if not impossible to pretend that
I am Mark with his father, of all people. If anything like this
happened with my Steve, surely I would know that something
bizarre was going on with him.

August 16 1994

It is our 42nd wedding anniversary. How sad Susan must
be today. If only I could do something. Can you imagine
sending her flowers? Who should I say they are from?

We never did explain why we were getting married in the
middle of August, though I am sure her parents were suspicious. Hey! We were horny graduate students very much in
love, and, if you wanted to cohabitate back then, you had
better get married.

Plus, the fact of the matter, we thought Susan was pregnant. The irony was that she then may have had some kind
of early miscarriage, and it was another eight years before we
were able to have Shelley.

I wonder what has happened to my wedding ring. I cannot believe it was burned up with the rest of me. Maybe Susan

has it in that box of her mother's with her other treasured jewelry—much of which I gave her, not least the ruby and diamond bracelet on our 40th anniversary.

And I wonder what women do with their wedding rings when their husbands die. I will wager that Susan still wears hers and will—at least for a long time.

In honor of the day I put more transmission fluid in the Corolla. It is obviously leaking and may not be long for this world either. It also occurs to me that I was 26 when Susan and I were married. Now I am 26 years old again and cannot imagine being married to anyone else.

Labor Day 1994

"Capital is only the fruit of labor, and could never have existed if labor had not first existed. Labor is the superior of capital, and deserves much the higher consideration." "Guess who said that?" I liked to ask some of my conservative friends, including son-in-law, Rob. None less than that very first Republican and perhaps most illustrious American President. I once used the quotation in an Assembly Day talk at Westview in the week just after Labor Day, but I never heard anything back, except one of the brighter students told me she thought it was from Karl Marx.

It is also Katie's third birthday, although they must have celebrated on Saturday. When I took my walk by, there were twenty or more Happy Birthday balloons tied to the porch railing and trees—some beginning to droop a bit. I think the party had been over for an hour or so—without any present from grandpa. I hope Susan said, "This is from your grandfather, too." I tried to peer into the backyard, but could not see or hear any of my beloveds. Maybe they were worn out from the party.

I am getting better at tennis and dared to join in a pick-up game of doubles last week when one of the foursome did not show up. Mark blew several easy shots at the net, but we did not do too badly as I guided him along. From the next court I recognized the voices of two colleagues I sometimes played with and against. Frank continued to curse himself every time he missed a shot: "Damn you, Frank. Whoever taught you to play tennis?"

The car is in the shop getting a new used transmission. I decided that was the most economical way to go. Much of last week I took the bus to work. I should say buses and a 10-minute walk. It gives one a new appreciation for the laboring poor.

I have asked Bill to help me sell the Suzuki. He tried to argue, but, after I convinced him I was no longer a biker, he told me he was thinking of giving it up too. I still owe on it, but he thinks I might clear $800, which should more than pay for the transmission.

Bill also told me, "Don't look now, but that's Cindy over in the corner with a friend." I felt my face flush and fought the urge to jump out of my chair and depart the new Cheesecake Factory which Bill had wanted to try out.

"Really," I said as disinterestedly as I could.

"She's watching you," Bill smirked.

"Really."

"She is a looker, Mark. I can see…"

"We're over," I interrupted him.

"I'm not sure she's over—the way she's watching ."

"Really."

"No, really. Take a peek."

Against my better judgment I glanced where Bill was looking. It was Cindy from the picture all right, but I quickly looked away, hoping she had not seen me look.

My biggest treat the last few weeks has been several trips to the Central Library. I feel more myself there among all those books and other readers. I thought I might find a book that could give me some insight into what happened between Mark and me, although I could probably better make use of a psychiatrist to help me sort out my conflicted feelings of guilt about having taken over Mark's life and anger or even sorrow about being killed off. "Let me see. Let me see," he would muse, peering at me over his half-glasses. "We have never seen a case quite like yours. There is apparently some identity confusion. Very interesting. Very interesting."

I read into a couple of books on reincarnation, but never have been able to put much stock in that stuff. There was one that claimed to be dealing with a person who had 87 previous lives. Of more interest were some of the references to the "Decade of the Brain," research—especially on the brain-mind relationship. Scientists were musing on how, while the mind is dependent on the brain, it is not the same as the brain or is much more than the brain. The human brain itself contains an unbelievable number of axon and neuron connections, at least billions in each brain—more than all the stars in the universe. But evidently each brain only uses a portion of all that potential, which, I thought— Dr. Frankenstein-like—could leave room for more than one mind in one brain. One scientist I read claimed that, while much will no doubt be learned about the mysteries of human consciousness, humans may never understand that "mysterious flame" completely.

But none of this could explain any manner of consciousness or mind transference from one brain into another. Moreover, Mark's mind was apparently gone. While I from time to time have this odd sensation of being observed, it is not any form of dialogue I recognize. Nor do I have any awareness of his consciousness or memories, except perhaps in his motor skills and bodily functions.

One might further speculate that if my mind waves and connections somehow transferred into his brain, his must have gone into Harold Barnes. There it would have "flamed out" as it were, unless, of course, it actually transferred to somebody else. But then there would be the further question as to why Marcus in someone else would not try to contact me.

It all seems absurd, does it not? It does to me, too, except I am apparently living some form of it. And, if, by some strange one-in-a-billion conduction or transposition of the mind, this happened once, might it have happened before or again? Could there be at least a few other transmuted minds and consciousnesses out there, finding it as impossible to communicate with the others as I do?

Meanwhile life goes on, or does not, as the case may be. Tomorrow is a day to labor.

Saturday September 24 1994

Today I talked with George. My heart was thumping as I first started to cross the street. It would have been enough just to see him out in front of his house on his bicycle with the training wheels. The last thing I wanted was to be thought of as some creep who chatted up small boys. But as long as it was in front of his house and I moved on in a minute or so I hoped I could get away with it.

"Hello, young man. Do you live here?"

"I'm not a man. I'm a boy...a big boy."

"You sure are. How old are you?"

"Five and a half. I'll be six next year."

"I like your bicycle."

"My dad is going to take off the training wheels, maybe next week. But I'm not scared."

"I bet you will do just fine."

"Grandmommy and grandpa gave me my bike when I asked for it." He rode ahead a few yards and did a tippy turn back toward me.

"Wow," I congratulated him. That was good."

"Grandmommy's birthday is tomorrow."

"Is it? Are you giving her something?"

"Maybe. My grandpa died. Did you know that?"

"Yes. I think so. I'm guessing he was a very nice grandpa."

"Do you want to see me ride fast?"

"Not right now. I better go on with my walk. Maybe I will see you again."

"O.K."

Jim was right about work picking up in September, and most of my new clients are over fifty. Randy called me the "geezer trainer." "Peas in a pod," I retorted, which made no sense to him.

But it does mean I am making enough to live on. Or at least it is close, barring some medical problem or the car giving out again.

I have tried to be firmer with Gabrie. "I will see Dad when I have my life more in order. I am really working on it."

"O.K., but please before Christmas and everything. The others want to see you too."

How many others? I wondered. "I know."

"Promise?"

"O.K."

"Cross your heart and promise?"

"I love you, Gabrie."

October 17 1994

I went on to work anyway today. Life has taken on kind of a routine. I have always liked feeling needed and my clients seem to depend on me to get them through their routines and to feel better about themselves, if not always better physically. But the whole side of my face ached, though it must not have shown much as even Amanda did not say anything. Well, she did say she liked my haircut and that one of her grandchildren has been diagnosed as "mildly autistic, but I don't believe it."

For the first hour or so I thought I might have to make a trip to that dentist. I could taste blood in my mouth, and it hurt the worst when I bit down or clenched my teeth in any way. Then my ear ached too. Maybe this is what molar extraction would feel like.

I knew it was probably a mistake—maybe a big one. But it was also something I almost had to do—since maybe this was a reason for me to be Marcus—to make something better if not right.

Last evening was the second time I had gone to the Cheesecake Factory by myself. This time Cindy was again there at that same table with the same or another Asian girlfriend. I ordered the cheapest hamburger I could find on the huge menu, aware that she was glancing over at me. Finally I turned my head and gave her what I meant to be a half-smile and then, inadvertently, a rather childish wave of the hand.

In less than two minutes she came passing by my table as though she were leaving the restaurant, but then smiled, "Oh, hi, Mark. Do you mind if I sit with you?"

I stood up like a gentleman: "Be my guest."

We both sat into a wordlessness that seemed fine with Cindy but felt more and more awkward to me. She put her chin in her hand and looked at me with those same eyes in the picture. I could feel a warmth through my body that must come from the chemistry that had been between them and now us.

"How are you?" I asked. She smiled in response. She seemed, I told myself, very feminine though still in some ways a girl. Mark must be nearly twice her weight, and I three times her age.

The waiter set down my hamburger, and I asked for extra catsup.

"I thought you didn't like catsup" Her English was natural.

"I like to try different things," I told her. "I am trying to be different."

"I like your hair," she responded, and the silence resumed. I took a bite from the hamburger and had difficulty swallowing.

"Have some water," she said. "I'm sorry about what happened. I love you, Mark."

I got the chunk of hamburger down and took my time with the water. "I am sorry too," I said in what I meant to be a kind tone.

We spent another 10 or 15 minutes in what would probably have seemed a lovers' dueling match to anyone listening in. She kept attempting to get me to say that I loved her while I was trying to find out what exactly had happened and if there was anything I could do to make things better. My questions became more awkward. I wanted to be sure that Mark did not have a half-Vietnamese son or daughter that I should be doing something about. Or if I had caused her to have an abortion.

"It doesn't matter, baby," she replied when I said for the fifth or sixth time how sorry I was.

"But it must have been so hard for you?"

"It was so hard for you. I didn't want them to make you do that."

Do what? And who was 'them'? "And then what happened?"

"What happened was that I couldn't see you."

"I know. I am so sorry. But..."

She looked down as though ashamed.

"Were you sick at all?" I tried.

"Oh, Mark." She put her slender, warm hand on mine, "I know you wanted to care for me."

But try as I might, I could not find out anything more. I became virtually certain there was no child. So there probably had been an abortion. Just possibly she had become sick and had a miscarriage like Susan once did? Or? There were other scenarios that I thought unlikely: there was another young man or boy who got her pregnant. She never was pregnant, and it was some scheme to get money from me or, as I guess it turned out, from "Daddy."

I paid for the mostly uneaten hamburger, aware that I did not know how to end the evening or how it would end. We walked out into the soft lighting of the mall plaza. It had become a little chilly, but was still a lovely Los Angeles in October. We walked about aimlessly, wordlessly. She slipped her hand into mine and walked closer to me. "I'm cold," she said.

"It is chilly. But still kind of nice,"

"To be with you."

"Hmmmm," I replied, thinking that it was, indeed, pleasant to be walking with this girl and that it would not be happening if it were not for the Vietnam War.

"We could go back to your apartment?"

I squeezed her hand as we continued our walk. My body was responding one way, my mind in two or three. I could imagine this lithe, little body on top so I would not crush her—her slender warmth bending over me. I told myself I was an old goat, and that I would only make things worse by resuming a relationship—maybe getting her pregnant all over again.

Without giving her any good reason that I could think of, I finally convinced her that we would not be going to my apartment that evening. As I walked her to her car, she grew a little pouty, and I realized that she could be thinking that I either had another girl now—even someone back at the apartment.

"Promise me you'll call me," she asked at her car door, tilting her face up to mine.

"I promise."

"Tell me you love me," she slid her arms around my waist then up my back. I held her close and closer. I could feel the erection rising and knew she could too.

"I love you," I broke away and marched off in what I hoped was the general direction of my Toyota.

I resumed walking about when I returned to the apartment—probably Ellie knowing that I had come in at half-past ten on a weeknight. Mark could do about eight paces in the living room, four or five in the hall, even fewer in the cramped bedroom and back again. I was frustrated and disappointed in myself. Maybe I had learned some things about the pregnancy, but I had not done anything to improve or heal the relationship with Cindy.

I got ready for bed. My body felt tired, but still I paced some more. I am afraid I masturbated, which only further divided body and mind: a dirty old man, indeed. But it helped me to know that I could not keep that promise to call her, or I had to find some way—for everyone's sake—to end our relationship decently.

This morning as I pulled out of the garage there was a young Vietnamese man who held up his hand in a stop sign and, when I rolled down the window, asked politely if he could talk with me. I must have had some intuition of what was coming, but I still shifted into neutral, pulled on the hand brake, and got out—thinking I would at least show him how big I was.

I was taller, but not by a lot, and he was burly. I remember thinking I was not aware that Vietnamese men grew that large, just before he (Cindy's lover? her would-be lover? her brother?) hit me, knocking me back against the car, after which I slid to the ground. I feared he would kick me as well. Instead he threw an envelope at me, said "You are a slow learner, Mr. Zito," and walked away.

I waited to be sure he was not coming back or I was not going to lose consciousness. I slowly stood, gently shaking my shoulders and fingering my sore jaw.

I hoped Ellie had not witnessed this altercation. I hoped no one had.

The note in a flowered envelope on flowered paper was in a girly hand. "Please, Mark. You must not see me anymore. PLEASE. Cindy."

Thursday November 9

I found out that yesterday was Ellie's birthday and took her to dinner. Believe me; we did not go near the Cheesecake Factory. Turns out that she likes Indian food, too, and I will train Mark to like it.

After we ordered, I reported to her that my work was going well and that Jim had become a good friend, teaching me things he had learned from an advanced physiology course he was taking. He was also trying to get me interested in the Raiders, and he and I were going to a game on Sunday. I confided to Ellie that, in fact, I was not much of a professional football fan and was doing it mostly to please him, whereupon she surprised me with some sharp words about the Raider's owner Al Davis.

This all led her, however, to lament her physical condition at the age of 72. "Nor am I about to attend one of your gym classes for old ladies, dear Mark. I'm not about to expose parts of this ancient contraption to you or anyone else."

I told her I could show her some easy exercises to do at home and she cawed a throaty laugh and said that would be "peachy."

She is a funny gal especially after two glasses of house Chardonnay, and I became so relaxed I am sure I must have made remarks that could have revealed my true age. She, however, complimented my knowledge of events that took place "when you were knee-high to a grasshopper."

We had two good arguments. The first started when she told me she was glad that the Republicans won the majority in the House of Representatives on Tuesday and that Bill and Hillary had "got their comeuppance." "I've spent my whole adult life with Democrats ruling the House and, despite all their palaver, they don't care for common folks either."

"You think Republicans do?"

"No, I'm independent. I just like some change. And I kind of like Newt Gingrich's swagger. Nor do I like politicians fooling around with my health care."

I accused her of being brainwashed by those silly Harry and Louise ads about the Clinton health care plan, and she was surprised I cared as much about it as I seemed to "at your age." "Wait until you get old and need it."

The second argument was about the bill. She was crafty and had close to the right amount in cash ready to set out on the table. But I won after promising that she could pay on my birthday.

"Well, O.K. When is it?"

"February 2nd."

"That's Groundhog Day."

"No, no. Actually I mean June 18th."

Lands sake. You must be like the Queen with an official birthday and a real one. You can't have two birthdays, sonny boy."

Thursday December 8 1994

Mark's father and I had lunch yesterday. Gabrie arranged for it after giving me the what-for because I said I "was not ready" to show up for a family Thanksgiving with what sounded like a gaggle of cousins and aunts and uncles. I asked her to warn "Daddy" that I had been trying to make some changes in my life and might seem different to him. "He'll like that, Markie. You wait and see."

Wait, I did, and grew anxious. I did not know what to wear and settled on my trainer's outfit since I would be coming from work and returning. My dark and now even slightly wavy hair I had cut conservatively. To me my head, at least, looked like that of a young advertising executive from the late 50s or early 60s.

God, I was nervous. I rehearsed a couple little speeches. One made me sound much like the prodigal son of "Father, I have sinned and am no longer worthy to be called your son," et cetera. Better would be one about how I was trying to make changes. "About time," he would probably say. "Which changes?"

Victorino Zito of Zito and Sons Construction and Rental Company was a near total surprise to me. His offices were in a one-story building attached to a large garage. Behind the counter in the reception area were two small secretary's desks. A matronly-looking Hispanic woman, who seemed over-dressed for the setting in a dark skirt and full blouse with a colorful necklace and earrings, hung up a phone, rose, and smiled. "You must be Mark. Your father is expecting you." She led me into what probably served as a conference room—a square table with chairs at various angles around it. On a smaller table in the corner there was a stack of hard hats. A large chalk board was on one wall, a bulletin board on the other—both covered with what looked like messages or schedules of one kind or another.

On the table there were two glasses of water, two paper plates each with a sandwich and what looked like small cartons of soup or slaw.

"Oops. I forgot the napkins," she said. "I hope roast beef is all right. Your father said that's what you like. He has the tuna." She bustled out.

"That's just fine," I told her when she returned with the paper napkins she folded beside each plate.

"Do sit down, Mark. Your father will be here in a minute or so, I am sure. I thought you would look more like him."

I sat. I fretted. I remembered an old trick I had passed on to my children. "Try wiggling your toes in your shoes. No one can see you doing it." I put my hands palms down on the table.

Victorino strode in, saying something over his shoulder as he did. I stood up, and he stopped and looked at me, holding out his arms. "Marcus, Marcus, Marcus, my boy." He clasped me in a hug. I did not know what to say or how to respond physically. I rather gingerly put my arms around him. He was a couple inches shorter but a strong man who then gave me a quick, tighter hug. "Sit down, Marcus. Hope you are hungry. Tell me how you've been. It's been too long."

"In the name of the Father, Son, and the Holy Spirit," he made the sign of the cross. "Bless us, Lord, in these and all your gifts. Give us grateful hearts and make us always mindful of the needs of others. In the name of the Father, Son, and the Holy Spirit." He again crossed himself and sat down, gesturing as he did so to my food. "Hope you like soup with your sandwich."

For a man who apparently liked soup for lunch, he had trouble opening the carton his was in. I was either better at it or luckier and offered to help him. "No, no," he said, finally prying his open and spilling a little of what looked like tomato soup. "So how have you been? Your sister has been worried about you, but says you've been doing better. You look like you've been taking care of yourself."

I cleared my throat. "I am," I half-whispered and then spoke up. "My work has been going better the last few months. I am trying to be more focused on the things that are important."

"Focused, focused," he replied. "Yes, focus is important," though he seemed puzzled by my use of the word. But he listened while I described my training work with the older clients. I emphasized my hope that I was helping them with their overall health and self-esteem. "Yes, yes," he affirmed just a touch impatiently. "That must be helpful."

I told him that I had given up the motorcycle, but I was not sure he ever knew I had one. Clearly we had been out of communication for quite a while, but there were no recriminations. He did say that he was disappointed in my not being around the family, but did not dwell on it. I tried twice to call him "Dad," but did not think I made it sound right and then avoided using any appellation for him.

He was both affectionate and rather business-like with me, and I guessed that was probably the way Marcus had been brought up—at least by him.

"You need some money?" he inquired. "Don't worry about asking. I've got enough of it. You should have some kind of health care plan."

"I am fine. I really am."

"Well, you just let me know. I've got it now and we love you. Maybe something at Christmastime."

It ended up that there were only two things he really wanted from me. One was a promise that I would come to be with the family for Christmas "get-togethers." The other was that I would go to Francis de Sales if I wanted to but he would prefer Our Lady of Grace "where we all used to go and where you'll really like the pastor. It's a good place to pray for your mother."

I had a hard time imagining it, but figured those were two requests I could go along with in some measure.

"And come and have lunch with me again. You can have a different sandwich if you want and no soup." He glanced at my half-eaten sandwich and nearly full carton of soup. He had downed all of his while doing most of the talking. "I want to tell you more about the company. It could all be yours someday, you know. Oh, and no tattoos," he laughed. "You remember that."

He stood and crossed himself. Above his aviator glasses his hairline had receded so far he was half-bald, his tawny pate shining like mine might some day.

The best part of his appearance was his smile. "Oh, my Marcus," he smiled as I got up. "We always loved you." He hugged me and then kissed the side of my neck. "Remember now. See you soon."

He grabbed one of the hard hats and left while telling, "Gracia, de regreso antes de las tres" or something close to that.

I looked down at the remains of my lunch. So I was a Roman Catholic or at least supposed to be, and the son of an evidently devout Catholic. For all my irreligion, it was hard not to think again about the story of the prodigal son, which he must know too—though in his case it might better be called "the prodigal father," who one would not want to disappoint again. After all, I was a father, too.

Gracia came in to clear away the lunch. I offered to help and she told me, "You know, Marcus, your father is a very good man. He really cares for all of us here."

She insisted on wrapping my half-sandwich in a napkin and handing it to me. "Next time we'll have something besides roast beef."

2

New Year's Day 1995

"Time heals all wounds," it is said. I have long doubted that. But I have become more accepting of the fact that Harold David Barnes, as a physical, interactive person, is no longer part of this world. I am to others dead and gone in all but memory. I might still hope that another miracle or whatever could take place, but it is more and more difficult to imagine my body or one like it somehow reassembling, and my walking back into the lives of Susan, Stephen, Shelley, George, and Katie.

I thought of it on my first Christmas without Shelley and Stephen since they were born—remembering the hastily wrapped presents, the tree with all the ornaments we assembled over the years, Stephen's first bike, the dollhouse built for Shelley, the dozens of books Susan and I gave to each other over the years.

No more. I hope and trust they had a nice Christmas without me. The wounds of not being with them will last as long as I live.

In lieu of them, however, I did have plenty of Christmas family and celebration—a half a clan full. The main party, Gabrie let me know with no question as to whether I would be there, was to be at Uncle Bart's and Connie's house—"just like we used to do," whatever that meant. Since Christmas fell on a Sunday, "we don't have to go there until about two."

My anxieties rose as the day grew nearer. Who would be there that I should know? And probably should know well? Were there to be presents? Who should I give presents to? What should I wear?

I tried to get Gabrie to meet with me ahead of time, but she pled being busy with "getting ready for Christmas." "Wear whatever you want that is nice. Just be clean and shave for Daddy's sake."

Thanks for that, I thought, and bought myself a nicely striped blue button-down to go with clean chinos.

"You don't have to get presents for everyone. Just Daddy and, of course, me."

"What?" I asked almost desperately.

"You know I want to be surprised, Markie. Coming from you, I know I'll like it. Maybe get Daddy a bottle of Christmas schnapps. He says he likes that. I don't know what it is, but I'm sure you do."

As far as the relatives were concerned, "Oh, you'll know them all," she told me.

But I wheedled. I begged. I really had been away too long. Some of them must have changed. I had forgotten things. I had changed. I wanted to be "the new me," and be sure I did not get anyone mixed up. Gabrie then began a list I could not keep up with, and I could hear the frustration in her voice. Finally she said, "O.K., Mark. I'll send you a list if you need it. It can be your family cheat sheet."

She did. It came in Mark's meager mail two days before Christmas but in time for me to begin memorizing. There were 26 names on the list, although she was not sure who all would be there. It was carefully done. Gabrie had beautiful penmanship. It was like calligraphy, and she had included a group photograph from some previous family gathering. Connecting lines were drawn with indications of relationship, although I could not tell for sure who was on Victor's and who may be from our mother's side.

Not wanting to be too early or late, I settled on 2:30, which turned out to be just fine. The house was already full, with more out in back and around the pool, and several others trailing in over the next quarter hour. I felt remarkably relaxed, having decided that I would make this into a kind of play in which I acted the part of Marcus Zito, beloved nephew and cousin, who had been away in the army and otherwise not seen for some time. Besides I had been to enough school and related functions where I had to fake remembering people. The trick was not to say much and listen carefully.

But for a minute or more, they were all so involved with each other no one took notice of me. I put my presents on one of the tables that was already overflowing and headed to what looked like a little bar with wine bottles and a punch bowl. Suddenly someone shouted "Marcus," followed by "Mark" and "Markie," and I seemed to be a celebrity. I kissed everyone who kissed me. Two of the tots clung to my legs thinking I must be someone important and then began pushing at each other. I was "fine," "fine," "Thank you." "Yes; too long." "Fine." "I love you too." "No, I'm fine." "I am a physical trainer." "Yes, I like it." "You look great too."

Before long, however, my celebrity was over, the adults going back to their conversations and the children to chasing one another, except for two of them staring in awe at the piles of presents—one with an arm over the other's shoulder. They seemed to be conferring. A grandmother snapped their picture.

I eschewed the wine in favor of the non-alcoholic punch and sidled over to Gabrie who was talking with, as I soon figured out, cousin Andrea, daughter of Uncle Bart and Aunt Connie, who was married to Ted and had two kids whose names I do not remember.

The one person who was so obviously missing was Daddy Victor. After all, my main purpose in coming was to be seen by him. I almost asked, but decided to keep quiet.

I did not need to wait long. To appropriate fanfare, in came Santa Claus wearing aviator glasses and, after due excitement among the children, there was a flurry of present opening. This was not one of those families that "ooh and ah" over each present. The adults went about it with as much gusto as the little ones. It was noisy and to me confusing with a number of shouted "thank you; oh thank you" and "I've always wanted one." In the end it seemed over too soon as I had been enjoying watching it all. And I was also a recipient. In the future I would need more presents if I were to reciprocate. I came away with a smart-looking sweater vest, a dress shirt, a tie neither Mark nor I would ever don, and several pairs of socks.

The children were soon outside with a young father who was trying to make function some manner of battery operated helicopter. Two of the cousins were stuffing the last of the wrapping paper into trash bags when large bowls and platters were brought forth from the kitchen. It seemed wonderfully orchestrated.

All were summoned and Victor once again took over, likely being the oldest of the Zito brothers or the most religious. Without any request to do so, all took hands, bowed their heads, and Victor began, "In the name of the Father, Son, and Holy Spirit..." More than half the group dropped hands and crossed themselves as Victor did and then took hands again.

I thought Catholics had shorter prayers than Protestants but Victor went on for some time. God was thanked for many things, most especially "for the gift of your beloved Son born this day of the Virgin Mary; for shining star and angel song, for the Word made flesh in a little child." The centerpiece of the prayer, however, was for "those no longer able to be with us." The list was only a half dozen or so names—two of them I assume the parents of Victor and his siblings. He paused, "and dear Mary." He steadied his voice, "and our dear boy Victorino." Then he added, "And how grateful we are that our brave and handsome Marcus is here with us again."

As the prayer ended about half the group crossed themselves, including, I noticed, Gabrie. I might have to learn to do it.

I was careful neither to be the first nor the last to leave the party. Victor shed a few tears as he held me and thanked me for coming. "It meant so much to us, Marcus, and for being at Mass."

I did, in fact, go to church (or, as I'm learning to say, "to Mass") twice in advance of the Christmas "get-together." I tried a 10 a.m. Sunday service at Our Lady of Grace and a 5:30 p.m. Saturday Mass at St. Francis de Sales the following week. Neither of them did much for me. I have only been to a handful of Catholic services in my life and found the music disappointing and the often short sermons...well, too Catholic.

For some time I have not necessarily thought of myself as a Protestant or even a practicing Christian, but, were I forced to go to church regularly, some form of traditional Protestant would be my preference. The Sunday Mass was well-attended although no one spoke to me the whole time I was there.

The Saturday version had the aura of being more friendly and congregation-oriented, but, when I introduced myself to the gentleman next to me, he seemed surprised and even befuddled by my greeting.

When I was talking on the phone with Gabrie about the Christmas party, I snuck in a question about whether she went to church. "Yes," was her quick response, but, after a pause, "lots of times." When I informed her of Daddy's request that I go, she said. "You don't need to go all the time, Mark. He just wants to be sure you still believe and pray. Someday we can talk about Daddy and church."

When I returned to the apartment building, it was just after five. I could see the light under Ellie's door, and, though I had guessed she was Jewish, thought it would be nice to at least wish her "Happy Holidays." The door opened but a crack. I could see she was in a bathrobe and appeared disheveled. We quickly agreed to talk tomorrow.

When we did she was her usual perky self and would not let me get near the question of how she was celebrating or not the holidays. But I concluded that one day we should have a more personal conversation.

Monday 2 January 1995

Cousin Andrea and Ted invited me to a Rose Bowl party and viewing of the game at their pleasant home in Northridge—bigger than any one I have ever owned. It too had a pool. Ted had an aerospace engineering job and Andrea a law degree, though I gathered she was not practicing full-time.

Having decided to try to be more social, I invited both Bill and Jim to come with me. Bill, however, had something else on. Jim was the only non-white at the party—maybe the only non-Italian besides Ted who, with a last name like Grabovac, was probably Croatian in background. He still looked Italian to me.

Gabrie, who thought it was "wonderful" I had come, was there with a young man whose name I have forgotten. He looked like a shorter version of me. As we were talking he put his arm on Gabrie's back and then slid it down until it rested just above her cute tail end. I resisted the urge to knock it away.

When Jim and I left, Oregon was losing to a school from the East that nobody seemed to like. On the way home he told me that he had joined the National Guard as one of his new year's resolutions. "You ought to think about it too," he half-lectured me. "Make some extra dough. You could use that. Make some friends. Serve your country without having to fight a war."

"I think I have had enough of marching around and being ordered about for one lifetime," I countered.

"Yeh, there's some of that crap. But you also might get a chance to ride around in a tank. It doesn't take that much time, and the worst that could happen is if you get called up to deal with an earthquake or maybe a nice urban riot."

Groundhog Day 1995

Can people still be said to have birthdays after they have died? I have continued to remember my parents' birthdays: Albert Stephen Barnes on March 16th, having died nearly twenty years ago now; and Phyllis Hames Barnes on May 8th, only deceased in 1988.

I am sure Susan is remembering, probably Shelley and Steve, at least first time around. I am or would be sixty-nine today.

My Dad had jokes about my birthday being on Groundhog Day. He would call me his little groundhog. He would rub my head and say, "You're a hairy little groundhog. Did you see your shadow today, Harry? How many more weeks of winter, little groundhog?" I know he wanted to take me to Punxsutawney one Groundhog Day. But we never made it.

Then came that Bill Murray movie and reliving February 2nd over and over again, until the arrogant TV announcer decided to make use of the time to better himself and help other people. So will I be reliving February seconds in order to be doing something for others? for myself? for Mark?

I did help four middle aged and two older women and men with their exercises today and spent some extra time talking to David about his health problems. He has got them, all right. If that is why I am still here, that is what I do most days—over and again.

Monday February 6th

Oh, misery, me! I have the whole thing: wheezing, sneezing, and coughing, runny nose and eyes, stuffed nasal passages, headache, probably a little fever. It is the first work day that I have missed in over seven months, and that means I will not be paid. Randy understood when I called in. He did not want me spreading germs either—especially to the older clientele. "Jim and I will try to schedule substitutes for you."

I have not had a cold like this in years. I think as one gets older, you develop some immunities—at least from different kinds of colds. Mark, being young and being bigger, seems to mean bigger symptoms. I am out of tissues and half through a roll of toilet paper.

I read somewhere that most of the symptoms from a cold are the result of the body reacting to the virus and trying to fight it. If so, Mark is putting up a great fight.

There was a knock on the door about 10. Wearing only sweatpants and a tee shirt, I hesitated. But it was Ellie. "I thought I noticed that you didn't leave for work this morning."

"I was not feeling so well."

"Oh, you poor thing. You sound awful. I'll get you something."

I told her I would be fine, but she was gone and back in less than ten minutes. I was better dressed, but still with bare feet and full of runny gunk.

She had actually brought chicken soup and crackers, dark syrupy cough medicine, lozenges that she said had zinc in them, "which will make your recovery quicker," and vitamin C tablets. After making sure that I had some of all of them, she settled down to "offer a little company. I hate to be alone when I have a cold."

I told her I felt a bit queasy, which made her more determined to stay "until you're feeling a little stronger. Keep the liquids coming too." She went into the kitchen and brought a tall glass of water. "It's better not to have ice," she informed me.

She had also brought a book. I finished the soup, started sucking on a lozenge and picked up Roth's *Zuckerman Unbound* which I was finally getting back to.

"And what do you make of Mr. Nathan Zuckerman?" she inquired. "I'm sure he's a stand-in for the author, don't you think? Sort of a way of reflecting on the ups and downs of all that introspection while you're doing it."

"So you like Roth?"

"Writer's are lucky. They get to lead vicarious lives through the character they create."

"Or characters. Sometimes one living through another a little like those Russian nesting dolls. Roth can be ingenious.

Maybe sometimes he seems too ingenious. So do you like him?"

"Wouldn't say that. But he's very Jewish, you know, and hard-nosed about all the hang-ups and issues he gets into."

"True to life?"

"At least a certain slant on life: Jewish boys and men trying to grow up and take on some responsibility. He is pretty naughty at times, but I think he's just trying to be honest about that. It doesn't bother me like some people."

"Hmmmm," I replied.

"Not nearly as bad as this O.J. Simpson thing. You been watching on the TV now that the trial has begun?"

"Mostly in the newspapers."

"I'm sure he did it. Both of them. Nearly cut her head off."

"There has to be something really wrong with him—after he had so much going for him: the Heisman trophy and his acting career."

"I don't care whether he's black or white or orange. You don't slash the throat of the mother of your children and then another guy just because he shows up to deliver the food."

"How's your health, Ellie?"

"Not so hot." She looked down and we were both quiet.

"But you're the one who is sick today." She shook her finger at me.

"Troubles of some kind?"

"A little arthritis, if you must know. But I manage. I'm all right. I'm fine."

"Some days maybe harder than others?"

"Oh, some days; some days it hurts like all bloody hell frozen over, and she began dabbing at her eyes. "Give me some of your blessed toilet paper." And it came pouring out:

it was in her wrists and back, but her neck and sometimes her shoulders were the worst. The doctors prescribed pain pills, but she hated loading up on them. And it was harder getting around, and she had been so lonely without Bernie, and they never did go to the synagogue all that often anyway, and she began listing old friends who had died or moved away or she did not hear from any more.

"How about your daughter? You talk to her."

"She's really very good. She calls at least a couple times a week. But I can't expect her to come and visit me. She's busy with her own family and her job, and none of us have any extra money."

"You can visit them."

"In Boise? I've done that," she responded a touch defensively. "I love those three girls. I always send them presents."

"Maybe you could go up to Boise more often."

"Do you think I'm Mrs. Moneybags?"

"No, but some things are more important than others."

"What they want is for me to move up there and move in on top of them."

"There could be something to be said for that."

"But they can't really mean it."

After a fit of sneezing and blowing my nose, I looked at her quizzically.

"They only want not to worry about me," she went on. And her son-in-law did not need his mother-in-law hanging around no matter how nice he tried to be about it, and this is where she and Bernie had always lived, and she knew where things were, and had her own things here, and it was too cold in Idaho.

"I bet those girls would like having their grandmother nearby. You could even help them. That is what I would hope to do some day."

"A lot you know."

"You should think about it, Ellie."

"I think you're an impertinent young man." She glared at me and then her eyes began welling up again. "Oh, ugh. I'm sorry Mark. Let's not talk about it. I shouldn't be bothering you with all my. . . my shit." She looked up at me to see if I had anything to say to that.

She pursed her lips and snickered, "Now I'm beginning to sound like Philip Roth. What I really think is that you should go to your room and get some rest. I'll just sit here for a while longer to be sure you're all right."

The former didn't sound like a bad idea. I decided not to tell her I felt like shit, too, and went off to my bedroom, firmly shutting the door. I had forgotten to take Nathan Zuckerman with me, but realized I wanted to sleep.

When I awoke it was well into this afternoon. Ellie was gone but there was a note reminding me to have more soup and crackers to keep up my strength, to continue drinking liquids, and to suck on the lozenges every couple of hours or as often as I felt like it.

Tuesday February 7

I am trying to convince myself that I am better, even while the flow of mucus continues. Perhaps that is a good sign and a result of all the water I keep faithfully drinking. Who knows? Maybe even the zinc is having some affect? In any case I am giving myself only one more day at home. That is absolutely all I can afford. Tomorrow, if I must, I will take some antihistamine to dry up my nasal passages so I can at least sound better.

I will also try to use some of this time off to do a bit of catch-up in this journal. I am not as good a journal keeper as I thought I might need to be

I can report that I have been quite regular in my weekend walks (usually Saturdays) past 2816 White Oak—Shelley's house, but I have not seen George again, or Katie. It is, after all, Southern California residential, and one rarely sees anyone else out on the sidewalks except occasional walkers like me. As long as I keep on moving and am white and reasonably well-dressed, I am likely pretty much invisible.

I did catch sight of Shelley in her backyard one Saturday. How I would love to have any manner of conversation with her—under whatever guise. But I could not just call out to her.

Several weeks ago I also caught sight of Rob trying to tie up a branch in one of their lemon trees. I felt less of an urge to converse with him, unless I could have pumped him for information about the kids. It is not a matter of disliking him. Shelley seems to love him and he her. And he cares about Katie and George even if he sets a lot of rules for them. Life is all about responsibility with Dr. Robert Longworth—a hard-working hematologist who, last I heard, was also considering pursuing a law degree in order to further his concern for defending the rights and responsibilities ("so they can be truly responsible") of the medical profession. He has been an officer of the county medical board and taken several trips up to Sacramento to argue against too much regulation or interference from either government or the HMOs.

Rob and I have gotten into several debates about the cost and economics of health care, though he does not seem to think I know much about it. "Wait until you have to meet a payroll."

"That is exactly what I have had to do at Westview," I retorted.

"I mean a for-profit not some non-profit institution" he almost sneered.

Tennis is a bright spot. I continue to think of it as a "we" sport: my crafty tennis mind and his height and muscles. We are not yet where I think we can get to, but I know we are already better than I was before . . . "the accident." We have a doubles game nearly every Saturday and I have begun playing some singles too. The Center has tournaments now and then, and Mark and I are thinking about entering, probably at the B level.

Except for the cold, I must admit to considerable pleasure in having our body. There are times when I suddenly miss the familiarity of my own, but I do enjoy the strength, the relatively pain and ache free composition of this one and, frankly, its attractiveness. I see women and men giving me a second or even a third look. I am working on it, too. I know I am not as hard-muscled as Mark's body was seven months ago. I do not do the heavy weight training he evidently did. But I have a strenuous routine and continue to run many miles a week.

Speaking of admiring women—or at least a woman who likes me—Ellie just marched right in a few minutes ago, bearing more soup, some toast "with only a little butter" and more zinc lozenges. She said she could not stay long, but was glad to hear "I am some better."

"You don't sound like it."

"I still have a cold, but..."

"Keep taking the zinc. That's what's helping the most. And the liquids. Drink. Drink. Drink."

"Yes, Ma'am."

"Mark, I'm sorry for yesterday; all the tears. It's not like me."

I put down my pen and turned toward her.

"Ellie, I do understand. More than you'll know."

"What are you writing?"

"Nothing important."

"I'll bet it is. She bit her lip. "Mark, I don't know why I tell you things."

"I'm glad you're my friend, Ellie."

"I've been thinking about what you told me."

"I am not sure what."

"Just what I should think about."

"We all have a lot of things."

"I will think. I promise. But there's one thing I didn't tell you.

"You do not need to."

"No. I've never told anyone. I think Bernie would die. God," she laughed, "he's already dead. Thank God."

"So you think he would care that much?"

"I don't know. Our Brenda is a Mormon."

"Is she?"

"Do you hear me? The whole family is Mormon. She converted when they got married. The girls are all Mormons."

"I had a number of Mormon students over the years."

"What are you talking about?"

"I just mean that I have a lot of questions about the Latter Day Saints, too. But they are very loyal to their families. Very family-oriented. They make good parents."

"I hang on to that. I'm actually fond of Micah and the way he loves the girls—and Brenda. He's a good husband and father."

"So there is a lot to give thanks for."

"Yes. I mean, there is. But it's just so . . ."

"Different?"

"A lot different. And I don't want to move up there and have them think I don't think it's different."

"And?"

"And that I'll keep on . . . I may not be very good at being Jewish. But that's what I am."

"I believe they'll respect that. The girls might even be interested."

"So then, what it is you are writing?"

"Nothing much. I decided to keep a journal a few months ago.

"Your deepest thoughts?"

"I cannot say that, but I do feel a lot has happened recently."

She smirked at me. "You wouldn't let an old lady read it would you? After all, I read *Portnoy's Complaint.*"

I half-giggled. "I am sure this would disappoint you."

"I'll never be disappointed in you, Mark. I don't know where you get your smarts from. You should stay home for at least another day—that's if you're really smart."

Maybe if I were really smart, I would be trying to make more out of what has happened to me and to Mark. Most of the time, however, I now lead a quotidian life of trying to fulfill basic human needs for food and sleep, work and rest, some recreation and—what s that other need? . . . ah, yes—sex, or at least relationships. I think Jim has begun to think I am a hopeless case, though he tells me, "I could find some girls who'd love to go out with you." The latest comes from Cousin Andrea: I should meet her husband's younger sister. No recent offers from Bill, but dear Gabrie, with her handsome beau Brett, has arranged for us to go to a concert together next week "with maybe a friend of mine." We shall see.

I am lonely.

Sunday February 19

The concert was a riot. The police came. Items of clothing were thrown at them; arrests were made; young people passed out. I did not see it myself, but I heard that two of them were taken to the hospital. I learned that it was not to be called a concert, and I quickly agreed with that. It was a "rave," whatever that was supposed to mean, though a not unsuitable name. The music was loud and very insistent. Lyrics were shouted and indecipherable, although quite a few of the audience seemed to know them and sang along, or, I should say, shouted back. Most of the youngsters also danced or at least waved their arms a lot and shuffled about—more vigorously as the night got louder. It all ended about when it was supposed to, but I am sure earlier than it otherwise would have if the police had not ended it.

No alcohol was served, but it was present in water bottles and flasks. More prevalent were whiffs of pot or, as I had learned to call it when it became a problem with a few students at the Academy "mary jane." The dangerous part was the stronger stuff—a powder they called "ecstasy." Brett seemed to have some of it.

By half-way through the evening there was an aura of hostility with Brett that I deliberately made physical when I several times bumped his groping body away from Gabrie, telling them I wanted a little chance to dance with my sister. Gabrie would say, "Really, Mark," and seemed puzzled but not wholly displeased with my chaperoning.

But most of the time I had to try to dance and to wave with Danielle. I felt clumsy and worse than a little stupid but came to find it far from unpleasant. She was an attractive, sharp-featured—even somewhat exotic-looking young woman, lithe of body with lots of wavy chestnut hair that had hints of red in it and smelled . . . nice. As she moved she rarely glanced at me, but, when she did, it was as though she wanted to tell me something special. The girl had a gift for men.

With all the noise we had little chance to talk, but I could tell she had a more serious side to her as we both— perfectly sober—rode home together in the back of Brett's car in which he drove us, somewhat erratically, home. She has plans to do graduate study at UCLA "in public policy or maybe anthropology." She also laughed whenever I tried to be funny. When I said, "Maybe we could sometime . . . maybe see each other," she gave me her telephone number. When she told me she had "a super time," I replied, "So did I." More as an observer than a participant, I think I did.

By way of contrast, I arose this Sabbath morning and went to church. This was the second time I had attended a Misa en Español. Not that I took in much of the Spanish, but I liked not being able to understand the sermon or the words of the ritual. I could sit and think my own thoughts, among them that I was doing this because "Daddy would love to see you again, Mark. He keeps asking when you are coming to see him again."

The people also seemed friendlier; several of them speaking to me in broken English—or even quite good English— when they realized I only knew a few words of Spanish.

What with tennis and attending the Rave yesterday, I actually missed my walk past Shelley's house. I may go later this afternoon or skip a week. It is frustrating so rarely to see anyone, much less to talk with them. But I am determined to keep at least a small part of my family life alive with me.

Tuesday April 11 1995

"Hi, ho; hi, ho/ hey don't you know/ Ellie goes to Idaho." We made a silly song of it with the three of us much of the time scrunched together in the cab of the U-Haul truck. Now and then Jim and I took turns resting or sleeping in the back, but I drove much of the way. When I first told Jim of my plan and expressed apprehension about driving a truck by myself that distance, he said, "Oh man, you used to drive a truck in the army."

"I did?"

"All over Germany, you told me."

"I guess I must have been good."

"You'd better be because I'm comin' along."

"You can't do that."

"Oh, yes. I can. You're helping out an old lady and I'm helping you help her. 'Love your neighbor as yourself' and 'Honor your father and mother' the good lord tells us."

"You go to church?"

"When I feel like it."

I half-heartedly tried to argue him out of it. We finally agreed we would leave after work on Friday, spending Thursday evening moving and packing what she was taking. I would have had a hell of a time moving her sofa around the corners and down the flight of stairs. Jim was strong and in good shape, but then so am I, and bigger.

The few remaining items Ellie tagged for a Jewish charity or for me to dispose of. Otherwise there was only her bed and a lamp for her one last night that we loaded up just before leaving.

And we were off—through the night and into early afternoon on Saturday—stopping only (in Ellie's elegant phrasing) "to eat and urinate."

Ellie was a brick. She slept some—once with her head on my shoulder. She occasionally seemed pensive, but there were no more tears. "Once I have made up my mind, that's it. It may be my last adventure, but all life's an adventure, isn't it?"

For several weeks there had been tears and flashes of anger. "This could be like dying, you know." One late afternoon she stood in front of me and stomped her feet up and down, up and down, until I finally held her and slowly persuaded her to take us out to the Indian restaurant where she could buy us dinner.

"I don't know why I put you through this, Mark."

"Not to worry, Ellie. I am your friend. Besides, I am a big boy."

"You sure are, but you don't need an old woman who can't make up her mind and doesn't know what to do"

"I love this Lamb Sag."

"Every time I call, Brenda says they really, really want me to come. She put her Micah on and then the older girls. "Grandmommy, please come and live with us?"

"Who could resist that? I would love it someday if I ever became a granddaddy."

"I don't know about you. You seem wise beyond your years."

"Not always about my own life."

She looked at me concerned. "You have girl problems? You hardly ever go out."

"Nah, I've been seeing a nice young woman lately."

"Her name?"

"Danielle."

"That's nice."

"But back to Boise."

"She's pregnant again. That's why she can't come down to see me."

"She'll need her mother more than ever."

"Those Mormon men! Now that they can only have one wife, they will . . . multiply."

"They like big families. Sometimes I could wish my children would marry Mormons. Lots of grandkids."

"Brenda says they've located an apartment less than a block away so I can have a little place of my own."

"A place of your own. That is perfect."

She toyed with her food. "Mark, would you talk to her . . . talk to Brenda for me. Help me to see if it's really the right thing to do. I'm sorry to ask you."

Brenda sounded like the daughter Ellie deserved. She also sounded a little stressed out, but repeatedly assured me that they really wanted her mother to come, that she'd love having her around to talk with and even help out from time to time, that they had figured out the finances, that there was a reformed synagogue only a mile or so away, a grocery store she could walk to.

We met Brenda, Micah, and the girls who, except for the younger one who was a little shy, were full of hugs and kisses for Ellie. Jim, Micah, and I moved her into her new apartment and set her up with some groceries. After dinner with the family, Jim and I fell asleep in "the girls' room"—getting up with the Idaho sun and heading south on the 95. We were back in Los Angles before midnight and to work yesterday.

Now I am missing Ellie and thinking I would like to move into a nicer apartment anyway. I checked to be sure this building was not owned or managed by my father Victor's company. I more than suspect that whoever owns this structure with the cracked walls and grubby hallways is planning to let it go until they can tear it down and finance a new building with bigger rents.

I cannot afford a move yet, but I did splurge on a new tennis racquet last week: claims to be made of titanium.—lighter weight, and I had it strung tighter. I have a tough match on Saturday.

Sunday May 21

Ellie has called several times, wanting to know "how my son Mark is" and how Blondie and Dagwood in 3-B are getting along. I told her I had actually talked with the young woman last week, whose name was Lori, and I thought she looked pregnant. "I knew it, "Ellie exclaimed. "Do you think they're married?" to which I could only reply that I did not know while telling myself I was not going to ask either.

She wanted to know what I thought about the business with the glove that Simpson's lawyers say does not fit him, and whether I was still seeing Danielle and what she was like, and to tell me that Brenda's baby was due early in June. She missed me and "some of my old haunts," did not much care for the weather in Boise but was "settling in." "My girls like coming over to my apartment and helping me make it 'my home'."

Marcus Zito finished third in the B level of the Center's April tourney. We have a strong first serve, though too often double faulting. I am going to have the racquet restrung a tad less tightly.

A week ago Saturday I saw George outside the house on his bike—without the training wheels. He was intent on his riding but seemed to recognize me and asked if I lived "around here." Suddenly Shelley came out to ask "Who are you talking to, Georgie?" and I had to do all in my power to seem nonchalant, and not to take my daughter in my arms or even just to ask how she was, or how Susan was, and Steve: just a little news of the family. I do not know what she thought of me wanting to stare at her, but then not looking at her in order not to.

"Hello. My name is Mark Zito. I live a few blocks away, but like to walk through the neighborhood now and then. Get a little exercise. It is a nice day, isn't it?"

"Yes, it is." She glanced up at the sky, then smiled and stuck out her hand, which I shook but then let go. "I'm Shelley Longworth and this is my son George."

"My Daddy is a doctor."

"Is he? Well, it's nice to meet you both. I may come this way again.. Bye for now."

"Bye, Mark," Shelley took George's hand. "Nice to meet you."

Then Gabrie came over yesterday afternoon because she wanted to talk with "my brother about a couple of things."

"What?" I answered as she went over and ran her fingers along the cracks in the walls.

"You ought to get these fixed, Markie."

The first was her "love life." Brett said that he wanted to get "more serious" and that he loved her, but she was concerned that maybe I did not like him.

"The main thing is whether you like him."

"Sometimes I think so. He's so attentive and keeps telling me how pretty I am and that he loves me. But then I'm not sure. He's got a funny streak in him."

"Like?"

"When he doesn't get what he wants."

"He gets . . . ?"

"Not exactly angry. I don't know. Sort of..."

"Petulant"

"More like sullen and hard to talk to."

I excused myself to go to the kitchen area and pour us the coffee I had brewed. She followed me in. In lieu of any cookies or pastries I had made little toast squares with cinnamon on them that Shelley used to like.

We agreed that the kitchen was far too small and talked some more about Brett and her feelings about him. I tried to get her to focus on her intuitions and how she liked him after they had spent time together, resisting telling her what I thought he was mostly after and asking whether they were having sex and how often. I felt a certain salaciousness on my part and confusion over who I was to be advising her.

"But I do want to know what you think, Mark. You are my brother and seem to be so understanding. It also worries me that Brett may not seem to like you. He makes remarks about you."

"Does he?" I felt a masculine irritation, but returned again to her feelings for him and what she liked and did not like about him.

The second matter for discussion, however, was me and my feelings about Danielle.

"She asked about me?"

"I think she really likes you, Mark, but says you puzzle her."

"Well, what to say? I thought men were supposed to be a puzzle. Sometimes even I cannot figure out who I am."

"She thinks you like her. She says she likes you a lot . . . likes talking with you and being with you."

"Me, too."

"But you're so . . . so . . ."

"What?"

"Unaffectionate."

"Me? What? What am I supposed to do?"

"Well, if you don't know, I'm not sure I can tell you." She scrunched up her eyes and her mouth at me. "She'd like you to kiss her, Mark. Speaking bluntly, maybe more than that. You know how to do that, don't you?"

"Of course."

"You're blushing."

"I am not."

"You are too, you goofus. You aren't gay, are you?"

"No."

"I told her you weren't."

June 21 1995 Wednesday

Tomorrow Hal Barnes will have been dead to the world one year. Mark Zito is now 27 years and three days old. To celebrate my birthday on Sunday "Daddy" (or "Dad" as I carefully have myself call him) took us to dinner at Marcello's Trattoria where he seemed to know half the staff. I learned that he especially liked Marcello because he knew how to prepare Northern Italian food along with all the "pizza, pasta; pasta, pizza." With this in mind I asked Dad to order for me, and Danielle quickly went along, which resulted in ossobuco for the three of us "which you will love."

Gabrie ordered her "favorite here," Fettuccine Alfredo, which Victor consented to since "Fettuccine burro e parmigiano" was a favorite in Northern Italy, suggesting she add some chicken to it.

Dear Brett just went ahead and ordered pizza.

Although Victor insisted on being the host and paying for the meal, I assumed Gabrie (who is always Gabriella to Daddy) was behind the occasion. She had phoned me and suggested that I bring Danielle, whose company I was glad to have. She looked particularly attractive in a long dark skirt with quite a slit up one side and what I would describe as a peasant blouse—white, with a semi-circular embroidered top, which showed off the near shimmer of the flesh of her throat and upper chest and the outlines of her youthful breasts underneath. I could see Brett taking that in and felt a sense of pride that made me want to appear handsome and manly as I sat beside her.

Victor was "Master of Ceremonies" of the evening, although Gabrie was her animated self. She gave me a beautifully bound book of blank pages of paper "on which you can keep just some thoughts, or a journal, or maybe even one of your stories." Much of the first part of the evening was, indeed, composed of stories—mostly stories told at my expense. I evidently sucked my thumb until I was almost six, which "would explain any ongoing oral fixations." This was the only time in the evening that I heard Brett join in the laughter except his was more of a snicker.

Evidently I could be a mean tease to Gabriella, telling her that her elbows and earlobes were fat until I got pimples and no longer wanted to tease anyone about their appearance. And then I often tried to hide from Daddy's frequent photo sessions—once "running away from home" for all of about three hours. Every time mention of our mother came up Victor crossed himself but did not stop smiling, trying several times to bring Brett into the conversation.

I mostly limited myself to "Did I really do that?" and was more interested to learn that I had liked to draw and to write what I claimed were science fiction stories but which I was otherwise rather secretive about.

Through the evening I noticed that Brett was keeping his hands to himself, perhaps out of respect for or fear of Victor or me, but I wondered with satisfaction if Gabrie had not drawn some lines for him. I, on the other hand, was keenly aware of Danielle's physical presence. Her way of touching me was to lean and bump her shoulder on my arm when laughing at what she found funny. I could smell her perfume and sensed the nearness of her whole upper-body.

Perhaps encouraged by the sexual tensions Victor may have sensed in the air, he said how pleased he was to know Danielle and Brett and how glad he would be to be a grandpa. Gabrie gave him a little glare, but he grinned right through it. He also wanted us all to know that he was happy that both his children were good Catholics, which caused Brett to gnaw on one of his pizza crusts and Danielle to tell him in a steady voice, "I am Orthodox," which was news to me and led Victor to smile and say, "That's wonderful."

The only difficult part of the dinner came when Victor announced that for my birthday he wanted me to get "your very own health care policy, which I will pay for." I do not know what part of me caused me to stammer, "I do not need . . . I do not want." Victor stopped smiling, but appeared surprised rather than angry, holding up and waving his hands palms up. "You're my son; why not?"

I could see both Danielle and Gabrie looking at me as I tried to sound reasonable, "I am twenty-seven years old, Dad. I want to take some responsibility for my own life."

"Not having health insurance isn't so responsible, is it?" he asked with some irritation in his voice. "Besides, if something bad happened to you, who do you think would need to come up with the money?"

I told him I appreciated that and would see if maybe I could get basic health insurance on my own.

We fenced for a while longer—he offering to pay some part of it if I could not afford it all. "So then," what else would you like for your birthday?" he asked.

I told him how much Danielle and I were enjoying the party and being with him and Gabriella and how good the ossobuco was. "This is a wonderful gift, Dad. Could not ask for anything more. And I will bet the spumoni is delicious here, too." And Victor was smiling again.

As we were getting into the Toyota, which I had washed and was behaving for the occasion, Danielle told me, "That was fun. I love your dad and your sister." She then slid over and put her head and soft hair on my shoulder. "Now take me home, birthday boy."

"I will. I will," I said too loudly and needed to clear my throat.

I had to brush her knee at the slit in her skirt as I shifted. The hint of perfume in her hair was so . . . nice. She was so nice—and warm. I took a deep breath and thought of just driving around for a while—wanting to think. It would not take more than ten minutes to drive up to Mulholland and find a place to stop and look from there down on the shimmering necklaces of the valley with just a few distant lights from the Santa Susanas in the background.

But that was best left for teenagers. And, anyway, then what? Groping each other in the car—getting all worked up? Asking her if she wanted to get in the back seat? Having a cop or more likely teenagers shining a flashlight in on us?

She sighed. She kicked off her sandals. Her toenails were painted a Chinese red. Even her slender foot looked lovely. If she had asked me to massage her foot, I would have. I wanted her to put her foot in my lap. Maybe I had a foot fetish. I sighed back—although it did not sound authentic to me. I was aware of myself acting the part of the young lover—with a lovely young woman on a lovely night.

Arm in arm, we half-staggered up the front steps to what was probably a townhouse. I am not sure. I was still trying to rationalize or be rational. Supposing I did go in. Supposing I discovered those breasts within that blouse, the legs beneath that slit skirt. What would I say? I did care for her. But I could not imagine. Would I say, "I love you?" Could it lead to more time together "making love?" How could whoever I was talk about a future together . . . more than . . . more than, I know not what?

She took out her keys. She put a key in the lock. She turned and offered me one of the nicest kisses any man will ever receive—her lips just slightly parted, all her warmth so near.

Yet there was no arousal in me. It certainly was not her. It was me—or whoever I was then—telling myself over and over again. *I am not ready. I am not ready. I am not ready.*

I half-ran down the steps saying, "Thank you. Thank you. Thank you."

And on the way home repeated, "You are a jerk. You are a jerk. You are a jerk." I so did not want to hurt her. I may have anyway,

Saturday August 19th
"The dog days of summer." I gather the phrase goes back to the Romans and has something to do with the Dog Star Sirius this time of year. But when I was a boy I pictured panting dogs lying around when it was too hot for them to move.

My tennis partner called off our match for this morning. He blamed it on his wife who said it was dangerous to play in the heat. Grant her a medical degree, I say.

We have had eight or nine days of temperatures over 100° in the valley. The clamoring air conditioner in my bedroom makes it at best tolerable at night. I bought a fan for the living room.

It does not take long to work up a sweat in the gym and work has been half of what it was in the spring. Jim is off on his National Guard duty. He is still so angry at Davis and the Raiders for moving back to Oakland, I could use the time off from his rants. I tried to distract him by talking about the Dodgers who are doing fairly well with a non-stellar club, but he is inconsolable about the Raiders, until I attempt my John Madden imitation for him.

The AC in the Toyota is no match for this weather either. I drove here to the Central Library this noon with the windows open. It is a tad cooler in downtown Los Angeles anyway but most spaces in the library are a relief and delight—in part because of the thick walls of the building and the spaciousness of the halls. And there are books all around me—arranged by topic in room after room.

I received a bittersweet letter from Ellie two days ago:

Dear Mark: I don't want to keep bothering you with phone calls. I realize my life is up here now. But I do want to pour out my thanks to you, and to dear Jim, for helping me move here. I do not think I could have done it without you.

The new baby seemed fine for the first couple of weeks. He is a darling little fellow they call Nathaniel. But there is something wrong with him. I so wish it was a heart valve or something they could correct these days, but they say it is in his brain. He may not be able to develop properly—even basic things like sitting up and seeing correctly and eating.

Brenda is doing the best she can and trying not to ignore the girls in the midst of this. But Micah is beside himself. He had apparently always wanted a son. He is not eating or sleeping well. He wants to be with the boy all the time. Brenda has to take care of him too.

I am doing all that I can. The two older girls often come over to my apartment to do their homework, and I sometimes feed them dinner and I have taught them how to play Tripoley, which I used to play when I was their age.

Please do not bother to answer this. But I know you go to church from time to time. I cannot imagine why in God's name things like this happen, but maybe say a little prayer for us—for poor little Nathaniel and Brenda and Micah and your grateful old gal friend, who sends her love, Ellie

And I, on the other hand, had a trip to Las Vegas. It was mostly Bill's idea. Apparently that was one of our destinations when we rode motorcycles. I would guess that it has been ten years since I was in what we used to call Lost Wages. Susan and I made several *excursions* when we were younger, but I did not care much for the shows and she turned up her nose at gambling.

The place just keeps building up. It is bigger, taller with more lights, glimmer and glamour and chintz. I saw more families with children than I remember earlier. That may or may not be good.

It turned out that my three friends needed my car as it was the only one that they were sure could make it. I wondered. They were, however, generous with the gas money—at least on the way up. Both Scott and Rod had lost their wages, and Bill and I had to pay our way home.

There were other downsides. I kept worrying about my money. I had set myself a strict limit for gambling, which I lost in the first few hours. And trying to sleep in a casino room, doors occasionally slamming, late night shouts in the hallway, and Bill half-drunk and snoring in the other bed was hard, though once this body of mine does drift off, I can sleep like the proverbial log. All in all, I would grade it a good trip. I listened a lot more than I contributed to the con- . versation. They told me that I was getting to be an old fart. A number of their jokes would classify as ribald. Scott called me "Mr. Maturity" and wanted to know what Danielle had done with my nuts. But I did my best to laugh along. It made me feel something like young again.

It sounds to me as though Bill's love life has gone bust again. He asked me several times "What is Gaby doing?" I reminded him that she is calling herself "Gabrie" now. I did not tell him about Brett, but wondered to myself if there might be someway of substituting Bill for Brett. I told Bill that he should ask her out: "I think she has always had a thing for you."

September 4 1995 Labor Day

Ever since I retired I have been restlessly conscious of the beginning of the school year. I feel like I should be doing something to get ready. I miss teaching more than administrative and leadership work. I should be getting something ready—a book list, notes for the first class, thinking of ways to entice the learning appetites of my students. Classes would start tomorrow, although teachers will have been meeting the last ten days or so. Maybe it was that anticipatory time with colleagues and my faculty I missed the most.

I drove out to Westview for the first time in at least three years. After retirement I had deliberately kept my distance—to let the new Head, who had asked for very little of my advice anyway, become established. I parked just beyond the new arch entrance, which I had helped to rebuild with our Latin motto "Pax et Bonum" inscribed above. I walked through.

The campus appeared well cared for. "It is as I left it," I said aloud. The yellow brick of the yet new looking science building sparkled smartly in the bright sunshine. I remembered the work with the planning committee: the different architectural firms we had for the structure itself and the interior design.

I passed two security guards whom I did not recognize, nor they me, of course. If they asked, I would tell them I was an alum of the Academy. After all, I still knew the school song by heart.

Ten minutes or so was enough. There was no sign or even a tree with my name on it. That is as it should be, I told myself as I slid my six-foot two, twenty-seven year-old self back into my eleven year-old car. My monuments are my students— many hundreds over the years. I wondered where Marcus had gone to high school. Maybe I should try to get us back to college, though I doubt I have much appetite for being a student in a lecture hall again.

October 3rd 1995

O.J. Simpson walked away a free man today. I cannot say I was totally surprised, given the way race and the years of discrimination by the Los Angeles Police had deeply penetrated into the trial.

I can hear Ellie's reaction. "Everybody knows that he did it. You would have expected the women on the jury to know better. The mother of his children: can you imagine?"

Jim said that "it was payback time all right. They just paid back the wrong nigger." I did not hide my shock that he used the n-word after experiencing years of controversy over Huckleberry Finn's use of it for his Jim.

"Just don't you use it, honkey," he replied, giving me a solid punch in the ribs.

Today I also received a letter from Danielle. I sniffed it for perfume, but knew what would be inside: what we used to call a "Dear John" letter.

Dear Mark,

I want you to know that I will always be fond of you and hope we can continue to be friends.

You are a great guy, but I need to find someone else in my life. I wish you well.

Please do not answer this.

Sincerely, Danielle

I looked for tear stains but found none. "Sincerely," I muttered to myself. But I was relieved while another part of part of me felt sad and even hurt. I will miss her company. I remembered the nearness of her breasts against me through her blouse when we kissed, but she needed and deserved someone who was really her own age.

Meanwhile, lo and behold, the Dodgers actually made it into the playoffs. They are playing Cincinnati in the first round this evening. Maybe there will yet be some good news today.

Sunday October 29th

It would be hard not to know that Halloween is nearly upon us. Ghost and goblin masks and gobs of candy have long since taken up at least one full aisle in the grocery store. When Steve and Shelley were little it was the busiest holiday of the year for Susan and myself next to Christmas. I miss carving up the pumpkins. I got pretty good at it.

Friday was lunch with Victor when I heard more than I needed to about the Catholic Church in Los Angeles: Cardinal Mahony and plans for his new downtown Cathedral, his support of immigrants, his hard line about abortion and contraception, and "God's preferential option for the poor." I was pleased to tell him that I had "been to Mass over the summer" if only a two or three times.

Señora Gracia, as I thought of her, looked the same. The little conference room of Zito and Sons looked the same. Gracia had a good memory. "I brought you a tuna sandwich like your father's this time, Mark. I hope that is all right." And soup was only for Victor, I noticed. I told her iced tea would be just fine.

Victor came in talking with a man about his age and height wearing a hard hat. Victor turned to me: "Marcus, me gustaría presentarte a Hector Carlo. Está a cargo de gran parte de nuestros trabajos de construcción.

"Encantado de conocerle." Hector shook my hand.

I knew enough to say, "Yo, también," but barely managed that.

"Marcus trabajo como entrenador de ejercicio," Victor explained.

"Muy bien," Hector responded. "¿Y dónde trabaja? ¿Aquí en el valle?"

I got the gist of what he was saying and am able to create it here from what I know of written Spanish, but at the time all I could manage was, "Gracias."

"What's happened to your Spanish, Marcus? You could speak it quite well."

I could? I rather desperately thought to myself. In fact, I was embarrassed that I was so poor at conversational Spanish. Susan was better even though I had once taken a basic course. "I am afraid I have forgotten a lot. Se me olvidó," I added uselessly.

I can't believe that," Victor replied. "I heard that you were good with German, too, when you came back from the army. We'll have to do something about this."

All I could think was what a hard time I had had learning to speak any language. I had two years of French in college but had forgotten most of that. And here Marcus was skilled at languages, but had deserted me when I needed him.

"Good to see you, Marcus," Hector told me, and he and Victor agreed to meet at a site in Canoga Park later in the afternoon.

As we sat down, and after Victor had crossed himself and said "grace for us," he did not try to hide his disappointment: "All those classes we paid for and the two months you spent in Mexico," he chided.

I held out my hands helplessly. "A lot has happened."

"Not that much. I'll bet you can relearn it quickly. I'll pay for a tutor or for you to take some courses. You need it here."

I told him he did not need to pay for it, but after more back and forth, realized that I would actually like to learn conversational Spanish.

That mellowed him as did my informing him that I had a health insurance policy now, without telling him how high the deductible was since, like anyone else who was 27 and in as good health as I was, I counted on never needing to use it.

"Dad," as I kept reminding myself to call him, again offered to pay the premiums or at least "help with it."

Fact of the matter, I was beginning to run up debt on my credit card account again and was not at all sure what I could manage over the next months. "I hate to take the money from you, Dad."

"It's not forever. I've got the money now." He paused and looked hesitant. "Whenever you want, you can come and work here you know."

He began his own work on his soup and sandwich. I told him I liked tuna fish. We exchanged commiserations about the Dodgers losing three straight to Cincinnati in the play-offs, but Victor did not seem that interested in baseball. He did not even know who was playing in the World Series. He asked me about Danielle, and I tried to appear sad when telling him we were not seeing each other anymore.

"Not to worry. She probably wasn't right for you. Someday you'll find a girl like your mother."

I thought he might cross himself again but instead began talking about Monsignor Martin at his church and where he supported him and sometimes disagreed, but "as a good Catholic."

There were times when I had to bite my tongue and others when I found myself nodding in agreement. But I realized that he was not just telling me about his own views and beliefs but also trying to instruct me in what I should believe and practice.

Half-way through, Gracia looked in to see if we "needed anything." Victor asked her for his check book and wrote me a check for $1000.

"Thank you, Dad. Very much. I will be careful with it."

"There's always more if you need it."

Gabrie told me that Daddy became "even more Catholic when our brother died, and even more so after Mommy went. But he was always devout. You remember how we all had to go to Mass every Sunday without fail—even when we were teenagers—even when I was 18." "'As long as you're living at home,' he told me."

Victor certainly believed in going to Mass, evidently more than "just Sundays," and in the efficacy of prayer, not least to "our Mother Mary." He had questions about the importance of "Mahony's Cathedral" but supported it because "the Cardinal is such a good man and really cares for the human dignity of our newcomers like once we were." He apparently had made a good-sized pledge for the cathedral. Both contraception and sex without marriage were "bad things," but the bishops ought to be more understanding, especially if people could not support "extra children." In a solemn tone, "I am going to tell you for the first time that me and your dear mother sometimes did use it. I agreed because I loved her so much." He crossed himself.

Abortion was also "terrible," but the Pope and the bishops "should get off their high horse" and understand that "women can't always control everything. And they make the church sound nasty when they try to dictate what everybody else should do and make it a big political issue when there are more important things."

Among the more important things were that "everyone who works for Zito and Sons gets paid what allows them and their babies to live O.K., and health care, because you can't live without it. That's what the Christian way is. That's the way I run it. I'm hoping maybe you will someday too."

I am sitting here thinking I had been given quite an agenda for one day.

Sunday December 17th 1995 Hanukkah

I think I have this right. Today is the first day of Hanukkah. We began to have so many Jewish students at Westview, I felt an obligation to better understand the Jewish holy days and holidays.

The timing gave me an excuse to call Ellie. I had actually used my occasional attendance at Mass to say a prayer for the baby Nathaniel and Brenda and Micah and Ellie. I did not see how it could do any harm even coming from someone like me.

She sounded both surprised and pleased to hear from me and began quizzing me before I could try to find out how she and the family were doing.

Yes. I had been dating a girl I really liked. No. We were no longer seeing each other. Yes. I was fine. She probably was not right for me anyway.

No. Lori and Dagwood had not had the baby yet, but I could see that it would not be too much longer. No. I had a hard time knowing where they would put the baby in an apartment that was not any bigger than mine or hers. Nor was I looking forward to hearing a baby crying at night. But, yes, they still could have their loud arguments. Maybe they would have to stop so the baby could sleep. I do not know if they are actually married, but they might as well be.

"Nathaniel died, Mark. I know you prayed for him but it was for the best. He wouldn't have had any kind of life. The poor little thing couldn't even swallow properly. They had to watch him slip away."

"I am so sorry."

"Thank you. But we're all getting on now. Micah was the one I worried about the most. He just sat there with the little tyke, hardly eating himself. But when the babe was gone, Micah was like King David. He started eating properly, got some sleep, and went back to work." And this shouldn't surprise you either. You know these Mormon men. Poor Brenda is pregnant, though she insists to me it was her idea, too, and the best way of healing. I surely hope so."

I finally got around to wishing her a Happy Hanukkah.

"To be honest with you, I wasn't really keeping track. But I have gone to the synagogue a few times. It's O.K. One thing for sure. I let people know I'm no Mormon."

"I can hear you now."

"No. I'm polite about it, just firm although I'm coming to think Mormons are more like Jews than Christians. The other thing I know is I am very much needed here. I don't even have time for the arthritis. Maybe this lousy weather is somehow good for it."

"That is good."

"But I'll bet it's really nice there, isn't it?"

"It's O.K."

"No. Don't tell me. I'm an Idohoh-ho-hoan now."

3

New Year's Day 1996

Say I lived to be 86. That was a number I picked when I turned 65. I would then have lived to 2012. Now it would mean I could live to 2054. Hard to imagine. But if so, should not I be doing something productive and useful? So I would counsel the Westview students: "What really interests you?" "What would you enjoy working at—learning and growing?" "What would make you happy and helpful to others so that you would feel you were contributing to life lived together?"

Good questions to ask—not easy to answer. First, I would tell them, one must develop a reasonable sense of the self. Who am I?

Who am I? I might try to become a teacher again. That is what I know. That is the way I was once able to contribute. It is what I still know, though I would first somehow have to accumulate several years' worth of college credits. Were I to go to college part-time, it would take even longer and still cost me many thousands that I do not have. And then what? Teach for another 30 or more years on top of the nearly 40 I had already taught? How much Joseph Conrad, Mark Twain, Hemingway and John Steinbeck could I take? Should not I do something different between now and, say, 2040?

So I have made only a couple of New Year's resolutions.

1) I will work on my Spanish. Indeed, I have already registered for an evening course that starts on Thursday.

2) I am going to take on more work. Jim has convinced me that I need to be on staff at a second gym, and I have posted an ad highlighting my skills in dealing with older clients.

I know. I ask myself: how can I go two or three days a week to the same Bally's where my body and much of my persona perished? Yet I do not feel afraid. It is, perhaps, a way of dealing with it—of saying that I am getting over it—whatever that might mean. I may also harbor some vague illusion that, if the unbelievable happened there once, something reversible—a time-warp of some kind could pop up again.

The ever-hesitant Bill informed me that his number one resolution is to ask Gabrie out. I did all I could to encourage him. I certainly noticed that Brett was not with my sister at the family Christmas party. He could have been with his own family or out of town for some reason. I did not ask Gabrie, but I have a hunch that she finally gave him his "Dear John." In any case, "Go for it, Bill." *You may not be every woman's heart throb, but I would much rather have you for a brother-in-law, if it comes to that.*

I am not going to the Rose Bowl party at Cousin Andrea's and Ted's. I fear Danielle might be there. I do not think she would want to see me, and I would not know what to say to her: "I am sorry that I could not be more affectionate. I would really like to have, but . . . you cannot understand who I really am."

That would help a lot! But I do miss her company, her conversation . . . the way she would bump against my shoulder.

I would love to have some female company, but maybe I am in the process of making a third New Year's resolution: no more young women, at least into the foreseeable future. In my heart of hearts, I cannot seem to imagine any uninhibited intimacy with a woman in her 20s. After Susan and I met, she was my only one. In my heart of hearts, she is the one I still wish I could be with in 1996.

February 18 1996

I saw Susan yesterday. It was the first time since our garage door closed behind her the day I died. She looked as I so remember her—if anything a bit younger: everything about her, her hair, her figure in the slacks and sweater. I heard her laugh...her low laugh. But I could not believe what else I was seeing. She was with Asa Demeter as they were coming out of the movie theater. He was holding her hand.

Anybody but Asa Demeter—or Ace as he sometimes asked me to call him. I had inherited him as Director of Development at Westview when I became Head. He did raise money. I cannot say he was dishonest. But there was always something self-promotional about him. The figures, after all was said and done, never matched what he was telling me or the trustees. He went through a long separation, and then a divorce, quite possibly his second one. I never liked the way he talked about the women on his staff— or even some of the younger faculty women.

I was with Bill. He wanted to see a rerun of Apollo 13, which "you absolutely have to see." But what he really wanted to tell me was that he thought he was in love with Gabrie and to ask whether he should ask her if she loved him, too. *After two dates*! I said to myself, but tried to listen and offer him something helpful.

But now, "There's something wrong." I stupidly shoved five bucks into his hand and told him he would have to go by himself. "Why?" he asked. "Did I say something?"

"No. No," I said, still looking at Susan and Demeter walking away together—he talking and talking as he always did. I did nothing to try to stop Ace when he said he had a better offer from Occidental College.

"Bill buddy, I just remembered something I thought I had forgotten." I stepped away rapidly—feeling a release of energy. I walked toward them—fighting the urge to give Ace a bump as I passed. I made like I was going into the Cheese Factory and let them pass. I did not want them to see me—though, I shrugged as I realized that they do not know me from Adam.

I followed them into the parking garage. They got into Susan's Volvo, the kind gentleman holding the door as she slid behind the wheel. I growled loudly enough that a young couple who had also entered the garage glanced at me.

I hurried into the next aisle, wheeled the Corolla about and spotted them on the way to the exit, and followed—soon obviously up toward 1848 Colina. *What could she possibly see in him?* Susan and I had talked so hypothetically: "Hal, if something ever happens to me, it would be all right if you found someone else—as long as you promise not to love her as much as you love me." She laughed her low laugh.

"Don't be silly," I told her.

"No. I mean it."

"O.K. I believe it." I took a sip of my Scotch, realizing it was my turn. "I would want you to feel the same way."

"I can't imagine it. I love you, Hal."

"I love you, Susan."

I blew out my breath and spoke aloud to myself. "No, no, no. I do not want Susan to be alone, if she does not want to be. But not Asa damn Demeter." God, I hoped, she was not having sex with him. "I would die," I laughed grimly. *And my house? My money? Even my dog. If they got married, wouldn't Susan lose my pension?* "She has to be able to see through his . . . his self-promotion."

The garage door went up. They pulled in. I stopped a half-block up the street. I felt sick.

The door stayed up. In another minute they came out of the garage and walked to a silver Porsche parked just past our front walk. Its tail and front lights blinked on and off.

I began to think of myself as a private detective, watching—ready to make a report. They talked. They smiled. They laughed. They talked. He put his hand on her arm and leaned toward her. They lightly touched lips. (Nothing like my kiss from Danielle Grabovac.) End of report. And I may never know what else had or would transpire between them or if there were to be someone else in Susan's life. "Nor should I."

Sunday June 23 1996

Sexual mores surely have changed since I was a young man: the sexual revolutions, more openness toward homosexuality, more sex before, outside of and after marriage. Mark's generation is the first to take "full advantage" of the changes if that is what it is. But, acting as Mark, I seem to be in some form of limbo or on the observation deck.

Trying to be age-appropriate, I have now gone on one ski trip up to Wrightwood and two more excursions to Las Vegas with the boys, although even one of the boys wondered "if we were not getting a little old for this" since other friends were married now and some had kids.

But, "no more ski trips!" Mark was apparently an accomplished and rather daring skier—and snow boarder. Hal Barnes had been skiing—other than cross-country—maybe a total of three times in his life. Moreover, I was scared of anything steep or fast. Bill tried to be understanding, but Rod made fun of me. I finally faked an injured knee and had a nice, long conversation with a blond girl from Carlsbad. We had cocoa in the living room of the lodge. She worried about my knee. She never liked skiing that much. We had two beers. (I still cannot get hard liquor down and two beers seem to be all I can take.) We had an early dinner, we were both tired. We went to bed in our own bedrooms. I never did find out whether she had come with someone or someones.

We exchanged friendly greetings in the morning, and she gave me a little kiss good-bye. If she was disappointed with me, she did not show it. Perhaps she was relieved to find a man who did not hit on her on first meeting. Perhaps she had decided I was gay.

I think others may be assuming the same—but that I am yet "in the closet" or have not been able to come to terms with my sexuality. There has been one awkward moment. The second night we were in Vegas, Rod (who I certainly thought was heterosexual, but maybe bisexual or "still coming to terms with his sexuality") put his hand pretty far up my thigh and kissed me. He had had a lot to drink and smelled and tasted like it. I let him go through with the kiss, but stood up and walked away—wiping my mouth with the back of my hand so he could not see me doing it. I wanted to feel sorry for him, though I did not know how to feel.

In the car on the way back to LA, it was as though nothing had happened. Much of the conversation was about girls since "getting it off" or "getting laid" was obviously an important part of these excursions.

Personally I had several encounters with young women, which I found amusing and even fun. I came to be well aware that I was an attractive mid-twenties man with good shoulders, nice hair, and, as one young lady in short shorts and a tank top told me with a little pat, "a great butt." The rest of my Las Vegas sex was, however, vicarious.

Bill had made me promise that, if I came back to the room and saw anything tied on the door handle, I would either find another room or come back much later. He solemnly vowed that he would do the same for me. "Bill," I wanted to tell him, "You say you are in love with my sister. What is this? Some kind of time out?"

What Bill had not reckoned with was that I would already be asleep in the other bed. At first I thought it was only Bill coming in tipsy until I heard her giggle, and they both collapsed on the other bed. Mercifully, mission was accomplished fairly quickly. I just lay there, trying not to hear. All I remember thinking was that I hoped she was practicing some form of birth control.

It was not long before Bill was snoring once more. I wished I had remembered to bring ear plugs. Were we alone I would go over and shove him around so he would stop for a while. I heard her whispering to him, "can't you be quieter?" and grunting as she tried to roll him over. "God," she said. I just lay there, trying to drift off—hoping I would not snore too.

"God," she said again, "who are you?" as she was getting into my bed.

"I am Mark."

"Oooh, I didn't know you were here."

"I was mostly asleep."

"I can't take his snoring. Can I just stay here with you? I'll keep way over here." She rolled away from me and—probably having had a fair amount to drink, was soon softly snoring herself.

"Way over here" on a double bed was not very far. I lay there trying to consider my options. After about ten minutes I took my pillow and a blanket from the closet and stretched out on the floor.

When I awoke, with a shaft of morning sunlight coming through a part in the curtains, my back and shoulder hurt. I tried not to moan as I got up and dressed quietly. Then, I realized, she was watching me.

"You're Mark, right?"

"Yes," I whispered.

"Where are you going?"

"I thought I would get some breakfast."

She yawned and sat up. Yawned again. "Can I come with you?"

"Why not," I shrugged. "I'll wait outside."

"Shhh. Let's not wake him up. You don't have to. Just let me go pee and get some clothes on."

Sabrina and I had bacon and waffles (hers with strawberry jam and whipped cream) in one of those casino restaurants that serve breakfast all day and all night. There were other customers, too, though I think they had been up through the night. She seemed like a nice girl. I did not lecture her.

I am writing this in my new apartment where there are no cracks in the walls of the two bedrooms with a real kitchen and a powder room in addition to the full bath. The second bedroom is not much more than a half-room which I use as a study. Zito and Sons manages the building. Victor helped me find it. I thought it might be a good idea if I sampled the product, but asked for no break on the rent since I am doing reasonably well financially in recent months—working pretty much full-time almost six days a week. Jim thinks I should rent a small gym space and go into business for myself as a trainer and therapist for older folks.

I was ready to leave the apartment on Libbet, though, hard to believe, I had been there almost two years. I only would miss Lori and Malcolm and that cute baby girl who turned out to be a pretty good sleeper.

Yes. Two years yesterday. Although I still have many regrets, I cannot say that I am always unhappy. I find things to do—am actually busy; I know I am doing some good for others. I read, play tennis, have people to talk with. But I am also...restless—trying to imagine if this is just to go on this way for years. How I long to be able to share with someone who I really am . . . or am becoming or am supposed to be.

Bits of the above may come up at my postponed birthday dinner tonight. Bill will be there with Gabrie. I will be alone. Victor will not approach that subject directly. He will say he loves me and then add, "You're twenty-eight years old. Congratulations, Marcus." Unsaid will be the innuendo that it is time to settle down, get married, have some babies. "You can always come work for Zito and Sons. The business is waiting for you. You should make something of yourself. And don't forget regular Mass and to pray for you dear Mother."

And speaking of family on this anniversary of sorts, I have fairly well kept my promise never completely to give up my own. Even if I talk with no one, I look forward to the opportunity just to see that their house is still standing and they have not moved.

I have only caught sight of George twice in recent months. He calls me "Mr. Mark." Once sweet Katie was on the porch—nearly four now and looking like it.

Occasionally Shelley is out in front or might even come out when she sees me pass or when I come back "on my way home." I am careful, but she seems to like talking with me. She is evidently active in the local homeowners' association and tells me some of its problems—most recently over "the second story Dr. Zalina wants to build that will ruin the Perry's view." I, of course, want to hear about George and Katie and to ask "How is your mother doing?" But I bide my time. I am not sure how much I want to know.

Sunday June 30th

Be careful what you even think about praying for. Yesterday evening I went to church. It was only the third or so time I had been in the last months, but I like being able to tell Victor, "Oh, I do go to Mass, Dad—maybe not every Sunday, but I go." I could add that it helps with my Spanish, which is coming along, though not as fast or easily as I wish it would.

But the mind does wander. I begin thinking about my feelings of restlessness and whether there ought not be more purpose and accomplishment to life as Marcus Zito, when darned if the priest did not start expostulating on that well-worn line from Augustine about "You have made us for yourself, O Lord, and our hearts are restless until they find their rest in you." He caught me up a bit further when he suggested that the Latin of "for yourself" could be translated "hacia si mismo," suggesting that human beings were created to be inclined "toward God."

It was a pious thought which maybe some people experienced, but my mind went on to reflect on the observation that most people do continue to feel a restlessness in life. I did when I was Mark's age and a certain measure of it was probably a good motivator, although "moderation in all things" I told myself now referencing Aristotle and Ben Franklin and dozens of other moderators in life. It would probably help if I understood a little more about who Mark was and any hopes or plans he had for his life. It was more a thought than a prayer.

Grateful that I live in Southern California, I had fresh sliced strawberries, banana and blueberries with granola and yogurt, followed by scrambled eggs and lightly buttered toast this sunny morning in my new kitchen. I read a thoughtfully hedged article about Clinton's chances for reelection and took off for a long run into Balboa Park. Back here, I cleaned up, admired my body—perhaps not so chiseled as when I inherited it, but "darn good," I said to the mirror. Maybe in its litheness even better. I dressed in new sweat pants and shirt and set about some rearranging in the apartment.

There were several things I wanted to put into storage or perhaps amalgamate or even toss. Among them were Mark's old file boxes that I had once called boxes 1 and 2. The files in box 1 held what appeared to be old school papers: short essays and several stories of a dozen or so pages—one that had been rather amateurishly typed, others in a fine, neat hand. A for penmanship. His grammar and sentence construction could use work, and I almost reached for a pen to offer a little advice and mark a misspelling until I saw that someone had already done at least a bit of that. I would have done more.

What I was reading was basically a science-fiction story about wormholes, teletransportation and the transplantation of the beginning of a human race in another galaxy—fantastic enough but more concerned with the fears and hopes of a Randolph and "his woman Mary" than the pseudo-scientific detail.

There were five or six scrawled but legible sentences in red on the last page, basically complimentary and encouraging, the grade of A minus, and the name, quite clearly, Grant Handsworth.

Grant Handsworth had taught at Westview ! I was his Master Teacher his first couple of years. *Marcus Zito. Marcus Zito.* I do not remember a name like that at the Academy, though we came to have nearly 400 students. Mark was 28. His ages 14-18 would have been 1982-1986—years when I was Head *Mark Zito. Marcus Zito.* I flipped to the end of another paper. The comments were unsigned with a B+. A third paper had comments signed by Grant Handsworth, but without a grade—instead "Why don't you try rewriting this, Marcus? With my suggestions in mind." That sounded like Grant.

Good God. But, if Mark had been at Westview when I was Head and doing some teaching of my own, he must have known me—at least to recognize me, even if I did know him.

In the past I could have just gone in and requested to look in the files—not many Zs, I could have checked grades, evaluations. Maybe I could write to the school now in my name. Would they send me my Marcus Zito files—or at least a copy of my graduation certificate— if I had graduated... if Marcus had really been at Westview? But what else would explain these papers? And Grant's name on them?

I have just called Gabrie, pleading that I needed to see her. "Can I come over soon—at least sometime today?"

"You can come over now, Mark. Are you all right?"

"Fine." I tried to take the urgency out of my voice. "I will explain when I get there. There are some things I am trying to figure out."

"About?"

"About myself. O.K.?"

"Sure. Love ya."

She had to give me directions to what turned out to be a rather classy condominium that I imagine Victor helped her get into. She had probably done some straightening up, but there was a cap that I recognized as Bill's on a corner table and what looked to me to be a man's shirt on a doorknob to what was probably a bedroom. Maybe Bill had even moved in. Maybe he was hiding in the bedroom. Right then, I did not care.

Driving over, I tried out several scenarios: pretending to some manner of amnesia would only lead to problems down the road. Nor did I want to seem overly confused or distressed. Nor did I want to make it seem like any kind of emergency.

What I decided on was the truth—always the best strategy—or, in my case, at least some of the truth.

I had found these papers I had written at Westview. It reminded me how much I had liked writing stories. "I know people change, but, do you remember any of my storytelling? I wonder if I should start writing again. I know you are my sister, but you still are the best friend I could ask."

It was a little lame, but got the conversation I wanted and needed going. From my side it was mostly listening. Questions I had thought I might ask were unneeded. It was as much about the family as it was me. "I think you are right,

Gabrie." "Yeh, yeh." "Thank you. That makes sense to me too." was my part.

I laughed when she laughed. I wiped at my eyes when it was time for both of us to cry—nor was I pretending.

Twice she cautioned to the effect, "I'm not sure this is so good for you, Mark. I thought you wanted to get away from most of it. That's one of the reasons you left for the army, isn't it? Are you sure?"

I was. But she surely wanted to talk, too, as our conversation became more intimate—sister caring for her brother, in sympathy. Both of us trying to understand.

More than an hour went by. She made us tea "just like we used to have" and found cookies that she apologized for. I liked them. I had not tasted chocolate covered marshmallow cookies in years.

Later she made a "pizza on toast" with sliced tomatoes, fresh basil, and cheese.

It was getting dark when I left with two or three hugs, a few more tears, and the kisses I suspect only brothers and sisters can give. "I love you, Markie." "I love you Gabrie."

I know I passed Bill's car as I was driving away. I am fairly sure I saw him slouched down behind the wheel.

So now sitting here in my newish apartment—on a day that had started so quietly—this is the gist of what I learned. Some of it, of course through Gabrie's filter—some, no doubt, through mine.

Our older brother had died of "a cancer" when I was about eight and she three.

I did go to Westview for my sophomore and junior years. It was mostly mother's idea. After a year at Woodland Hills High where she taught, she thought I would benefit from new friends and challenges. Daddy went along. Everyone agreed it was great: "Expensive but great."

"You loved it."

"Then Mommy got sick. Daddy sort of got sick, too. I mean he was wonderful, but he was so worried about us and the business and money."

Fearful that there was not going to be enough money and that he needed me more at home, he took me out of Westview. "He still blames himself, Markie. But I know you know why."

And then that next summer Mommy died: our Mommy. "Our Mommy who helped us so much with our homework in history and everything, especially you, Mark. She doted on you. You remember that. Who can blame you? She was so great. I love her."

"So do I," and I did, but apparently I was a mess, barely graduating from high school—angry that I had not finished at Westview. And without my Mommy. I was sent to a psychiatrist until I quit going. I did a year or so of community college until I quit and went into the army.

July 1st 1996

So here is what I think. Actually I am not sure what I think, even though I spent much of the day mulling it over—distracted at both my gyms.

Most of it makes sense. I mean I can understand much of that happening to a teenager, and what he experienced as traumas helps explain his subsequent behavior. The two surprises I am still trying to put into focus are his interest in writing and storytelling, which he appears to have abandoned. And the distinct possibility that Mark (which he spelled Marc on several of those Westview papers and maybe subsequently for all I know) would have recognized me just before what happened two years ago.

I can see his mouth slightly opening, just as our eyes locked. Was he going to say something? Possibly "Mr. Barnes, I . . ."

But what then? Did he have some part in it? Why and what happened to him? Did he commit suicide? Did he at all know what he was doing? Did he have any idea I would have to die—at least physically and to the world and my family?

O.K. Here, you try being me. Mr. Barnes? You try telling the story of my life.

He, then, may be at least as responsible as I am for my death, his apparent loss of conscious life, and what I or we are now.

And it can become spooky if I sit here long enough trying to understand and get an inkling or suspicion that maybe I am not fully alone. Someone is observing? Someone is reading what I am writing?

Of course, for some people in the past that has been God—watching one's every move: "you miserable sinner." But I do not believe in that.

Or is it one's conscience or some manner of super ego? Or the imputed future reader? Or my alter ego or the writer's own critic and/or author in some form of relationship with the actor and author he is creating a la Nathan Zuckerman? However, one tries to imagine what has happened I am two lives—one trying to live and act through another.

But there is also only the here and now. I can wonder if Marcus Zito is completely gone. One thinks of the enormous capacities of the brain. At any given time the brain's mind is using only a relatively small percentage of its vast capacities. Could that leave room for more than one mind?

I knock my forehead. "Hello, Hello. Anyone else in there?"

But I find so little of Mark's consciousness, his language skills—of his memories other than what I have learned of them and what we have done together for two years.

I know. I know. We are always losing the past, and we never do have direct access to what has gone by. We are always making it up as it were, in the stories of our lives we knit together. But this is different from that.

And here is another slice of puzzle, though I cannot make it fit. I think of it as a piece of jigsaw puzzle that appears like it ought to go in nicely somewhere in that horizon where blues of the sea and sky blend with one another, but at least not yet.

Earlier this morning I read through several of Marc's (I am going to adopt that spelling unless I learn differently) stories and essays. One seemed to be a version of his story of humans beginning lives on another planet but this time with their minds transported into other life forms. I am not sure I would have been quite as generous as Grant had been with the grades, but I can understand why he was encouraging him. Marc had quite an imagination.

Also back in box 1 was his copy of *Tess of the d'Urbervilles* (which looked to me like he had not read his way through to the end) and Conrad's novella *Heart of Darkness*, bound together with the shorter story *The Secret Sharer*.

To the best of my memory none of my colleagues at Westview had students read Conrad. But I did in the seniors honor course. I am sure I would remember Marc had he been a student in any of my classes. But one could guess that he had been hoping to take the honors course his senior year. Maybe he had talked to students who were taking it when he was a junior—possibly gotten hold of a book list.

I prided myself on that course that introduced students to some of the world's great literature and challenging stories. I had used *Heart of Darkness* in previous years, and it might still have been on the supplementary list, but had decided its psychological explorations of tragic evil were too bleak and overwhelming for twelfth graders. I had even had a complaint or two from parents.

Instead we read *Lord Jim*, of which Marc also had a copy. *Lord Jim* could be read as an adventure story even though it also explored dark themes of human guilt and the cost of redemption.

Marc had pored over all the Conrad. His yellow high-lighter had been active, but when it came to *The Secret Sharer* more than half the text was highlighted. Some parts of this impossible but haunting story of a sea captain who takes a naked swimmer aboard and hides him from officers from another ship who held the swimmer responsible for a death at sea were underlined in ink as well. Whether Conrad had read Freud or not, he was also exploring the human psyche and the dark or other side that persons may have in them as a form of alter-ego. Some commentators have found hints of homosexual attraction.

Strong stuff for a 16 or 17 year-old. I would not have used it in class, but it clearly appealed to Marc's imagination and perhaps even some of his own psychological insights. He may well have forgotten his interest in the story, though he had kept it. I will probably never know if or how it stayed with him, but his youthful fascination with the story gives me a greater sense of sharing with him.

Thursday October 10 1996

My first surprise, when I went to have lunch with my father today, was Gabrie sitting at Mrs. Lopez' desk. "Can I help you, young man?"

"Gabrie, what are you doing here?"

"You can call me Gabriella. I work here."

"You do?"

"And I ordered you a roast beef sandwich. I believe that is your favorite."

"Wheat bread. Lettuce and tomato. Light on the mayo?"

"Pretty much. And, get this: Daddy and Gracia are getting married."

"What!"

"Isn't that wonderful? And she is going to retire after we work together for several months. And don't think I just get sandwiches and answer the phone. This is a big job with a lot of responsibilities."

"I am sure it is."

"Talking to subcontractors. I'll write all the checks and keep records. Daddy calls it "command central" and says we will need to hire an assistant for me next year when Gracia retires."

Victor came in, wearing his hard hat with his aviator glasses. "How about them apples?" he beamed. "I would have told you earlier . . ." He interrupted himself to give us both kisses. "I would have told you earlier, but first I had to talk her into it. She is a good Catholic woman and a wonderful mother."

Sunday October 13th

There was more to our lunch meeting. Gabriella sat with us until someone came in needing directions. She had pictures of our new half-sisters and brother-to-be: Miranda, who is married, and Isabel. "She and I are almost the same age. You'll really like her."

Victor affirmed the importance of Gabriella's position, first telling me that Gracia was "almost irreplaceable but deserves more time for her children and for us." He went on to describe the ways in which "the company is doing very well, Marcus. There's room for you, too, you know. The contracting side has plenty of work but a lot of it has to do with the apartments now. We own two and manage seven of them—one quite a complex. You should come take a look with me some day. We may convert the apartments at Ventura and Downey into condominiums. Sell 'em off and probably make a bundle."

I told him that Jim and I were thinking about going together into starting a personal training facility and maybe adding a physical therapy program to it.

"Good for you," he smiled and offered to lend me money, "if you can come up with a good business plan. There's always risk in something like that. A lot of work, too. Has Jim got a good head for business and any of his own money to put into it? And be sure that's what you want to do with your life."

Along about then, he wanted to be sure I was registered to vote.

"Always," I said.

"Not last time Clinton was elected, you weren't. I'm voting for him again."

"Me, too."

"Not easy though. I wish we could get someone who was really on the side of the working people of America. So much of it is special interests and money. I would vote Republican in a minute if I thought they really cared about that. They say they do, but where they get their money from us is all the rich fellas who want to bust unions and keep wages as low as possible to increase their investments."

I satisfied myself by saying, "Good for you, Dad" with a vehemence that surprised him.

"I love you, Marcus. You're coming along. Still going to Mass, I hope. Your Dad prays for you every day."

"And be sure that's what you want to do with your life." That is a good question for any 28 year-old. Jim is a hard worker and trustworthy, but he does not have any investment money. Even with Victor's help, we would start out with considerable debt for purchasing or renting all our equipment. It will take time to develop a client base. And I would hate owing my father a bundle of money if it did not work out.

And is that what I want to do with my life? Maybe thirty-five years as a personal trainer? Maybe learning physical therapy, too. Running the business? Maybe hiring others? Having several facilities? "Lord and Zito: Physical Therapy and Personal Training."

We did not do that much career counseling at Westview. Almost all the kids were headed on to college. They still had time to think and plan about "what to do with my life." "You can be anything you really want to be," we sometimes told them. I worried we could give them a false sense of optimism about life. Before long they would be making choices that would start limiting their options. Things could happen that would limit them further. And everyone has to do something to make a living.

"But the quality of life is not just found in your work and career," I would counsel the students in my assembly talks. "Many of the best parts will be with family, friends, colleagues, neighbors—in mutually caring relationships."

One of the challenges of teaching and education is that one keeps losing relationships. The students graduate. They leave. One may see them again from time to time, but not often. And they will have changed. Then one has to start over again with a new group of students. Over and again.

Something of the same, I am learning, is true with personal training. Amanda disappeared at the beginning of the summer and did not come back in September. I tried not to take it personally. Any number of things could have happened. I hoped not tragic.

And David died—my oldest client. He had his first stroke six years ago, but he kept coming. To him our relationship was probably almost like grandfather and grandson. He did not know that Hal Barnes was much closer in age.

I went to his service at Valley Beth Shalom. The rabbi asked who I was.

"I was his personal trainer."

"Well, thank you, for that, young man. That, I think is a first, but I know the family appreciates it."

"It happens all the time," was all I could think to respond. I found parts of the service somewhat incomprehensible but also moving with its deep-rooted sense of Jewish history and community.

Yesterday I decided to take my run still in my tennis clothes up in the hills and past Shelley's house. I came back walking and she was outside in her garden gloves trimming her roses.

"Hi, Marc. I saw you run by a few minutes ago. But you're hardly out of breath. You look like a tennis player."

"I love it. Do you play?"

"No, but my brother does. He's good."

"He probably took lessons when he was young."

"He used to play a lot with his father."

"I imagine that was fun.

"Dad was good, too."

"I bet he was. So what is your brother doing now?

163

"He's teaching in San Francisco. He comes down to visit Mom and see George and Katie. He was here a week before school started."

"How is your Mother doing?"

"Oh, she's fine. Well, sort of fine. She is in China right now. Can you imagine that? It's a tour sponsored by the university with lots of lectures and things."

"That is brave of her."

"She always goes with a friend or two."

I left it at that.

One of my tennis partners yesterday was a young man who teaches what is now called "Life Sciences" at Westview. He would have started there after I retired. I told him I had gone to Westview for two years. I wanted to ask him how he liked the new science building, but realized he would not consider it all that new. I did not ask him if he had ever heard of Harold Barnes.

4

Wednesday One January 1997

William Jefferson Clinton will soon start his second term as president, but with a Republican majority Senate and House. Victor will wait and see how well any of them will do to help out the average and lower paid workers of America. According to Gabriella, Zito and Sons (I told her it should be Zito and Daughter) is doing well in this regard. We have made some new hires, and she has ideas about reorganizing the business. "Among other things we must get everything on computers. The company is bigger and more complicated now than Daddy realizes. It's almost double the size it was five years ago. You should really come to work here, Marc. You could get training. Daddy would love it."

Meanwhile Jim and I are no closer to starting Zito and Lord or Lord and Zito. "Maybe we should call it Lord Gym," I tried to joke with him.

"How so?" he asked.

"It has a literary ring to it."

"I like it," he responded. "But better Lord Personal Training and Physical Therapy."

So we talk about it, but I notice we do not talk about actual numbers. I tried floating $50,000 as what we would need to get going and have enough cushion for the first six months. In one sense, that is not a lot of money, but it is to the two of us. Try as I might I cannot do much better than pay the bills on what I take in and, while Jim says, "I've saved some," I cannot believe it is very much.

Nor do I believe the matrimonial prospects of Bill and Gabriella are making progress. Each of them has come to talk with me. Bill says, "Yes. I love her." Gabriella says, "Most of the time. I think I do." Clearly Bill has moved in to her place.

"Why don't you marry him?" I tried.

"We're O.K. for now. He is very sweet. There are just some things about him. He keeps complaining he's in a dead-end job with the sound studio. But he won't do anything about it."

"How is his pot smoking?"

"You know about that. I don't mind, but I won't let him do it in the house. And we sometimes fight about that."

"I guess the important thing is that you don't get pregnant. You do something about that?"

"That's none of your business," she scowled at me.

I had never seen her look that way and tried to laugh it off. "I am your brother."

"Brother shmother," she let me know.

On the brother hand, as it were, Danielle seems to be doing just fine according to Andrea when we talked at the Christmas gathering where there were at least two additional children, maybe ten altogether with a new baby. "She's begun her Ph.D. program at UCLA."

"In Anthropology?"

"I think so, and she's getting married next month. I know she'd want you to know, Marc. She really likes you."

Easter March 30 1997

My biggest regret will be losing the opportunity to work more closely with Jim. We do plan to stay in touch, and I am going to continue as a part-time personal trainer for at least a few months. Jim is taking over several of my clients. Our stumbling block was lack of capital. We could not come up with a business plan that I had the courage or confidence to present to Victor.

There is a lot to Jim—smart, steady. I particularly appreciate his patience with other people and with me. We might have made the enterprise work. What I could not tell him is that I had had ten years running a large institution with almost a hundred faculty and staff. I, however, had a lot of help and it was an established, endowed institution

I start with Zito and Sons on Tuesday. It was mostly Gabriella's enthusiasm that did it. That and being repeatedly reminded "how much it would please Daddy." Of course, if it does not work out, I could severely disappoint Daddy.

So I am nervous but also excited. I like the challenge of it. Gabriella says the company is doing well, "but we need better business practices." She has hired a young woman with a business and accounting degree that she says is "really tech savvy." "We have some debt for the two apartment buildings but certainly can manage more."

My interest in the figures surprised her, but she appreciated my help in convincing Daddy that we could afford to invest in getting the whole business—perhaps especially the apartment rentals—on computers.

I, however, begin as a carpenter's apprentice—working in both new construction and remodeling and repairs. It was my idea. "Let me start at the bottom, Dad. Learn some of the trades. Learn to know some of our men. We will see how it works out, but let me try six months with the carpenters and maybe the same with the electricians and plumbers. I think it will be fun, and I will like working with my hands and learning the skills—learning how things work and can be fixed and put together. I have always wanted to do that. Then maybe I will get into the apartment management side—rather than starting there."

Victor also agreed that I could continue to work up to eight or ten hours a week as a trainer in addition to my time with the company. I want to keep my hand in that work—perhaps knowing I have a fallback—but mostly not having to give up several of my longer term clients who, I believe, need me.

And Victor smiled that winning smile, "Now I know you'll have good health insurance."

Sunday June 8th

I have my own computer. Not only that, I am learning how to use it. I even have my own email address: marcus29@zitoco.com. The 29 is for my birthday in ten days. Another year and no one under 30 will trust me, or so the erstwhile hippie generation was wont to say.

Carol came over and helped me get set up and going. She knows her business, all right, and the company already has its own website including pictures of much of the staff—most of us smiling, although Gabriella already wants a different picture. I think the site will be particularly helpful in presenting a friendly and informational face to our renters. We next need to set up a way for them to contact us with concerns and complaints and for us to notify them when their rent is due or overdue.

Carol is also working on her Spanish and tells me I can be her tutor. I do not know about that. My Spanish is a long way from where I would like it to be. She is not far behind and corrects me from time to time. We laugh at our mistakes; not least *embarazada* for *embarazosa*.

I am still very much an apprentice at carpentry, but the best part is the guys seem to like me and have stopped calling me "boss's boy." They appreciate the fact that I want to learn, and who does not like to teach a good student? Maybe more important is that I can lift and carry my weight.

Saturday June 14 1997

"Hi, Mr. Marc."

"Hi, George. How are you doing?"

"I'm fine. My sister's sick."

"She is? Got a cold?"

"Yeh. And she has a fever sometimes and amemia."

"Anemia?"

"Uh-huh."

"That is not good."

"I don't know."

Shelley came out looking tired.

"Hi, Marc."

"I hear Katie is . . . that she has been sick."

"Yes. We don't know."

"I am sorry."

"Yep. Yep. Yep." She started to wipe at her eyes.

"Oh, Shelley."

"She's in the hospital now. They're getting ready to do some more tests. Thank God Rob's a doctor. He . . . he." I could not help it and neither could she. She came into my arms for maybe ten seconds and then collected herself. "I'm sorry," she attempted a laugh. "It's . . . been hard."

"I can barely imagine." "And your Mother?" I asked.

"She just doesn't get better. I think they think she could have childhood leukemia. Rob says whatever it is they can treat it—even if she needs a bone marrow transplant. I may not be able to teach this fall."

"Wow. Darn. Darn. That is . . . I am sorry."

"Thank you. We're going to be very brave, aren't we, George?" who had been taking this all in, watching both of us carefully.

"We are, Mommy," he replied bravely.

"Good for you, George," I told him. "Look, Shelley, if it turns out she does need a transplant I could give it to her."

"Oh, Marc," now she did a half-laugh. "That's so sweet. Why would you do that?"

"Because you will need a donor with a close genetic match."

"Pooh. Rob says that usually takes a relative unless we're just lucky."

"I . . . well, I . . . just wanted to help."

"What you can do is say a few prayers, if you'll do that. And give me your phone number, and I'll tell Rob of your offer."

I gave her my phone number and my email address.

Friday June 20th 1997

I should get a mobile phone. Dr. Robert Longworth left me a message yesterday afternoon. I returned the call this morning. At first he could not be reached, but then he came on the line—still talking to someone before he broke off. "Mr. Zito. This is Dr. Robert Longworth. My wife told me of your concern about our daughter. I appreciate that. May I ask the nature of your concern?"

I finally got out: "I'm a neighbor. I just came to know them on my weekly walking routine, and I . . . I was concerned and wondered if there was anything I could do."

He half-laughed, "She said you offered to be a bone marrow donor if that should be necessary. But trying to get a right genetic match is very tricky. It usually takes a relative and even then, we have to be lucky."

"I understand that."

"But if you're serious, we can always take a look, and we can put you in the National Bone Marrow Registry. Are you in good health?"

"Excellent."

"And your age?"

"Just turned twenty-nine."

"There is a bit of discomfort, I'm afraid, if you're up to that."

"O.K.," I replied, and he gave me a number I could call to make an appointment.

Fourth of July 1997

They certainly seem to be in no hurry about taking a sample of my bone marrow. It took a couple of weeks just to get an appointment. Then they called yesterday morning to postpone, saying something about "personnel scheduling." The Fourth being on a Friday this year, I suspect it had to do with the long Independence Day weekend. They rescheduled for the 10th.

I have not been able to find out anything more about sweet Katie. I realize I have only seen her once in three years.

She would have to be five or so now. I am not sure I would even recognize her. How could a child like that have leukemia?—if that is what it is.

I have dawdled as I passed the house. Last Saturday I went by four times. I thought of knocking on the door, of calling Shelley, and of going by Susan's house if she still lives there.

And, yes, I have prayed. What else is there to do? She is even on the prayer list at Our Lady of Grace. God, Jesus, the blessed Virgin Mary and a couple of saints are all being beseeched. I love Katie. I love George and Shelley and Susan, but now I feel so very far away and helpless and unhelpful.

But I am helping to build a house—under fairly close supervision, mind you. I have built doorways and windows, put up joists. It is going to be a well-built house, and it is good to make and build with one's hands—not that I do not have to think about it too: getting everything plumbed and straight. It can get wickedly hot on site, too. One prays for "June gloom." From the waist up, I am bronze.

This afternoon Gabriella and Dad and Gracia are hosting what Gabrie calls a Fourth Folly. Everyone is to wear something red, white, and blue. Much of Zito and Sons will be there—Carol too. I am assigned to charcoal wieners and bratwurst.

Sunday August 10th

Finally I received a call from someone at Children's Hospital. Could I see Dr. Longworth there at 10 a.m. on the 8th?

"Yes. Can you tell me what it is about?"

"I'm not certain I know. He wouldn't ask you if it wasn't important."

"I understand. Does it have to do with my bone marrow sample?"

"You will have to ask him."

"Can you tell me anything about Katie . . . Katie Longworth?

"I'm afraid patient information is always private."

Dr. Longworth was seated behind a small desk in what was more like a cubicle than an office. Though without stethoscope, he had on the white jacket and looked very much the medical professional.

"Ah, Mr. Zito. Please do sit down. Just a moment." He continued to write on a chart he had before him.

"Very good of you to come in." Now he looked up.

"Glad to do so. I . . . was my bone marrow all right?"

"I have some good news and what I hope you will find good news too."

"Yes?"

"Without going into detail, your bone marrow turns out to be an extraordinarily good match for a youngster we have here at Children's."

"You mean Katie?"

No, no. He is a boy of Italian-American descent with acute lymphocytic leukemia or ALL. We're at the stage where he very much needs to have a transplant."

"But what about Katie?"

"Katherine is getting the best possible care, you can be assured."

"Won't she need my bone marrow?"

"No. No." He laughed. "You're no match for her, and we still hope to avoid a transplant in her case."

"So how is she going to do?

"I believe she is going to be just fine."

173

"Radiation and chemotherapy?"

"I don't want to go into details with you, Zito. Let's just say she's getting the very best care possible. Thank God, we have the finest health care system in the world."

"And who helped you, and Shelley," I wanted to ask him, "get through those years of residency?"

He tapped his pen twice on the chart and then flipped and caught it and smiled. "The important thing is that you can save a life."

"That is pretty important."

"His parents will be eternally grateful."

"I was wondering if there is some kind of relationship."

"Nothing direct as far as we can tell. There must be something, however; perhaps back in the land of pizza and opera."

"And the Mafia."

"Sorry. I didn't mean to be ethnically incorrect."

"Would you do it?"

Again he tapped and flipped his pen, but missed it this time. "Yes. Yes. I would. There are two ways to make the donation. It can be done through a blood stem donation. But in this case we want a direct bone marrow donation. It is a surgical procedure. A syringe is inserted into the pelvic bone, but you will be under general anesthesia."

"Doesn't hurt at all, huh?"

"There may be some aching afterward, but it goes away in a day or two. And within a week one can resume all normal activities."

"And it will save the boy's life?"

"No promises. But, yes. I think I can assure you."

"All right."

As I drove back into my underground parking garage, a car followed me in. I did not think anything of it until it stopped right behind my space. It was Bill's old BMW and Bill got out. He told me that he had been sleeping in his car since Sunday when he and Gabrie "broke up." "I know you're her brother, but you're my best friend too. I need a place to crash for a few days until I can find something else."

I helped him carry some of his belongings upstairs and made up a bed with the sleeper sofa in the room I was using as an office—where I had been writing this. There he promptly crashed.

He was still sleeping when I went to work yesterday morning before tennis in the afternoon and what was mostly a run all the way up past Shelley and Katie and George's house. When I got back Bill was halfway dressed, had bought himself a couple of Taco Bell burritos and was watching the Dodgers get beat by Cincinnati on my television, although, as Bill rightly noted, "Piazza's doing great." I noticed Bill had been putting on weight.

This morning we had a long talk in two segments about the break up with Gabrie. When I returned from the gym, he had decided that "it was mostly my fault, although maybe you could talk to Gabrie for me." Then there were his problems at work, "that I wasn't saving anything," "no pot in the condo," and how much he appreciated having a friend like me and wanted to keep on talking.

Sunday August 24th 1997

I had Bill drive me for the "procedure" (I love their word) and later return to the hospital to bring me home.

The first thing I remember post-operation was the pain in my pelvic region and back. Then I was nauseous—probably from the anesthetic. But there was not much of anything to bring up since I had no food and little water since midnight. Yet I never took more than ibuprofen and today there is only residual pain in the area where they went in. Although I am supposed to "lie low" for another two days, I am thinking about getting back to work tomorrow and restless to return to the gym. As far as I can tell the minor trauma has done no damage to this good body, and, I trust, they got some great bone marrow.

Bill did almost all the talking, especially on the way back when I kept wishing he had had something done to the shocks in the BMW. On the way to the hospital it was, "I can't believe you're doing this for someone you don't even know." "Are you sure it's not going to hurt a lot?" and "Every operation poses some degree of danger, you know." On the way back: "You don't look so good—kind of pale and you're awfully quiet." "It must be something to get the bone marrow drained out of you. I wonder what that does." And "I can't believe you did this for someone you don't even know. Wow."

I had, however, awakened a care-giving side to him that was rather sweet. He was solicitous—offering to share his Jack-in-the-Box hamburgers and fries with me and managing to warm up some soup when I told him that is what I really wanted. On Thursday and Friday I was able to feed myself while he was gone and since then have been back to preparing food for myself and for him when he would eat it. I gave him the shopping list yesterday morning, which he mostly followed.

And have we talked! I retreated to the bedroom Thursday evening saying I wanted to read and he mostly left me alone. Friday night, however, he brought in a chair from the kitchen and said, "I'll keep you company."

More talk on Saturday. He retained the TV remote by his side of the couch, but eventually became bored and asked, "Whatcha reading?" When I told him I was rereading Faulkner's *Absalom, Absalom*, he said, "Gee, I tried that once. And I'm the one who finished college."

I mostly listened, trying not to make it sound like a father with son and having learned that, with perhaps a few suggestions framed as questions, many young people will get around to telling themselves what needs to be done and even asking what they hope for out of life.

Bill wanted a better job with an opportunity for more responsibility and promotion. He wanted more friends like me and ways to have fun without a lot of drinking. He wanted to get off pot and eat better. He wanted some money. He wanted a better relationship with his father. He wanted a girl who really loved him, whom he could love and maybe marry and have two kids.

He hoped he might be able to get back with Gabrie again. It sounded like they had some pretty good fights about marijuana smoking, his "not picking up after yourself," sex, money, and his "lack of ambition." I let him play that out to when he observed, "I guess I sort of . . . really cooked my goose."

We talked about what women "really wanted." I put in a few thoughts: "good sex, yes, but probably not the first thing on the list." Perhaps more important was an intimacy that involved respect and good conversation. Companionship? Women today wanted someone who would not "only bring home the bacon and take out the garbage" but also put in honest time in around the house and with the children and their school.

"They want someone who will listen to them, don't they?"

"Who doesn't?"

The only area where I pushed a little was on the job skills front. "It sounds to me like your work is beginning to require more and more technological proficiency. Even if you finished college, maybe you need more computer and related know-how applicable to sound equipment and the sound stage."

"More courses?"

"Why not? Or a good mentor. I have a woman who is helping me to learn some computer skills."

"Is she cute?"

"Not the first question, Bill."

"I have to get serious?"

"You have to want to."

"So how come you don't even have a girlfriend?"

Sunday September 21 1997

I passed 2816 White Oak yesterday for the second time on the way back to my car when I heard Shelley call out. I walked back as nonchalantly as I could.

"Rob told me what you did for that boy with the leukemia. That was . . . that was classy."

"Classy?" I ducked my head and tried to look humble. "My great bone marrow was such a great match for his."

"It was a very kind and gutsy thing to do."

"How is Katie?"

"She's doing O.K."

"Does O.K. mean she is home now? Can she go back to school and other activities?"

"We're in what Rob calls 'watchful waiting.'"

"A kind of remission?"

"A full remission, we hope. Even a cure. She has a lot of her energy back, though we have to be careful with her."

"Is that your mother's car?"

"How did you know that?"

"A lucky guess, I guess."

"I don't know how I could have gone through these last couple of months without her. She's been wonderful."

"Must be a classy woman."

I made Bill play tennis with me. He was not much competition and, even though it was early morning and not yet hot, he tired too easily. He needed to rest and talk after every fourth game or so. But he said he liked it and agreed to go to the gym with me later today.

I have to get him into a place of his own and have the apartment back to myself. I think I can help him better that way. Among other things, I do not want to ask Carol over for any more computer lessons while he is still here. Part of the trouble is that he is so clever and as good at "yes…but" as any youngster I have ever dealt with.

He has more than hinted at "being willing to take a small loan for just a few months." What I have told him is that, while staying with me he should be able to save enough money for a deposit on his own place that I can help him find along with a little cushion of savings.

I have not breathed a word to Gabriella about Bill staying with me. On the other hand, she has not said anything about their breaking up. I bet she kicked him out. I wonder what she would think if she found out he was here. I wonder what she would think I would think about the end of their affair.

Meanwhile Bill is in the living room frequently changing channels, and I am sitting on my bed with the door closed writing this.

Sunday October 26 1997

"We will never be able to thank you enough. You were a gift from God to our Nathan and the answer to a thousand, thousand prayers. We know we have to continue our prayers, but the doctors have given lots of reasons to believe Nate is regaining full health and will have a long life. He looks perfect. You should see him running and eating and with his beautiful dark hair almost grown back. It is a miracle and you and the doctors are miracle workers.

Please sometime come see us. Come meet Nathan. We love you, Mr. Zito.

Very sincerely, Ellen and Mark Provezano"

The address was in West Hills. I could easily drive out—perhaps another Sunday. But somehow I do not want to claim too much credit. It was the doctors who worked the miracle—that and some bodily material I was quick to replace. In retrospect, it cost me little relative to what was accomplished. I did not want them to feel beholden to me and wrote them that in a nicer way, not closing the door on the possibility I might meet Nathan someday.

After I mailed the letter, I realized I was not happy with it. Maybe I was short-changing their hope to express their gratitude personally. Maybe I was short-changing myself.

I am now an electrician—or, thank God, just an apprentice electrician. I miss the work of carpentry and building and the guys I was working with, although I see them from time to time when we are on the same projects. I especially liked installing new windows. Electricity makes me nervous. The main thing I focus on is to be absolutely sure the power source if off before making add-ons, repairs, changes. In another life, I repaired several lamps and changed a few plugs—more than once blowing fuses and, on another such occasion sparks everywhere. My present work is often at higher voltage, but I am learning and it is good to see the lights go on.

Lights are going on after work, too. I sometimes stop by and talk to Gabriella and Carol. Carol teaches us more programs we can do with our computers and Gabrie both enthuses and worries about the company: "Daddy has more happening here than even he knows. He's done it a lot with his contracting skills and because people like him and like working for him, but it needs better organization, business, and accounting procedures. That's what we're putting in place; at least we're getting there."

Several times we have gone out afterwards for beers. After we shared a second beer last week, Gabriella decided it was "time to let us know about Bill." I was not sure Carol knew much about Bill, but Gabrie was remarkably frank with both of us. "It was a mistake to let him move in. I kept thinking the problems we were having were mostly my fault and trying to be nicer, and I still do like him. Actually, I worry about him. Do you see him, Marc? For whatever reason, he looks up to you."

"Yes. Some."

"How's he doing?"

"I can worry about him too. But better, I think."

Carol appeared sympathetic, looking at whoever was talking. It turns out that she played tennis in college, but I am not getting mixed up with that one. She is too young for me. I cannot afford to get emotionally involved with someone I might only end up hurting. Besides she might be able to beat me. Since Carol works for Zito and Sons, I should not think she would want to become personally involved either.

5

New Year's Day 1998

"Maybe next year we'll have a float in the parade," Gabrie gushed. Victor only beamed, but I asked how much something like that would cost. Nobody knew, but consultation with willing experts in the crowd came up with a figure of around $40,000. That I thought would put an end to it, but after a posse of ponies from Arizona, a huge float with a giraffe that would turn its neck and gawk at us, and a flashy high school band of over a hundred from Texas passed by, I noticed Gabrie and Carol conferring and laughing about a cartoon draft Carol had drawn of a chariot drawn by two horses, driven by a character waving a whip. The notation read, "Zito Builds It Best," which was crossed out and replaced with "Zito Does It Faster." I shook my head, attempting an "Oh, you girls" wide-eyed look, to which Gabrie responded. "Don't worry, Marcus; we'll dress you up as Charlton Heston to be the driver. You'll look great in one of those short togas."

It is now nearly 8 p.m. after a full Tournament of Roses day. Gabriella had laid out some company money for a group of us to have seats (getting there shortly after dawn when the temperature was not much over 50°) and then to take in Michigan outlasting Washington State while sitting on the more than toasty side of the stadium and having our faces sun-burned. The game ended with Washington State fans shouting in a ruckus about whether time had actually run out before the Cougars could get in a last play.

This year's top New Year's resolution belongs to Bill, though it is mine as well. I did not phrase it this way to him, but I will be so glad to be an "empty nester" again. Glad, too, not to listen to his snoring even with two closed doors between us. Last night I wanted to stuff a sock in his mouth. He claims he is determined to go, and I am more than ready to help him find a place. He has enough money saved up for a deposit and a couple months of cushion. A bed and some kitchen equipment can be bought second-hand. I told him he could get along without a TV for a while, to which his response was "I don't need anything big." If Victor were to overhear us, he would ask about health insurance, but I decided Bill had made enough of a resolution for now.

He is better physically, too, and, I hope, emotionally. He claims his second resolution is to keep on with the running. He wants to set up a schedule with me, which I may do if that is what it takes.

I duly attended our family Christmas party. Gabriella whispered that people were talking about us since we were the only cousins there who were not married or engaged to be.

My best Christmas present was a surprise just before Christmas. Shelley came out with a Christmas card to give me. On it was a great picture of Shelley and Rob with George and Katie taken up at Big Bear last winter "before Katie's illness."

"What a great family, Shelley."

"I would have mailed it to you. You should give me your address."

"How is Katie doing now?"

"Rob says so far so good. She's starting back to kindergarten half-day after New Year's." And then out of the front door came *my son, my son,* Steve. "This is my brother Steve, Marc. Here for the holidays. He teaches in San Francisco."

I think I have become a great actor. "Glad to meet you, Steve." We shook hands.

"You, too, Marc. Shelley told me of your offer for Katie and what you did for that boy with ALL."

"I..."

"Big stuff, if you ask me. Thank you, man."

He looked so good to me, handsome, kind of a Dutch jaw like Susan's father, blondish hair, athletic. There was a sore of some kind just below his lower lip. I wanted to put ointment on it.

I have made another resolution to go see Nathan and his parents—telling myself it would be a kindness to them, but, recognizing I was denying myself the pleasure of shaking the hand—or maybe high-fiving—a lad whose life I had helped to save.

Three more months as an electrician and, under expert tutelage, I have not even come close to frying myself. Having learned on the job what a red, black, white and green wire mean and do, I have even been sent on my own to make a couple of apartment repairs and (cross your fingers) have not started any fires. Probably I now know just enough to be dangerous, but I brag to Gabriella and Carol and wish there was some way I could show off to Susan: "Look, honey, what

I can do. Do you have any lamps than need fixing? Maybe a toaster?"

My Dad Victor and I have started having regular monthly lunches where we talk about the business and he describes some of the work he has begun with Catholic Charities. A couple of weeks ago there must have been eight of us that piled into the company van, and he drove us up to Pacoima where we helped cook, serve and clean up for a church sponsored meal for several hundred mostly immigrant men, women and lots of children. One of the younger men with us in the van had been hired from there earlier in the year to work for Zito and Sons.

But it is late. More on all this in 1998.

Groundhog Day 1998

Well, what did I expect? You could guess. I spent a good part of the afternoon with Nathan and his family yesterday. He is a great eight year-old—just a few months younger than George—still a bit small for his age, but full of freckles and a boyish smile he cannot quite control. I am not sure how well he understood the significance of my bone marrow donation, but, after he shook my hand and said, "I'm Nate, Mr. Zito," he held my lower half and buried his face in my stomach in a wordless hug that left me speechless too.

His parents were older than I expected with two teen-aged daughters who had sweet little speeches of thanks to offer me. The subsequent, almost flirtatious behavior of the older one somewhat unnerved me. Maybe a half-dozen times Ellen Provezano thanked me for what I had done for "my baby" which endearment clearly embarrassed Nate, but I managed in my interaction with him to convey that I regarded him as a young man.

Nate showed me his penny collection. Mark Provezano, who does something in a laboratory for a pharmaceutical company, took us to a park where we played catch. Nate loves the Dodgers and dislikes the Angels. Mike Piazza is his favorite player. He showed me his Piazza 42 jersey. Mark and I talked about being of Italian ancestry, and I told him of my spelling of Marc—short for Marcus. He said he had heard of Zito and Sons.

Nate and I agreed we would stay in touch, and he promised to send me a letter with pictures of him playing baseball. I left reminding him of his promise.

Sunday February 8 1998

Bill leaves later today. I will help him move with a few last of his clothes. His apartment is small and not in great condition. I did, however, check the wiring and also made sure it was not a Zito and Sons-managed building. He and I do not need any more family entanglements.

We went out for beers and had a last long talk this evening. He told me, "I think I'm really over Gabrie. I guess I never did figure her out." We talked about what it would mean "to figure someone out" and whether that was even a good idea.

After his second beer he was profuse in thanking me "for everything:" the bed, the food, the exercise and conversations. And then, "You know I kind of have trouble figuring you out any more, Marc. We used to have so much fun screwing around. I don't mean you aren't any fun, but, just hanging around with you, you seem so . . . I don't know. Like you know who you are . . . or, I don't know, just older. Even in the way you talk."

I shrugged. "We get older."

"And wiser?"

"Maybe wiser, too."
"That's what I'd like."

Jim helped us get Bill set up in the apartment last week. We do not see that much of each other lately. I gave up my last clients just before Christmas, but we agreed to stay in touch, and I had dinner with him and his new "special," Tiffany. She was, as we used to say, a "doll," vivacious, very well-dressed, her hair and nails expertly cared for, and she would not let go of "Why you wouldn't let me bring Norrie along for you to meet. She's great."

I guess I will never know if Norrie is a black or white woman, some of each, or something else. I have wondered what it might like to be attracted to a black woman. But I am staying determined not to get involved with any woman my age or younger. If pressed too hard, I will say, "I have identity issues," which is true enough whatever they may think I mean.

I can imagine what floated through Tiffany's mind, though she does not act like she has accepted that about me. Women, I have noticed, have a pretty good sixth sense—or whatever sense one wants to call it—about whether a man is gay or not.

That being said, I have, however, agreed to tennis with Carol. I swear she almost dared me. "I'll bet she can beat your pants off," Gabrie joined in as they laughed at my expense. When we were alone, I clumsily attempted to let Carol understand, "I am only good for tennis."

She laughed her sweet, young laugh, "Me too."

Sunday February 22nd

As I suspected might happen, Carol bested me in our first match. She has been playing tennis since she was ten and has great ground strokes, so consistent, moving well from side to side, some top spin on her forehand. I have trouble outlasting her rallies, and, when I dash to the net to volley, she is good at passing me or hitting a lob that leaves me panting in the back-court and her laughing in triumph. Her serve is no great shakes, but she regularly gets my return back and then just steadily wears me down into an error. 6-2, although then 6-4, 6-4.

However! Yesterday I used my strength and a few drop shots: 4-6, 7-5, 6-4.

Gabrie tells me Carol has a boyfriend, which makes the relationship a lot easier for me. She is a great young gal and a lot of woman. Her hair is really red and becomes even curlier with the perspiration and all. Her laugh irritates me but then gets me laughing too.

Gabrie does not ask about my love life. She may have given up. Nor have I asked or she volunteered about hers. I am grateful she is my sister. Someday she is going to make some man happy as a companion and spouse.

Instead we talk about the business, sometimes with Carol there. Gabriella is putting in a lot of overtime and is full of ideas and, evidently, a bit frustrated that Daddy seems less interested with "growing the company" than she thinks he should be. My hunch is that Dad may want to keep it a size where he can know everyone.

I try to regale them with adventures of "my life as electri-cian." Last week I impressed Gabrie by rewiring an antique lamp she had recently purchased. Piece of cake!

Yes, and I still go to Mass now and then. I figure it helps to keep me on good terms with Dad. I tell him that I espe-cially like praying for others.

"Who?"

"Oh, a boy who seems to have fully recovered from leukemia and a girl who I think may have had it too."

"And your prayers are answered?"

"So far so good."

"And always pray for your mother and your brother."

I forgot to record Victor's and Gracia's wedding last month. It took them some time to arrange the necessary decrees, or whatever they are, from the church bureaucracy. Apparently Gracia's husband went back to Mexico eight or so years ago to visit relatives and was never heard from again. She feels sure he would never have deserted her or the children and must have met with some "terrible accident." The Mass and vows were rather quick at Our Lady of Grace, and I then enjoyed dancing with daughters Isabel and Miranda at the reception in the banquet room at Marcello's. I had forgotten that I had liked to dance, and decided I looked at least a bit dashing in the black tie outfit I rented for the occasion. There must have been over 200 people there with much food and wine and a great cake. I dutifully danced with Gabriella, too, and cousin Andrea and more.

Gabriella sometimes joins us for the lunches. We talk business. Dad quizzes me on my work as electrician and carpenter. He can get very detailed and exacting. He tells us more about his involvement with city-wide ecumenical "Hope in Youth" program Catholic Charities has begun. He has also been invited to be part of an advisory group in the building of the new downtown cathedral. "No contracts for Zito and Sons, but I tell the Cardinal and Father Vosko what I think. To begin with, I think they are spending too much money. Some of it should be for the poor.

The Cardinal says it is a church for the poor. Doesn't look much like it to me."

He also wanted to know what we thought of Bill Clinton and "whatever he did with that Lewinsky girl." I kept my mouth shut.

Gabriella wonders, "whatever she could have been thinking of. And in the White House! Awful for Mrs. Clinton." Victor said he was not surprised by Clinton being "so self-centered." "I just pray he doesn't get hamstrung and can still work for the good of everyone and not just these rich types he seems to hang out with more and more. As if they don't influence his policies. Hah!"

Sunday May 31

Young Nathan phoned me two weeks ago. "My dad said it would be O.K. to call you, Mr. Marc."

"Sure is, Nate. How are you doing?"

"I'm fine, but I wanted to ask you about the Dodgers trading Mike Piazza . . . about what you think."

"Well, I did not much like it."

"He was their best player." His voice broke. "I...I..."

"It's going to be all right, Nate. Players get traded all the time these days."

"But I loved him. I've got his jersey. He was Italian too."

Ah, what to say? He did not need my "'Baseball is big business now and Murdoch's News Corporation crew and Fox Sports were mostly interested in the TV rights where the biggest money is, and, no doubt, thought young Piazza was asking too much, and hoping to get as much as they could for him, and the hell with the fans like Nate and team loyalty. With the O'Malleys gone, it is going to be all about money. Watch what happens to the price of the tickets and the concessions and the parking. Let's switch our loyalty and start

rooting for a good minor league team like the High Desert
Mavericks or the Rancho Cucamonga Quakes."

And Nathan was too young for "Time heals all wounds,"
even though it would be mostly true in this case. Instead I
said, "You could still pull for him. Do you know to whom they
traded him?"

"To the Miami Marlins. But now he's with the New York
Mets." There was disgust in his voice. "I'm going to throw
away his jersey."

"Don't do that, son. Here is what we could do. Let's go to
a Dodger game together. Wear your Piazza jersey if you want.
I will bet there will be other fans there with theirs on. And we
can root for their new catcher.'

"Really? Could we do that?" "Dad, Mr. Marc says we can
go to a Dodger game."

I fixed on a date with Mark and told him I would order
four tickets and to find a friend for Nate to bring along,
only to have him call two nights ago and say Nate's classmate
could not come. "Can you find someone?"

I could and called Shelley with the story. George and
Nate were about the same age and, I told her, it would be fun
for Nate to make a new friend.

When Mark, Nate, and I pulled up in front of 2816 White
Oak yesterday the family was waiting for us—George with his
Dodger cap on. He spotted Nate's Piazza jersey immediately.

I worry that Rob worries that I may have the wrong interest in boys and so gave George a good slap of a high five and
backed away, thinking I may need to cut back on my walk-bys.
But maybe he should transfer his worry to little girls because
Katie decided I was someone worth hugging and grabbed my
leg, her hands alarmingly upward around my thigh. Her full
dark hair came up to my belt and I tousled it—noting how

good her color looked. I wanted to pick her up and swing her about.

Rob shook hands with Nate and Mark, giving Nate a good medical look. I introduced Dr. Longworth as one of Nate's consulting doctors which, if Rob wanted to correct, he did not.

And then we were off to the game in the always startlingly beautiful Dodger Stadium with the San Gabriels as backdrop. I found out from George that "I like my sister a lot but sometimes she's a pest." He and Nate agreed that most girls are pests.

Hot dogs were eaten, followed by ice cream. I learned what George thought of fourth grade and homework and his teacher, Ms. Schneider. He and Nate joined us in shouting "Ra-ooul, Ra-ooul" every time Mondesi came to bat. George decided he was his favorite player. Nate reserved judgment but said, "I might like Tom Prince" (who caught that night), "but he never hits any home runs." Mark and I argued over who would pay for what until I realized it was not generous of me to insist on being the fairy godfather or whatever. We split the tickets. I paid for the parking and he for the food. The total tab, with our beers, was nearing $200. The Dodgers lost 7-3 and two nine year-olds fell asleep on the way home.

Sunday July 18 1998

Here is one for you: Two girls and a guy go away for the weekend. I am the guy, escorting and driving them in my new used Ford Probe GT listed as one of the best cars of 1994. Proceeding up Route One, the fabled Pacific Coast Highway, we stay in a motel in Morro Bay and then at the Big Sur River Inn.

Saturday evening is a postponed celebration of this older man's 30th birthday. He is unmarried and for a long

time without a girlfriend, thought by some to be gay or perhaps confused or stunted in his sexuality. One of the young
women is 26, the other 25. They are also single; they are quite
attractive, occasionally date, and are presumed heterosexual,
though you would not know that for the manner in which
they laugh and carry on together, ignoring the guy's masculine presence except to make jokes at his expense. Their
favorite took place in the Villager Motel in Morro Bay when
the guy, who is presently working as an apprentice plumber,
was asked to come to their motel room to see about what they
thought was a leak under their sink. After he had turned on
the faucet, knelt, and professionally checked the pipes, he
heard the click of a camera, followed by what could only be
called giggling and claims (false, I believe) that they had a
good view of "the crack in the back."

The only other untoward moment in what I otherwise
regarded as a thoroughly enjoyable mini-vacation with some
challenging driving, great views of the coastline and ocean,
and a visit to Hearst Castle, occurred when I was invited to
come to their room in Big Sur for "some wine before dinner."
I entered a little warily. The one young woman, attired in a
sweater and designer jeans which nicely showed her athletic
figure, gave me a chaste kiss and poured us both some wine.
The second came in from the bathroom with an open shirt
over her bra and panties. I am not sure what color I turned
as I stood and looked toward the door. "For heaven's sake,
Marc. I'm your sister."

The other girl—you guessed it—was my sometimes tennis opponent and sometimes partner: always fun, although
I realize that can be a put-down of a young woman; "She's a
lot of fun," and not much else. Believe me, there is a lot else:
smart, unbelievably savvy technologically or whatever you are

supposed to call it these days. By mutual agreement we have cut back on some of our matches, so that I can play with "my buddies," but have also played some mixed doubles. Carol wanted to put us into the spring tournament, but I was not ready for that.

What else? Not a lot. Plumbing is boring compared to electricity, but, one quickly realizes, just as essential in an emergency, maybe more so.

Bill tells me he has a new girlfriend and that "work is better." I told him he needs more exercise and better eating habits. Evidently Jim has a new girl, too. Despite his talk about "settling down and having kids," I think he backs away when affairs get too serious. Maybe he is looking for just the right girl. Probably I should say "woman." We all three are thirty or getting there. "Once upon a time" that was old for an unmarried guy.

Sunday October 4 St. Francis Day

My father, that is, my Pittsburgh father of blessed memory, would tell me that time goes faster as one grows older. He was probably thinking of 72 year-olds rather than someone who was 30, but, either way, the summer seems to have shot by. I would have to press my memory to recall what happened to August.

I finished my plumber's apprenticeship last week and begin tomorrow morning working with Uncle Tony, who oversees all the rental properties for Zito and Sons. My dad Victor wanted to get me started here earlier as "I can see this being your future and where I'm going to most need you."

We will see. I shall miss working with my hands and using my physical strength. Although there were several weeks when I assisted with installing the plumbing in two new houses, much of the time was "problem solving" with repairs in the apartments, which can be rather grubby work in basements and under flooring—once putting in a new sewer line. Then there were the stopped up toilets. When I returned a call from an older lady in the Hayvenhurst building and asked her what the problem was, she said, "It's the toilet. It won't swallow." I understand we receive more complaints about plumbing problems than any other issues.

I wonder what Francis of Assisi would think of that. Our Padre sermonized about Francis for a while last evening. In the past I have thought of him as a curious mixture of down-to-earth lover of the world and its creatures and an impractical innocence. I could see him on his hands and knees working on someone's plumbing, for which he would not charge anything. Maybe he would say something kindly to a passing rat.

Gabriella still has her ideas about "growing the business," to which our father listens patiently, often smiling, but I think more in appreciation of her enthusiasm and ambition than in agreement. He lectures us both on the importance of good relations with all our workers, fair compensation and the importance of health care. "That's the first responsibility. Not the only one, but then the rest will work out."

She also has begun work on an M.B.A., attending evenings and with "a day course I can fit in now and then." I had taken two summer courses in school and business administration when I became Head at Westview, and would not mind learning some more, but, then, I am the sibling who has not even finished college.

More problematic is Gabriella's "seeing" Darin from Dana Point, "a nice guy in his thirties, divorced and with a five year-old son." I can understand that he is good-looking and charming in his way, but I do not think he would be at all right for Gabrie. He also wants to advise her on the business. Carol and I had a "date" so that we could go to dinner with Gabriella and Darin and size him up. I have a hunch that Carol's opinion of him will weigh more with Gabriella than mine. Fortunately she did not seem enamored with him either. During dinner I thought Darin showed as much interest in Carol as he did in Gabriella, which I found doubly irritating.

Carol and I talked ourselves into entering the mixed doubles tournament at the Tennis Center. So far so good as we won the first two matches rather handily. Tougher matches to come, but Carol is a good competitor. I love it when she holds her racquet in front of her face and whispers to me her next strategic ploy. She can make me look slow out there.

The Dodgers did get into the play-offs, but Nate has switched his loyalties to Paul LoDuca. I plan to get him a LoDuca jersey for Christmas.

Sunday October 25th

We won. Actually the semi-final was our toughest match—against last year's champions, a married couple. The woman was not pleased, making remarks to me so that Carol could overhear about my pairing up with "a little Stanford lassie pro." Her husband may have been embarrassed but perhaps did not dare to say anything other. The missus tried to give Carol a withering look as she shook her hand, which Carol countered by complimenting her on her backhand and the effectiveness of her serve.

The final was a relative breeze: 6-4, 6-2. That is the good news. The other news is that after they accepted the trophy, the still elated and lightly perspiring pair held each other in a kiss that lasted long enough to draw whistles and a couple of hoots from the little crowd of witnesses. Then there was the look in Carol's eyes, and likely in mine—a shock of recognition that we had become more than friends. Whooooah. Where do I go from here?

6

New Year's Day 1999

"Negotiations," is what Carol and I have decided to call our caring if sometimes wary conversations. In fairness, it is probably more my word than hers. We hold hands. We kiss when we part, often finding it difficult to let go. She can be quite direct with me. "Marc, you don't have to be afraid to be more affectionate. I'm a big girl."

Or, "I can understand if you're not sure about making a long term commitment. I'm not asking that from you. But I do want you to love me." And, "Believe me. I never intended to fall in love with the boss's son. Maybe it was your seeming lack of sense of privilege. That and the way you so innocently came charging up to the net the first time we played." She laughed. I smiled and the warmth of her hand flowed up my arm and into my chest.

"And believe me; I never intended to fall in love with a man who didn't finish college. Wait until my father finds out about that, after all the money he and mother spent on my education! 'What are you going to talk about afterward?' he'll ask me."

"Emily Dickinson? 'Tell all the truth / But tell it slant / Success in circuit lies.'"

"That's the point, you weirdo. You can win him over, but there are parts of you I find deliciously mysterious. And the stuff you read and that you care about the world around you. And you've been such a quick learner with the computer. You must be some kind of autodidact."

"Who is still trying to find out who he is."

"Pooh. Who isn't?"

"I mean . . . I mean; I want to be fair to you, Carol. There are things about me that I cannot explain even to myself."

"There are things about me that I can't explain."

"I mean more than that."

"Tell me."

"Oh, bumblepuppy."

"What? Marc! Talk to me. You can't tell me that you don't love me."

"No, I can't."

"What?"

"I cannot tell you that I do not love you because I do."

"Why was that so hard?"

"It's not. I love you. But I do not want to hurt you."

"You're not. Give me a kiss, a nice kiss, your best kiss."

"I'll give that a five," she graded it. Maybe you don't find me that attractive."

"Oh, no. You are very attractive, Carol. You are beautiful."

"Ah, men. I'll bet it's only my body."

"That, too, for sure."

"Well, in case you're wondering, it's mutual."

"Oh, that is nice to know."

"Ding, dong. That's what you are, sweetie."

She admits she talks to Gabriella about me. She knows about my mother dying and my dropping out of college and the army and then not being close to her or Daddy and then "the big change that happened in you several years ago."

"That is true."

"Did something happen?"

"Yes. Sort of."

"Like?"

"That is what I find hard to understand."

"Maybe I can."

"I do not think anybody could."

"Try me."

"Oh. It is like...I don't know. Let us say a change in personality."

"But you're still Marc."

"Yes."

"And?"

"I can't explain."

"If you mean it's kind of like being two people at times, that happens to everybody. Sometimes I'm nice Carol, sometimes mean and selfish Carol."

"Well, me too."

"And I want you to have both of me, just the way I love both of you."

"Oh, Carol. Carol . . . Carol."

"Oh, Marcus, Marcus, Marcus. It's not like you killed somebody."

Sunday January 3rd

I should add that we are at least a semi-public couple. From the sidelines, if not edging onto the playing field, Gabriella has been cheerleading our "affair," though I asked her not to call it that. She thought it would be a "grand idea" if I brought Carol with me to the family Christmas celebration. If one measures by the measure of her reception, it was, indeed, grand: "She is lovely, Marc," "What a great catch," Uncle Tony whispered to me. "Best looking non-Italian woman I've seen in a long time." Gabriella had a present for her and Dad Victor claimed it was from him, too, which may have embarrassed Carol more than it did me. She looks so sweet when she blushes.

This relationship of ours ought to be a no-brainer. Part of me is very much in love with her. Part of me would love to make love to and with her. And that is where part of the trouble comes in. How can I be fully intimate with someone without sharing all that I am? How could I keep such a secret from her?

Carol is different from Susan. Some of it is, of course, generational. Dear Susan was 25 in 1954. Carol knows technology and modern styles of music and has traveled—all sorts of things neither Susan nor I would have guessed then.

Her coloring—her hair and skin—are quite different too: lovely red hair and light, slightly freckled complexion. Taller, fuller figured, while I was so infatuated with Susan's womanly slenderness.

But there are other ways. Carol's laugh can make me think of Susan, maybe especially when she pokes fun without intention of hurting. And (and this sounds strange even to me, but) I once read that men can be attracted to women and visa-versa by subtle smells—something about pheromones that couples are not even aware of.

So what? Why should that make any difference one way or another? The moral law says (if I remember correctly, I think St. Paul says) that when one partner is dead the other is free to marry—and that must mean have sex—with another. And "gadnabit"—as I would sometimes say to avoid swearing, I was a faithful to one-woman for 42 plus years. Susan can make love to someone else now. I ought to be able to make love to someone else. And how about Carol and her feelings?

Fact of the matter: I am scared. Bottom line: the bottom line again is I love her, though I am not quite sure how. She is like a daughter, a sweetheart, someone who loves me.

So just do it. Be Marcus. Love her. Maybe marry her. Maybe have children. Explain to her later. Never explain. She will not care. Susan cannot care. Why should I care? Make Marc happy. Make me happy.

Sunday January 17 1999

A steward of this body is one way I have continued to think of myself. I can still be proud of it at 30: no longer so hard-muscled, I can get a pinch of love handles, and I have to suck it in to see my abs. But the running, tennis, and gym workouts keep it well-toned. Looks good, as I pat my mostly flat stomach.

I cannot say the same for the life of the mind. I read less fiction, perhaps because I have no one with whom to discuss it. On the other hand, I do keep up with the newspapers and again have subscriptions to the *New Yorker* and the *Atlantic Monthly*. I find more and more I like biographies. I enjoyed Cole Porter's biography. It made me feel nostalgic, though surprised that such clever breeziness could come out of so complicated and often pain-filled a life: talk about being two people! John Nash's brilliance, schizophrenia and loneliness in *A Beautiful Mind* were even more problematic for me. He may have been gay, too, though his sexuality may just have been stunted in some way.

A fair amount of mental energy goes into daily work. Uncle Tony runs the supervision of the rental properties out of an office he has connected to his ground floor apartment in our Sherman Oaks building. His daughter Nora is good at keeping track of payments, billing, repairs, and the like, but it is not as efficient as it should be and the business has grown over the last years more than Tony realizes. With Carol's great help we are beginning to get it computerized, and I find myself in the thick of it. I also find that a lot of what I do is personnel work, listening to people, helping them to understand that Zito and Sons does, indeed, care about the demands of their schedules, the broken elevator, the lights out in the vestibule, the noise of the repair work in the garage.

Last week it was reported to me by one of the guys I had worked with that another of our employees "might be here illegally." I pretended not fully to understand and took it to Victor.

"Is he paying taxes, social security and everything?" Victor asked.

"I think so, I can find out."

"Good. I'm sure he is. Government's glad to have his money. Then get him a lawyer."

Body, mind, and soul, if I have one, are scheduled to go on a "tennis weekend" to a resort Carol knows about in Ojai. We have agreed to see if we can take our relationship to "the next level." What a nice euphemism that is. I am excited and scared.

Sunday March 7 1999

We played tennis. We shared nice meals—one breakfast in our room looking out over the 9th hole of a golf course. It has been hard to find words for the rest. Of course she was warm and young and coy. I almost immediately ejaculated and made a mess. For the rest of our time together I could not keep it up.

Carol was understanding and tried to be helpful. The more she tried the worse it became. I retreated to the

bathroom and cried. We tried a warm bath together. She con-
ducted what she called "a full body search" and discovered
my two tattoos. Then she cried. She was not pretty enough.
She was not sexy enough.

"No, no, Carol. It is me. I am messed up."

"You could see a doctor. Maybe it's something physical
that can be fixed."

"Maybe." But it is not. *I can masturbate all right, although it
is a lonely and almost entirely physical experience.* But I could not
tell her that. *It is in my head. The mind is the major sex organ.*
But I could not tell her that either. I could not tell her that a
major part of me was still a 72 year old mind, quite probably
with inhibitions he does not understand.

"Or a psychiatrist?" she tried. "Something that can be
fixed."

"I cannot be fixed," I burst out. "I am not good for you.
Can't you understand?" and got dressed and walked out, not
returning until after dawn, determined to try to convince her
that, though I did love her and she was lovely, I could only
be trouble for her—that there was something wrong with me
and she could and would find someone else.

We drove back in near silence. In the last stretch on the
freeway I think she was getting angry, which I convinced myself
could be good for her, whether she was angry with me or God
or life or all of the above. I got her red suitcase out of the
trunk and took it up the five stairs to her front door. She said,
"Thank you" and took it inside. No kiss. No good-bye. I have
not seen her since. I do not imagine I will ever see her again.

She called Gabriella the next morning and quit her job,
volunteering to come in and help the new person with the
transition. I think Gabriella still talks to her from time to

time, though I dare not ask. Gabriella is furious with me, possibly more because Carol quit her job than about Carol not having any future relationship with me. In any case it is my fault, and I cannot come up with a defense that would make any sense to her.

Or to Victor, though I see him as more disappointed than angry. He does not realize how hard it is for Gabriella to find someone that companionable and smart. He worries about me. He thought I might finally have found someone with whom "You could settle down. She was a good one, Marcus. She reminded me of your mother." Then, "I hope there's nothing wrong with you. You can always talk with your Dad, you know. There could be something about losing your mother, Son—not to speak of your brother."

I switched the subject to the rental business of Zito and Sons and some of my plans for it. Victor often surprised me with the detail he could into with any aspect of the company. It was good for both of us to change the subject. It had taken a few days for it to sink in that there will be no more tennis with Carol either.

April 21 1999

Yesterday two deranged youngsters with easy access to guns killed twelve students and a teacher in a high school in Colorado. Twenty-four others were wounded. I hate guns around young people. I well remember the April day in 1985 when we learned that our own Tyler Donner, only weeks from his graduation, had killed himself with his father's gun in their garage. We had to do a lot of soul searching: Why was Tyler depressed? Why had we not known about it? Had at least an inkling? Provided better counseling opportunities for him?

But even his friends said they did not know. A year later his parents divorced. His sister did not return to Westview in the fall.

We held a memorial service. We had conversations about better counseling and mental health services. We talked about better gun safety, safe storage, training, licensing. There was a time when even the National Rifle Association emphasized some of these steps, and I guess they still offer classes and produce instructional materials. But then Wayne LaPierre and now Charlton Heston and all the money from the gun and ammunition makers has shifted the emphasis to the ready ownership and access to guns, guns, guns—several hundred millions of them in a country where some 12 times more children are killed by a gun that in 25 other industrialized societies put together.

Sunday Fourth of July 1999

I attended two Fourth of July parties this year, and I might have wangled my way to a third. The third was a party that Shelley mentioned they would be having today, but I quickly told her about the company party that Gabriella seems to have made into an annual tradition. I may also have been afraid that I would see Susan at the family gathering. I am not sure why I was afraid: to see her aging? That she did not think of old Hal that much anymore? She had a new guy now? That she could somehow intuit what I had been up to . . . or not up to? What would I say to her?

I only go by Shelley's house every three weeks or so now. "I think George has grown an inch in a couple months," I told her. "What is he? Ten now?"

"He is taller than most of the other boys," Shelley replied. "It's hard to keep him in shoes."

Yesterday's party was at the Provezanos. I want to stay in some touch with Nate. He is growing, too, though he seems to me short for his age. But full of beans. Eric Karros is now his favorite Dodger, although we had to agree that "the Dodgers don't look so hot this season." I did not tell him that I seem to have lost some of my interest in the Dodgers. We talked more about his learning to play shortstop for his Little League team, the Agoura Hills Tigers.

I will again dutifully wear red, white, and blue to the company Fourth Folly this afternoon and at least help charcoal the hot dogs. Dad says he is thinking of coming as Uncle Sam. Gabriella and I are talking again—sort of like brother and sister, but mostly about business. She is making "great progress" with her M.B.A. Alan, a young man –younger than she is—seems to be a capable replacement for Carol, if a bit unpredictable in his work habits and social skills. His ambition, however, seems to be with what he calls "the dot com" companies, and I am not sure how long we can keep him.

I think Gabriella has decided that there is something odd about my sexuality and hopes "you'll get straightened out someday. No pun intended." I do not hear anything about her dating or love life. No mention of Darin. She sounds a little infatuated with one of her teachers in the M.B.A. program who has been "so extra helpful and knows his stuff." But I gather he is older and married.

She respects the fact that I am working long hours for the company. I pretty much have to as Uncle Tony seems to have health problems. Fortunately Nora is now full-time, too, and catching on to the computer programs. We do need more help.

I should take some vacation time. Victor Dad says, "It's a bad example for the company not to."

I would have to do it alone. Both Jim and Bill have their women. Bill's sounds more serious: "She's really good for me. Keeps me on the straight and narrow."

I have thought about driving up to Idaho and seeing how Ellie is doing. It has been almost two years since I have heard from her. Maybe better would be to head up to Oregon or Washington and even into Canada. Maybe I could learn how to fly fish. I always wanted to do that.

7

New Year's Day 2000

The world did not end. Some computers required repro-
gramming, but there was no great information technology
crash. Technically speaking, of course, the new century and
millennium begin with 2001, but today seems to be the popular choice. Interesting questions are raised about calendars
and how time is measured and even the relativity of time.
"How did you spend your time?" people ask each other.
Spend. Time is like money; in many ways more valuable than
money. One never wants to waste it. Yet we need our distractions just because time keeps on going no matter what we do.
I remember a little poem: "It's not that time goes so fast / It
never stops that makes it past."

I lost in the quarter-finals of the fall tennis tourney. Not
bad, but I doubt if I will ever get further than that—even if
I *spent* more time on it. The couple that Carol and I beat in
the semis last year won the mixed doubles. The woman was
so unctuously sportsmanlike in her little acceptance speech
that I felt like throwing up.

No more talk from Gabriella about having a company
float in the Rose Parade. She would rather invest the money
in new company ventures. Her M.B.A. studies are paying
off. But we do have tickets for the game this afternoon: the

Stanford Cardinals (or correctly, I guess, Cardinal; I can remember when they were the Indians) versus the Wisconsin Badgers. Carol would have had me rooting for Stanford.

Tuesday January 4 2000
Unbelievable. "It's not your business," Gabriella informed me. "But I thought you ought to know." On the last day of the century, she attended the rather hastily arranged marriage of Carol to Darin Dunning— that Darin from Dana Point. Carol told her that "No, I'm not pregnant, but Darin wants us to be married for the new century—for the 'next millennium.' Isn't that sweet?" There was also something about Darin wanting to do it in 1999 for tax reasons.

"Carol really seems happy. They make a great couple. They're going to Hawaii for their honeymoon."

"Uh-huh."

"Her parents were able to get there so her father could give her away. They're really nice, though Dr. Campbell took me aside afterwards and asked me what I thought of Darin."

"And?"

"I told him I thought he was a good guy. He just said that he wished he had had a chance to know Darin better."

"Smart man," which earned me a withering look from Gabrie, and, "you had your chance, bucko."

"I'm glad she is happy," I got out.

April Fool's Day 2000
We had good fun with this day at Westview: a joke edition of the school paper, an announcement from me that we would be inverting the grade order for the rest of the semester, but the students were not to tell their parents until after the final report cards were sent out. I pulled tricks on young Steve and Shelley too: the arm in a sling that I broke

while turning the steering wheel too hard. For whatever reason Stevie was more gullible than Shelley—or maybe he just liked going along with the joke. It would have been fun to have some grandpa tricks for Katie and George today.

I hope it will not turn out to be an April fool on me, but I saw that the old apartment building of Marcus and Ellie and Lori, Malcolm and their baby was up for sale. After my own cursory inspection (they at least had done some repainting), I took Victor, Gabriella and Hector over to look at it. Evidently the structure was sound, but it would need a complete rehab and remodel. Gabriella was enthusiastic and had ideas about the kitchens and bathrooms. I suggested we might make the three first floor apartments into two larger ones.

It will require a good-sized loan, but Alan figures that the stream of income we could have if we worked quickly would pay it off in five years, by which time Zito and Sons would have another strong income-producing asset. My dad shook my hand: "You're in charge, my boy."

Sunday April 15 Easter

Mass was full of flowers and bells and Easter finery this morning. It was a packed house with people streaming in for the next service as we were leaving ours. Victor also wants me to come and see the progress of the new cathedral with him one of these days. Easter on a spring morning does seem to lift people up. I caught a taste of it myself.

Alan gave a week's notice on Maundy Thursday: "The day Jesus was betrayed," Gabriella muttered. He is going to work for something called Open.com. I will not miss him that much and encouraged Gabrie to think she could get someone better, "but soon, I hope." All easy for me to say. I told her and Dad that I am going to need more help soon too. Uncle Tony had another trip to the hospital last week. "Tricky heart," he says.

Monday May Day 2000
Gabriella handed me a rather banged-up package this noon: stamps all over it with a second or third label addressed to me at Zito and Sons. "One of your girl friends," she smiled.

It was from Ellie, a book: Philip Roth's *The Ghost Writer*, with a flowered *ex libris* label pasted inside the front cover and neatly stenciled Eleanor Harvey Hubbard. And a note: "Thank you, dear Mark Whoever You Are. Love, Ellie."

I called the number I had from two or now three years ago: "The number you dialed is out of service." This evening I was able to reach Brenda. "I'm sorry Marc. Mom died just after the New Year. She asked me to mail it to you before she went. It came back the first time, and I'm afraid it took a while to get is to you."

"It could not have been her arthritis?"

"No, that actually was better. She had a heart condition she wouldn't tell anyone about until last year. Marc, she was so grateful to you. And I am so grateful. The girls too. We are so thankful she was able to be here with us." "And then I could care for her," with a little sob.

"Me, too, Brenda. Believe me, she was my friend."

Yesterday I ran into Bill at the car wash. He showed me his "new" powder blue BMW which is "only five years old." Then he said he wanted me to meet his "new girl." I demurred: "Not again, Don Juan."

He begged. "She is gorgeous." He cajoled: "You'll love her too. I love her forever." He insisted: "Five minutes, no more."

I followed him to what I suspected was a fairly new address. The yellow brick apartment building looked in good shape to my now practiced eye. He was virtually giggling as he ran up to the second floor ahead of me, unlocked the door and then told me to "wait to see if she's presentable."

I waited. There was some whispering. I was invited in to meet a comely, rather tired looking young woman rocking a baby. "Only three weeks old. Isn't she a doll?" Bill burbled.

"Hello. I am Marcus Zito," I said to the mother.

"Oh, sorry. This is Noel." The ever-tactful Bill then added, "we're going to get married someday."

"And who is this lovely little girl?" I inquired.

"Eleanor," Bill carefully pronounced.

"Really?" was my response.

"Why? It's a nice name."

"It's a very nice name. I love the name. Maybe you will call her Ellie."

"Eleanor," Noel spoke up. "I'm very glad to meet you, Marcus. Bill has told me all about you."

And so life goes on and is even renewed with another of its little coincidences. But what had my Ellie been guessing or hinting at? She knew I was keeping this journal, while any comparison between me and Philip Roth or Nathan Zuckerman is more than far-fetched. In one way or another everyone is spinning stories about themselves as they try to imagine who they and others are in their overhearing and seeing. I just have a peculiar problem or, if you will, an extraordinary opportunity in the telling.

Fourth of July 2000

It is good to have a break. Fortunately Victor has come over almost every day to help direct the rehab job, which is bigger than we expected: especially the foundation problems that require the whole building to be jacked. It is amazing how they can do that. There is some asbestos, termites, mold. Victor remains unperturbed, like he has seen it all before. His foremen know what they are doing, marshaling workers from other projects when they need them. I have opportunities to talk with some of the guys I worked with before.

Gabriella, who looks fetching when she comes over in her yellow hardhat, tries to be encouraging, but I can see the added costs concern her. She seems satisfied with Robert Odin, a C.P.A. who says he is in his mid-forties but appears older. He is not so strong on the I.T. side, but Gabriella has enrolled him in a class. He smokes and ought to lose 30 pounds. I would be glad to enroll him in a personal training program with Jim.

Both Robert and Gabriella could probably use more help. Finishing up the M.B.A. is clearly wearing on Gabrie. She is also putting on a smidgen of weight, and I worry spending too much time with "my mentor professor." But I keep my mouth shut except to be sympathetic about the work load.

I have to have more help too, particularly on the rental supervision side—someone who is good with people –not least complaining people—as well as detail. Victor and Gabriella agree and say it is my hire. I have an idea.

Sunday July 30 2000

Beginning as soon as he finishes his two week stint with the National Guard, the new Assistant for Rental Operation at Zito and Sons is to be James R. Lord. (He says the R does not stand for anything, that when he was young his parents called him J.R., which they told him was a "family name.") It was not that hard talking him into it. He was ready for a change: "I never did want to be a personal trainer forever," and the money is steadier, if not better. Plus better health insurance, worker's compensation, and opportunity for pension enrollment in six months. "Sounds like a real job." He has a lot to learn, but then he taught me a lot about being a personal trainer.

Labor Day 2000

Plenty of labor for me. Today I am grateful for the labor time off. I am grateful for Jim, "I love my new job." But there is, of course, a learning curve. My assignment has been to offer support and do a little tweaking of that curve. Working hard and being liked is not the problem. Victor seems fine with him, and Jim easily gets Gabriella laughing, which is good for both of them. "And he's good-looking, too," she offered.

I have had a few complaints: "I'm an hour late and he doesn't get it that I can't be sure how long the previous job is going to take." "Who does he think he is to be bossing me around?" "He doesn't know his place."

I am mentoring. "I know you get complaints from the renters, Jim, when our people do not show up on time. But you need to cut some slack on the other side. Most of the time our guys and the gals are doing their best. Even our renters understand that. Just keep in touch with both sides. Go see them if you need to. Stay friendly like you are."

I understand that Jim is used to setting and keeping his own schedule and prides himself on being punctual. Victor thinks there "could be a touch of racism. No matter how far people say we have come, some guys still bristle at taking orders from a Black."

"But you have Hispanic foremen?"

"But, I don't know; it can still be different—even with the Mexican and Central Americans. There's still prejudice.

Then there's competition for jobs, too. But it'll work out. He probably is wise to this better than we are. I think it helps that guys know he had to do his National Guard duty this summer. Several of our men are in the Guard, too."

I decided it would be an annual event to take young Nate and George to a baseball game. Mark Provezano could not make it, and, for whatever reason, Rob bowed out. But Shelley wanted to come and then, of course, Katie begged, "Why can't I go?"

I then enlisted Ellen Provezano as well and loaded the troop into a borrowed Zito and Sons van (free advertising), everyone complete with Dodger hats. Yesterday on a hot Sunday afternoon the Dodgers, who are doing O.K. in the new century, completed a three game sweep of the Phillies 6-1. Chan Ho Park pitched, and there must have been at least ten thousand Korean Americans, mostly in the right field bleachers, chanting "Chan Ho, Chan Ho," and clacking little sticks together. With all its problems, what an amazingly diverse region this is. Even George, Nate, and Katie got into the chanting.

Nate decided to call George "Georgio" because he has a friend with that name. George agreed enthusiastically: "Good. You're Natio."

Halloween 2000

I carved myself a pumpkin with a toothy grin—even bought little bags of M&Ms and small Milky Way bars, but I have never seen kids in this building, and hardly anyone knocks on apartment doors on Halloween anyway. I will put the Milky Ways into the freezer. I like to cut them into thin frozen slices and eat them that way.

Although he still is more of a work in progress at Zito and Sons than I thought he would be, I do like seeing and kidding around with Jim most days. I have also been to a sports bar with Jim and Delsey, his new girl who has two little children and is either divorced or never married. I think Jim better look out for her. She comes on rather sexy toward me, too, but I imagine that is her way of trying to check me out. I tell her I am between girls.

"How long is between?" she wants to know.

"Oh, it has been a while."

"Somebody must have broke your heart good."

I doubt that Victor was serious but he claims he was considering voting for Bush: "Like to see if he means it about 'compassionate conservatism.' But Gore is my man for now. Hope we can elect a few Democrats who will do something for the working poor in this country. Only way to get a strong stable economy going: bottom up."

"Daddy thinks most of the company is for Gore," Gabriella believes. I am far from sure. Of course, some of them just will not vote, but, particularly from some of the white men, I hear a kind of grumbling leaning Republican.

Shelley is voting for Bush too. If nothing else it may be for peace in the family because Rob has been sending money and working for "Doctors for Bush." I feel confident Susan will quietly be voting for Gore. I so hope she is well. Maybe it is Halloween family memories that make me think of her now.

Good news on the rehab of the Libbet Street building. The heavy work is done. Victor and I estimate three more months for the new flooring, further repairs, painting, and installations. Gabriella estimates we are "only twenty percent over budget." Robert Odin, C.P.A., says "We can handle it."

Wednesday December 13

Bush vs. Gore, hanging chads, Florida courts and politics: all decided today—some say preempted today by the Supreme Court. Victor is blaming Nader for taking votes away from Gore, "and some on Clinton with that poor Lewinsky girl." He thinks Nader was "only pro-consumers anyway," but says "the sky won't fall." I am more concerned that an election of a president of the United States has been decided by five judges selected by Republican presidents versus four judges selected by Democratic presidents. Does not look good for future respect for the Supreme Court of the land.

Last night Victor and Gracia, Uncle Tony and Nora, Robert Odin C.P.A. and I attended a small graduation ceremony and party for Gabriella and five other new M.B.A.s She stayed with it, and I am impressed. I also met her favorite "mentor professor," thinking I might tell him to stick to his teaching. He, however, was friendly, not that good-looking, and I decided my suspicions were questionable. He and Victor got into a lengthy conversation. He seemed genuinely interested in Zito and Sons and suggested that he might one day consider doing a study of its methods and policies. Victor was visibly proud of Gabriella, and I wanted to suggest he should change the name to Zito and Daughter and Son.

8

New Year's Day 2001

Not sure why but it seems appropriate that the new year should start on a Monday. It is, of course, the actual beginning of the new century and the new millennium, though the media have not made nearly the fuss over it they did a year ago. There ought to be more curiosity and excitement. Will there be a lessening of wars and a more lasting peace in the world? In the decades to come will humanity be able to overcome many more diseases? Provide more education—for girls as well as boys around the world? Alleviate the worst forms of poverty? Perhaps the greatest challenge will be to keep the environment supportive of a world population that should peak around mid-century at 11 or 12 billion. Billion!

I never thought I would live to see that day, but now I just might. Harold Barnes would be 75 this year. Viewed actuarially, he would likely die sometime during this decade, if he already had not.

I, Marcus Zito, will be 33. Should I live to be 85, I could get to mid-century—even beyond. Together we will have seen more of human life than anyone. Hard to imagine.

Right now the world seems relatively peaceful. No big wars anyway. The stock market has taken some hits, but the stockbrokers and most of the pundits assure us it is only temporary. There will always be work to do at Zito and Sons, but that is what makes it a strong company. People need good places to live.

Another Rose Bowl this afternoon: Purdue vs. Washington. Who cares? I say. But there will be a lot of folk from Washington and Indiana who do. Jim is coming with Delsey, and Robert is bringing his teenage son and daughter. I did not realize until several months ago that he is a single parent raising two kids. It reminds me that there is often much we do not know about others. It causes me to think differently of him—imagining the schedules and finances he must have to juggle daily. I guess Gabriella and I will be bringing ourselves. I try to convince myself that I am becoming quite used to being a single man, whatever others may think of me. Gabriella tells me that I am more handsome than ever as I grow older, but then she is my sister. I know, however, that I should lose a few pounds. One New Year's resolution anyway.

Sunday February 4 2001

Ground Hog Day was the official opening of the Libbet Street apartments. We are having a kind of open house this weekend. Three are already rented and I feel confident the other five will be soon. I wish Ellie could see her old apartment and mine made new: all those cracks in the wall gone; the hallways so clean, well carpeted, and softly lighted. I am proud to the point of feeling smug that I had an important role in the restructuring and complete redecorating. As Friday was what I now think of as my "other birthday," I had a secret desire to rename it the Barnes Apartments. That way old Hal could have something named after him.

Uncle Tony officially retired the last day of January. Victor kept him on for as long as he could. Tony seems happy with it: unable to work much of the time the past year. But now says he wants to travel. With Jim's help and Nora's (absolutely could not do it without Nora and her experience) I am now in charge of all our rental operations.

Sunday April Fool's Day 2001

An appropriate day to think about the stock market, I suppose. Gabriella apprised me that Alan called last week to see if there was any chance of returning to his former position or any job with the company. Open.com seems to have fallen into an open pit. Robert tells me that the NASDAQ is "sucking gas" and that a "dotcom bubble is deflating quickly." I am grateful I have not had much to lose in the stock market, but I gather from his tone that Robert may have—probably trying to get a good return for his little family. But while some people are losing important money, you can bet others are walking away with it.

I am back to playing tennis most Saturdays and getting in my runs and trips to Bally's at least twice a week. Also more fish, green vegetables and less ice cream. Susan would approve.

Easter April 15

More "bells and smells," as they say, songs and joy. I went to Easter Mass with Victor, Gracia, and Gabriella and then to a pleasant, if filling brunch at Marcello's afterwards. Victor was so pleased. He wants me to come with him and take a tour of "Mahony's Cathedral" which is "five-sixths" done. He and Gabriella also say they want to talk with me in a few weeks about a surprise. How can a surprise be a surprise if one is to talk about it first?

Bill is getting married a week from Sunday. He wants me to be the best man.

Sunday April 29 2001

Yesterday in the chapel of what I think was an Episcopal church Noel Anne Phister and William Spencer Drummond were united in Holy Matrimony and, after vowing to remain faithful to one another "as long as you both shall live," were pronounced to be husband and wife. It was the first wedding I have attended where underneath her simple white dress, the bride was rather evidently pregnant. They tried to get one year-old Eleanor to be a ring bearer, but she would have none of it—starting to put the ring into her mouth and, when Noel tried to take it from her, casting it upon the chapel floor. The woman minister laughed and kept smiling throughout as though these things happen all the time.

Bill looked so pleased and proud and happy, I was ready to cry for them. To tell the truth, I did tear up a little. What can I say? I have always had a romantic streak.

Sunday May 20 2001

Here is the surprise: a company reorganization. Dad and Gabriella took me to Marcello's for lunch on Thursday. Gabriella brought a folder complete with charts: fruits of her M.B.A., I should think. Victor ordered the full special lunch with a veal chop and baby potatoes. Gabriella asked for a salad, and I tried for the middle with a rotini and broccoli dish that was labeled "heart healthy."

"Daddy will be President of the new Zito and Sons. You will become Vice President for Rental Properties and

Secretary. I will be Vice-President for Business Operations and Treasurer." There are to be goodly-sized pay raises for the Vice-Presidents Zito too.

I had some questions about lines of authority and how major decisions would be made, which I kept mostly to myself. Evidently Victor would retain final authority, head up the contracting and new construction side of the business, which is where he began it. Being secretary meant that I would sign a few official letters and approve of the minutes of our annual meeting and not much else. It certainly would be a family business, and I would have considerable scope to organize, advertise, set rents, write and sign leases, and, of course, deal with all the complaints and make everyone happy. That should keep me well-occupied. After coffees, we stood and shook hands like good business colleagues, followed by hugs, a kiss on the lips from my sister and another on the neck from my father. Call me what you want, but also call me Vice-President.

4th of July 2001

Scheduling is a mite awkward when the 4th falls in the middle of the week. Still it is the day for fireworks, and this afternoon Gabriella with Victor and Gracia are hosting the traditional Fourth Folly poolside "in Daddy's backyard." There, she reminds me, is where we grew up, showing me a framed photograph of a scrawny "Markie" and a pudgy little girl in their swimsuits.

I have not heard any mention of Delsey for at least six weeks, so Jim and I will be making a couple. It will be good for him to have a beer and dog and conversation at a non-business company event. With his personal skills he and his position are more accepted now. He has the gift to get people laughing. He comes prepared, and co-workers have learned he follows through: hard combination to beat. Plus he is good company for me. His sense of humor brings perspective on life's problems.

There are serious problems in Asia and Africa and the Middle East, but at least no major war and this free and independent nation of ours seems to be at relative peace with the rest of the world.

Last week Victor took me with Gabriella on our tour of the nearly completed Cathedral of Our Lady of the Angels. As neither of them seemed to know the best way to get there, I drove—secretly pleased with their surprise of my knowledge of the freeways and the city.

The view of the structure from the outside put me off. It appears fortress-like, as though a place of protection rather than invitation. Our guide responded that a great church is meant to be both. Certainly the interior was breath-taking— the expanse of the plaza, the size and height—the filtered light in the church. "Imposing, isn't it?" commented a white-maned, very Irish-looking older priest walking beside me, and I realized that whatever protestant streak was still within me was irritated by that sense of the grandeur and power of the church. "Indeed," I responded.

"Next month the glorious new altar will be placed here," the guide informed us, pointing to a large incised rectangle on the raised dais.

"I hear it will cost five million dollars?" a young woman asked.

"It will be the heart of the Cathedral and our worship," the guide answered.

The distinguished-looking cleric leaned toward me and muttered, "We call this place the 'Taj Mahony'."

Our tour ended in the crypt several levels below. Here, the Cardinal and future distinguished Catholics would be entombed. The state of the art seismic engineering on huge hydraulic pads elicited several questions from Victor.

I was glad to escape upstairs and outside and asked Victor and Gabriella to walk with me to the Central Library. "This is wonderful, Marc," exclaimed Gabriella. "I didn't even know it existed. When did you come here? While you were in school?"

"It is sort of another kind of temple," I told them. They may have thought I was making a joke.

I concentrated on my driving on the way home, letting them talk about how impressive and beautiful the Cathedral was. Before long, however, they got around to the cost. Victor again came to his defense of "the Cardinal's support of the immigrants and the poor right from the start. If he says the new Cathedral will help us do that, I want to believe him."

Labor Day 2001

Everyone came to Dodger Stadium yesterday: Nathan and George, both sets of parents and their sisters. We had to take two cars and meet there. Although I bought the tickets and organized the event, they insisted I was to be their guest. As such, I insisted on sitting with George and Nate. We engaged in a lot of Dodger talk and some about 6th grade, which begins Wednesday. "More homework," Nate observed. "But I don't mind."

"Homework can be good for you," I tried.

"Yeh. I kind of like homework, except for too much of it," was George's comment.

"Just like me," Nate agreed.

George was maybe three inches taller than Nate. He was going to be a tall young man. But Nate looked fit and had some young muscles on him—telling us of an adventure he had "with a huge, really huge snake while hiking with my dad in the mountains." It warmed my heart to think of my bone marrow in him, helping make his blood, though by now the healthy bone marrow must surely be all his.

I had a second hot dog with mustard and relish, which meant they wanted seconds just like mine. When I saw Shelley and Ellen grimacing, "they'll get sick", I talked them into sharing one. The Dodgers beat the Cards 7-3, putting them 13 games over .500. Nate was sure they would make the playoffs and got into an argument with George when he would only repeat "maybe."

Here's one for you. I first noticed that Jim seemed to stay on the phone longer than necessary, sometimes laughing and dropping his voice when I passed by. Then there were extra trips back to the company office. Then there was the sharing of sandwiches in the little conference room. I am not sure they were yet admitting anything to themselves, but I was not born yesterday. And twice last week, when I got back to the office, Gabriella was gone, but her car was still there. Maybe just a brief, little office friendship, but, oh boy.

Tuesday September 11 2001

I am an early riser, but I do not often turn on the radio or television, at least until I have shaved, had breakfast and looked at the newspaper. What an odd hour it seemed for the phone to then ring. It was Jim: "Got your TV on?"

"No."

"Turn it on. This is terrible."

"What channel?"

"About any channel."

We stayed on the phone for a few minutes, trying to make some sense of it. A plane they think came from Boston had flown into the World Trade Center. Another plane had crashed near or into the Pentagon. Rescue crews were rushing from all over New York. No one knew how many planes were involved. The announcers tried to remain calm and professional, but were clearly out of their depth. There was confusion and a growing horror.

"What time does your sister get up?" Jim asked. I told him I would call her, and we agreed to meet at the office as soon as we could get there. "No one should be watching alone."

Victor and Jose Lopez and three other workers were huddled around the little TV in the hall that served Zito and Sons as a garage and equipment storage areas. They had on their hard hats. Contractors are regularly at work from before seven. Jim and Gabriella came in five minutes after I did.

A second plane had crashed into the south tower. Another had apparently crashed in Pennsylvania—perhaps having been headed for the White House. The president might be in Florida but was safe, we were told. All other flights were being aborted and grounded, but no one was sure if there might be other attacks. At least one of the planes had been headed for Los Angeles. We began to think about possible friends or relatives who could be on board.

One tower then seemed to pancake into a huge cloud of dust. All any of us could say was "Unbelievable." "God." Then the other tower collapsed. "How did they build those things?" Victor asked. It was hard enough to understand what had happened. The who and why questions were only beginning to be formed. There kept running through my head Kurtz's "The horror! The horror!" and then Franklin

Roosevelt's words just after Pearl Harbor. Finally I said aloud: "A day that will live in infamy." There was a general murmur of assent, but also a look of puzzlement on several faces. Perhaps it was the word "infamy." None of them were born when the Japanese snuck up on Pearl Harbor. Harold Barnes was going on 16 and would fight in the war to follow.

Wednesday September 12 2001

Not much work was done today, except for a couple of emergency repairs which I managed myself. Victor, Gabriella, Jim and Nora came in for most of the day. We needed each other. I needed what family I had. I wanted to look out for others, but decided not to walk by Shelley's house.

We had learned of the deaths of the firemen and the police as well, of the emergency rooms ready to receive the wounded and injured, of which there were none. We had heard stories of people leaping 80 stories to their death, of last minute phone calls to loved ones. Evidently all the death and destruction was accomplished by four groups of Saudi Arabians in their twenties with box cutters for weapons. Their low-tech appropriation of our fuel laden jets is proving a puzzle and embarrassment to just about every security agency, government spokesmen, the media, the airlines and maybe most Americans. Fingers have begun to be pointed.

So far no one has pointed to God except maybe the perpetrators. Victor has gone to church with Gracia and Gabriella and Jim asked to go along. I said I would come back to this apartment and say some prayers. What to pray? "God have mercy on everybody."

Sunday September 16

No planes are flying. It is strange to be here is San Fernando Valley without seeing plane after plane taking off

from or heading into Burbank or Van Nuys. I imagine everyone is haunted by the pictures of the jets seeming to glide
into the Trade Towers.

I went to Mass this morning. The priest tried to be con-
soling: God would care for the bereaved. We should pray for
them. The beloved dead were borne to heaven by angels.
They were with God. Jesus rose from the dead. And then
something about we could be sure there was a right and
wrong and a moral order to the universe, but we must never
be a vengeful people. We could "stamp out evil" but not seek
revenge. We all must pray for peace.

President Bush—bless him—has made a valiant effort to
rally the American people and spirit. And no doubt we will,
just as we did after Pearl Harbor. Fortunately, in this case we
were not attacked by another nation-state to which we would
need to respond with some great war and mass killings.

I found myself wondering what the Head of Westview will
say to the students and faculty in Assembly this week. I wonder what I would have said. I worry about the fact that the
attackers were all Muslims.

I jogged and then walked by Shelley's house yesterday
afternoon, but did not see anyone. I have never felt so alone
in my life.

Monday December 31 2001

Gabriella finally convinced Victor that today ought to be
a holiday from work since no one wants to come to work on
a Monday between the weekend and New Year's Day. Victor
complained that he had never not come to work on anything
but official holidays and would set a bad example to others
if he did show up today. Furthermore, Gabriella persisted,
all the company workers would love him if they could have
the extra day in peace. She graciously added that I would be

available should there be emergency problems at any of our properties. Victor tried to look at her disapprovingly, but, as he turned, I saw a smile on his face.

That is the only uncomplicated piece of good news as 2001 comes to an end. I think the worst news is that Osama bin Laden got away. Now there is no one specific to punish and take out vengeance on. Our soldiers are in Afghanistan without any clear sense of why we are there or what our goals are—fighting an obscure enemy the United States once helped to arm so they could fight the Russians.

Meanwhile there are lingering fears and a mood of frustrated patriotism abroad in the country that are subject to manipulation and exploitation. The "go shopping while we are at war," "relax but stay alert" philosophy elicits nervous laughs. I imagine this will be evident at the Rose Bowl tomorrow: patriotic song, perhaps a guard of honor, flyover by fighter planes, cheering fans for Nebraska and Miami on a crisp, brilliant Southern California day—the Goodyear blimp, all hovering over palpable concerns that there might be another terrorist attack, perhaps right here at the Bowl where bags will have to be searched and anyone who looks Middle Eastern or just too foreign should cause one to spring from relaxation to alert.

I wish we could have avoided the phrase "war on terror" and even just the word "war." It opens the doors for further war rhetoric and an escalation of "whatever is necessary" thinking. Any good English teacher knows that.

The complicated good news is that Gabriella and Jim say they are engaged, though not publicly—perhaps only to me and, they at least hope to be, to Victor. They have taken me out to dinner to tell me and do a fair amount of hand-holding, hugging and kissing when I am around. "But we're not living together," Jim wants me to know. "I don't believe in that."

"Neither do I," Gabriella put in, caressing his forearm.

Tempted to wink at my sister, I only agreed, "That is nice."

They are in love. They want to be married "in the spring or summer." I am happy for them, if still rather surprised, and a touch . . . what should I say? "Wary," though I also have the smug satisfaction that comes from knowing they never would have met without me.

The wariness comes from knowing that any two human beings will have problems meshing their needs and expectations into a caring and committed relationship. Then there is the interracial dimension.

In theory and, I trust, in practice, I favor interracial marriage. I see it as a solution to racism in America. Already in Los Angeles the population is becoming more and more various shades of tan.

Jim is a handsome brown man. I know white people are not meant to talk about African Americans in these terms, but I understand Blacks do all the time. As with most African Americans who have been in this country for a few generations, there has already been some mixing of the races. But he is still fairly dark-skinned with hair and facial features most white folk would identity as negroid.

The problem is Victor. "He says he respects me. He likes me. He even loves me," Jim tries to keep the emotion out of his voice. "But he has to think about it—if it is best for Gabriella." He leans over and kisses her. She tears up.

"That's what Daddy says to me too."

They want me to talk to my father.

9

Martin Luther King Day 2002

Today is also the eighth anniversary of the Northridge earthquake. Angelinos are still grateful that the earth shook early in the morning on a holiday when not many people were on the soon to be fractured highways, bridges and overpasses. It also seems an interesting day to reflect on the conversation with my Dad Victor on Saturday.

Just to have the talk took some negotiation. He knew what the topic would be and put me off for a week. I told him, "There are a lot of things we could talk about, Dad. We can talk about business and the company and, sure, about Gabriella and anything we would like to." Not wanting the conversation and whatever else might happen to be in a public place, I suggested I could come to the house or I would be glad to have him see my apartment. "We could even have a little inspection of the building while you are there."

After thinking it over for three days, he chose my apartment. Possibly he wanted to be out of earshot of Gracia.

I prepared. I jotted a few notes and thought about approaches I might try. But my most important prep was to talk with Jim about religion. "He will want it to be a Catholic wedding, Jim. Have you and Gabriella talked about that?"

"That's fine with me."

"And you will probably have to agree that any children will be raised as Catholics. You will need to sign an agreement that says that."

"Why not? Look, I've told Gabriella I'll be glad to become a Roman Catholic."

"Really? You would have to take instruction."

"Yes."

"And believe in all those doctrines and things."

"Gabriella says I could do it just like she does."

"It is still a lot."

"How about you then? You're a Catholic."

"I am hanging in there."

"Two things more. I love Gabriella, and they've got Jesus. That's more than enough for me."

Victor may have tried to prepare too, but I was not prepared for what came out of him in bits and pieces and then more. First we toured the building. He admired my apartment. He told me he loved me and was proud of me. We chatted about my end of the business and how grateful we were to have survived the dotcom bust and the market downturn after 9-11.

I got us some coffee and suggested we "talk a little about Gabriella and Jim." He said, "Fine," and was quiet.

"They want to get married."

"Fine."

"They need your blessing, Dad." And he was off, rambling about how he was not prejudiced; had learned to work with all kinds of people; liked Jim, thought he was doing a good job. He loved Gabriella; he wanted her to be happy; to marry anyone she wanted; was sorry I had not found the right girl; was O.K. if I was gay; wanted some grandbabies;

loved Gracia; was sorry for what happened at the end of my high school, but never did understand why I did not want to stay in college. And he would not "stand in the way of their getting married if that is what she really wants. I love my little girl. Always have; always will."

"That is so good of you. But they need a little more, Dad."

He turned in his chair and frowned. "You shouldn't talk to me like that. Who do you think you are to lecture me? Haven't seen a woman you liked yet. What do you think your mother would think?" He began to cry. "You know she wouldn't approve."

"Of Jim?"

"No! Yes! No!"

Silence. More tears. A sob. "I'm sorry. I love you both. You ought to have kids by now. She should have kids."

"Maybe she will."

"But...I know it's O.K. but it's not supposed to be this way . . . this mixture."

"Do you know that Jim wants to become Catholic?"

"How do you know that?"

"He told me."

"How . . . are you sure?"

"Yep. All the way. He means it."

"Really?"

Think of it as advancing the faith," I laughed.

He did not. "Catholic wedding?"

"Catholic wedding. Catholic kids."

"Baptisms?"

"Maybe two or three or four. They will be beautiful children, Dad."

More tears. "I don't know. I don't know. I never meant not to give them my blessing. I just wanted them to be sure."

Sunday January 27th 2002

"I don't know what you did, Markie, but I'll love you forever," with a long embrace from my sister on Thursday. "At first I thought maybe Daddy was faking it. That he really didn't mean it. But if so, he's a good faker. Thank you. Thank God. Thank you."

I gently explained the problem with mixed race babies.

"But he already has two Mexican-American grandchildren . . . I guess step-grandchildren. He loves them."

"I am sorry; I haven't met them yet."

"They're dolls."

"I'll bet, and I promise you: Do not worry. Wait until Dad sees that first grandbaby of his very own. He will love it, I promise you. I have seen it before."

"Ha! Where have you ever seen it before?"

"Well, just wait and see. No hurry, mind you. But Uncle Marc is looking forward to this too."

Sunday March 31

Jim and Gabriella have set the wedding date: June 15th. Gabriella says she always wanted a June wedding. It also gives Jim time to complete his instruction and be blessed or accepted or whatever they do in the Catholic Church. Apparently he does not have to be baptized again since he has a certificate proving he was baptized at the age of ten in the Name of the Holy Trinity. "It was a real dunkin', too," he claims. "None of this sprinkling stuff."

Victor is hoping he can arrange for Jim to become a Catholic at a service where Cardinal Mahony will preside. I may or may not go to that one but I will be a best man again on June 15th.

I have been trying to think of some April Fool's joke I could pull off tomorrow—maybe something about the business. But the company is going well enough, I do not want to jinx things. Moreover, while Robert has become nearly indispensable in our business operations, he is so serious about his work I am not sure he would find some prank of mine about losing rental checks or whatever funny.

With Robert's considerable help Gabriella and I have decided to sell the Libbet Street apartments to a couple of dentists who want it for an investment. Zito and Sons will continue to manage the building and then look for another we can perhaps rehab and start the whole process over again. It certainly looks like a good way to make money and also keep our workers well employed.

It cannot hurt that everyone now knows that Jim is to become the boss's son-in-law, but I believe he would have come to be regarded as my full associate and colleague anyway. We both are certainly working long enough hours. Last month we promised to do workouts at the gym together at least twice a week. I am not getting in enough tennis either. The old body looks good but could lose a few pounds.

Sunday May 19 2002

I don't know. I do not know. It is probably a prudent investment. I am making enough money, and with prospects for more, to handle the mortgage. It looks like a propitious time to buy. The question is how wise is this for me to purchase a house two doors down and across White Oak from Shelley, George, Katie, and Rob.

I walked by two weeks ago and noticed the "For Sale" sign but do not think I gave it any thought. It was on the way back that I stopped. It was the smallest house on the block, but still at least three bedrooms and likely a fourth that could be used as an office or room for a little gym. It was far more footage than a single man needed—and to keep up. I think I was imagining having a dog again when I heard Shelley calling to me.

"It's a great house, Marc."

"Hi Shelley. No. It is nice, but way too much house for me."

"Well, look anyway. We hate having Matt and Karen and their boys move, but they've really kept it up. No pool, but a nice back garden and a bit of a view of the valley. You'd make a great neighbor."

My offer was accepted Friday. The Billingtons will stay until the end of June so their boys can finish school. Gabriella says, "Now you'll have to get married and have kids." First a dog, I say.

Sunday 16 June 2002

My good friend James R. Lord and Gabriella Teresa Zito are now husband and wife. I thought the service itself was on the brief side, but I understand there were three other weddings that day. The reception, on the other hand, went on for hours. I had no idea Jim had that much family—mostly from the Crenshaw and Leimert Park neighborhoods. His father died in an accident working for Caltrans, but his mother, both grandmothers, aunts, uncles, two sisters and a brother, cousins, nieces, nephews, and more were there. Champagne and wine flowed, all manner of food, a cake of four or five tiers. Daddy Victor put on quite a party. Nearly half were Italian relatives and friends, with some Mexican Americans from work, and half African American. And now the happy couple is off on a honeymoon, refusing to tell us where they are going—Jim insisting he was old-fashioned in that way. But he promises to be back in time to help me move.

July 4th 2002

I had hoped I would be in the new house by now, but Matt and Karen had some problem with the former owners of their new home in Santa Clarita—so it will be at least another week or two. It is a bit like a game of musical houses. But, as everyone seems to say these days, for me it is "no problem" or "no problema" or, as Carol would sometimes remind me, the correct Spanish is "no hay ningun problema." The lease here in my apartment is not up until the end of the month, and I am in charge of leases anyway. Nor do I have all that much to move. 2823 White Oak will be sparsely furnished, probably for quite a while.

I do have one problem: Minnie. I thought I could time this right, but made the mistake of visiting the animal shelter "Just to see." And there she was wagging away—I swear almost smiling at me: half lab, like Barney, and half wire-haired Vizsla, which turns out to be a Hungarian hunting dog. I was looking for a male, but Minnie was looking for me. I tried to keep her here for several days but was getting disapproving looks from residents for whom I was supposed to be setting an example. "Just for a few days," I tried. Fortunately George and Katie learned of my plight and Shelley took mercy.

Minnie is a mite hand shy, but does not snap or bite and is well house-trained. She is a sweetheart.

I look around. Leaving here will be harder than I thought—where Carol first came to help me get set up with a computer. Where Bill stayed. I am used to the nooks and crannies—the view of the street. It is hard to believe I have been here more than four years. Anyone changes in that amount of time: a part of me recedes; another grows with memories.

The Fourth Folly has been moved to Saturday. The stars of the show will be the newlyweds who I hear are coming as Uncle Sam and Madame Liberté. Evidently it was a great honeymoon. Must have been. I know it is a cliché, but the two of them are nuts over each other. That will have to change if it is to endure, but it surely is nice to witness.

Sunday August 11 2002

No doubt I talk to Minnie too much, but she seems an attentive listener—sometimes putting her head down and then looking up quizzically if I go on too long. My biggest problem is getting her enough exercise, driving up to "dirt Mulholland" when I can and jogging along the road while she chases rabbits and the little ground birds. Some days Katie will walk Minnie after school.

Shelley cannot get over my knowledge of basic carpentry, electricity and plumbing and the fact that I have access to Zito and Sons workers if needed. She has learned that, while I am glad to listen to her thoughts about remodeling and decoration, I often know more than she does. She has been helpful, however, about helping me find some second-hand furniture, and then there is always Ikea.

My first major project is to build a small loggia in the back, setting in large paving stones, and lining it with planters and two or four large flower pots. I know Minnie will approve.

Active in the homeowners' association, Shelley tells me that the basketball hoop over the garage door is not appreciated by all the neighbors. "Matt put it up for the kids, and I understand because my Dad had one for us when we were kids. Mother had him take it down when we left home."

The implication seems to be that I should take it down, but I have other ideas. I bought a ball and yesterday went out to shoot a few hoops. Within a half hour, George, who must be 5'8" now, and a friend joined me. I could not believe that they did not know how to play "Horse," but I taught them.

Sunday August 25 2002

It ended up being "men's night" for the Dodgers game this year. Nate and George mostly talked baseball and other sports with each other: for George basketball and Nate cross-country. As the junior member of the threesome I mostly listened as Dr. Rob and Mark veered away from the Dodgers and Braves to muse about their work and then more generally about health care. Mark seems to be some type of laboratory worker with Amgen. You can imagine that Rob did most of the talking, much of it complaining about government, health insurance companies, hospital bureaucracy and interference with doctors' prerogatives and the best practice of medicine. I put in "my theory is that the biggest problem with health care is the cost—with too many people making too much off of other people's health, partly because there is no real price competition." That did not go over too well, and I again remembered some of the conversations I had had with my then fairly new son-in-law about the Clinton health care proposals when I was several times reminded that I had spent my life working at a not-for-profit institution and did not know much about how the for-profit world had to operate.

When Rob lectured Marc and Mark to the effect that well-trained professionals should be rewarded with good livings and that free markets helped to create "the best medical system in the world," Mark put in, "Amgen is a great company, but the price of some of their medicines can knock your socks off."

"But those proposals for Medicare prescription drug coverage aren't going to help that one bit," Rob seemed to half agree. "Just more government interference in the markets."

I contributed that "I was not talking about people making a good living, even a very good living, but fortunes, large fortunes and even gross fortunes being made off people's need for health care."

Rob laughed. "I'm glad you're in the business you're in, Marc. I suppose landlords like you don't make big money building and renting apartments."

"And I do have good health insurance and am thankful for it. And who is not grateful for what you were able to do for Nathan," was my response.

"Right," Rob replied.

Mark bumped my shoulder with his, and there was a short silence before he continued rather hesitantly, "You know, I don't know whether it makes any sense but my boss thinks it would be smarter to have health insurance really be just insurance for serious medical problems—injuries and cancers and things, and then find cheaper ways to deliver the rest of medical care which people would pay for."

"How would they do that?" Rob asked with a note of suspicion in his voice.

"I guess clinics and things with more doctors and nurse practitioners."

"I can't see that happening," Rob responded. "But, something needs to happen to fix the convoluted payment system we've got. I agree that there are problems with unnecessary testing and procedures that need attention. Part of the problem here is the lawyers and all the lawsuits. It makes the practice of medicine unnecessarily defensive."

"I thought at one time you were going to get a law degree?" I asked him.

"How did you know that?" he responded. "I did take more than a year's worth of courses—enough to learn how lawyers make their money. Probably just enough to make me dangerous," he laughed. "But I am a doctor first and foremost, caring for everyone who needs help as we try to do at Children's."

"My Dad loved to quote Florence Nightingale. Do you know who Florence Nightingale was?" I asked them.

"Of course," Rob responded. "You even learn about what she accomplished in medical school."

"I like that," I told him. "Anyway what he quoted was 'When the poor become sick, they become our brothers.'"

"'And our sisters,' we better say, too," Rob agreed. "That's very romantic sounding, but most of the doctors and nurses I know got into what we do because we want to care for everyone. I'm sure that is true for Mark here, too."

"I believe that," I told him.

"You have no idea of how hard we doctors work," Rob went on. "But the economics of this whole business has made it enormously complicated."

"I believe that, too," I agreed as we were interrupted by Eric Karros hitting into another double play with two men on and my trying to convince Nate that "a lot of good hitters hit into double plays just because they hit the ball so hard."

"But he's so slow," Nate complained. "He's not a good runner."

Halloween 2002

Several pirates and a vampire. One princess. One Mr. Spock. A Zombie, I guess, and assorted ghouls and ghosts, one having lost its head. I had carved my best jack-o-lantern and bought more candy than I needed. Twice I did what Susan had scolded me not to do: "Don't do that, Hal. They don't know what to say." When the kids shouted "Trick or treat, mister," I responded "Trick," which was met by silence, or as one little girl primly reprimanded me, "You're not supposed to say that." So I apologized and handed over the Tootsie Rolls and the little packets of M&Ms.

George and Katie were among my first visitors—George informing me that he was only coming along as Katie's older brother this year and that he was being "careful to eat only a little candy because I need to stay in shape."

10

New Year's Day 2003

I was in bed and probably snoring when the new year began. No one is here to tell me whether I snore or not. If it bothers Minnie, she is not talking. For the moment her eyes are closed, sleeping soundlessly, though her hind legs twitch now and then—perhaps dreaming of chasing rabbits. I guess dogs do not snore. Barney did not. Maybe older ones do.

I saw Susan a few minutes ago. She drove up in front of Shelley's garage in her same gray Volvo, took a bag out of the back seat and used her key to walk in. She looks . . . well, different, and, I suppose, older. She is in her seventies now.

I have thought about buying binoculars. I could sit here in the living room and watch the comings and goings at 2816 White Oak: a genuine voyeur, particularly if some neighbor spied me spying.

I might take Minnie and walk over and accidentally meet her. I would shake her sweet hand and wish her Happy New Year. And then I might cry, "I never told you one last time how much I love you." Instead I tell Minnie I love her.

Instead I could think about praying for Susan. Perhaps she still prays for me. There are churches that pray for the dead. Victor certainly does.

The Rose Parade is on the television with the sound muted so that I need not listen to the perky commentary of that woman and guy who sound like the Pasadena Chamber of Commerce. I am not going to the game either. Nor are Gabriella and Jim. They are going to some party "with friends"—probably all of them married. Maybe Bill and Noel are too. I have not seen them since their wedding. I do not even know whether their second was a boy or a girl.

"We do not watch much television, do we, Minnie?" Not much good news: though they are cutting taxes for the wealthy so the economy can grow even while there are wars and rumors of war. We have not even begun to help Afghanistan and now they are talking about taking on Saddam Hussein. Saddam Hussein, Minnie." She lifts her head and looks at me. "Do you think he has weapons of mass destruction?"

"Freedom and democracy," we say are our motives, never admitting the others that are perfectly obvious to the peoples of the Middle East. "See if these bombs and guns cannot help you get freedom and peace." Minnie's head goes back down. And even if the means of war were not bound to get out of control once again, who is thinking ahead about the geopolitical consequences with more suspicion and hatred from much of the Arab world? "I could tell those neo-cons a thing or two, could I not, Minnie? Or do you think I am just feeling sorry for myself and for our world? . . . an old fart at 34?" Minnie, without lifting her head, eyes me as if to say, "I'll do the farting around here."

So wait a minute: I do at least get to see my grandchildren from time to time. How many dead grandfathers are able to do that? Minnie and I may not watch much television, but I have an old set of Hitchcock movies. They do not make them like that anymore.

My health is good, and I am resolved to keep up my trips to the gym, with Jim's encouragement, if often without his company. I do see both him and Gabriella on an almost daily basis. My dad likes my work even if my marital status and lack of regular Mass attendance disappoint him.

In fact, I do find the work keeps me on my toes, as they say. With his good employee relations and slow growth policies, Victor has established a company with considerable potential. The net is steady in good times and those less so and, so far, keeps ticking up.

I like keeping the house clean—making the occasional repair. The large paving stones are down in back and the loggia is half-built. The bougainvillea is beginning to pink. In an hour or so I will put on my new Christmas sweater and sit out in the crisp, sunny Chamber of Commerce morning and read the paper—skipping the parts I do not like, maybe doing the crossword. I should resolve to do some more serious reading. Perhaps it is because I have no one to talk with or teach.

"Of course, there is you, Minnie," who gets up, yawns and stretches. "What do you say if we go for a jog, my girl?"

21 March 2003

A "light and thunder" show in Baghdad last night and "we" (almost entirely U.S. forces) are invading Iraq—which the first President Bush wisely did not do. I cannot imagine how they cajoled Colin Powell into going along or how otherwise thoughtful senators could have voted to allow it. They must have been afraid of what they would be accused of if they did not. How many people will have to die as though to atone for the 9/11 victims?

Shelley wants me to start coming to the homeowners' association meetings and to consider being on the architecture committee. "You'd be great at it, Mark. Most of the neighbors are really nice. You'll like them and they'll really like you."

I am sure, if I did, that I would come to know my neighbors better and such would be a form of service. But I also already know something about neighborhood architecture disagreements: mostly about somebody building "so as to obstruct our view," or "too close to our property line" or "not in keeping with neighborhood standards." It is nothing like the terror in Baghdad, but perhaps a distant third.

Yet I told Shelley I would do it. After all, she could almost always get me to do what she wanted.

Sunday May 4 2003

It looks like I will soon be a Rotarian. Victor invited his Vice-Presidents daughter and son to last week's meeting of the Rotary Club of Tarzana and Encino, and we asked Jim to come along as well. Victor had evidently been an officer for several years and then president in 1998. He knows everyone: mostly local retailers and business leaders, other professionals. I can see why it can be good for business to be members. I also learned of their scholarship and literacy programs and what they have done to eliminate polio in the world. The only other members I knew were Marcello and his son Mark from the Trattoria, but I shook hands with other interesting folks—mostly older but a few in their 30s who were particularly warm in their welcome.

Jim and I joined a couple of others in surreptitiously checking our new Blackberries for messages. Gabriella ordered them up for us last month. I am still a learner. I once would have made fun of such gadgets, but I can see how useful they can be. I felt a certain sense of status in noting other people noting that I had one.

Sunday May 18

Victor said that he wanted to have lunch with me on Friday—just the two of us. I was not sure what to expect: had I done anything wrong? Was there something about Gabriella or Gabriella and Jim or Jim? Or something else about the business? My church-going or lack thereof? My sexuality or lack thereof? His health?

We had some preliminaries. He has concerns about the company becoming too large—that Gabriella and Robert might be too ambitious for growth. Bottom line, I believe, he wants to have some form of personal relationship with all the employees. Then he wanted to know what I thought of the problems the church was having. He wanted the perspective of "a thoughtful younger Catholic."

What was the purpose of that flattery? I asked myself. Or was it wishful thinking on his part? Thoughtfully, I played dumb: "What problems, Dad?"

"Well, you know, the thing." He hesitated. "Whatever it is, the thing with boys—even altar boys—the abuse and hiding it. I know everyone is human, but I'm disappointed. It makes me sad about our church and some of the priests that we always look up to."

The old debater in me wanted to see if it would be helpful to explore the other side: "I understand, but some of this could get exaggerated by lawyers and the press. They love it: big scandal. After all, it happens in schools, Boy Scouts, other places. And much of it took place when church officials thought priests with problems could be cured psychologically and could find new strength in their vows to resist further temptations."

"You know what?" Victor's eyes flashed behind his aviator glasses. He paused. "If it were up to me, it would be like a pilot who had a problem with alcohol. You don't let him fly planes again, no matter what. That's what I'd tell them."

"I don't disagree, Dad. It was a bad mistake."

"More than a mistake. Think of these boys, though a few of them may be just after the money."

"So?"

"So I don't like the church having to give up hundreds of millions that ought to be helping the poor and schools and charities."

"One thing you cannot accuse the Catholic clergy of is feathering their own nests," I tried to put in positively.

"Except maybe for the new cathedral?" he half asked.

"No, I meant that unlike the heads of some non-profits and charities they do not take home big six-figure salaries. Plus, what they are probably most guilty of is trying to protect the reputation of the institution. You can understand that. Businesses do it. Even Zito and Sons might do it if they were being sued about something."

He gave me a look, but I went on: "I have seen schools and other institutions do it. Corporations. Banks."

"But you're supposed to be able to trust the church. Trust the bishops."

We went on in that vein for a while longer. I noticed he did not mention Cardinal Mahony's name, but I did not press him. As far as I could tell, he had not lost any of his faith in God or in the goodness of many of the priests. He repeated that he understood about sin and that he was not someone who could cast the first stone. I told him that the real measure of the church's change would be in strong new procedures and policies they enacted and enforced.

"Confession." "Atonement." "Reparation." "Maybe new leaders?" Victor slowly pronounced. "The Pope is too old."

"Do you think married clergy would help, maybe even some women?" I dared.

"No, I can't see that. I wish I could. If that is God's will, whatever it takes. And a lot of prayer."

"I could not agree more. Prayer always helps."

Victor eyed me a mite dubiously, but then put his hand on mine and said, "Thanks, Son." For just a moment I thought he might ask me to pray with him.

Sunday July 6 2003

I could have squeezed in two Fourth of July parties this year: the Fourth Folly, put on by Gabriella and Jim, Victor and Gracia and me again as the grill man, and a late afternoon family and neighbors party at Shelley's.

I declined the latter using as an excuse my duties at the Folly, but also afraid of meeting Susan: What I would say? What might I say? If husband Hal Barnes was completely dead and gone, it would be one thing, but I cannot escape some feeling of responsibility—to protect, to care for, to find out how she is. "How are you, Susan dear?

After most of the patriotically decked out crowd had left the old homestead, Gabriella took Jim upstairs with her and wanted me to come along. She showed us the room where she grew up—still with her bed, her little dressing table. "They painted it, and the curtains are new, but I can almost walk back in here and be my whiny teenager again."

Jim laughed, "Glad I didn't know you then," and ducked as she threw a forearm at him.

My room was next. "What's the biggest difference, Markie?" she asked.

"Look at that old Raiders pennant," Jim pointed out. "I thought you didn't like them." The Dodgers were there, too, and Westview Academy and Woodland Hills High School. I walked over to peer at a framed picture on the dresser of me, I guess, smiling uncertainly in a tuxedo with a dark-haired girl in her prom dress looking barely into womanhood.

"The big difference," Gabriella explained to Jim "is that the bunk beds are gone. For several years Marcus wouldn't let them take them down after our brother died."

"Big brother," I put in.

"You must have really missed him," Jim said.

"Mother worried you were always hoping he would come back. Sorry, Markie, I shouldn't have reminded you."

Late yesterday morning George and Katie came over with "Uncle Steve who flew just to see us from San Francisco." And there he was again—still handsome with his mother's dusky blond hair and an easy athleticism about him—the son I had only seen once and barely talked to in nine years. For an awkward moment I neither responded to his greeting nor took the hand he reached out to me—finally shaking it too vigorously and exclaiming, "Shelley has told me all about you."

Katie politely interrupted to ask if she could take Minnie for a walk. George fetched the basketball from around the corner of the garage, dribbled past us and made a lay-up. I widened my eyes, "Your nephew is getting good, Steve."

During 15 minutes or so of free throws, longer shots, occasional fakes and dribbling, I learned that Steve was dedicated to teaching science at the Giannini Middle School and still plays tennis like he did at Westview, shortly before I became Head, and then at Berkeley. Four or five years older than I am, he seems to be quite unmarried.

"I still play some tennis," I told him.

"He's really a good teacher, Mr. Marc," George informed me. "He shows me good experiments to try."

"Maybe when I'm down sometime we could play tennis," Steve suggested.

I gave all three of them quick, somewhat sweaty hugs as they left.

Sunday July 27 2003

Bob Hope died earlier today after living 100 years. I saw some excerpts from Monsieur Beaucaire and the Road to Rio and the Road to Bali on television and tried to explain to Minnie why we thought his movies with Dorothy Lamour and Bing Crosby were so funny. They also showed clips from his USO tours, and Minnie watched me laugh and then grow nostalgic and a little sad, finally putting her paws on my leg and giving my face a lick. "He had a regular radio program," I told her. "There was a skit about a train conductor announcing that one of the stops was Rancho Cucamonga which he would draw out and make sound even odder than it was—Rancho Cucamonga, Minnie." At which point Minnie not only got down from my leg but left the room

Some of his movies I had seen with Susan. Steve and Shelley wondered why we wanted to see them again when they were teenagers. I once made them popcorn and had them watch one of the road movies with us. Bob Hope could make them laugh, too, but I could also see them finding it amusing that we found his rather predictable predicaments and escapes and accompanying banter with Bing as funny as Susan and I did.

Sunday August 24 2003

I have not enjoyed a baseball game so much for a long time—sitting there in the second deck, just behind first base so we could see into the Dodgers' dugout, with my grandson and a boy whose life I may have saved. I like it that they have become pals even if they see each other only once a year. "Georgio," Nate greets him. "Natio, how ya doing?"

No parents could fit it into their busy schedules, and Shelley took the blame for telling Katie it was "just for boys this year." The Dodgers won a tight one over the Mets 2-1 with Gagne stalking in from the bullpen to make the save. All three baseball boys loved that.

I had to drive out to West Hills to get Nate but did not want to bring him back home late at night, offering to have him stay with me. And Ellen Provezano said she could pick him up in the morning. For reasons I can only suspect, it was Rob who insisted on Nate sleeping over with George.

The two young men are headed into eighth grade. George is already talking about going to Westview next year, "if I can get in. I bet I will. My grandfather used to be the boss of the school. You should come too, Nate. C'mon. We could rock the place."

I have not yet told them of my two years at Westview. I think I will wait to see who goes.

Friday Thanksgiving weekend 2003

"I played tennis with Steve this afternoon, didn't I, Minnie? We like Steve, don't we? He gives you tummy rubs." He beat me fair and square, but I kept him running to the point he complained about "getting old." "You hit that damn backhand slice like my father used to."

I could have told him he still has a hitch in his serve.

We had a beer afterwards and agreed we would play again sometime. I am sure we would play more often if he lived closer by.

I think Gabriella is pregnant. Maybe she does not want people at work to know yet. I cannot wait to see the look on Victor's face when that first grandbaby comes.

11

New Year's Day 2004

The best news for 2004: Gabriella and Jim are expecting in April.

The mood of the country feels confused. Neither war seems to be going well. Both Iraq and Afghanistan are full of sectarian strife, which we seem ill-equipped to understand, and most everyone there is suspicious, if not angry, with the United States. With no weapons of mass destruction to be found and the archenemies Osama bin Laden and Saddam Hussein still on the loose, and body bags passing regularly, if surreptitiously, through Dover Air Force Base, and gazillions being spent, the reasons why we are there seem hazier yet. "Freedom and democracy" are the fall backs. I think President Bush half-believes them or has talked himself into believing. In fact, I kind of feel sorry for him. He is not that unlikable but seems out of his depth. Or maybe it is better to say he does not seem to think very deeply and gets led around by those who tell him he is "the Decider."

"So, Minnie, what are your resolutions for 2004? Catch a rabbit? How about not rolling in mud holes, especially when they have deer or coyote scat in them?"

"Ohhh, sorry. It's all right, sweetie."

Here are mine: Do more serious reading—maybe sub-
scribe to the New York Review of Books. Lose five pounds
and keep up the gym routines.

"What's that? Yes, more runs and walks with you."

Maybe take a vacation—perhaps on some group tour to
Russia . . . or to China. Maybe meet someone?

Shelley would like me to meet someone in 2004. She
wanted me to meet someone last year. Now I just tell her I
am an old bachelor—kind of set in my ways, but I do not
believe she is ready to buy that. She also encourages me to
become more active in the homeowners' association and to
consider "coming to church with us some Sunday. You'd like
the new minister and meet some people." Good old Valley
Presbyterian—where my memorial took place—where Susan
probably goes. "I am Catholic," I tell her.

"Well, a good Catholic ought to have at least three kids by
now," she tries to kid me.

Steve and I are playing tennis this afternoon. Maybe I can
take him. We may later catch the rest of the Rose Bowl. I do
not remember who is playing.

Sunday April 4 2004

A boy! Marcus James Lord. I am to be his godfather, too.
And a girl Mary Elizabeth Lord—Mary being the name of
the mother's mother and mine, and, I am reminded, of our
Mother, the blessed Virgin.

Born yesterday. Healthy but still in special natal care
because they are so tiny. They came a bit early. Victor says
Gabriella and I did so as well.

Thursday April 9

It is late in the evening with Minnie and me in front of a gas log fire I installed to take the chill off nights like this one. I pull her bed nearer. She watches the flames flicker and dance among the fake logs, looks at me in gratitude and, after two turns, lies down.

Victor, Gracia, and I had our first viewing of Marcus and Mary today. They are so small and yet seemingly so perfect in every detail. Gabriella looks exhausted, maternal, and happy. Jim is walking on air. Victor swears Mary smiled at him.

Afterward, Victor and I repaired to Marcello's to talk business over ossobuco and wine. We agreed to insist that Gabriella take at least three months of maternity leave and then return to work on a part-time basis for a while, and only if she wanted to. We agreed that she and Jim would need to have some sort of part-time nanny, which we could pay for as necessary. We did not agree on which of us would do that.

Nor did we agree on a further raise he wanted to make in my compensation. I told my father that coming to work for Zito and Sons was the best financial decision I had ever made. I was doing very well. The company is doing even better.

"Hard to believe. After all these years," he smiled and ordered a second bottle of Tuscan rosso. I decided I might need to drive him home.

"No doubt we have to mind our Ps and Qs, Dad, and, like any business, we will hit some rough patches, but we have a solid base. You have built a revenue machine."

We toasted Zito and Sons. For the third or fourth or fifth time we toasted Marcus and Mary and then Gabriella and Jim.

I could see Victor trying to sober himself. "And to Mary mother of Gabriella and Mary Mother of God," he lifted his glass, and then added, "on this most holy Thursday."

I had not paid attention to the fact that this was the Thursday before Easter. Evidently Victor had gone to church earlier and asked me point blank if I had. I lied point blank. He gave me a searching look, and I compounded my lie. I do not think of myself as a liar, but telling myself it was a white lie and that I had not wanted to break the mood, I steered us back to business, commending Robert for the work he was doing, suggesting additional compensation and having Robert hire another person to work with him, especially in Gabriella's absence.

Victor agreed enthusiastically and thanked me profusely for "all you're doing for our company, Marcus. It's what I have always dreamed of. And, especially while Gabriella is recuperating, I am going to work extra hard for us. I know you will, too. Tonight I am the happiest man in the world."

I drove Victor home and then myself back here carefully, "didn't I, Minnie?"

Tomorrow I need to record something about Nathan and Westview but "I need to take a pee before hitting the sack, Minnie. You, too?"

Easter Sunday 2004

I can truthfully tell my father that I made my Easter communion early this morning. When the subject of forgiving sins came up, I remembered my Holy Thursday lie. I can think of worse sins.

Steve went with the family to the 10 a.m. blowout at Valley Presbyterian. I gather he is otherwise not much of a churchgoer. He may think I am a devout Catholic.

If he only knew! If only he knew what a pleasure it is having him stay with me this weekend since Susan is staying at Shelley's. I may have seemed a bit rude about turning down invitations to eat with them, but have had the good excuse of wanting to check on Gabriella and the babies.

They brought the babes home from the hospital on Friday. What a scene. How could two tiny creatures require so much attention? I tried to joke with the mother that now I understood why women come equipped with two breasts. My sense of humor was not appreciated.

I should trade houses with them. Actually I do not know what I can do to be helpful. I feel in the way. "Moral support," I tell myself.

I will need to put this away before Steve comes back. Imagine if he started reading it.

We said we would play tennis again this afternoon if he is not too full of Easter ham and scalloped potatoes that he remembers as a boy. I came close to winning the second set yesterday. He is tough.

We would make a great doubles team if he came down from San Francisco more often. If I had a magic pen, I would enter us in the father and son competition.

I do not know what will happen with Nathan and Westview Academy. George, of course, had no trouble getting accepted and Rob and Shelley can handle the hefty tuition. Without asking anyone's permission George sent Nathan a brochure about the school and then they talked on the phone. George should become a school admissions officer.

Next his mother Ellen called Shelley and asked whether she thought this made any sense. The distance from West

Hills was a problem, especially given the morning traffic, and she doubted whether they could make the tuition or would qualify for any scholarship assistance.

Next, George, who must be nearly five foot ten by now, lures me outside by practicing his jump shot and tells me that "Nate could even stay over with me sometimes if they can find enough money."

In between shots I casually let drop, "You know I went to Westview…"

"You did! Did you like it?"

"Only for two years, but yes; I liked it a lot."

"You got to tell Nate."

I did better than that. I told Shelley and asked her to get some ballpark figures from the Provezanos.

Shelley first wanted to know, "When were you there? Were you there with Steve?"

I played dumb. "I did not know he went to the Academy." And that makes another lie, but not on Marc's part.

"Well, you probably wouldn't have been there at the same time. But how about my father? You must have known him."

"Who is that?"

"Harold Barnes. He taught there and was Head in the 80s."

"Oh, sure. I can remember him. Nice man."

At some point I will tell Steve, too, if Shelley does not spill the beans first.

Meanwhile, I have an appointment on Wednesday with someone in the Development Department at Westview Academy. I think I know which buttons to push.

Sunday April 18 2004

Development, it turns out, is now the Advancement Department at Westview. I had to wait but briefly for an attractive woman, exceedingly well-groomed and dressed in a crisp blouse and well-fitted skirt, who introduced herself as associate for Advancement and invited me into her corner office. I thought of trying a taste of my handsomeness out on her, but could see she wanted to be quite professional.

I told her I had attended Westview for two years and, now that I was vice-president of a large firm in the valley, I would like to do something in gratitude. "Maybe something like forty or fifty thousand dollars over a several-year period, depending to some degree on business conditions."

"That would be very generous of you, Mr. Zito." Her professionalism did not waver. She put her fingers together and waited.

"Possibly on into future years when the gifts could increase, though I would like to play some role in where the funds would be directed."

"I know we would be glad to have your ideas."

I informed her that I was particularly interested in scholarship assistance and "while I understand gifts cannot be specifically directed to any particular student . . ."

"You are, of course, quite right. Especially relatives."

"The youngster I might like to see helped in some measure is not related at all unless . . ."

"Yes?"

"Unless someone would say that sharing bone marrow makes a relationship." I went on to tell her the story as her eyes widened and softened, and I knew I was also talking to a mother.

"That's . . . that is an interesting story, Mr. Zito. Would you mind . . . just a moment."

She came back with "our Director, Barry Cranston"—a tall, balding but also well-groomed man in his late 40s who I quickly sized up as at least two cuts above old Ace Demeter.

We exchanged greetings and Tiffany (as it turned out) told Barry my little story. Barry congratulated me and thanked me for my "generous intentions" and asked if I would mind if some publicity was given to the "extraordinary generosity of a former student." By this time I was feeling almost in charge but resisted asking if anyone remembered Harold Barnes. Instead I modestly insisted that I did not want any publicity about the bone marrow gift in the "Westview Academy Arts." If everything worked out, perhaps it would make a good story when Nathan Provezano graduated. In the meantime, Zito and Sons and I would be glad to know "should you ever need any contracting work here at the Academy," and understood completely that there could be no specific commitments of scholarship aid to a specific student based on other than an identified need, but that, as Barry expressed it: "You can be sure that the school will give every consideration to a qualified student."

We shook hands. I liked them. In another time I would have been pleased to work with them. Memories accompanied me as I walked out under the twenty year-old entrance arch that we had rebuilt when I was Head.

Tuesday June 22 2004

It is a little after 9 p.m. I have a handful of broccoli spears in the microwave, and have cut up a tomato, which I will put on toast with mozzarella. And then bed. It has been another long day at work, including the Rotary meeting where I have allowed myself to be put on the program committee. Robert and I have had to spend considerable time conferring and planning. In the last three months we have sold one apartment building and bought another. In the past we have never had more than two new houses under construction at one time. Now we have three, and Robert claims they will sell as fast as we can build them.

Jim is one man more tired than I am. They first had to supplement the breastfeeding with bottles and are now using them more and more. "Little Mary is a sweet sleeper, but your Markie is finding his voice—it seems every time I get back to sleep."

KUSC is playing Mozart's clarinet concerto. The dulcet melody soothes the tired spirit. Is there any sweeter sound in the world? And imagine that fingering. I wished I had kept up with the instrument as a young man. It is probably too late to teach Marcus, even if we had the time.

For all known intents and purposes Harold Barnes departed this life ten years ago this afternoon. I have been Marcus Zito for that long and have ten years of combined memories—the stories of our lives that tell us who we are. Hal lives on while his past recedes, and there is more and more of Marc and his future to imagine. We are one in this tired body with its occasional tummy aches, long-disappeared abs, a little gimp in the left knee and sometime athlete's foot. Sometimes, now, I feel much more Marc writing this. Tonight, it seems to me, we are writing together. And as I observe their lives and stories I am author of us both. "Good night, Hal." "Good night, Marc."

Friday the Fourth 2004

Although Victor, Jim, and I have insisted that Gabriella play no other role in the Fourth Folly, she is bringing the stars to the party. Knowing Gabriella, Marcus and Mary will be decked out in red, white, and blue.

Steve and I are to play tennis tomorrow and perhaps Sunday. I have not been playing enough to be sharp, but I am yet determined to take him one of these times.

He wants me to come up to San Francisco and play with him there one day.

Labor Day 2004

George and Nathan start at Westview on Wednesday. There is some trepidation on their parts, but I have encouraged them to have as good a time as I did there. I know there have to be excellent teachers, several of whom I once helped learn the craft.

I took last week off and drove North, first up to Tamales Bay and then through Sonoma and Napa valleys, dropping in at several wineries. I had not been up that way in years and was pleased to see it still looks much the same, though with a few more houses, several new wineries and most every slope mantled in vineyards.

I stopped in San Francisco and visited Steve where his school year had already begun. He had had a long week, and I bested him 3-6, 7-6, 6-4. Then I took him to the new SBC Park, and watched the archrivals Giants demolish the Diamondbacks 18-7. It was fun seeing my son down a hot dog again—even if he says he has become a Giants fan.

I am so proud of him and his dedication to his teaching and public school students. It would be nice if he could find someone, though. He seems lonely to me. Susan must worry too.

Sunday November 7 2004

I am neither surprised that "W," as some have begun to call him, won reelection nor by the relative closeness of the vote. The country is in a quagmire of a war—uncertain about its rationale while afraid to pursue it and afraid not to. Even if confidence is limited, it is hard to change leaders in years like these. At the same time the electoral map is startling with all of the West coast, North Central and Northeast in blue and otherwise the whole West, Central, and South in red.

Most of the country can go on living as though there were no war. Those in the lower echelons of the economy still struggle for enough to live on, while everyone is encouraged to borrow. It reminds me of the "guns and butter" slogans of the Vietnam War era. We can have both without making any sacrifice.

Except that the sacrificial news for us is that Staff Sergeant Jim Lord's National Guard unit has been called to active duty. So much for the volunteer army being able to "easily win this war!" Gabriella is beside herself. You would think Jim could get some kind of exemption with the two little babies, but, oh no: "Your country needs you." I am not sure Jim would accept one anyway. Although I do not think he has a war-like bone in his body, he feels protective of the guys—and a few gals—in his unit.

12

New Year's Day 2005

Jim has been with his 1st battalion of the 84th Infantry in a desert training camp in New Mexico and then at Fort Bliss for two months. He tells Gabriella that they are eating and living well and that he is in fantastic shape and hopes they will not be deployed outside the country. He tells me, however, that a number of his Bravo group are grumbling over the way they are being treated by the regular army officers and that they may well be headed for the Middle East before much longer.

I am here at Gabriella's for the weekend as I try to be one or two nights a week—at least to be company, though I am not all that bad with the diaper and feeding duties. They are such cute babies. I love being able to hold them.

I make up the sofa bed in the little den and can use the powder room down at this end of the house. Fortunately Gabriella has found some good help so she can be at work parts of days. Some nights and holidays are hard, though the other big support has come from Grandmother Lord, or as she has invited even me to call her, Granny Pearl. She works in the billing department at King-Harbor Hospital during the week but manages to be with "my daughter-by-love and these two little rascals" parts of many weekends.

Victor and Gracia are coming over this afternoon and we will all watch Michigan battle Texas in the Rose Bowl. Gabriella will lament that we cannot be in Pasadena at the game but I will be quite content to stay at home with this family.

Steve is at my house for the weekend. We hope to find time for tennis tomorrow. He beat me fairly readily at Thanksgiving. But, then, he is able to play more often than I am.

He also found out that I went to Westview several years after he did. It was bound to come out. While we were shooting hoops out by the garage—talking of sports and school, George half-shouted "And did you know Marc went to Westview just like us, Uncle Steve."

Of course, Steve wanted to know if I knew his father and George's grandfather. I gave him what is by now almost my standard line: "I wish I had taken a class from him. I know he was a fine man, but I did not have a chance to know him that well then."

Then George added, "But you only went there for two years. You didn't finish."

"Well, I did finish high school," I firmly maintained as I drained a twenty-footer. "We had a family problem."

"Sorry for that," Steve said, whipping the ball back to me.

"But how 'bout college?" George stole the ball from me. "You said you didn't finish college. Uncle Steve is getting a Master's degree."

"Yes, that was a mistake," I told him as I tried to steal the ball back.

George shot and missed. "But you know a lot about history."

"I have read a lot," I informed them both.

Sunday January 23 2005

All we know is that Jim is in Kuwait. Gabriella is praying he can stay there, but it seems likely this is only a staging stop.

We had an impressive presentation at Rotary today on the progress being made in eliminating polio world-wide by the end of the decade. There are only a few places where it is hanging on now: northern Nigeria and, I think, Pakistan and a couple of others. When I was a teenager in my former life we had a polio epidemic in our neighborhood in Pittsburgh. One of my friend's father died, and Darrell (cannot remember his last name) on my baseball team ended up in braces and crutches. He was not the only one. We heard that another kid would have to be in an iron lung for the rest of his life.

March 27 2005 Easter

I had forgotten that Easter could come this early. It has to be the first Sunday after the first full moon after the equinox, or something like that. All based on a lunar calendar of ancient religion.

Steve seems to think I am a devout Catholic and offered to come to Mass with me. I did not disabuse him but sent him off to Valley Pres with Shelley and crew. That way he was also able to tell me that "our mother seems to be doing O.K. She claims she is getting "a little flaky," but looks good. She is such a great mom and grandmother."

We called our tennis match a tie yesterday. I won the second set and we had enough rain during the third that the court became slippery, and I did not want to go on with my knee. I think Hal may have had better knees at 68 than I do at 36.

This afternoon we were able to sit out in the back under the completed loggia. I had to confess that I "borrowed" a couple buddies from the company to get it finished, but Steve was impressed and, truth be told, so am I. The whole back—now set with desert grasses and plantings—needs very little water. Yesterday's rain should keep it going for weeks. Minnie also adds her contribution. She has also become a great fan of Steve—fickle girl that she is.

Steve had a surprise for George and me. He has set up a short biography of Harold David Barnes, complete with picture, on Wikipedia. "It's a way that Dad and your grandpa can live on a little."

The picture I cannot even recall, but I look pretty good. That's when George informed us that he sometimes gets Nate to walk the "Barnes way" (or, I guess "Barnes Way") with him at school.

"What's the Barnes Way?" I asked.

Almost everybody knows, Mr. Marc. You know, it's the walkway from the arch to the science building that they named after Grandpa. There's a plaque that says so."

"Isn't that great?" Steve gave George a high five. "I'd almost forgotten that."

"Isn't it, Marc?" he said to me. "I should add it to the Wikipedia entry."

I am at Gabriella's as I write this. Jim's Bravo group is somewhere in Southern Baghdad as part of "Operation Iraqi Freedom" and he is able to send an occasional email—one complete with his smiling picture in helmet and battle fatigues. Gabriella showed it to the babies to their mystification. I fear that one of these days they will start calling me "Da-da."

Jim claims they are mostly engaged in security details and that the hardest thing to deal with is boredom. The newspaper reports do not make it sound all that boring with the sectarian Sunni and Shiite violence increasing—sometimes even when one group is celebrating one of their holy days.

I have decided that my main job is to talk to little Markie and Mary—make a lot of eye contact, show them things, look at books. I read somewhere that this is very important for even the littlest of babies and toddlers. Gabriella agrees, but she is so busy that it is hard for her to give them all the attention they need. With young Isabel as almost full time day help, Gabriella is also back at work as much as she can, insisting "the place could fall apart without me." Robert, Victor, and I try to convince her otherwise. "Let's concentrate on what we have, or only add slowly," I tied to sum up. "Zito and Sons is fine."

I heard Victor arguing with her last week—almost ordering her to be at home more, until she began crying. I told Victor what he already knew: "Some of this is her trying not to worry too much about Jim."

Sunday April 3 2005

Marcus and Mary are one year old today. I have bought them each a Dr. Seuss book—probably not "age appropriate," but I will have fun reading to them *Green Eggs and Ham* and *One Fish Two Fish Red Fish Blue Fish* in anapestic tetrameter as I did to Shelley and Stephen.

On Friday Shelley had to take Katie to some appointment and asked me to drive George and Nathan (who had stayed the night with them) to school. After I dropped the boys off, I took a walk along Barnes Way with a gaggle of today's teenagers and stopped to see Tiffany in the Advancement

Department. I told her that Nathan Provezano very much liked being at Westview and wrote out a substantial check as my annual contribution to the scholarship fund.

On my way off campus I found the plaque: "This Barnes Way honors Harold David Barnes Master Teacher and our President Head 1981-1991."

Fourth of July Independence Day 2005

We once declared ourselves independent from foreign powers and kings and now find ourselves bogged down in two foreign wars and a battle with Al Qaeda and terrorism that seem to be causing more and more intrusions on our liberties and costing us enormously in treasure and now hundreds of lives—not to speak of the damage done by Abu Ghraib and Guantanamo Bay.

I would not be surprised if Victor wanted to say a prayer over the wieners, brats, and beer at the Folly this year and go on for a while about our hopes for peace and concern for our brave fighting men and women and especially Jim— husband, father, son, colleague—who has not been home or seen his wife and children for more than eight months. He says he is still very safe, but I will bet their security details go beyond Baghdad. I hope not out toward Fallujah. What a mess we have made there. That picture of the four burned American bodies hanging from a bridge still haunts. And what will Iran do now that it no longer needs to worry about Iraq?

Steve was down for Memorial Day weekend but stayed with Susan and told Shelley his shoulder was bothering him. Apparently he did not come at all for the 4th. It seems funny not to have heard from him at all when we seemed to have become good friends as well as tennis competitors.

I do, however, get occasional visits from his 13 year-old niece and my granddaughter. Katie walks Minnie and sometimes likes to stay. Once she brought homework from her summer school class, but I think she mostly talked on her cell phone and then to me. I told her, however, that she could not be on my computer without her parents' permission. She did not protest. She is, in fact, perfectly pleasant, if rather subdued. She may just like being away from her mother some of the time. Last Saturday Shelley called and told her it was time to come home.

Sunday August 28 2005

Realizing we missed last year's game together, George, Nate, and I were eager to see the 2005 version of the Dodgers on a lovely summer evening at Chavez Ravine. The sun had not yet set on the San Gabriels but the stadium lights were on, and one again had that sense of walking into a cathedral—seeing the expanse of grass and the manicured diamond and readying for "Ladies and gentlemen, your Los Angeles Dodgers," the national anthem and then "play ball."

The lads had brought their own money for hot dogs and all and reminded me that next year they would be old enough to do the driving—a daunting thought in more ways than one.

They described to me their good teachers and then funny ones, of plans for basketball and tennis for George, soccer and cross-country for Nate their sophomore year. The Dodgers lost to the Rockies and are 13 games under .500. I did not tell my young friends what I thought of the Dodgers' new owner and the way he kept raising prices and his business ethics generally.

Monday August 29 2005

Jim is in a hospital in Germany. We do not know much more. They informed us only that he was wounded—not in danger of dying, we pray. I told Gabriella I could go for both of us, but, understandably, she insisted she had to be with him. Brother and sister fly LAX to Frankfurt late tomorrow.

Sunday September 11

In several ways the flight over was the hardest part. Neither of us had gotten much sleep. The babies were with Gracia and Victor, with Isabel to help care for them. But Mary had an earache, and their mother did not stop worrying about being away from them. Unspoken was the fear of not knowing what to expect—how badly Jim was injured—even if he would survive or how he would be surviving.

I could see my seatmate going from worry to worry and then to why: Why did he have to go fight in a war half-way around the world? Why were there people like Saddam Hussein and Osama bin Laden? Why must people kill each other anyway? Why did President Bush listen to Cheney and Rumsfeld and Feith and Wolfowitz and the rest of the chicken hawks? Why didn't Colin Powell or Condoleezza Rice do anything to stop them? Why Jim? Why God? Why do Sunnis and Shiites hate each other and then hate us and try to kill somebody as nice as Jim? Why could not people get along?

I was surprised at how carefully she had been following the war. She knew about the Kurds—where Kirkuk, Tikrit, Mosul, Baghdad and the Green Zone, and Basra all were. But that would happen when one's loved one is in the midst of it all.

Or was. Now Jim was in a small ward with three other wounded soldiers in the Landstuhl Regional Medical Center. Jim was asleep. He did not look gruesome, but the first appearance was hard. Gabriella put her hand to her mouth. His left arm was bandaged almost to the shoulder and his face was puffy with contusions and what were probably stitches—especially on the left where his eye seemed swollen shut.

The room was immaculate and quiet. Morning sunlight came in from east-facing windows. A male nurse moved quietly about. My dumb thought was this was nothing like MASH and that I should not expect Hawkeye or B.J. Honeycutt to come joking in. No: our soldiers were getting the best medical treatment possible. Hundreds—even thousands of lives were being saved. What the reports rarely told was how many thousands were now maimed, traumatized, blind. One of the patients kept calling for the nurse.

The doctor did not look at all like Alan Alda—rather Middle Eastern himself, handsome, about our age, considerate—ready "to answer any of your questions, as I can." "Was it an I.E.D.? An Improvised Explosive Device?" Gabriella carefully pronounced. I wanted to put in, "roadside bomb."

"Yes," said Dr. Nasralla.

First he wanted us to have the good news. "Sergeant Lord, I can almost promise you, is going to live. In fact, he's going to live well. Right now he looks worse than he is. The facial swelling and wounds should all clear up in a few weeks. He'll be handsome as ever," he smiled at Gabriella.

"I am told they can save the sight in the damaged eye," he told us. Gabriella started to cry. I put my arm around her. "I am her brother," I explained.

"I understand. I have two sisters." Dr. Nasralla went on as assuredly as he could. "There may be some damage to his hearing—particularly on the left side. You see the bandages on his arm. There are no broken bones. He nearly lost a couple of fingers, but they were able to save those too. Lots of good news, you see. Not all of them are so lucky."

"Thank you," I got out for both of us.

"You'll see, too, that his spirits are not at all bad, all things considered. He is a remarkable soldier."

"Thank you," was all I could say again. I gave Gabriella a shoulder hug.

"No abdominal wounds. The genitals are perfectly intact," Nasralla continued in a doctor's matter-of-fact tone. I had not even thought about that and looked about the room, wondering how the other three were doing.

"And that's about it. The only other news, the only hard news is that we were not able to save the left foot above the ankle. That was amputated."

"Oh God," Gabriella cried and started to shake.

"I am sorry, but more than half the leg is fine, and with modern prosthetics..."

"That's good," I tried.

"He'll be able to walk again. I'll wager even jog some, if he wants."

"He was a personal trainer. We both were," I added, thinking it might somehow be helpful.

"That is excellent," Dr. Nasralla responded, standing and giving Gabriella a kindly smile.

Jim's first words to Gabriella were "I'm sorry," as she bent over him and softly kissed his forehead. I could see she was being careful not to touch him otherwise.

"Don't you be sorry, Jim. I just love you and you're going to be O.K . . . better than O.K."

We stayed for a week, visiting Jim every day—I often left the two of them alone. Jim was still on heavy medication and slept quite a bit.

I took Gabriella for walks. We visited the Sickinger Schloss and ate in neighborhood restaurants, several of which had menus in English—except for the local favorite: wiener schnitzel. It seemed half the town were Americans with families of medical personnel and airmen. One could see and hear the planes in and out of Ramstein Air Base almost 24/7.

I persuaded Gabriella to try some of the regional Gewürztraminer and, after a glass or two, found myself *in Bits von Gesprächen* with the locals, recalling for Hal several weeks at a Goethe Institute as a young man and reminding Gabriella "of my army duty in Deutschland. One learns some interesting colloquial German driving about in a truck."

Even better were the beers—stronger and more substantial than American beer. It only took one to feel a little intoxicated. I wished I could smuggle one in for Jim.

Dr. Nasralla was right about his spirits—with an emphasis on "all things considered," while I could also see he was making an effort for us—especially for Gabriella. "You'll see. Old Jim will be back soon—right as rain. Can't wait to see my babies." And he could still flash his smile—if a bit lopsided.

They need to do at least one more operation on his eye. It will be another month or more before they may be able to fly him back to a hospital in the States.

Later this afternoon Jim's mother Pearl and two of his sisters are coming over to see the babies and to listen as we try to reassure them that their son and older brother—minus a part of his leg— is going to be just fine.

Sunday November 27 2005

Jim is still in the hospital in Landstuhl, but there is some hope he will be transferred to Walter Reed in Washington by Christmas. The operation on his eye was apparently a success, although they will likely need to do another. Apparently shrapnel from the I.E.D. crushed parts of the eye socket. Walter Reed seems like a good place for him until we can get him home. The only thing that concerns me is that, when I was looking up Walter Reed on the internet it told me that a number of their patients from Iraq and Afghanistan were suffering from T.B.I., which, I then found out, is one of their shorthands for Traumatic Brain Injuries. No point in bothering Gabriella with that information, and she claims that his mind seems clear when they are able to talk on the phone.

Jim will have been away for more than a crucial year in the life of his little family: another of the often hidden costs of going to war. In the meantime I am back staying with them two or three nights a weeks. I have taken to bringing Minnie with me to the delight of Marcus and Mary, though Minnie, after sniffing them, shows little interest in their attempts to play with her. Each night Gabriella says a prayer with the twins and tells them "it won't be long before we have our sweet Daddy home with us. Maybe by Christmas." I sing them silly songs: "Rock-a-bye babies, in the tree top / Soon will be home your dear loving pop / When he is here, all war will be done / and Marcus and Mary will have lots of fun."

Earlier this afternoon I drove Steve to Burbank to fly back to San Francisco after he had stayed with me three nights and we played tennis on Friday and then with George and a buddy from his Westview tennis team on Saturday. The two young men have good strokes—George's friend a remarkably powerful two-hand backhand, but we managed to beat them. George is almost as tall as his Uncle Steve and has taken to calling me "Uncle Marc."

Otherwise, Steve was with his family much of the time, though we had a couple of friendly conversations. It was as if nothing had happened, but when I returned from Germany, there was a strange message on my answering machine from Steve—emotional and as if he could have been drinking. He was full of apologies about not visiting me since Easter and practically begging me "to see if you can fit in a quick trip to see me around Labor Day. We can play tennis."

I called back and explained about Jim's injury and the trip to Germany. He said he completely understood and apologized for bothering me. I told him it was no bother and hoped he could come down around Thanksgiving which he then did.

The rest of the time it has been, as they say, work, work, work around here. It is impossible completely to replace Jim and Gabriella, who tries to be a whirlwind when she shows up, but has been half-time at best, and does not always understand the latest projects and problems. Even Victor, while putting in long hours, prefers to be out on the sites and seems less interested in overseeing the whole operation. It has been left to Robert and me to think through the bigger decisions and put out a couple of fires—not least—speaking of potential fires—dealing with an alcoholic electrician.

The biggest decision involved whether we should purchase several lots so we can begin building more than three houses at a time. More and more people are buying homes, which is driving up prices, and at the same time, putting some downward pressure on rents. More houses would also mean expanding the work force, which could be a problem if at any point we had to cut back. Gabriella was all for it. Victor said that he was satisfied with things the way they were. Robert was cautious and looked to me for a decision. In the end we bought two additional lots and sold one of our apartment buildings that we will, however, continue to manage. But I also have my eye on another small apartment complex that we could completely rehab and possibly have a store or two on the street level.

13

Sunday New Year's Day 2006

Today I will cook for my father, step-mother, sister, nephew, and niece—or at least help feed the latter two. And they are all staying the night, which meant buying two more beds, more sheets, pillows, pillow cases, and towels. Some of the food I have bought prepared from Gelson's, but I have already begun cooking a beef bourguignon that was once one of my specialties.

I have also put everything and anything that looks breakable away or up on shelves. Marcus and Mary are in full locomotion and exploration mode.

I have invited Shelley and Rob over tomorrow to meet my family and have a sort of browsing picnic with, however, no Rose Bowl game to watch. This year's game is for the national championship, and the powers-that-be have apparently moved it to Wednesday for the TV audience or something. So much for tradition!

It has meant kicking Steve out, but he said he wanted to leave early tomorrow anyway: "Get ready for those 2006 seventh and eighth graders with a couple of eye-popping new science experiments." He also is only one course short of completing his Master of Arts in Education at SF State. Evidently he is being tempted to think about becoming a school principal but so far wants to stay with the teaching "Where I believe I'm more needed."

Except for his nearly demolishing me on the court yesterday, I am proud of him. There also remains something sweet and affectionate about him. He wants me to come visit him in San Francisco, but given the work load here, we will have to see.

Jim was transferred to Walter Reed three weeks ago and Gabriella was with him for four days just before Christmas. She brought back a picture of him with a patch over his eye that makes him look like a pirate. Otherwise that is Jim's smile and he is standing with his fists up like a boxer. He tells her that it is mostly physical therapy now, being fitted with his prosthesis, some counseling, "and getting home to see my babies." Gabriella did not find the care he was getting at Walter Reed "as good as it ought to be."

New Year's resolutions? It is tougher, but I still get in my gym time and my runs—often by getting up at six. I certainly could work on my tennis game. I would actually like to spend less time at work but do not see that I can for the foreseeable future. More than ever I feel responsible for Zito and Sons and its future for everyone's sake. They want me to become an officer at Rotary but I am resolving not to do that in 2006.

I could watch my diet better: more green vegetables and fruit. Also watch out for the noodles with the beef bourguignon and the peppermint stick ice cream afterward.

February 20 2006 Presidents' Day

It seems tragic for our country to realize that those regularly remembered as our great presidents—Washington, Lincoln, Wilson, Roosevelt—were our war presidents—General Washington, of course, becoming president as a war hero. One can well argue that the wars were thrust upon them, but they were not able to avoid them either. Then add to them Jackson, Grant and Eisenhower who became presidents as victorious generals, and maybe, too, Colonel Teddy Roosevelt, hero of the Battle of San Juan, and dear Lyndon Johnson whose war on poverty ran up against the war in Vietnam. That is a lot of war for the United States of America and does not count our wars against the Native Americans.

Our war hero came home today. His United flight from Dulles landed almost exactly at noon. On behalf of our grateful country, I was his designated greeter. I felt like I should shout something to the crowd as he descended the short escalator into the baggage area. I may have imagined that he appeared unsteady, but he looked very much like Jim. No one glancing at him would know of his war injuries. God, it was good to see him.

Unfortunately it was not one of Southern California's finest days. It was bordering on chilly with a fine mist in the air. One could not see the mountains as we headed up the clogged 405. Jim was quiet as I drove—twice saying "Man, it's been a long time." Then, "Traffic's same as ever." I imagined he was apprehensive if not fearful. It had been 16 months since he had left his house. The toddlers were barely six months old when he left. It had been 16 months since he had intercourse with his wife. One probably had to take the prosthesis off first.

I pointed out the Getty Center to him. "You gotta speak up brother," he tried to laugh." You got my bad side. One good ear and one good leg left of old Jim."

But he surely got a hero's welcome at home. It would be some time before Marcus and Mary would figure out how important he was in their lives, but there they were, bravely waving flags and competing with one another in shouting "Daddy, Daddy." Gabriella broke down in tears twice, repeatedly told the children, "It's our Daddy; he's home," and was flushed with happiness and, I guess, a kind of relief. Victor gave Jim a father's hug, and Gracia kissed him solidly on both cheeks. There was chocolate cake and vanilla ice cream, and soon we left the reunited family to begin its new life together.

First Sunday of Easter April 16

That is what Monsignor Gallagher called it at Mass this morning, reminding us that the Easter season has seven Sundays in it. Afterwards we all repaired back to Victor's and Gracia's for our Easter brunch—huevos rancheros con chorizo on corn tortillas as the main dish. Her daughter Miranda was there with her husband Carlos and two rambunctious boys about five and seven. Daughter Isabel was also there—perhaps for me, I worried. She is a bit on the heavy side, but quite attractive. I may have imagined that she was flirting with me. I was polite, but I have trouble fabricating a story in which I am dating again, much less in a serious relationship. For one thing, I tell myself, I do not have the time for it, but I also do not feel I can afford it emotionally. If I let myself fantasize, I am aware of a longing for a woman in my life—even a deep sexual longing, but I can make it go away. Other men are single—stay single, "confirmed bachelors," as they say, and manage to lead productive and useful lives. And I do have family—sometimes more than one.

I guess we could not have expected Jim's "reintegrating," or whatever we want to call it, to be all that easy. My biggest problem has been colluding with Gabriella to persuade him not to come back to work right away. He had assumed that was how it was going to be. Gabriella, however, envisioned him as taking some months at least at home where he could "get your strength back and make up time with Mary and Markie," while she was able to put in more time at work.

"I am not cut out to be a house husband," Jim retorted. "I'm a man, and I'm alive. There's no reason."

Gabriella reports that he does have nightmares and trouble sleeping through the night. She finds him in the kitchen, lights on, half-listening to the radio. "When I try to talk with him it's as though there is some secret he is carrying around with him that he cannot tell anybody."

I have tried to get him to come to the gym with me for a "buddy workout." He says he will, but is having difficulty with the prosthesis and has to return to the veterans' hospital once a week for rehab and what he calls "adjustments." I know he is worried about the amount of pain medication he takes.

I can look at him and tell myself that he appears the same, but it is not true. He moves more slowly. A measure of vitality has gone from his body. His face looks older. There is a kind of squint to his left eye and one can see some of the scarring around the socket. He has to see that every time he looks in the mirror.

But he is my friend—my best friend. Somehow he is going to get through this. I know he is determined. There is a goodness and strength to him that . . . I know is going to be better.

The compromise arrangement that I—as the one who seems to be making the decisions for Zito and Sons these days—made, begins tomorrow. Gabriella will come to work three days a week and Jim for two. We will see how well it works out for them and for us.

I should add that we had a grand birthday party for "the terrible two at two" two Sundays ago—grandparents, aunts and uncle all gathered. No, they may be terrors some of the time, but they are not terrible. What smart, beautiful children! Of course, they are my nephew and Godson and little niece Mary.

Saturday April 22 2006

I came back from whomping Ned Coburn in early morning tennis and topped it off with a good run with my faithful Minnie up on dirt Mulholland. It was still not quite 11 when I returned and saw the light blinking on my message machine. I decided to let it blink while I showered and debated whether I would drop by the office or take the whole weekend off for a change. I had asked Jim to check the phones and websites in case there were any emergency apartment problems. It would give him something to do. Maybe the call was from him. There was nothing important on my Blackberry or cell.

The message was from Shelley. She started out light, but "there's something kind of important I'd like to talk to you about. Really. If you've got the time, Marc. Maybe at your house. I can bring some coffee, if that's O.K."

As is my wont, I began to have dark worries: something is wrong with George or Katie; there is trouble with Rob and the marriage; I have done or said something wrong. Maybe it is only some problem with the neighbors. I know she thinks I have not done enough with the homeowners' association, though I did help settle the argument between the Zellys and Rouhanis over their fence line and even had the company build the new fence for them. The only lingering part of that was old Zelly's ostensibly friendly message to the neighborhood that he had a new gun permit.

I called and she came right over with a thermos and paper cups, the over-organized Shelley (nee Barnes) Longworth. She looked a little worn—no make-up—in her mid-forties now: actually 45—still attractive. She looks otherwise healthy.

I asked about the kids. I asked about her mom.

"O.K. in most ways, but we have to worry about her forgetting things. I'm not sure about the driving anymore and that would finish off her independence for sure. But that's not what we need to talk about."

I waited.

"Marc, I don't know how to say this but I love my brother."

"He's great. So do I."

"Yeh. Well, there we are."

"Which is?"

"You do realize that he's really quite shy?"

"Some of the time. Maybe. Not on the tennis court."

"Yes." She sighed. "You know that he's gay?"

"Not really. But . . . that is fine if he wants to be."

"He's not had an easy time with it, but he's 'out' now to his friends, to his sister—now to his mother who's really been wonderful about it."

"And to Rob?"

"Why should that matter? But Rob's figured it out. But here's the thing that does matter: Marc, are you gay?"

I looked at her. "No, I do not think so, but no. They say everyone's sexuality is . . .is . . . can be different. But no—not really at all. I have only been interested in women ever since I can remember."

"I didn't think so. But you do know you're quite attractive to other women and, I suppose, some men as well. I'm sorry to get so personal."

"It's all right."

"So, here it is. He thinks he's in love with you."

"Oh, boy."

"You didn't know?"

"No."

"Ah, men."

"Oh, boy."

"You're two grown men."

I told her how sorry I was—that I really cared about Steve. I asked her if he knew about her talking with me—if there was anything I could do.

Shelley would not let me completely off the hook. She told me I should be more careful about "whatever vibes you send out."

I promised I would. She said she had only hinted to Steve that she might talk to me, but now she would tell him.

I again protested that I had not known—that he never really said or did anything.

She tried to lighten things up. "You're something, Marc Zito. How would you like me to find a girlfriend for you? I'm pretty good at that."

"You always were."

"How would you know, Mr. Stay-at-home."

I told her I did not want to lose Steve as a friend—even just someone to play tennis with. "After you tell him, let me know. Let me know if it would be all right that maybe I could talk to him too."

Wednesday May 10 2006

When I got home late this evening there was a message on the answering machine from Steve. I imagine that he wanted it that way, and I had earlier decided it would be better to write him a letter—no phone calls where I might not say it

287

right; no emails. It took me three versions until I realized brief was better: I was sorry about any misunderstanding, I wrote to him. I very much liked him as a friend. I hoped we could see each other again on his visits to his family—that we could play tennis—that maybe I could finally pass him at the net.

He would never know how much I wanted to keep seeing him.

He could not have been more considerate of me, more mature sounding in his recorded message. I felt relieved and curiously proud of him—reconciled in ways I do not understand. It makes no particular sense to me, but, for the first time in years, I wanted to have a Scotch—neat: Glenlivet, single malt preferred.

He ended by saying he would call me the next time he came down—that we could play tennis—that he was determined to "solve that backhand slice of yours."

Fourth of July 2006

Probably it was just me. The others seemed to be having a good time. Marcus and Mary were all over the place and into everything. Jim was not dressed as Uncle Sam but wore sky blue pants and a red bow tie on a bright white shirt. His main job was corralling his kids and the others that were there. He seems more confident. He wants more work and has been spending a day a week at a rehab center at Veterans' Hospital helping other amputees. He tells me that their biggest problem is lack of employment opportunities. "But," he also grumbles, "some of them need to try harder."

Gabriella was back in her role as cohost of the event. What she does not know is this could be the last time we hold the Fourth Folly at the old homestead. Victor picked my 38th birthday to tell me that he wants to retire next year. "Been in the contracting business in one way or another for over 40 years—a few more if you count those first years when I was mostly a painter—if you can believe that. I'm darn proud of what we built here. But enough is enough. I always dreamed my son would succeed me. We'll work together for a year and then that's that. I'll get into my rocking chair and, after a few months, and if I feel like it, I'll start rocking just a little." He laughed. "Get it? It's an old joke!"

I cannot picture him in a rocking chair. He is already volunteering a day a week with Catholic Charities and clearly plans to do more, "particularly helping out with some of their property issues. But I want to work with high school kids, too: help them think about their futures."

Nor do I think he will stay away from his company. He will want to talk with his foremen and check up on some of the projects. But I do believe that he no longer wants to feel that he is running the place. Indeed, that has been evident for a while now and certainly to me when decisions have to be made.

There was a time when I believe Gabriella would have wanted to try to run the show—or at least be a kind of co-president. But I think she is too wise to want that now, if I am wise enough to treat her as a partner in some of the planning.

And how about me? It makes me feel a little nervous—perhaps especially wondering if this is what I want to do for the next 25 or so years. A few years ago I could never have imagined being head of a company managing apartments, building and repairing houses and apartments. I have learned, however, that much of what I do is personnel work—encouraging and helping people to do their jobs, to know what their job is and to be good at it, to work together—to take some pride in what they do and accomplish. And to see they are properly compensated for their work. That may sound like Business 101, but it is something I feel reasonably good at and can get better at. And the finances? That may be a bit tougher, but I know something about that too.

The phone rang an hour or so ago. It was Shelley inviting me to come over and watch the fireworks from their back deck.

In fact, most of the fireworks were just occasional sprays at a great distance out in the valley: Tujunga, Studio City—Woodland Hills in the other direction. The ones at Hansen Dam might have been nearest. We saw a couple high sprays from as far over as the Hollywood Bowl. Then there would come the muted delayed booms.

With that it was mostly hushed—no other munitions: a world seemingly at peace with those of us observing talking in subdued tones. George and Katie were there with their parents. Katie had a neighborhood friend she whispered and giggled with.

Steve was there. He apologized for not letting me know. He was down for barely 24 hours as he is using the summer to finish his Master's degree. We would definitely play tennis next time. We embraced each other.

And Susan was there—sitting in a deck chair. We were introduced. It seemed the easiest thing in the world to sit down beside her. It was dark. She seemed almost another person—which in some ways she was—as was I. She felt like somebody who needed someone to hold her hand. She asked me how I knew Rob and Shelley. I explained I was a neighbor.

"And do you have children?" she asked.

I laughed.

"Did I say something funny?" she wanted to know.

"I have a wonderful nephew and a niece."

Rob asked if I wanted anything to drink. "I would not mind a splash of Scotch," I told him.

"On the rocks?"

"Oh, sure. Why not?" Nor did I care what kind it was.

Sunday August 6 2006

Fifty-one years ago today the Enola Gay dropped "Little Boy" on Hiroshima and changed human history and the world forever.

Last week Fidel Castro announced he was turning over the power of government to his brother. He has some kind of bleeding illness—the nature of which no one is supposed to know about. It takes me back to those terrifying few days of the Cuban Missile Crisis when we thought there could be nuclear war—escaping by what Dean Acheson attributed to "plain dumb luck."

And it is close to 50 years since Fidel forced a dictatorship on the Cuban people while yet managing to provide at least forms of health care and education for everyone. It is hard to believe how ineptly we have handled him for so long. Some even believe young Fidel might have allowed a few democratic institutions to arise had he not been afraid the CIA would infiltrate them as it had done in Central America and Iran. Fast forward to Bush's 2000 election, which would not have happened without the support of the Cuban community in Florida.

Nate and George are taking me to the Dodgers versus the Rockies tomorrow night at "the old ball yard," as they claim I once referred to it. I gather they have rather gone their separate ways at Westview, but yet are friends and insist that "tradition be observed." They have even bought the tickets, albeit in the bleachers, which is fine by me. I still got to drive, however, as they cannot yet drive at night. Thank goodness.

Labor Day 2006

I hear the words of that old hymn: "Come, labor on / who dares stand idle?" I do not remember any more of it.

It is good that we all have the weekend off. We have our problems at Zito and Sons. There are so many new houses being built in the area that we have had trouble keeping some of our best craftsmen. Victor wisely began an apprentice program several years ago, but we have even lost several of the best of them.

Victor announced the transition last week: that he will be officially retiring on June 1, 2007 and that I would be "assuming some of the leadership duties in the interim." That was, I thought, on the vague side—not even making it clear that I was to succeed him. Yet everyone seems to assume that and already comes to me for advice and decisions. I can imagine that there is some chatter in the ranks, but I think they respect me and the company in my hands.

Perhaps my biggest immediate problems are Jim and Gabriella. Jim shows up, does his work, is friendly enough most of the time, but his mind is not fully engaged. He is on a three day-a-week schedule, and there is certainly enough work for him to become full-time. I have told him that, but he says "This is good for now." He wants to spend some of his time with veterans' rehabilitation programs. We will talk some more.

I think Gabriella is more frustrated than anything else, although it can come out in flashes of anger. After all, she is the one with the college degree and the MBA with many of the growth ideas for the company. It has to be hard for her.

I have tried to convince her that there are and will be many opportunities for us to work as a team in the years ahead. Unfortunately she shows up with bursts of energy and ideas, but not always the follow-through on detail and planning that we need or the time to supervise and help others with the work.

And she is pregnant, or maybe I should say the two of them got pregnant. I cannot believe that it was planned though maybe Jim felt he had to show something after his trauma and injuries. Or maybe they are such "good Catholics" that they relied on rhythm control that went off-beat.

Better news for me is that I took Steve in a spirited three-set match Saturday, though he evidently had not played much this summer. But then, I had not either. It was followed by conversation over beer, in which I tried to show myself open and understanding. He only "suspected I might be gay in college. It took me a long time—longer than most, I guess. I certainly had opportunities where I was living, but I was so awkward and, I guess, inhibited. I began to think I was really screwed up."

"I went to a psychiatrist who told me I was perfectly normal, and that I clearly was attracted to men more than women, and that should not be considered abnormal. He kept using that phrase 'perfectly normal'." "He asked about my 'family of origin' and suggested that I come out to my sister and then my mother and would be surprised by how accepting and understanding they were."

"Which was true?"

"In spades. But I still . . . I think I was afraid because of my job. And I am pretty sure my father would never have approved. We never really talked about sex, but I knew how he felt."

"Did you?"

"Well, whoever knows? But he's dead, and I can't come out to him."

"But he was a good man. I told you that I knew him."

"Yes. But you said only a little."

"I did, but I have been thinking about it. I can remember at least a couple conversations I had with him. I know I looked up to him. There were probably ways in which I wished I could be like him."

"Really?"

"Yes. Really. Some of the conversations were about literature. He had read so many novels, I could not believe it. I think it was what made him understanding about people."

"That's amazing."

"That I would know all that? I guess so. This is a good Biersch ale—made right next door in Burbank."

"So he might have understood having a gay son?"

"He loved you, right?"

"I sure believe that." He bit his lip. "Sorry, didn't mean to get weepy after one beer."

"Steve, let me tell you something. I have a dad, too. He loves me whether I am blue, pink or orange. He does his best to understand me—even if I do not get married . . . even if I do not go to Mass very often. Whether I am gay or straight."

"But does he understand?"

"He does his best. The love is more important than the understanding. Maybe love is the understanding."

"I'd like to believe that."

"Believe it. I bet if your Dad were here right now, he would tell you he understands. He understands that you are gay. He loves his gay son. He loves you."

"That's nice. This must be strong beer."

"It's more than beer."

14

New Year's 2007

"What do you think of the dinosaur, Minnie? Look how it swings its neck back and forth. It isn't scary, is it?" The Rose Parade floats are as elaborate as ever—some of them operated by computers. "It's computerized, Minnie."

And the game will be played this afternoon as it should be: our very own USC against Michigan. Mary and Marcus, Gabriella and Jim, and the one-to-be are coming over to watch on my new 48" TV. I have invited Rob and Shelley, George and Katie, too, though I gather they will be coming without Rob. I particularly want Shelley to have some time with Gabriella and Jim, and, of course, see how fast my half-namesake and his suddenly shy little sister are growing.

They hanged Saddam Hussein by his neck a couple of days ago. Finally caught him hiding in some hole in the ground. While the media kept reminding us of what a villain he was—cruel dictator, persecutor of the Shiites and Kurds, who, along with "Chemical Ali" gassed his own people (though we did not seem to care much back when it happened), one could almost feel sorry for the trapped and diminished human being who had been afraid to admit he did not have any weapons of mass destruction and, we found out, wrote romantic novels when he was not being so evil. Meanwhile, we may be near to losing the war there, although no one seems to be able to define what losing it or, for that matter, winning it would be. Jim just shakes his head. "It has to be for something."

Jim and I had coffee after work today. He surprised me by being in favor of "the surge" of 20,000 additional troops into Iraq—what President Bush announced this morning as "The New Way Forward." "Gotta see if we can make something out of the mess we helped make," Jim held. "Maybe double down. I'd hate to see it all go to waste."

He also told me why he sometimes has to get up in the middle of the night: "It's a kind of nightmare, I guess. But I don't really remember the explosion or right after. I'm not sure . . . maybe the noise of it. What I can't get out of my head is right before: me shouting, "Keep going" to the guy at the wheel of the Humvee even when we see the Arab running away from the road, and then my throwing the grenade after him and seeing kids there."

"But you do not know if you injured any of them. They were probably running."

"I have no idea. Never will."

He went on for a while about how much he loves his family and knows he has to support them and is grateful for his job. "But somehow it's not enough anymore. I've got to do something. Can you understand, Marc?"

"I think so."

"Aw shit! I wish I could."

Meanwhile, not many are even thinking about poor Afghanistan—continuing to grow its poppies and new Taliban.

Easter April 8 2007

Pearl Anne Lord was born on Holy Thursday, two days
after Marcus' and Mary's third birthday—too close for comfort for them, but they will learn to love sharing birthdays
someday. In spite of war and Jim's months in hospital, this
must be regarded as pretty good family planning. I told my
sister it was just as well she did not have a litter this time, but
I do not think my effort at humor was appreciated.

The baptism will be in a week or so: another Catholic for
Victor.

She is, by the way, a little cutie with a surprising amount
of dark hair. Needless to say, her grandmother Pearl finds
her quite special.

I think Gabriella and I have worked things out. I have
told her that after maternity leave, she is welcome to come to
work when and as often as she feels like it. We will keep a desk
for her, her job title, phone line. She can also work on-line
and by phone from home. Robert will actually handle and
direct much of the financial management as well as accounting and related decisions, but will view her as a partner in as
many ways as she wants. "After a few years you could resume
your full responsibilities and authority. Who knows? After a
few years, I may be glad to have you run the show."

Victor is having trouble with his transition into retirement, but I can humor him about it—at least some of the
time. I have certainly seen it before. Even Hal Barnes had to
go through it. One looks forward to retirement, but then, it
is somehow too . . . quiet or something, perhaps especially if
one has had a good deal of responsibility with other people
looking to you for leadership and guidance.

Victor comes in almost every morning by seven as usual.
"I may only stay for a while." Then there are questions: "How's

the Woodland Hills site coming along?" Or "The Moorpark Apartments are nearly finished aren't they? I'll go out and check on them for you."

The more complicated conversations have been about health care for the employees. The cost of health insurance just keeps going up, and some other contractors around here do not even offer it to their lower paid workers or they use day laborers. Robert and I are looking into cheaper plans with higher deductibles and also asking employees to pay more for their policies. Victor hates those ideas: "Zito and Sons has always been known for putting its employees first." But he does not fully understand the spiraling cost and market forces.

I went to Mass with Jim, Victor and Gracia this Easter morning, and then Jim and I brought Marcus and Mary up here to play. They are disappointed that Minnie has so little interest in their stuffed animals.

We also looked at a house around the corner that I know will be coming up for sale. I am sure the seller will be asking too much for it, but the Lord family could use some more space. It probably would make even more sense to let them move in with me, but I do not think I am up to that: those sweet but noisy kids.

Monday April 16 2007

A deranged young man—apparently a graduate student with ready access to guns—killed 32 fellow students at Virginia Tech today, and wounded another 23. He shot a total of 55 human beings—32 dead, 32 grieving families.

Sunday May 13 2007

Having what sounded like a reasoning conversation with a girl about seven and a toddler boy too big to have been riding in the grocery cart, a woman with lovely chestnut hair that looked like it would feel and smell nice preceded me along the aisle stocked with colorful boxes of cereal. I was having trouble finding my favorite bran flakes with almonds bits and raisins. "Let the man by," she said to the children and turned. I swear in our surprise we almost kissed.

"Marc, that's you. Hey, you look good. I'm so glad to see you."

"Me, too. Gosh, Danielle. You look great." And she did, and pregnant. She had finished her doctorate three years ago and was teaching half-time at UCLA where her husband was also on the faculty. Her thesis was recently published in some scholars' series.

I shared in turn, I was about to assume the presidency of a contracting and apartment rental firm that my father founded. "You remember him . . . at that birthday party."

"Of course," she smiled, with her face if anything more attractive, matured, her sharp features softened, yet still hinting at the exotic. Her eyes were warm and smiling too. They glanced down at my left hand on the handle of my cart. I wished I could have hidden it. "Did you ever get married?" She asked.

"Ohhh, not yet," I tried.

"Somebody's missing out then," she nodded her head, still smiling.

The children were getting restless: "Mom, Mommy, why are you talking?"

We agreed it would be wonderful to see each other again. "I'd love it," she smiled emphatically.

At the checkout counter I realized I had forgotten my cereal. I was, no doubt, thinking about Danielle and what if

I had married her, though that probably could never have worked out. And I was pondering whether I would or should ever have a love in my life, and that Shelley had tried to inveigle me into coming to two dinner parties at her house where I could well imagine there would also be a single woman— perhaps another teacher from her school or a friend from Valley Pres, and we would engage in conversation and perhaps find a number of interests in common.

It would not, however, be someone quite like Danielle. Or for that matter dear Carol. Maybe she would be a divorced woman with children. Maybe she would talk my ear off and start calling me at night. Maybe she would be hefty with warts. Or too young. Or too old. Or too beautiful and vain.

Still, I should probably give it a try, if only to satisfy Shelley. And myself.

I have poured myself a finger and a half of Scotch and given Minnie her dinner—telling myself that I feel in many ways satisfied, perhaps even a touch smug. "Just the two of us, right Minnie?" However I think of Danielle now, it was more like a daughter at the time. I am pleased that I did not get in her way. I am not jealous of her husband. Look at all she has done.

With another sip of Scotch, I want to take pride in her— more like her parent—more like an observer of life's passing stage which I depict and describe.

Sunday June 3 2007

Jim has applied for a job in veterans' services of some kind. I am all for it, but not sure that I understand it completely. Not sure he does either. Still, I will be writing a letter of reference for him.

He would be assistant or associate of a program that works with veterans who have incurred disabling wounds and assists them with rehabilitation and employment where possible. Sounds like an excellent fit for him.

The major problem is with funding. Despite all the fine rhetoric about caring for its veterans, Congress does not intend fully to fund the program but rather for it to be a public-private, government-corporation partnership with businesses providing money and also employment opportunities. Among other things it is meant to offer participating companies opportunities for good public relations.

It could be a win-win situation. We shall see. The director and, I imagine, the associate director or directors will likely be expected to do at least some of the fundraising.

I did go to a dinner party at Shelley's and Rob's last night. I had not been to a dinner party for couples for many years. I could see their dining room table nicely laid out, the plates I remembered as a wedding present that family members had given them. Shelley greeted me in her apron, managing to appear both gracious and relaxed. Her mother must be proud of her. I felt proud of her as she gave me a surprisingly warm hug. Rob was on doctor's call of some kind and several times was off in the study. I felt a bit like a co-host. There were two other couples—friends, I gather, for many years: a doctor Rob had interned with. I knew the second couple from the neighborhood association.

Then there was, indeed, the single woman—or at least single at the party: quite pleasant, about my age, a lawyer who Shelley knows from church, who had served in child protection services and now was with a small firm that "dealt in family law and, I'm afraid, quite a number of divorces." She expressed an interest in my business and asked whether

we ever had need of lawyers. I told her there were two that
we had called on for a number of years when we were sued,
or had contract disputes or the like. Together we enjoyed the
roast lamb and the rest of the dinner Shelley had made and
the conversation with the others. I tried to imagine some further—even intimate—relationship with her. My imagination
did not get that far. I think she has even less interest in me.
Strike one, Shelley.

July Fourth 2007

In lieu of a Fourth Folly Gabriella, the company and I
hosted our father's retirement party at Marcello's on Sunday
afternoon—renting out the whole of the Trattoria and with
a tent over half the parking lot. I think almost everyone who
ever worked for Zito and Sons was there with families. There
were Rotarians, other local business types, representatives
from the Chamber of Commerce and from city councilman
Weiss's office. County Supervisor Zev Yaroslavsky stopped
by for a few minutes, sampled the fare, and made a brief
speech about how fine a man and citizen Victor was. Victor's
doctor came, his dentist, our two lawyers, Sister Catherine,
Monsignor Gallagher who read a letter from the Cardinal
and (I thought Victor was going to fall down) a message
from the Pope that Mahony had somehow obtained for him.
The Monsignor offered a surprisingly lengthy prayer, and
we might have expected a choir to break out in anthems.
Instead there was a mariachi band serenading us as we ate
hundreds if not thousands of pizza squares, meatballs and
chicken parmigiana and drank considerable vino rosso and
bianco, Coca Cola and Marcello's special punch. The whole
affair cost us upward of $20,000, even with Marcello's son
Mark trying to give a discount. But, hey, Victor had founded
and grown the company for which he worked over 40 years

and which was probably worth a couple hundred times that by now. Over the years he had provided employment for, let us guess, several hundred people and housing for hundred if not thousands more. One of the things I like most about Victor is that he was not greedy. He ended up making quite a lot of money, but, though he might have been able to, he never seemed to need multimillions for himself.

If Victor had any regrets about retiring, there was none of that on Sunday as he beamed and ate and drank and seemed to know everyone there, kissing most of them.

At seven on Monday he showed up at work, "just to thank everyone and look around. To see if an old retired guy is needed for anything." He greeted me as "Mr. President" and gave me a hug and a kiss that ended up on my ear. He put on his hard hat, which he keeps on a peg in the conference room and now has his name on it, and walked into the garage and storage hall. I think he went home about lunch time.

Sunday July 22 2007

Jim did not get the veterans' services job. Apparently it went to a man who is neither an amputee nor a veteran. Hard to understand.

He and Gabriella have decided not to make an offer for the house on Oak View Drive. I tried to help them with the financing, but it would have been quite a stretch for them. They do not need to be stressed out about money too.

The company provides sufficient stress for me. We are understaffed for some of the things we are trying to do, even while there seem to be so many opportunities in the housing market. We have four houses under construction as of today, with two more lots waiting for us. It is hard to believe we can keep selling them for these prices—two of them even before they were finished. But money for mortgages is out there as well as for a lot of refinancing. Meanwhile the rental market is relatively flat, while we try to continue with a regular plan of renovations.

Monday Labor Day 2007

Katie—or Katherine as she sometimes prefers to be called—begins at Westview Academy on Wednesday. Nathan and George start their senior year.

The four of us saw the Dodgers eke out a 4-3 victory over the Washington Nationals. Former Giant Jeff Kent hit a home run. He is one tough guy but probably the mediocre Dodgers' best player right now. Certainly Nate thinks so.

Seeing the Nationals play for the first time made me think of Washington teams of yore: the Washington Senators famed as "First in war, first in peace, and last in the American League."

George drove us in the family Mariner SUV, which seemed like a huge car to me, but he maneuvered it through the 101 traffic and the stadium parking lot flawlessly. I rode in back with Katie and tried not to pay too much attention.

Katie had enlisted me in her insistence on going. I think she would like to have Nate pay attention to her, but to this he was not paying much attention.

She is a young woman now—or perhaps better described as an older girl becoming a woman. She appears rather gawky at times but knows boys look at her body. Several times this summer she came over to see Minnie and me, and I felt like sending her home to put on more clothes.

Pressures on these kids to test out their attractiveness and to be sexy must be even stronger than they were in the 80s. I

304

wonder how the Westview administration handles it or seeks to help them. Of course, we had our "sex club" scandal back then too.

I fear Katie likes to try out flirting with me a touch as well. Last week she rubbed her finger in the hair of my left temple and told me she could buy some Grecian Formula for me. I denied any interest but did not need to look in the mirror. There is definitely graying there. I hope it makes the *head* of Zito and Sons look more mature—even distinguished.

George and Nate are already thinking about college. George has hopes he might get a basketball scholarship. He is already as tall as I am and may not be finished growing. Rob took him on a college tour in the East in the spring— some of the big ones: Princeton, Yale, also Wesleyan and Amherst, which might make more sense for him—and Rob's Georgetown. *Hey, how about your grandfather's and grandmother's University of Pennsylvania?* I gather Nate is looking mostly at in-state schools.

I should add that Mary and Marcus begin school this week too: half-day at a Jewish nursery school Gabriella thinks "will be just right for them to begin with. We won't tell Daddy." Neither will I, but I would love to be a fly on the wall to watch their first days.

Thursday October 4 2007

It was dark when I drove under the basketball hoop and pulled into the garage. The message light was blinking on the phone answering machine and before I had my jacket off the phone rang. It was Maryam Rajavi from across the street, hurrying to get her words out: "You should know that Shelley and Rob's boy—young George—fell down playing at your garage. They took him away in an ambulance we haven't seen in this neighborhood in a long time, with a siren and lights. They put him in and I saw a look of pain, though he wasn't making any noises. His face was pale, I saw. I heard he broke his leg."

I thanked her and sat in the dark kitchen. Minnie came and sat watching as though to console me. Basketball season would be starting soon. "How badly was the leg broken, Minnie?" How did it happen? Would it somehow be my fault for having created an "attractive nuisance?" "I should take it down"—after the damage was done? Maybe I could be sued! But, darn, I hoped George was not in too much pain. How long did it take a broken leg to mend? He was young.

I thought of calling, but instead marched myself over to 2816 White Oak and rang the bell. Who would answer? What to say?

It was Rob. "It's you, Marc. Sorry about this, but it is going to be O.K. Come in."

"I am the one who is sorry. I've tried to keep the pavement there in good condition."

"It's a fairly straight-forward break of the femur," Rob went on. "They'll probably set it with a few screws. That's what they do these days."

"Good. But I am sorry."

"Of course. We all are. But he's going to be O.K."

"Will he be able to play basketball this season?"

"Should. By the New Year anyway."

"Do they know how it happened?" I asked.

Not for sure. But I think he was hot-dogging it. Apparently started out in the middle of the street and then tried to dribble over the curb and around one of your trees."

I kept rehearsing some of Rob's words as I boiled water and found left over broccoli and chicken in the refrigerator.

"Hot-dogging it." In the rank of accidents that can happen, this evidently was far from number one. "My George is going to be O.K., Minnie. But he is going to hate missing part of the basketball season. Let's hope he will get lots of sympathy from the young ladies at Westview. Maybe he will have a cast they can sign and draw pictures on."

Sunday October 28 2007

Jim got the job with veterans' services after all. Something happened with the previous hire. From what his new boss said Jim thinks the young man may have been foisted off on the program by one of the cooperating companies and never really wanted it.

He does not start until December first or possibly the new year. There are still problems in getting the money together. Nor will it pay him as much as I am paying him. But he says that he feels affirmed and that this is what he wants to do. That part seems right to me.

Now I need to find someone to replace him. There was a time I thought Jim might head up all our rental operations, but, especially after Iraq, the work never did get his full attention. I will need someone with strong personnel skills as well as good at scheduling and with some overall knowledge of repairs and renovation. I may even need two people the way things are going—perhaps a younger one who can be trained.

Meanwhile Victor is off in Italy. "You say you always wanted to go," Gracia told him. "Well, now's the time." I saw them off at LAX. Victor looked a little dubious. "First time I've ever been across the Rockies," he said.

"Bring home some parmigiano," I told him "and do not worry about your company. We are doing just fine," which was basically true. The stock market had dropped a little but was still up there and, while some people think the housing market is too strong, we just sold two of our houses—one of them that is not yet finished.

Halloween 2007

It was a fun Halloween for me. Katie helped me carve two jack-o-lanterns: one scary, one friendly, and I put her in charge of doling out the Tootsie Pops, little Milky Way bars and assorted other candies. She dressed up as Countess Dracula for the occasion.

Meanwhile Jim and the twins came up because I thought it might be a safer neighborhood for them, and I took them to a dozen or more houses, just to be sure everyone knew this was my brother-in-law and my nephew and niece costumed as the Cookie Monster and a fairy angel.

Jim and I looked at some of the houses, speculating about their moving up here one day.

Sunday November 25 2007

It was certainly one of my best Thanksgivings. Steve flew down with his "personal friend," which was the way he introduced him. Bryan Chen is my age, a few years younger than Steve and a "super techie" of some sort. I put him to work showing me how to download to my iPod, but his skills obviously go far beyond that as a programmer and design engineer. I do not understand it all, but it was interesting to listen to him.

They stayed here and we also had several long conversations about state and national politics, in which they are both involved, even to the extent of donating money to campaigns. Of that, I confess, I have done very little, scandalized by the money that has now permeated the electoral process. With

Bush's approval ratings so low and no strong Republican candidate yet visible, we agreed it could be a good opportunity for Democrats. Steve says, "I am really behind Hillary. She has the experience, and I always thought of her as wiser than Bill and just as smart."

Bryan is interested in the articulate senator from Illinois who is coming along fast, though it is hard to imagine a man with a Kenyan father and a name like Obama getting nominated much less elected president of the United States. He is also relatively inexperienced. We did agree that Biden, Edwards, and the others are beginning to look out of the running, though I think Biden could make a good president, especially with his foreign policy experience and long history working with the Senate.

With George out of action, we made a foursome with Bob Tappen who I have played with before at the Tennis Center. Bryan is somewhat of a neophyte—probably doing it to be companionable with Steve, but they were obviously having fun together.

We "ate the bird," as Steve put it, with Shelley, Rob, George and Katie and Susan. There is clearly something going on with Susan. I have to remind myself that she is 77. I think she looks good for 77, but she can grow very quiet and then seem agitated about not knowing where her purse is or something. Then she will ask me again what it is that I do and make polite conversation before again falling silent. I fear she could be beginning to get Alzheimer's or some form of dementia. I will have to figure out a way to talk with Shelley.

George is still using crutches and I gather has not healed as rapidly as he and Rob had hoped, but "I'll be back in January for sure. Coach Ryan is counting on me. The Eagles are going to win it all this year." I told him that I used to be a personal trainer in case he need help getting back into shape, but they evidently have an excellent training room and program at the Academy now.

Rob at least feigned surprise in Steve's and Bryan's interest in Democratic politics and "the Clinton *frau* or some Barak *Hussein*, for heaven's sake, *Obama*. You wait. The Republicans will come up with somebody. We have a good bench."

15

New Year's Day 2008

I was asleep when the New Year rolled in and up just before 6 as I do almost automatically after these years at Zito and Sons. I had toasted the New Year begun in Times Square with a Scotch, was brushing my teeth when it hit Chicago and likely snoring before it reached Denver.

I have now done a decent home workout, and Minnie and I ran the better part of two miles. I could resolve to lose a few pounds but the body looks good, although the left knee is a bit sore and, I must say, there is a surprising amount of gray in my hair. Come June I will be 40 years old. Doc says I should think about giving up running and take up cycling or swimming. That would be tough. I'm going to try some new exercises to strengthen the muscles around the knee.

George came over this morning to shoot a few hoops with me. He still has a bit of what looks like a limp or a hitch, but he may just be being cautious. Someone taught him the phrase "Get back on the horse" and so we played a good game of Horse in which he thumped me. His coach plans to work him in carefully, but he is sure he will be back at point guard before the playoffs. Go Eagles! I swear he has grown another inch in rehabilitation.

Otherwise it has been a quiet New Year's. If I watch the Rose Bowl, it will be by myself. Steve came down for Christmas, but he and Bryan are now with friends of Bryan's family in the Bay Area. Bryan told Steve that his family, which has been in denial about his being gay, has been won over by Steve.

Although this is an election year, and the unexpected always has a way of happening, it could be a relatively quiet year, too. The war in Iraq is still a wild card, but whoever becomes president will have to try to extricate us and then figure out something about Afghanistan.

It still looks to me like Hillary will pull out the nomination and could become our first woman president, though Obama is not giving up easily. Despite some of the grumbling about him by "the true conservatives" McCain looks like the Republican fall-back candidate— but with Bush shackled to his ankles.

Now that I have had a year *de facto* running Zito and Sons, it is second nature for me to worry and try to guess about the direction of the economy—particularly the housing market. There are a few gloom and doom sayers out there—worrying that we have become a nation of borrowers. "Fear and greed," they say are the great motivators of the markets. That is too cynical for me, but there is, I guess, truth in it. That other me can remember growing up in the Great Depression, which was only ended by all the borrowing and spending on the world war. I am glad I am not an economist. In any case, we went along with two new hires, one to replace Jim: a smart young Filipina woman. I like her calm efficiency in dealing with complaints, repairs, collection problems. I have tasked her to complete the programming so that our renters can turn in work and repair orders online. We will still have a phone line for the elderly or those who do not otherwise want to use computers, but all the orders will be programmed from beginning to finish, including opportunity for comment and evaluation. Robert will supervise her and his son who graduated last year from Northridge and is working on becoming a CPA. Why not? This has always been a family business.

Saturday March 1 2008

The Westview Eagles men's basketball team had a good season. They were knocked out of the second round of the regional play-offs last night—a tough loss in overtime. But they won every other game but one after George returned. He steadied the team at point guard, drove often and well at the game last night—in the athletic facility I had once helped to build—and no one could tell that his leg had ever been broken. I also wanted to take some credit for helping him learn how best to take his jump shot from the top of the circle. He must have done—what?—a couple of thousand of those by now in front of my garage.

I spoke with a father of one of the other players who told me there was talk of a new gym and athletic facility because of the expanded enrollment and the attendance Westview was getting for basketball and other events. "This one isn't yet twenty-five years old," I complained. "I'm afraid that's the point," was his response." And. of course, it will be another fundraising opportunity. Apparently, according to this man, they have somebody ready to put his name on it.

Nate was there with a girlfriend. We sat together for much of the second half and overtime. I almost did not recognize him. He seems so suddenly a young man—with an emphasis on the man: a fashionable dark stubble on his rather swarthy face—his shirt unbuttoned enough to show the hair on his chest. He gave me a hug and introduced me to Kelsey as "the man who saved my life when I was a boy." Kelsey called him Nathan. He told me that he had decided to go to college in-state and evidently could go almost anywhere he wanted. He thought he wanted UCSB but was being counseled to think about UC Berkeley.

Kelsey told me confidently that she was going to Pomona where her mother had gone. I found sitting with her both a pleasurable and disturbing experience. For a time Nathan left us to see "who we might hook up with after." I explained in part how I knew George, and Kelsey let me know that he was a great guy who her best friend used to go out with.

I asked her about her classes and one of them turned out to be the senior seminar on the novel. This week they are reading Toni Morrison. I asked her if they were going to read any Joseph Conrad and drew a blank. I felt an urge to tell her about *Lord Jim* and the *Heart of Darkness*. Instead I told her that I had gone to Westview "a ways back" and was jealous of her because I had not been able to take that senior seminar.

I was jealous for another reason. I realized I was jealous of Nate for being able to be with her—perhaps to kiss and fondle—if not more. I reprimanded myself. The girl was half my age, but she exuded a youthful attractiveness. I had trouble not glancing over at her from time to time, almost touching when we together cheered a Westview basket. It may have been my imagination, but I did imagine that she had the feminine intuition to be aware of my attraction to her and to at least want to play with that. When George made the shot that sent the game into overtime, we jumped up and she gave me a full hug and I had to fight myself not to hold on.

After we told each other how sorry we were the Eagles had lost and she shook my hand and said "How wonderful to meet you, Marc. I hope I'll see you again sometime," I handed her over to Nate and came home feeling alone and embarrassed and with a longing that was sexual in ways that hurt. Even Minnie sensed something was bothering me when

I repeated several times "perfectly normal, perfectly normal." 'That's the way a man is supposed to feel from time to time, isn't it, old girl? I did not do anything wrong, did I?"

Easter March 23 2008

Surely this must be the very earliest Easter can come. Perhaps because I paid so little attention to the season of preparation and fasting, I tried not to look surprised when Victor and I were at Marcello's last week and he asked me to come to Easter Mass and brunch with Gracia, her daughter Miranda and Carlos and Isabel and her new husband Richard, and Gabriella and Jim. All the children would stay at Victor's and Gracia's house with a sitter he had hired. He has also has turned the house into kind of a grandchildren's paradise, complete with old-fashioned blocks and new legos, stuffed animals and other toys. Needless to say, he dotes on those kids.

But my good father Victor has been diagnosed with Parkinson's disease. I did not notice anything until he held up his left hand and arm. It is early stages, and he seemed to be taking it in Victor stride, talking of some of the treatments he could be given—remarkably sanguine. Indeed, I thought as we talked, what a remarkable man he is, having lost a son and a wife, loving me through my travails and missteps as a young man, building his business with the respect and loyalty of his employees, loving Gabriella so, overcoming his prejudice, caring and working for the poor. I found myself telling him that and telling him that I loved him. He teared up and wanted me to know that "though you're a bit of a putz, you're the best son to me—all I could have hoped for."

For a moment I thought we would hug and kiss right there, but the waiter set my Reuben sandwich down before me. The hug and kiss could come later without my telling Dad that I had gone off ossobuco for a while.

We had a fairly brief conversation about Zito and Sons or Z & S as one of our lawyers has suggested we might relabel ourselves. I did not tell him that.

Victor has been into the offices all of twice since the New Year—once to consult with Robert about his retirement fund and another time "to see if there is anything new." He decided "not much," but liked the "swell" office addition and remodeling we had done. He had, however, kept up with the news and at our lunch he wanted to know what I thought of the collapse of Bear Stearns: "When a financial company like that goes belly-up for two dollars a share, there has to be something rotten in Denmark or more likely on Wall Street. I've been reading about all the over-leveraging and complicated financial tricks and bets—some of it with housing loans. How are we doing there?"

I tried to reassure him that Zito and Sons was sound, although I could worry about the borrowing for the six houses we had in various stages of construction, but two were already under contract. We had sold another apartment building recently, though we had a few more vacancies than I would like. Victor now, however, switched gears and went over for the third or fourth time their itinerary in Italy, particularly the days in Firenze and the side trips to Assisi. "I wish we had a Saint Francis now for the church."

He had liked it so much that "another trip is in order. Gracia and I are going with a tour group to China in June. Why don't you come along?" I demurred. "Could not leave the business for that long, Dad."

"Well, business, business," he responded. "When you get to be as old as I am, you learn that some things can take care of themselves. And you've got Robert and other good people.

We'd really like you to come with us. I hope you don't inherit my Parkinson's. You only live once, you know."

"Maybe so. O.K." What else could I tell him? I love him. I have always wanted to see China.

On another front the news is not at all happy. Back in February, Shelley had another of her dinner parties and, while I found the petite Italian American woman attractive, we were a conversational mismatch. She thought of herself as quite an intellectual and, finding out I did not finish college and worked in the contracting business, turned her attention elsewhere. She may also have thought I was a little old for her.

Susan was again there. I imagine Shelley wants to keep her around people. She actually seemed to be doing better—tracking several of the conversations but with what appeared to be effort. Still she looked good to me. But yesterday I found out from Shelley she has been diagnosed with something called Lewy Body disease. I wish I had not gone to WebMD on that one.

Shelley hopes to "keep her in her own place for a while longer . . . with help during the day. "She will be happier there; I can check on her fairly often. And she has her little studio."

"Oh, I am glad she is still painting."

"Then maybe when George is off to college, she can be with us a few years. I don't know. I don't know what is best for her . . . and for us." She choked up.

"It's going to be O.K., Shelley," I tried. "I mean it is not O.K. I am sorry."

"Thank you. You're a good neighbor. I think Rob will be all right with it. I don't want to put her in some home. Not yet. She has so many good days."

"That's good."

She tried to laugh. "He can be so clinical about it. He was that way about George's leg, you remember? He's that way about everything."

"Maybe that's best."

"But this is different," she looked at me plaintively.

"I understand."

Ah, but it is Easter: time of new life and hope. And soon there will be the baseball season with Joe Torre as the Dodgers' new manager. And it is time for me to take Minnie for our walk.

Tuesday June 24 2008

Fourteen years after Head Harold Barnes' death I attended a Westview Academy graduation ceremony for the first time in 17 years. I would not have missed it. We returned from China on Sunday so I knew I would make it—if a bit jet-lagged.

It was the same Pomp and Circumstance brass, the same school song, although people around did not join in the way I thought they should. There was what sounded like the same prayer. From a distance the faculty even looked much the same in their black robes and hoods of many colors. Madeline Masters, Ed.D., presided with aplomb. I shook her hand at the reception, which also seemed much the same. I told her what a fine job I thought she was doing as Head. She did not ask my name, which I thought a mistake, but otherwise she seemed friendly and poised.

In their gowns and mortarboards George and Nathan appeared every inch the young, handsome graduates, which—in George's case particularly—is a lot of inches. I also congratulated Kelsey and met her parents—three of them. As it turned out her father was remarried. Her mother and father were not that much older than I while Sondra (as Kelsey called her) looked somewhere between my age and Kelsey's. There was a younger brother, too, who would graduate in two more years. I tried to imagine that I once looked something like that when attending Westview. Together they all made an attractive and good-looking family, while I got the impression that her mother was quite happy to have passed the father along to Sondra's responsibility.

Nathan is headed to UC Berkeley, probably for an engineering degree. I had not seen Ellen and Mark Provezano for several years. They thanked me "for all you have done for Nathan, including helping to steer him to this wonderful high school, which we never would have thought about." I refrained from telling them that I received a call from Barry in Advancement some weeks ago asking me if Westview might run a story about how one graduate once gave his bone marrow to help another "Westie" live and graduate. I did not remind Barry that I was not, in fact, a graduate and, after some reflection, disappointed him. I told him I did not want to embarrass Nathan or his family in any way, though I realized I was more concerned that my way of influencing Nate's tuition assistance could somehow leak out.

Rob and Shelley, with Katie likely having the most fun at the reception, thanked me for my friendship with them and George over the past years. George had passed on Stanford to go to Wesleyan—his choice. There, though without scholarship assistance, the coach had encouraged him to try out for basketball, and he had been told by a friend a year ahead of him there he would get better attention from his professors. They were all bursting with pride, as, more quietly, was I.

I am quite sleepy now. More on the China trip later. Suffice it to say, I was easily the youngest member of the tour and popular for that, especially with the women who took to calling me "young Marc." We tried to cover too much territory in 12 days, but imagine being able to see for the first time the Great Wall of China, all the new building in Shanghai, Tiananmen Square, the great Yangtze Dam, one of the redoubts of Mao in the early days of the Communist Revolution, and more. The apparatus of the controlling central party was discreetly evident, especially in our conversations with English-speaking Chinese, but so also was the rise out of poverty for millions. Several of the tour guides gave me kudos for my questions and knowledge of Chinese history. Victor expressed his surprise. I told them I had done a lot of reading in the past and in preparation.

And, lo and behold, Zito and Sons was still standing when I returned. I do not know what I would do without Robert, and Gabriella was there almost every day while I was gone. More on that later, too, but I am still two-thirds on Beijing time. Good night, Minnie. Good night, dear diary.

Sunday July 6th 2008

When I become king, the 4th of July will always fall on Friday. It seems to make for the best three day weekend with the patriotism and fireworks mostly on Friday and more time to rest and reflect on the weekend.

Victor was already in a reflective mode as we were cleaning up after he generously hosted the Forth Folly again "at the old homestead." He had been far more interested in the present-day China than in its history. "Don't know what to think for sure. Lots of good economic news—a miracle in a way, but bad stuff too with the crazy form of half-government and half-new-rich capitalism, the pollution, and the way they treat so many of their workers."

"But you have to compare it with where they were 20 or 30 years ago," I reminded him.

"Some of it has been done on our back," he contended. "I mean almost literally, with our companies shipping jobs over there and the huge trade imbalances we have with them just so Walmart and the computer and gadget people can sell us cheaper goods and make a lot of profit and even lower their taxes to do so."

"Hey, Dad, it's the Fourth of July," Jim laughed.

"I'm as patriotic as the next guy," Victor retorted. "But mark my words; you cannot build a good company or a sound economy without a labor force where most people have good jobs. You don't have to be a brain surgeon to know that. Even the Popes have said the same thing. Every good Catholic ought to know that." He lifted his aviator glasses onto his forehead and squinted his face at Jim and me as though expecting agreement.

"It's the American way, Dad." Jim responded. "Make as much money as you can. Give some away to good causes. Invest the rest to create more jobs. I used to hear that even in church."

"Yes," Victor conceded. "But not so true lately and not jobs at decent wages. A lot of the economists in the country are millionaires or want to be anyway. What do you expect them to say?"

"I do not disagree either, Dad," I spoke for his putatively good Catholic son-in-law as well. "Do you think the next election can do anything about it?"

"Ha," he responded. "Talk about crony capitalism in both parties. The politicians can't resist all that money themselves. How do you think we got where we are? But I don't give up. Hope springs eternal. The Republicans don't look so good right now and the Obama character has the nomination locked up. He talks a good game. Fact of the matter is I like him. Good for Black Americans in our country, don't you think, Jim?"

In the evening I again went over to Shelley's and Rob's to watch the distant bursts of fireworks from their back deck. Susan was there sitting quietly. I made conversation about George and Katherine. She told me several times how proud she was of "my grandchildren." Occasionally she pointed to one of the far away bursts of light. "They look like flowers," she told me.

"Showers of flowers," I agreed.

It seemed so quiet and peaceful—far away from the wars in the Middle East—only the delayed, muted booms from the showers of flowers reminders of wars past: "the rocket's red glare, the bombs bursting in air." Rob brought us all a Scotch and sat down with us. "Hers is mostly water," he confided to me.

"How's the practice of medicine?" I asked.

"Still practicing," he replied. "Actually it's good. We can't save them all, but it's remarkable the progress we're making. We could do more. There are too many middle men."

"In the hospital?"

"No. It's everywhere: government, regulation, the health insurance people, lawyers, even when it comes to the new drugs we need. Way too expensive. And the health insurance types are always looking for ways to cut money out of hospitals and doctors' fees. We have our problems at Children's, but it's the bean counters at the for-profit hospitals who are changing the way medicine is done in this country and not for the good. It's when profit becomes not only the driving force but practically the only force."

"Big Pharma say they need the millions in profits to stay in business."

"Hard to tell. They do so much advertising: 'Tell you doctor about the latest pink pill or something or other.'"

"I can understand the frustration. It's getting harder to provide good health insurance for our employees. Do you think Obama will be able to do anything?"

"Puhhh. I'm not voting for him."

"He is campaigning that he has some ideas about health care reform."

"If he'd listen to doctors, we might get somewhere."

"Do doctors have a plan?"

"There are some good ideas out there. We need to get rid of so many middle men. Costing too much. Excuse me. Hey, Susan, you all right? That one was pretty, wasn't it? But it's late. I have patients to see tomorrow. Still practicing. Still practicing."

Labor Day 2008

This morning I flew back from a long weekend with Steve and Bryan. We drove up into Sonoma and did some wine-tasting. We stayed in a B&B just outside St. Helena's that I want to remember. We came back on Sunday in time for our tennis game and played a somewhat unsuccessful doubles match with a friend of theirs. Bryan has been taking lessons, but I am not sure he has the tennis gene. I could teach him a thing or two, as I once did Steve, but that is not my job. The important thing is that the two of them get along well together. I wondered if they were thinking about getting married someday now that it is legal in California, although there is a ballot measure that would oppose it again. I do not think it will pass now.

Then Steve and I had a set of singles that I won rather handily. I think playing with Bryan has thrown Steve somewhat off his game. He did not seem to care.

Obama and McCain are out furiously campaigning. A couple of guys at work say they get a kick out of Sarah Palin, but I cannot understand why McCain chose her. If Victor is listening to their speechifying, I can imagine what he would say about their Labor Day rhetoric. Nor do the economic indicators look good. The housing market is getting softer; has been for a year. Fortunately we have two newly built houses under contract but have had to reduce the asking on another. We may slow down on the construction of the others. I would feel better if we had not run up our line of credit for them and our new apartment on Dover. The Dow is trying to hang in there but lost big on Friday.

On this Labor Day I can, however, report that Jim says, "I feel back on my feet now," which is his bad joke, not mine. Although he is the Associate Director, I have the impression he is pretty much the driving force for the whole public-private program to aid wounded and disabled veterans rehabilitate and find employment in Southern California. He's too polite to say so, but it sounds to me like the Director is a political appointee more interested in running for office than directing the program. Jim does complain about needing to spend so much of his time trying to raise money from businesses and corporations and educate them about veterans' employability. The Department of Veterans' Affairs provides only a part of their administrative budget. "The businesses are as much interested in getting good public relations for what they are doing as employing vets, but I can work with that. I just wish there were more time to work with my buddies and now even a couple of gals." But Jim is certainly back on his feet and believes what he is doing makes a difference.

Meanwhile, Mary and Marcus have reached the fearsome fours and will be full-time pre-Ks in their Jewish nursery school, and Pearl has day care at home and occasionally comes to work with Gabriella—which I do not like. Gabriella thinks we should have a nursery for our employees, but there are only three or four other kids under five right now. And it would be expensive. But, as she says, "I want to work and we could never get along with what they pay Jim," and I must admit I like having her around to talk about Z & S (we do sometimes abbreviate it) with her. My overburdened sister has a good business head on her shoulders.

Monday 15 September 2008

The hot news today is that Lehman Brothers is seeking bankruptcy protection. This is Lehman Brothers which has assets of something like 600 billion dollars—or maybe it is liabilities. One can sense the panic in New York and Washington.

Sunday September 21

Evidently many if not most of the Lehman's funds were invested in the housing market in one way or another. Hard to tell what it all means. Not good.

Shelley tells me they hear from George at least every other day by email. She thinks he is a little homesick and has already told them how cold it gets some nights.

"Wait until the southern California lad finds out how cold it gets in the East," I chortled.

"When did you live there," she asked, but then gave me his email and suggested I might write to him. "He really respects you, Marc. Send him something newsy and encouraging."

I think they forget that I never finished college. But I will gladly write.

Meanwhile, sophomore Katherine—now also sometimes Kate, sometimes Katie again—has become something of a problem child, at least to hear Shelley tell it. It is at times about clothes on the weekends, other times going to church, and dating. The list went on.

"I don't want to yell at her, but there are times when she just won't listen and she's sneaky. I try to get Rob to help. I know she worships him. Yesterday she said she hated me."

"I think most mothers go through something like this with teenage girls."

"Sometimes you amaze me."

"It is stuff I have read about. You find it in novels and the growing up with mommy memoirs."

"I guess. The big issue with us now is body-piercing."

"Ooooh. I have seen some of that on television."

"Fortunately, Rob is really on my side here. 'Ears and no more,' he insists. 'It is not hygienic.'" "'Only on my navel,' Katie begged him. 'Nobody will see it.'" "'Not safe. Not right. Not my daughter,' Rob told her. 'End of conversation.'"

"Good for him, I say," I said.

"I hope so. If she ever asks you, please tell her that too."

Monday September 29 2008

Black Monday or whatever we are supposed to call it: the stock market, they are reporting, lost over a trillion dollars— the largest one-day loss ever. Some predict the slump is not over. In the past year, I figure my 401.K is down more than

25%. I know it is worse for some. And I am relatively young with, one can hope, time to build back up again. We have employees who are retired or near retirement. What in the world were the gurus thinking? It is almost funny listening to the pundits scrambling to explain what they never foresaw—in some cases were cheering on.

Jim is afraid he could lose his job. I am sure a lot of other people are as well. But I am determined Zito and Sons is going to see it through and put a brave face on it—for Victor's sake, for Gabriella's sake, for Robert, for Anilin, and for every one of our employees.

Wednesday October 15, 2008

The Dodgers' run ended this evening with a 5-1 loss to the Phillies. Joe Torre got the Blue Crew into the series for the National League pennant but the Phillies and Cole Hamels were too much for them. 56,000 were there, but I have not been to a game for some time now. Nobody to go with. Maybe when Marcus and Mary are older.

Sunday October 19 2008

I must confess that I have not made a Rotary meeting for some time. Victor, who often still attends to "keep my hand in" and, no doubt, to see friends, asked me to come with him. "It's also a good support group, Marc. And we can all use that and maybe gain a little of the old perspective on things." I asked Robert to come with me for my own support.

There was a lot of anger and bitterness at the meeting—more than a few references to "us versus them." It was not always clear who the 'them' were other than the "big guys versus the small guys." Sometime the aim was at Washington who should have been watching out for this, or the Federal Reserve, but more fire began to center on "Wall Street versus Main Street" and the banks with all their leveraging. The word "casino" came up more than once.

I had certainly heard they were leveraging their money
20, 30, 40 times in order to make huge amounts of money
when the bets went right. What I do not understand was how
these new derivative instruments—the mortgage-backed
securities and collateral debt obligations—enabled them to
magnify their debts and so their bets many times over. "They
are complicated," Robert explained, "but that is one of their
main purposes—so regulators and even stockholders cannot
see the size of the wagers. Whatever else they tell you that is
why a huge part of the Wall Street debt bail out has to go to
AIG. The other investment banks were using their so-called
insurance to insure their debts except that they never had
anywhere near the insurance. They were gambling too."

"That may be right as far as it goes." Don Larson, a retired
banker who is even older than Victor, commented after many
of the others had gone: "But everyone was doing the borrowing and the new bankers were letting them have the money
for houses, for refinancing, for vacations, and boats and
more—a lot of people who had no business getting loans. In
my day, that would never have happened. What about you,
Victor? You've built good houses with sound mortgages in
your time."

"Proud of it," Victor told him. "But we hardly ever had
trouble with people taking out bad loans. In any case, that
wasn't our business. We weren't making loans and we never
got in over our heads, did we Marc? But I tell you one thing
from my experience. You watch: when this thing is over the
people who had the money will still have most of the money.
It's the people who didn't have much to begin with who will
be out of jobs or out of houses."

Victor asked to come back to the offices with Robert and
me. I figured he wanted some reassurance from us about the
company. As we drove, he offered to return to work. "No pay.

Just another head and set of hands. These are tough times, but we've been through other ones. How much debt do we have anyway?" I let Robert do most of the talking. He first thanked Victor for his offer, but "you built a strong company here, Mr. Zito. Marcus, with Gabriella's help, can handle this bubble. Here's how."

Out came the spreadsheets and a discussion of debt to assets and income projections. Robert and I had been through some of this before, but it sounded more convincing as he was explaining it to Victor. There were only four houses for which we did not have buyers. While we owed for the land they are on, we should probably go ahead and finish them or at least get them to a place where they were safe to let sit for a few months. We could either finish them then or wait a few more months or even a year to see if the price improved—perhaps refinancing if we could.

The apartments and the apartment management business were our greatest assets and backstop now. We owed on two of the buildings, but had the income to manage that debt. If necessary we could sell a building or two, but he advised against that. "Counter-intuitively." he advised, "and especially if interest rates stay down, maybe we should become buyers rather than sellers. If people keep losing their homes, the rental market should get stronger. People need somewhere to live."

"You make it sound almost easy," Victor responded.

"No," Robert said. "There's work to be done and we must carefully monitor. No one knows where this is going. We should plan for a recession."

"I agree, Dad," I put in.

"And our work force?" he asked. "My employees?"

"We will do the very best we can," I told him.

"We will," Robert added, "but if we are not building houses it will be a challenge. We can shift some people to the apartment work especially if and when that picks up. And hire people back when we can. Some of the younger ones may have to go for a while. It's going to be tough. We're not immune."

"That's what makes me mad," Victor told us. "Those damn fancy-pants bankers," which was about the strongest language I had ever heard from my good Catholic father.

December 24 2008

Shelley came over this afternoon with a beautifully wrapped present "to put under your Christmas tree." After telling her that "She shouldn't have" and that I did not have a Christmas tree, she readily agreed that I could open it. I recognized instantly the artist working in water colors and charcoal.

"Mother wanted you to have it. She began it after that night watching the fireworks from the back deck."

"Showers of flowers," I remembered.

"They do look like flowers, don't they? She isn't the painter she was."

"I don't know. This is beautifully imagined—more abstract perhaps."

I have not decided where to hang it yet. I may keep it in the kitchen.

16

New Year's Day 2009

Obama gets to give it a try—officially in about three weeks. What a mess he has inherited. But then it was probably the mess that enabled his election: two wars, both partly paid for with huge debt purchased by the Chinese, and the economy headed into a deepening recession. But we must not give up hope for America, both Victor and Jim are reminding me, though I worry that a measure of desperation defeated McCain, and we shall have to see whether the Democrats or Republicans are better at either managing or manipulating all the deep concern and fear that is out there in the populace.

It will be an historic day when Michelle Obama and those two girls move into the White House with their half-Black, but to many Americans, Black father. It will be a great day in this book, but also open to political and media finagling—some of it subtle, some not so subtle.

Meanwhile it is a chilly Southern California morning, though headed into the upper 60s in time for Oregon to play our USC Trojans in a sold out Rose Bowl where the ticket price for seats is $125 and the game is sponsored by Citi. That stands for the Citigroup, Inc., which is one of our huge financial services corporations, whose shareholders include large funding from the Middle East and Singapore, and which recently had to be bailed out by the government—that is, us.

How do I know these things? I *google* them. For a man used to having to go to the library and encyclopedias to look things up, it seems almost like cheating. I thought I had seen a lot of change in my lifetime from almost everyone owning a radio, cars and then on to TV and digital television, the jet airplane, penicillin and antibiotics. But, with the internet, information technology, Wikipedia, Google and who knows what else, change seems exponential.

Robert has suggested that our management team and foremen should switch from our Blackberries to new iPhones, which is fine by me since I have never used my Blackberry that much. But someone will need to teach me how to use a "smart phone." Maybe that person will be Katie, who desperately wants one of her own. She has also suggested that I join Facebook. The last "Facebook" I remember was a picture directory the students put together at Westview. Katie's is an online social networking service where people trade profiles and pictures and probably gossip as well as "liking" each other. How do I know? I googled it.

Rob thinks I should be on "LinkedIn, which is social networking for "professionals." I am far from sure I can keep up with it all.

Katherine (as she has asked me to call her most recently) came over to wish me a Happy New Year and to see "if you wanted to talk." I get visits like this maybe as often as once or twice a month. Ostensibly, I guess, I am the lonely one.

She sometimes asks me what it was like to be a sophomore at Westview "back then:" what the guys wore, what the girls wore, whether I dated. She asked me when I got my first kiss. I told her I did not remember and that the question was out of bounds anyway—being concerned where that line of questioning might lead.

I did tell her that none of the girls then had tattoos and would not have liked body piercing, and that I did not think that was attractive. This information she took in without comment.

Today, I suggested we should treat Minnie to a walk. I asked Katherine about the classes she would be taking in the winter/spring semester. The answer was more interesting to me than it seemed to her.

We talked about George and agreed that he looked good. Katherine expressed surprise that "he didn't date anyone and just hung out with the guys" when home for Christmas. I told her that was "perfectly normal."

"But," she replied, "I don't think he has a girl at Wesleyan either, but he says there are nice ones out there." That also, I told her, was perfectly normal and perhaps made sense for a freshman in college.

"And for sophomores in high school, I guess?" she half-asked.

"Yep," I responded. "'Perfectly normal and good for you. Have you made any New Year's resolutions?"

"Not really. I should probably study harder."

"Maybe more efficiently. Sometimes it helps not to have distractions or be thinking of two things at once."

"Did you make any resolutions?"

"Hmmm. Probably should. Not to work any harder. Maybe more time for tennis. Get to the gym more regularly. And, of course, more time for you. Right, Minnie?"

"You're talking to a dog, you know. Don't you ever get lonely?"

"Oh no . . . maybe a little."

"Mom thinks you are. We both think you ought to get married."

"Oh do you? Nice of you to be concerned."

"So have you ever tried online dating?"

"No. I do not think that is right for me."

"So do you think you'll ever get married?"

"Possibly. But what if I told you it was none of your business, young lady?"

"Maybe you should try dyeing your hair. It's getting a lot of gray in it."

"I guess it is."

"You don't want to look old."

"Thank you."

"I mean, you don't look old. You just don't want to."

Monday Groundhog Day 2009

Today Harold David Barnes would be 83 years old. Today Marcus Ditmar Zito, the CEO of Zito and Sons Construction and Rental Properties notified three employees, one of whom has been with the company over eight years, that their services were no longer required as of the end of the month. Five more were told that their hours would be reduced to half-time. All of this was done in the name of corporate responsibility. I have not told Victor. Unless he presses me, I will not tell him. Still, he must have had some slack periods in the past.

We are down to five houses—having sold the one. I let the Brennans out of their contract for the second one. In the name of corporate responsibility I should not have, but their mortgage would already have been more than the new assessed value. Two of the others houses are nearly finished, and we may just keep the other two unfinished until we see how the market goes.

Robert was right about rentals. Our few vacancies are quickly relet, but we do have a small rash of delinquencies—probably mostly from people who have lost their jobs. We have not had to evict anyone . . . yet.

I will confess that I did look at several online dating services the last weeks or so. I cannot seem to get to the part of entering my personal data: single, white, male, well-built. Did not go to college. Graying hair.

Easter April 12 2009
We all went to Mass at Our Lady of Grace this morning where it was standing room only and we sang and heartily proclaimed "The Lord is risen indeed." And, indeed, parishioners seemed full of Easter happiness and hope.

Victor waited until afterwards to tell us that "your Uncle Tony died yesterday, Holy Saturday."

I felt ashamed. "I am so sorry, Dad. I did not even know he was that sick. How many years did he work for us?"

"It's all right son," Victor put his arm on my shoulder. "He didn't want people to know. In the midst of life we are in death," he added as though to console us both.

It must be awkward for the priests to have funerals shortly after Easter, but, then, they must be used to it. We will say good-bye to Tony and commend him to this risen Jesus on Thursday.

Sunday April 26 2009
On Thursday, from somewhere deep in space, there was a gamma ray burst that lasted all of ten seconds. It may have come from the explosion of a massive star. It was the oldest and furthest distant such burst ever detected—like from 13

335

billion years ago when the universe was only 600 million or so years old. That ought to bring perspective on what goes on here. Maybe too much perspective, if you ask me.

Memorial Day May 25 2009

The last of the British troops are leaving Iraq this week. I guess that leaves only us—down to about a dozen or so of "the best of America" dying a month to add to those we remember this Memorial Day. And, as Jim would be the first to point out, twenty times that number are getting wounded, not counting the ones with Post Traumatic Stress Disorder, PTSD as we are learning to call it.

Obama laid the customary wreath at the Tomb of the Unknowns in Arlington Cemetery and then felt he had to continue the practice of sending one to the Arlington Confederate Monument, to which a number of people objected as they felt it honored as heroes those who had fought to maintain slavery in America. Obama then also sent a wreath to the African American Civil War Memorial to honor all the Blacks who fought and died during our Civil War.

I guess it is still true that more Americans died in the Civil War than in all our other wars put together. Perhaps in some sense we are still fighting that war, which may be an indicator of how hard it will be to extricate ourselves from the ones in Iraq and Afghanistan. I wish it all could be ended by sending out wreaths.

In the meantime North Korea has set off a nuclear "device" and rumor has it that General Motors is about to file for bankruptcy. I would say President Obama has his hands full. General Motors! I must have owned five or six General

Motors cars in my lifetimes and have a 2005 Buick LeSabre now.

I have been using Katherine as my best informant on her grandmother's status and health. Using the key I gave to Shelley and "for Katie when she feels like giving Minnie a walk," Katherine lets herself into my place perhaps more often than she should. The door opened again yesterday, "to see how you are doing and if Minnie wants to go out with me." Of course, Minnie wanted to go out and jumps up and begins wagging furiously the moment she even guesses it is Katherine at the door.

There was a lot of Katherine to see on a pleasant late May Sunday afternoon. I hoped that the neighbors understood that I was a friend of the family.

The good news is that there is no sign of body piercing or even tattoos anywhere visible, which included a glimpse of her belly button.

The news on Susan seems to be more mixed. Through Katherine's eyes she still gets around all right: "just kinda slow and she shuffles her feet. But she's so nice."

"Forgetful?"

"Sort of. I remind her of things and she will laugh. Sometimes I don't know why. But Dad thinks she's doing pretty well. Mom says she is strong-willed about keeping her independence."

"That does not surprise me. Good for her."

"So she has this woman who lives with her in her apartment."

"So what happened to her house?"

"I don't know. That was a year or so ago. I loved that house."

"I can understand. It was a nice house. Do you know where the apartment is?"

"No. But not too far."

Tuesday May 26 2009

I checked. Susan is not in one of our apartments. I wish she were.

Fourth of July 2009

The bad news is that the drop in housing prices has hit pretty hard, even here, and caused Victor and Gracia to postpone their plans for downsizing. The good news is that they are holding on to "the old homestead" and we can again have the Fourth Folly there this afternoon.

We will be festive, but it will be hard not to notice several fewer of our employees and their families there to eat the hotdogs. I told Victor about the Zito and Sons downsizing last month. I figured that I had to. He was more sad than angry and wanted to encourage me: "Use it as a time to plan ahead to when you'll be able to rehire. Smaller can be smart if it can be stronger, but then build back slowly."

He also told me to try and stay in touch with the people we had to let go. "See how they're doing—especially about their health care. They may be putting odd jobs together. If you can even give them some occasional work, let 'em know. It will pay off some day."

"Maybe, too," he went on, while rubbing his chin and looking a bit sly, "there is a way we could help out with some of those houses that are getting repossessed. The banks are crazy just to let them sit there. Better to let people live in them, but maybe we could be the ones to look after them and keep them in shape until people come to their senses."

Jim has been worrying about his job, too—not so much about keeping it as its effectiveness in "really helping my vets." "Have you heard about the suicide rate among the young ones?" His boss, he says, has to spend too much of his time "just holding on to the budgeted money from the VA," and Jim "too much of my time with the businesses and corporations, raising dough and helping them with their PR."

"Another problem," he went on, "is with the competition. There are hundreds, if not thousands of charities that have "Veterans" in their name—some of them out-and-out scams or ways for telemarketers and a few so-called executives to make big bucks." Apparently hardly any of it is getting through to the veterans. "I don't want to be any part of that," says Jim slamming his fist into his other hand.

That, I think, on the Fourth of July, is about as patriotic as it gets.

I, on my other hand, have convinced Jim and Gabriella to come with me tomorrow and look at a house a couple blocks from here. I found out the Donatellis are moving and the prices may be about as good as they are going to get. It is still a reach for Gabriella and Jim, though I could make them a loan if they would let me. It is a good house with "good bones" as they say and four or possibly five bedrooms, which they need.

Then this evening I shall again stroll over to Shelley's and Rob's to watch the distant fireworks from their back deck, have a Scotch, and, I hope, sit with Susan—making my own assessment of how she is doing. I know Shelley, and Rob too, are seeing to her care as best they can. Were it somehow possible, I would take her in myself.

And maybe "big George" will be there. We have only had one brief hoop session since he came home for the summer, but it sounds like a good first year at Wesleyan. He did play freshmen basketball and "am pretty sure I'll make the varsity next year." Not sure what he wants to major in or "to do with my life but I'm thinking about one of the life sciences."

Labor Day 2009

I am scrawling this on a bumpy plane back from San Francisco—after spending three days again with Steve and Bryan—perhaps having become our Labor Day weekend tradition. School, at least for the teachers, had already begun amid cutbacks in teachers, staff, and programs, and larger classes. Steve believes that before too long he may have to use his own money for some of the class science experiments: "Madness," he griped. "We ought to be spending more on these kids. Sure, we could pull back on some administrative stuff and save here and there, but they're cutting into the flesh now."

Perhaps it was love more than economics, but Bryan piled on about the importance of education and complained about the cuts to the community and state college budgets. "Companies like mine have a lot of money saved up. Just sitting there. We could pay more in taxes for a while."

"An old economic theory was for governments to tax and save during good times and cut taxes and spend in tough ones. We seem to do the opposite," was my contribution. "Maybe just human nature."

But mostly we had good times together. I do like their friends. It is not hard to believe that gay men enjoy one another's company more than straight men. That could be because many of them have fewer family responsibilities, but I think there is more to it.

Although neither one of us is playing as well as we did in past years, Steve and I may have enjoyed the tennis and companionship more. At least for the time being, Bryan has given up on tennis and gone back to his first love of swimming, which Steve says he hates. In this they are not unlike other married couples which they are not yet legally. Two of their friends were married before Proposition 8 was voted in—I gather to the surprise and then ire of a number of them. The hope now is to have it overturned in the courts.

Sunday October 25 2009

I am tired for a different reason this evening. Uncle Marcus was allowed to baby sit for the weekend with little Marcus, Mary (who are now kindergarteners at Our Lady of Grace), and Pearl. It took me several weeks to talk them into it: not sure whether Gabriella and Jim thought I was incompetent or did not really mean it or both. Fortunately, Granny Pearl was there much of the day on Saturday. We made a good team, although it was still three against two. My best tactic was to arrange for Mary to play with Pearl and then make up some game for the two Marcuses: probably rather sexist but it sometimes worked.

One of the rules in the Lord household is practically no television. I am making up for it now by watching my Angels play the hated Yankees for the American League pennant on my large digital television on which one can see almost every blade of grass. They are *my* Angels because the Dodgers have been knocked out again by the Phillies. I did however, go to my first Chavez Ravine game in several years and saw the Dodgers win their one game in the series. The losing pitcher in relief was no less than Chan Ho Park, once the Korean hero of Dodger Stadium.

I was taken to the game by a woman I know through Rotary—and her two children—when her husband suddenly could not make it. I found myself wishing she were not married.

They interrupted the game tonight for a quick news summary, the lead item being that bombings today in Baghdad killed 155 and wounded more than 700. Now that we are slowly getting out, they are killing more and more of each other.

Looks like it will be the Yankees and Phillies in the World Series.

Veterans' Day November 11 2009

My contribution to Veterans' Day was to have Jim come yesterday and speak to our assembled Rotarians. He was good: tough, dedicated, emphasizing the positive and the opportunities, but not skipping the problems. Only in the Q and A did some of the negatives come up: criticizing politicians for too much talk and not enough support for wounded veterans and the lack of employment opportunities generally in "our wounded economy." Jim's response was to appeal directly to those of us who were employers "to make a sincere effort to hire one or two of these boys and women—some of whom have literally given an arm or a leg for you. I know you're going to give it a shot, aren't you, Marcus?"

The conversation also veered into the new health insurance and expansion program, which looks like it might be passed. Veterans apparently have their own program with its problems, but Jim opined that the new act could also help veterans and their families. The general verdict was that something had to be done but that the various political and special interest forces might be making it too complicated for ordinary folks. I sang my song about the burden of rising health insurance costs on small companies like ours and that the most basic need was to do something about the huge profits that some individuals and companies were making out of other people's health problems. I saw several friends nod their heads but no one hummed or sang along.

Jim also made an appeal for our club to support his work financially. The request has to be dealt with by a committee— a committee that I was elected to in September. I will see to it that we give him something.

17

New Year's Day 2010

Chesley B. "Sully" Sullenberger III, the captain who landed that powerless jet in the Hudson River, is the Grand Marshall of this morning's Rose Parade. He seems like one cool customer and hero. Maybe we should put him in charge of the economy.

2010 has to be a better year. Maybe I am slower than others, but only now do I see how much of a mess all these sub-prime loans and "tranches" of CDOs have made of the housing market and people's lives, with Countrywide—one of the chief culprits and predators—headquartered practically down the street in Calabasas. "Countrywide is on your side," was their *ad nauseam* jingle. I cannot imagine why Bank of America wanted to take them over. "I'm sorry now," will become their jingle one of these days.

Zito and Sons is, however, going to survive and maybe better than that. If we do decide to become the Z & S Corporation it will not be because any damage has been done to our name like that of Countrywide.

Our salvation is that people do need places to live and renting is a smart move for now—not least for younger people. It is tempting to buy more buildings at these low interest rates, but also to sell when the price is right to investors who are looking for a steady stream of income and probably tax write offs. We can both buy and sell and often continue to manage the sold building. Renting houses is looking profitable, too, and both Robert and Gabriella think we might do more than get our feet wet.

It will help everyone if the economy improves and we can get the unemployment rate down, but those who call themselves conservatives seem to think the best way to do that is through austerity budgets and preaching fear about future deficits. Unfortunately, that is what will get them a deeper recession and future deficits. Once there is recovery will be the time to deal with the deficits, especially the costs of medical care and probably then raise some taxes too.

Meanwhile the effort to get something even approximating health care for everyone in America struggles on. Victor has discovered the internet and how to do email attachments and links. He is kind enough "to keep you informed, Marcus. As you can see the lobbyists are having a field day and the longer it takes means more payoffs for the politicians."

And then, "Read this: the conservatives who once thought individual mandates would be wonderful are now against them."

"Read this: Republicans who say they want to hold down the cost of Medicare are calling attempts to look at end of life issues and costs 'death panels.'"

"Look at this: The Democrats have caved again. Nothing will be done to hold down rising rates or the cost of drugs. Rube Goldberg rides again."

Gabriella gets them too. I feel some responsibility to respond. But when I see her and Jim and my fetching nieces and high-octane nephew this afternoon, she will say, "I am so glad Daddy keeps interested in things and has something to do." Jim will be more interested in the football game.

The gym is open on New Year's day—probably for people full of New Year's resolutions after a couple of weeks of overeating and perhaps a night of debauchery. If I am going to be "the silver fox" (as Shelley, I hope searching for a compliment, called me a few days ago), I better at least resolve to keep this body in shape.—for whom I do not know. "I will do it for you and me, Minnie. I will be the sleek silver fox."

Sunday January 17 2010

Over 300,000 Haitians were killed in an earthquake last week. What else could happen to that impoverished island? I googled to find out that we do have a club there. "Le Rotary est une association de membres issus des milieux d'affaires et des professions libérales qui se consacrent à l'action humanitaire et encouragent l'observation de règles de haute probité dans l'exercice de toute profession ainsi que l'entente entre les peuples." My French is at least still up to that. I hope our Rotary can reach out in *l'action humanitaire* to them.

Palm Sunday March 28 2010

They finally got the Patient Protection and Affordable Care Act passed and signed. It looks like progress, especially in covering a number of the poor and uninsured and making certain that people will not be rejected or dropped for "prior conditions." That has been a problem for us when making new hires, especially any older ones. And, I would hope, they can improve on it as it goes along.

But the fact that not a single Republican voted for it is worrisome. The state of American politics is something. There ought to have been at least a few Republicans who thought it was an improvement on balance, but I guess they could not stand letting Obama and the Democrats have any credit for it. I would believe them more if they had alternative proposals.

I thought Rob might be apoplectic, but he is too clinical for that. He did find some good aspects and knows the A.M.A. supported it, "but it doesn't solve the major problems and looks like government bureaucracy on top of private insurers bureaucracies, all costing us money and trying to tell doctors what to do. And we won't have enough doctors to treat all the added patients."

I thought about asking whose fault the shortage of doctors was, but instead said, "Then maybe we should get more doctors."

"Easier said than done," he replied. "And a lot more money just to educate them. And it doesn't help to lure doctors from other countries. What about the state of medical care there?"

I will be interested to hear what Victor thinks. I am sure I will.

Easter April 4 2010

This was different. Last night I went to an Easter liturgy that lasted over two hours in what must be a quite progressive church. The place was full of gays and lesbians. It started off solemnly with a long series of readings from the Bible and then broke out into shouts and bells, songs and incense with a baptism of two adult men. Steve told me that he and Bryan do not get to church that often, but they go to St. Gregory's when they do.

We again had a good two days together. They are in some ways my best friends, and I have come to know several of their friends. I am, however, finding it awkward at times—even painful. Their friends understandably seem to assume that I am gay, too, and I do not know how to be deftly polite in turning away their advances. I just move away or say something stupid about not feeling well. I should ask Steve or Bryan how to help me with this, but have not figured out quite how to ask them. On the other hand, I was very attracted to one of their female friends—but she would have had the opposite problem with me.

I have an email from Victor wishing me a Happy Easter from Haiti where he—Parkinson's and all— is with some church group. Evidently they have plans to help rebuild a school: "school first, then the church."

Sunday April 25 2010

Jim has a new job: with Walmart. I could not believe it either, but, to hear him tell it, the position made a kind of sense. Apparently he was having more success getting veterans—and especially his veterans with amputations and other handicaps—employed with Walmart than anywhere else. The problem, of course, is with their pay and benefits, but at least a couple of them that have stuck are rising through the ranks. His job is to help them get employed ("Hey man, it's better than being unemployed!") and with on the job training and then some publicity and public relations. He says he does not mind the latter as long as he has some real successes to talk about. Maybe I will have to get off my high horse and start shopping at Walmart. But we shall see. The Walton family did not make all that money by putting employees first.

Meanwhile, British Petroleum—or someone working for them—has blown a hole in the floor of the Caribbean off New Orleans that is pushing out 5,000 barrels of oil into the ocean every day, though some say it may be ten times that amount. Worse, eleven people were killed and others injured. When Susan and I were young marrieds we had a short vacation in Biloxi. I wonder what all that oil is going to do to the tourist and fishing industries?

There may not have been enough regulations, but one might suspect the rules in place were avoided or gamed in some way. Evidently the rig was being operated under a Marshall Islands flag of convenience. It is not hard to guess why that was so. When there are that many billions of dollars involved, there must be a lot of motivation to try to take short cuts and hold on to chunks of it. And we do have to have our oil, almost no matter the cost.

The rig sank to the bottom on Earth Day.

Memorial Day 2010

So far so good with Jim and Walmart. Every once in a while I remind him that I am a veteran too. "Not one who got shot at or blown up," he laughs. "Those are the ones who count the most."

"Well," I think to myself, "I could tell him about my purple heart and the Battle of the Bulge," which makes me wonder how many veterans are still left from that war. They would all be in their mid-80s or above by now.

Victor was born during that war and then never had to serve in the military. He chuckles and says, "I'm a patriotic peacenik who loves our vets," and gives his version of a salute.

I try to have lunch with him every few months—sometimes at Marcello's. But last week we met in the same—but refurbished conference room, where Gracia brought us sandwiches, and he was so good to me those years ago. That is when I learned that he and Gracia were moving, "to a nice townhouse in Woodland Hills. Come see it. Extra bedroom if you want to stay. Also a sofa and a blow-up bed if those little tykes want to come visit their gramps."

Although he did not get all the money he wanted for "the place we raised you kids," and the price of the townhouse was "no bargain, but pretty good," I would bet he still has close to half a million to put in the bank.

"This way we can travel more, and, though the medicine is doing me good, I can't work around the place like I used to. Not fair to Gracia." So, he tells me, he is going back to Haiti in a few weeks and Gracia is making plans for a trip for them both to Mexico in the fall. It looks like I had better make plans for hosting the Fourth Folly.

Monday July 5th 2010

Whew! I am recovering. 2823 White Oak is recovering. The way Minnie is lying around, I think even she is recovering, especially after having Mary, Marcus, and Pearl here too. But I pronounce the first White Oak Fourth Folly to have been a success.

Gabriella and Jim said they would help and tried to, but they have their hands more than full. Victor is in Haiti until Wednesday. I hired a couple who advertised online and they helped cater and do much of the setting up and clean up. But I—in my new red, white, and blue "King of Grillers" apron—cooked the brats and wienies on my also new outdoor gas grill. It was crowded and I imagine the neighbors were not thrilled. We may have to try something different next year.

It was a relief to wander over to Shelley's and Rob's after dark—with a sweater as it had cooled off considerably after a day in the low 80s. Rob soon had my Scotch for me and the distant boom and flowering of the fireworks had a sameness that was comforting—almost soporific.

It was just the four of us. One reason I had come was to thank Susan for her painting. She did not seem to remember.

Instead she took my hand and ran her fingers over its back as if exploring it.

Shelley and Rob caught me up on George and Katie: George, with a summer job at Children's Hospital and planning on majoring in molecular biology at Wesleyan; Katie, having become a more serious student and now taking two summer school courses. We agreed that the influence of peers, beginning themselves to think about colleges in their futures, can be stimulating and constructive in teenagers' lives. It is one of the advantages of going to a school like Westview.

Then they shifted to talk about Susan in the way people do of one another when they believe the person is not able to understand. "It's no longer working well to have her in her apartment, even with a live-in companion. Viola herself is getting on and mother is more difficult to manage just in the day to day things," Shelley explained.

"We're thinking about her moving in with us . . . to see how it goes," Rob added.

Shelley lowered her voice. "I'm just not really ready to put her into some care facility—even if it is the best we can find."

"Though we know that day will come." Rob put his arm around Shelley's shoulder. "But maybe she can still have a good year or so."

Susan leaned closer to me and whispered, "They're talking about me, you know."

Sunday August 28 2010

Jim and Gabriella and, of course my nephew and nieces have a new house—on a cul-de-sac less than three blocks away. They spotted it when they were driving home from the Folly. Not many houses have been on the market in the neighborhood as people are hanging on hoping their prices will come back up. I still think they may have paid too much, but it is yet a good price and a good house for them. We had some of our team check it over and will do a couple quick modifications and some painting. They want to be in by Labor Day and have the twins start first grade at the local elementary school to see how that goes. "And Marc, I want to be back at work full time. I know you need me and we need the money. It helps that Granny Pearl is retiring and can spend more time with the kiddies."

"Could not agree more," I told her, but I do have a few concerns. I like to consult, and get as much input as I can, but I have been making the major decisions pretty much on my own for some time now, for the most part cautious ones in this economy. But Zito and Sons is solid and still managing to add to our inventory here and there. I do not want to rock the boat.

For the moment, however, my bigger concern is that Jim and the children with Gabriella be accepted if not welcomed into this neighborhood. We have a lot of ethnic and religious diversity, several Muslim families, and it is pretty much live and let live around here. But I have never seen a Black in the entire neighborhood. It will help that I am fairly well known; they are my relatives—which I will figure out how to make known to their neighbors and mine. Early on I should give a little party for them.

Meanwhile it has already been something of a moving day across the street. The biggest problem turned out to be George, who did not like giving up—even to his beloved grandmother—the room in which he was raised and that

gave him some sense of security and "home." Nor did
Katherine or Katie (she seems to be firmly Katie again) want
to be relegated to the bathroom down the hall. But, once
again, it was Zito and Sons to the rescue: Grandmother now
has her own room with her own bathroom, and George has
temporary quarters in the unfinished attic area which we will
finish for them in the fall—presuming we can get a permit
and the homeowner's association architecture committee to
agree. I should be able to pull that off. And I bet grandson
George will come to like his new space, even if the big junior
in college and hot-shot on the Wesleyan basketball team will
be unlikely to make much use of it.

I invited Steve and Bryan down for the weekend, suggesting to Steve that it would also be good for him to have a little
time with his mother. Indeed, we took her to the Getty, got her
a wheelchair, saw a photography exhibit, in which she showed
some interest, sat out in the gardens, took in the view down
to the Palos Verdes peninsula, and treated ourselves to lunch.
I think what I enjoyed the most was watching how attentive
Bryan was to Susan even after she had given up trying to figure
out who he was, except for telling Steve several times, "He is
such a nice young man," and then asking loudly enough to
turn a half-dozen heads in the Getty cafeteria, "Is he Chinese?"

Last evening I had Jim and Gabriella and the children
over so Steve and Bryan could meet some of my family. I have
enough Legos, toy cars, and an old-fashioned box of wooden
bricks to keep Mary, Marcus, and Pearl occupied part of the
time—plus a Curious George video for them whether their
parents wanted them to watch it or not.

We had a conversation that I did not fully understand about
Proposition 8 and the prospects of gays being able to marry

legally in California. I do understand that the courts have overturned—or nearly overturned—Proposition 8, but that it is still in effect in some measure while it is being appealed. Rather unhelpfully (I think it was the Scotch) I interjected that I remembered a time when gays and lesbians would be rather critical of "the heterosexist institution of marriage." The four of them looked at me as though I were some kind of Neanderthal and rather impatiently explained to me that it was a matter of human rights and equal treatment under the law.

Jim appropriately used the eve of Labor Day to make a little speech on behalf of employment for veterans—especially those who had been wounded, and concluded it (he had had a Scotch too) with his disappointment that "my wife's and brother-in-law's company has not yet employed a single one of them."

I gathered my senses and explained that, because of the recession we had not been able to make many additional hires and also that the kind of contracting and construction work we did was not very—I think the word I used was—"conducive" to other than the able-bodied. I looked to Gabriella for some kind of support or confirmation. I did not get any.

Halloween 2010

It was fun to have a Halloween visit from my neighbors Marcus, Mary, and Pearl. Marcus was an astronaut, Pearl said she was a fairy princess, and I am not sure what Mary was, though it was meant to be scary: perhaps a zombie of some kind. With ice cream and cake I bribed Katie and a friend to "staff" my house while I then went around with Jim and the kids to a dozen or so other houses. I thought Jim might object but he agreed: "I get it, Mr. Zito. I don't want anyone calling the cops or whipping out their guns. My mother kept me home on Halloween."

Thanksgiving 2010

I have some catching up to do in this journal and also a number of things to be thankful for. I have employment, however many challenges it brings. If there are lonely nights, I still have more family than many people—and have had to choose where to eat the Thanksgiving feast. We will do so in Victor and Gracia's new townhouse. I am bringing the candied yams that I bet they did not know I could cook and which I hope will be a treat for Marcus, Mary, and Pearl.

Zito and Sons is doing—let us say—B+, thank you. Gabriella is fully back with some new ideas where we can "take advantage of the housing market." They actually make good sense as long as we do not borrow too much. I like working with investors on repossessed housing to provide rental homes for the fortunately employed.

Speaking of cooking, I have had two neighborhood parties for Jim and Gabriella, one with the members of the association architecture committee and spouses. Of the six other members besides myself there is a Persian, an Indonesian and an Armenian. They have become my neighbors, if not friends, and I enjoyed letting them know that Jim is my brother-in-law and father of my nieces and nephew.

The second party was mostly for my immediate neighbors including Rob and Shelley, although Rob could not make it at the last minute. I especially wanted Shelley to get to know Gabriella better. For both occasions I purchased a smoked ham that I then carved before the amazed eyes of my guests. I overheard Shelley and Gabriella in an exchange about how their fathers liked ham.

Another of my secret family members has been over to talk with me at least three times in the last month or so. The newly seventeen Katie, and a senior at Westview Academy, has discovered "the amazing amount you know about literature and poetry and things. Did you learn all that at Westview?"

I did not share with her Huckleberry Finn's rationalization that he just told "stretchers" rather than lies, but I imagine I did stretch a bit on Marcus' time at Westview. The course she is taking now is on the short story, and I let her do most of the talking about how much she liked Flannery O'Conner but was finding "A Good Man is Hard to Find" "a little weird and gruesome. Ms. Samson tells us to see if we can find 'a moment of grace' in it."

Students can, if they wish, try their hand at a short story, and Katie asked me if I had ever done one. I had to tell her that I did not remember, when I suddenly did remember young Marcus' quasi-science fiction stories in the storage box in my attic. The next time she came over I gave her my "Two for the Money," which I claimed I had written for a Westview class. I volunteered as well to read and critique her story if "you decide to try your hand,." and added, "If you end up taking a course on the novel next semester or in college, I can tell you about Joseph Conrad, who was one of my favorites. I still have my copies of *The Heart of Darkness* and *Lord Jim* I can loan you."

"I'll bet you can write really interesting stuff," was her reply.

"You can't know that," I told her.

One can also be thankful that we yet have a democracy, but the price is getting higher, which I mean as something of a joke since so much money cascaded into the November elections—a lot of it from unknown sources in the name of free speech. I guess I am old fashioned, but I thought, if one were for some candidate or issue, one ought to have the guts and the sense of responsibility to say, "Hey, this is what I am for" instead of trying to hide.

The other price is in divisiveness and the angry, name-calling rhetoric clothed in deceptive advertising and given media loud speakers by all the money. I try to see the positive in the calls for fiscal and personal responsibility. Who does not want those? But should the people who have different ideas about how best we strive toward that be called "not true Americans" and "taking our country away from us?"

Saturday December 11 2010

I confronted Katie early this afternoon. I hated to do it, but I also had to know what she knew. I was aware that I was angry with myself for not realizing how curiosity might get the better of her.

The last several years I have been keeping this journal in the second drawer of my dresser, usually under a reasonably neat pile of boxer shorts. This morning I found the shorts all arranged with the tops to the left. I have never done that. My heart seemed to skip a beat and then speed up. "What?" I exclaimed loud enough to bring Minnie in to see what might be what.

Twice a year I have a cleaning service come but otherwise am my own housekeeper and laundry man. "It wasn't you, was it, Minnie? Who else could it be?"

I saw Shelley out in front of her house trimming down her rose bushes and drove past asking if I could get her anything at Ralph's. She came over and we chatted for a moment: something about Rob being given more supervisory responsibility at Children's and that George would be home in less than two weeks for Christmas vacation. I told her that I might also need to stop by the office for a few hours.

I did go by the office but came back in under an hour, letting myself in quietly. There was no Minnie at the door. The house seemed ominously silent.

I went in to the kitchen. "Minnie," I called, and she came wagging in from the direction of my bedroom. I waited. I waited.

A toilet flushed, and Katie came from the hallway into the kitchen. "Hi, Marc. Sorry I had to use the bathroom."

"You can use the powder room, you know, whenever you want to."

"I know. I'm sorry; I should."

"Katie, I need you to tell me the truth."

"Of course." She reddened slightly, but I had to admire her apparent poise.

"Were you in my bedroom?"

"No. Why would I be?"

"I really need to know the truth. Do you ever go in there."

"Oh, probably I glanced in a couple of times. You're pretty neat. Not messy like some guys." She tried a little laugh.

"More than that, Katie."

"What?"

"Maybe you were just curious?"

"Why do you need to know. I'll be honest with you if we have to. Maybe just a little. I've never seen a man's bedroom before except my brother's and that doesn't count."

"And . . .?"

"Now who's being curious. Why should you care. There's nothing special about your things. No special guy's perfume or anything else special at all."

"Like?"

"I don't even know." She gave me a disdainful look. "You're being a kind of bully."

"No, Katie." I paused and tried to soften my voice. "It's not that I am mad or angry or want to hurt you in any way. I am not going to tell anyone. It's because I need to know the truth."

"What is truth?"

"I hope you did not learn to say that at Westview."

"You learn that truth can be relative. That's important to know. Facts can be manipulated when they are even facts."

"Did you come across a journal of mine—my diary?"

"No. What diary?"

I waited. She looked away. I held her with my eyes as her poise faltered and she began to cry. I wanted to stop the inquisition, but told her, "Katie, dear, I have my own reasons for needing to know. I need to know the truth from you. I'll even say, please. I really do have my own reasons."

She wiped her nose with the her forearm and managed to get out, "You shouldn't leave it lying out like that."

"We both know where it is kept. Have you read very much of it."

"Only a little."

I tried to keep anxiety out of my voice. "What were you looking for?"

"I don't know." She looked up at me. Maybe I was hoping you had secrets. Things you didn't want to tell anyone. Frankly, I think it's pretty boring."

"I appreciate that review. All of it?"

"I told you I didn't read all of it. I started with the last parts to see if you had a secret lover or something interesting."

"I am sorry to disappoint you."

"I don't mean that. Maybe I sort of feel sorry for you."

"And did you keep going?"

"I skipped around some. I found that awful part about the girl you played tennis with. That certainly didn't come out very well. She seemed really nice." She tried to give me an adult look combining disapproval with sympathy.

"So you read quite a bit."

"That part and some others I don't get. You seem to think you're too old and then younger like at the same time—even mixed up." She squinted at me as though she might be expecting agreement.

"Yes, well; maybe that's the human condition."

"At least yours. Perhaps you should get some help. I didn't think you handled that situation with Uncle Steve very well either. You have to be pretty naïve not to have figured out what was going on. And I get it that you didn't want me to do any body piercing and took a look at my navel. Maybe you're sort of naïve about a lot of things like sex and stuff."

"You did read a lot. It must not have been all that boring. Anything else?"

"Not really."

"Stuff about your family."

"I didn't really get that part. You seem to like us and granny. Mom says she likes you, and she told me about that time you were ready to give me some bone marrow if I needed it. Of course, I don't remember any of that."

"Or your grandfather?"

"He died when I was only two. Why do you like us so much. It seems you liked him a lot too. I know you knew him."

"Maybe I just do. Maybe because you are all so loveable, even if one of you is a little sneaky. But that's enough. Promise me you will not go looking for my journal again."

"O.K. I promise."

"And I promise not to tell on you. You and I can forget this happened."

"Cross your heart and hope to die."

"Cross my heart anyway."

"And not to put any of this in your journal?"

I laughed. "Your job now is to get out of here and take Miss Minnie for her walk."

18

New Year's Day 2011

And so on into the second decade of the new century and millennium. It certainly has begun quietly for me. No invitations to parties either—which is fine. I may walk over and watch part of the Rose Bowl with Jim: the Wisconsin Badgers versus the Texas Christian Horned Frogs. I doubt whether he even cares about this one, but it brings a lot of visitors to Los Angeles. The parade rolls by on Channel 5 without commercial interruption. Unless one pays close attention, it tends to look and sound the same as previous years, though there do seem to be even more salutes to our soldiers and sailors this time around.

But quiet is good. "It is nice to have the weekend off, isn't it, Minnie?" We are feeling quite domestic—Minnie lying in front of our fire. "Maybe getting a little old and lazy, though."

She gives me a soulful look and wags her tail just two or three times as if to say "it takes one to know one."

"O.K.; we'll go for a walk in a minute—maybe even a run." That is about the extent of my New Year's resolutions. I could eat better—get to the gym more often. But I am in pretty fair shape. Probably no more than seven or eight added pounds since I took this body on." All right, Minnie. Maybe ten."

My greatest admirer has decided that "the silver fox" looks quite distinguished. "It's sort of like your face is tanned and the blue in your eyes stands out."

"Well, thank you, Katie. Really?"

"You should have been a teacher," she tells me. "You look and sound like a teacher."

I—or I should say Gabriella and I—have, however, made one resolution. In 2011 we will hire at least one wounded veteran. Jim insists, "I can find as many as you can take. I even have a couple I'd like to help from the Vietnam War, though a lot of them are either already on or trying to get on disability. The VA bureaucracy gets so clogged with them it makes it hard to help our newer ones."

Sunday January 9 2011

There are far more deaths and wounds of Americans from gun violence and accidents in America than from all wars. Yesterday in a mall in Tucson a U.S. congresswoman (this time a Gabrielle and someone's sister and child as well as wife) and eighteen other people were shot by a mentally ill young man with easy access to guns. Six of them are dead. There is the usual flurry of pious wishes that we could have reasonable gun regulations.

Valentine's Day 2011

Neither of us has given anyone a valentine in years. I do not know whether Marcus ever did. He must have when he was a youngster.

But yesterday I did. I asked Shelly for permission and she said, "It is sweet of you." Indeed, she says it is "sweet" of me to come over every few weeks and sit with Susan in the back—sometimes on the deck—in the sun but often with sweaters, even a light blanket for Susan. Last week I brought Minnie, and Susan seemed eager to pet her—even to talk with her.

"It is sweet of you, Marc. She is so much calmer when she's with you. But you don't need to . . . well, it's kind of you. But why?"

"I think," I told Shelley, "I think I do not know why. I think maybe it is because I lost my mother when I was in high school. And she reminds me of her."

"Well, that explains something. But I don't know what.'

"I hope you don't mind."

"Mind? No. I'm glad. I think it is kind, though she doesn't know who you are. After you leave she looks a bit worried and asks me."

"I don't want to worry her."

"No. I don't mean really worried. Puzzled. She has enough trouble with Steve and sometimes I think even with me," she bit her lip.

"I'm sorry."

"I'm so sorry," she began crying in earnest. I fought back my tears.

Sunday March 20 2011

Zito and Sons (and Gabriella insists, "no name changes while I'm around. Certainly not while Daddy is alive") has hired a one-armed and one-legged apprentice electrician with two prostheses. Jim brought Manual Ramirez to us from his Walmart employment. "He's married. Has a son. Excellent work habits. And he's smart."

"So," I said, "one leg is no problem. It isn't for you. But I do not know about the arm." I tried to laugh. "I had enough trouble with two hands."

"Give him a shot. He's a learner. Can adapt."

"But there's metal in this . . . his other arm. He could electrocute himself."

"Hah. They've figured that out. Call him Sparky."

Two weeks ago Jim brought us Dwayne Richmond—a muscular, almost tough-looking African American with no legs. He has a motorized wheelchair, but mostly uses a lightweight chair he whips around in with his hands. Jim tells me he plays basketball in a wheelchair league.

We are training him to help supervise our rental repairs and problems—how to do that by computer and phone. But he insists on going around talking to people, "Get to know them; check for myself."

I already have thank-you notes from two of our residents and realize how helpful Dwayne could be in dealing with some of our access and handicap-ready issues.

Meanwhile, another kind of springtime seems to be springing up in the Arab world. At least that is what they are calling it. The Tunisian dictator was forced to flee. Egyptians were then in the streets and Mubarak had to resign. There are rumblings in Yemen, Kuwait, and now Syria. The Saudi princes are sounding nervous. Certainly hope is in the air, but it is difficult to know what we can do to help. Given our past role of supporting dictators, in standing by Israel right or wrong, and invading Afghanistan and Iraq, almost anything we do or even say will be regarded with suspicion in that part of the world.

Easter April 24 2011

There are good Catholics and bad—or at least not very good Catholics. I am afraid I fall into the latter category. I have never made my confession, or at least not in the 17 years I have been Marcus. I do not know what Marcus did before that, but I suspect not much "did we Marcus?" Perhaps when he was a boy or even a teenager he was made to go. "Father,

I took a half dollar off the kitchen counter when my mother wasn't looking." "Father, I had impure thoughts."

"Did you act on them, my son?"

"You figure it out, Father."

You can see I do not know much about the confessional. But I did go to Mass on Ash Wednesday. I was having lunch with Victor the next day and wanted to be ready in case he asked. Each year I am surprised about the crowds of people streaming in and out of church on a Wednesday, though even I can feel the emotions—the need: "Have mercy on me, O God, in your goodness." "Wash me from my guilt." And even if I cannot come up with a lot of personal guilt, there is the shared guilt that we as a people have not done enough to care for one another: "Be merciful, O Lord, for we have sinned."

But now this morning we were all at Our Lady of Grace for the Mass of Easter with the Alleluias and message of hope and new life on a splendid San Fernando Valley spring morning. Afterwards we repaired to the Woodland Hills townhouse for terrific Spanish omelettes of Gracia's. Victor, who I know is frustrated by the increasing difficulty in using his hands for minor repairs and even cutting his food, was nevertheless his more ebullient self, especially with his grandchildren. He has given up on plans to go to Haiti later in May, but nevertheless hit me up for a donation to support the school there and another to "help out Father Boyle and his Homeboy Industries. Jim's coming with me next week to see what he might do. You want to come along?"

Gracia has scheduled them for a trip to Spain in the fall. This Easter I give thanks that my father has Gracia to be with and to watch over him.

Tuesday May 3 2011

A brave and daring group of Navy Seals killed Osama bin Laden yesterday in a villa compound outside Islamabad. While claiming they had no idea he was there, the Pakistanis are apparently more than miffed. Some reports are giving credit to Obama for what Bush could not do. Yet it all seems so anti-climactic. He is dead. Is anything better? Perhaps if they had caught and killed him in December ten years ago we would not have had to occupy Afghanistan and invade Iraq. We would have had our villain.

Viewed more darkly, Osama bin Laden may have gone to his grave believing he had accomplished what he set out to do, enormously complicating and weakening the U.S. role in the Middle East—perhaps for generations, and, at the same time, harming America's economy by causing us to borrow so much money to pay for wars. And we live spending untold billions on "homeland security" with long lines and spying on one another.

Monday July 4th 2011

I think we had a better Fourth Folly at my house last year, but dear Gabriella insisted. I can understand that she wanted to show off her new home, and they do have more room in the back. In some ways, however, it was more work for me on their small grill, especially after Jim had a difficult time getting the charcoal going. "Come get your hot dogs everyone. Finally!"

And then brother Jim and nephew Marcus had some kind of water and air pressure propelled rocket that would not work and then did, spraying both Granny Pearl and grandmother Gracia on the way up. On the way down it lodged on the roof behind the chimney where it could well have stayed until the roof needed repairs. But, oh no! Marcus and Mary and then Pearl were crying and guess who had to clamber up a ladder and risk life and limb to retrieve it?

After doing a lot of the clean-up, I came home, took Minnie for a walk, cleaned myself up, poured a Scotch and jotted this—feeling suddenly very much alone.

I had no invitation from across the street, but it was as though I was expected. I soon had another Scotch in hand while Susan took my other hand and began exploring it as if to discover whose it could be. If I did not know who she was, I might have almost not recognized her. She seemed old and...wizened. I hate writing this.

George is in Senegal for the summer. I am not sure exactly what he is doing. but working in a rural hospital and studying. It is a Wesleyan program, though I gather Rob helped to arrange it.

But Katie was certainly there—looking every inch the bright and handsome 18 year-old honors graduate of Westview Academy who would be going to Stanford in the fall. Indeed, she did a good deal of the talking about "how much I love the novel and just literature generally, but I am probably going to continue with Mandarin and who knows where that will take me?" I told her a little about my trip to China and seeing the colossal Three Gorges Dam, and it was Katie who brought me my second—or, actually, my third Scotch.

Her graduation should be the last time I will ever be at Westview unless that is where Marcus and Mary and maybe even Pearl end up going. I again shook the hand of Madeline Masters, Ed.D., and told her what a fine job we all thought she was doing. Again, she did not ask my name. For whatever reason, old Philip Dorn, whom I had first brought to

Westview to teach American History—but did not know me from Adam—came up and confided, "I think next year will be her last. I know it will be for me." So Dorn will be gone, and, should Dr. Masters leave, that will be two Headmasters down since old Barnes retired—who has trouble holding his Scotch like he used to.

Sunday August 28 2011

Muammar al-Gaddafi: another Arab dictator is gone—this time a rather megalomaniac one dispatched with the assistance of U.S. and European weaponry. Libya now has some opportunity for a less oppressive and at least semi-democratic future. All the tribal divisions and surfeit of guns may make it difficult. Tunisia is struggling. Yemen is a mess. Egypt looks like it may have the best chance.

Labor Day 2011

News on the local labor front: Zito and Sons has made several new hires, one of them one of Jim's veterans, not disabled but with a history of post-traumatic stress disorder. So far so good. We are also making use of more subcontractors as, "at these interest rates," Gabriella continues to push expansion and we have bought a new apartment building and—I think we are up to four repossessed houses for rehab and either sale or, more likely, rental. I have to respect the fact that Gabriella may have a better head for business than I do. Perhaps it is Victor's influence on me, but I still would like to run a company where I can know everyone working for us. Actually, however, if someday Gabriella wants to take over as head of Zito and Sons, I think that would be fine. I can at least imagine other things I might do.

Manuel is doing fairly well. He has not yet electrocuted himself or any of his colleagues. As far as I know he has not even blown a fuse, which is better than I did with two good arms. It helps that his co-workers have taken a shine to him and that he knows how to ask for help when he needs it.

Dwayne, on the other hand, is gone. He may have left for another job, though I think it was mainly the push back he was getting—not from our clients but from our workers and staff. He could be very aggressive. Whether out of a commitment to see that the job and clean-up were done right and on time or some anger issues, or both, he could become enraged when the work "did not meet my standards and schedule." I wish I could have done a better job helping him to use all that energy and dedication more constructively.

Robert had heard that Dwayne may have developed an addiction problem with pain pills. Jim tells me that he still hears from him, although Jim is having his own labor problems—or at least challenges. Walmart clearly likes Jim, and it likes having a reputation for hiring veterans. They have Jim go around and speak at several sites where they hope to open new stores. Jim, of course, thinks they could do more and is particularly pressing them to open up more paths to promotion and for better pay and benefits generally. His bosses may accept that as a fair trade-off, but for his sake, I hope he does not get caught up in the attempts to unionize Walmart employees. I hear Sam Walton's successors can be ruthless then.

Sunday 9/11/2011

Ten years ago. I cannot watch the reruns of the planes gliding toward the Trade towers. Again the buildings collapse with their fast expanding clouds of dust and debris. And I do not know how anyone can listen to the phone calls from those soon to die or the messages sending the "first responders" (as we have learned to call them) up into the doomed buildings. The question the commentators keep asking—after ten years of seemingly unending war or terror, our longest wars in history in Iraq and Afghanistan, the Patriot Act and all the information gathering on "foreigners" and us—is whether "we are safer." The polls suggest that many think "yes" and many more are "not sure."

Sunday October 2 2011

I am myself having a hard time with the "empty nest" across the street and two houses down. I know Katie and George will return home from time to time, but they are grown and flown. I do not know how Shelley and Rob are dealing with it, but I remember how it was when Shelley and Steve were gone. One expects a door to open, a voice or noise to come from the kitchen or down the hall; instead it is quiet.

Susan is there but is herself so quiet. She is in a wheelchair—often bundled up even when it is warm—pretty much all skin and bones underneath the sweater, jacket, and blanket.

She will still take my hand and look at it, but then seems to forget she is holding it. Sometimes she smiles.

I once read that the parts of the brains of people with dementia deteriorate or become clogged up at different rates. The author of the article had learned that his mother, though she could not remember what she had read, could still read words. He found that she was able to try to play tic-tac-toe and enjoyed a simple card game like "War." I wish I had tried that with Susan. She seems past that now.

Instead I tried just quietly talking to her. I talked of Shelley and Steve. I told her a story or two of them. She seemed to listen and would smile at me and then surprised me by carefully pronouncing "Stephen" and "Shelley."

Although I hardly sing well, I tried snatches of old songs I could remember—mostly "You are my Sunshine, my only Sunshine / you make me happy when skies are gray," and darned if she did not move her head in a little rhythm with the music. I told Shelley that she might try playing her songs from one of the "oldies" stations or to see if she had some old records to play for her.

Friday October 28

Gabriella has been diagnosed with breast cancer. I cannot believe it. It is the worst rotten luck. She is frightened. Jim is acting brave and frightened. I am just stunned. "Yes, of course I will pray for you. No, we will not tell Daddy yet."

It cannot be good for someone this young to have breast cancer. But they say they have caught it early.

Sunday November 6 2011

The doctors are planning chemotherapy and, I guess, radiation, too, to see what they can do. They want to at least reduce the size of the tumor. Or maybe there is more than one. I don't know. As I understand it the plan might then be to do a mastectomy—or maybe a partial one. Damn! Damn! Damn!

I have checked her health insurance and asked Robert to do it too. We seem to be in good shape in that regard. I have heard these stories about health insurance companies cutting people off, claiming it was a "prior condition" or finding some other reason. They, of course, only want to insure healthy people. That is something the Affordable Care Act is supposed to fix. One way or another, Robert worries our company rates will go up.

Gabriella keeps coming to work. I have told her she must take as much time off as she needs to—especially when the chemo begins. She said she would, but only when she had to. I told her we would pay her anyway—only put her on sick leave if we have to. Maybe we will get something from all the workman's compensation taxes we have been paying.

Somehow we started arguing about it and then she was crying. Nice going, brother. I have to realize that coming to work is a kind of therapy for her—making life feel at least somewhat normal.

Sunday November 13

Susan and I sat out on the deck this afternoon. Again she took my hand. Again I sang to her. I told her about Gabriella. I told her a silly story about Shelley trying to make potato pancakes one Mother's Day years ago. We were quiet for maybe five minutes. She squeezed my hand and squinted her eyes, smiling at me. "Hal, is that you? Is that you Hal?"

"I . . . I love you, Susan."

She giggled and was quiet again. I sang, "I dreamed I held you in my arms / When I awoke dear, I was…" and broke off, but then went on, "You are my sunshine, my only sunshine / We can be happy when skies are gray."

As I left I told Shelley about Gabriella.

Monday December 26 2011

Shelley and Rob, George and Katie came by last evening to visit Minnie and me, to bring us some Christmas cheer: a rather large packet of turkey breast, a Tupperware container of Shelley's "Christmas pudding," and to ask "How is your sister doing?" Minnie was first interested in the turkey and then Katie who said she had brought a little piece of dark meat for her. When I reminded Katie that Minnie was not allowed human food, their disappointments were palpable, and Katie called me "a Grinch."

I was, however, deeply touched. I turned on the gas log fire and offered drinks—some Scotch to reciprocate for all I had had to drink at their house, but they said, "We're stuffed and only came by for a few minutes."

I learned that George was captain of his basketball team and thinking seriously about medical school, but "may take a year off—maybe AmeriCorps or something."

Katie likes Stanford, is going out for the women's lacrosse team, loves her girlfriends but says most of the boys are "stuck up."

I laughed. I have not heard that phrase for a long time.

"Well, it's true." She looked at me indignantly. "Ask anybody."

I told Rob that it looked as though Gabriella would be having an operation in the new year. "Maybe further exploratory. But quite possibly more. They seem to think they should treat it rather aggressively."

He inquired about her doctors and said, "I know Sprague. She's in good hands. If at some point you want me to, I could talk to him. May I ask you about her health insurance? People get pretty concerned at a time like this." His tone was so gentle, it surprised me.

"I think she is pretty well covered," I told him. "I sure hope so."

"Good. But watch it. The hospitals especially. They often do a lot of overbilling at this point. It's how they make their money."

"But," I almost plead, "The insurance will knock that back, won't it? I mean they will fight them."

"Yes. They will," Rob agreed. That is another problem Obamacare will have a tough time addressing. Gabriella and Jim just don't want to get stuck somewhere in the middle.

"Oh, brother," was all I said.

As they were putting on their jackets, Shelley offered to have me join them to "walk some of this food off." I demurred, but it was too late as Katie already had Minnie's leash and they both were headed for the door.

As we were walking together, Shelley asked, "Marc, has my mother ever called you Harold or Hal?"

"Uhmmm, She might have once. I wondered about it."

"I'm afraid she gets very confused. That was her husband's name."

"I am sorry."

'You don't have to be sorry. It's just one of those things. She loved him, but that was quite a while ago."

"Yes."

"I'm sorry for you. I think other times she knows you're just a friend."

"I could stop coming to see her."

"No. She likes you. Besides, it doesn't make any difference now. Maybe it makes her feel a little better."

"I knew him, you know. Way back when I was at Westview."

"That's right, you did. He was a good man. A wonderful father."

"I am really glad to know that. In any case of mistaken identity, it is nice to be mistaken for someone nice."

"It's funny." She gave me a little shoulder punch. "You don't look at all like him."

19

New Year's Day 2012

It is Sunday—a good way to start the new year, except the aficionados have to wait for tomorrow for the parade and football game. It is Wisconsin against somebody from the West coast. I thought it was Wisconsin last year. I cannot keep track.

The priest loved that it was New Year's Day and Sunday and wanted us to make our new year's resolutions and bring them up to the altar in our hearts. His suggestions were mostly along the lines of coming every Sunday to Mass and giving more to God.

I went with Gabriella and Jim and the kids. I wanted her to know I was praying for her, which is about all I can do . . . and maybe help with those rapscallions a little. I cannot tell how Jim is handling it, but I am going to be his friend as best I can.

That is it for 2012 as far as I am concerned. *Please God, if you do pay attention to things like this, make my sister well. It would be nice if you could improve the economy some too. The stock market seems to be doing rather well, thank you. Zito and Sons is not bad either. But a lot of people are still without jobs or stuck in jobs that pay them pitifully.*

Martin Luther King Day January 16 2012

We do not seem to do much to honor Dr. King and his dream other than to take the day off. But, I guess, that is not quite fair. The media takes note, and I am sure there are events commemorating the day, perhaps especially in Black churches. TV runs snippets of his dream speech.

On occasion we would do that at the Westview Assembly on the day following. "I have a dream," Martin would dream again, "that one day little black boys and girls will be holding hands with little white boys and girls." Of course, that is what terrified not only the segregationists but other white folk as well, while we probably had only a couple dozen or so upper class Black students at Westview. Ratio-wise it is not even that good in Mary and Marcus' second grade. "Black and white together: hell," I can imagine another Mark—Mark Twain commenting. "All those two would have to do is hold their own hands together."

Little Marcus announced to me in the fall: "Uncle Marcus, I am going to be Mark now."

"Is that with a 'c' or a 'k'?" I asked his mother.

"Sorry, Marcus. He spells it with a 'k'."

"Good idea," I told her. "What's in a name?" Actually, lots.

I have sat with Susan several times since she asked, "Is that you, Hal?" But she hardly says a thing now. She smiles and looks at me a little quizzically. It is hard to watch the tremors: her head, particularly in her lower arms and hands. When I give her my hand, she will take it with both of hers and that seems to steady her, though then I can feel her tremors on my hand and up my arm.

But Shelley told me last week that, after I left, Susan reported rather matter-of-factly, "I talked with Hal today." On the internet Web MD indicates that along with both Alzheimer's and Parkinson's-like symptoms, hallucinations can come with Lewy Body disease. "Maybe I am an hallucination," I suggested to Shelley.

"Oh, I don't think so," was her response.

Breast cancer is no hallucination. Gabriella's surgery is scheduled for Groundhog's Day, or, as I have been told, for the purposes of my prayers, it is the Feast of the Presentation, "when prayers to the Holy Family are especially appropriate." Help from all three of them would be good.

Her surgeon is still calling it "quite possibly exploratory but has warned it could result in a mastectomy or even a double mastectomy. "Just to be safe," whatever that means.

Gabriella is trying to be brave. "It may be bye-bye boobies," she tried to laugh. "Don't need 'em anymore anyway."

Jim may not feel that way, and it is hard to believe that Gabriella could. The whole thing is hard to believe . . . hard to understand, certainly for a man. Maybe it would sort of be like losing your testicles. But not even that. Susan once had an older friend who had a double mastectomy, after which I believe there was some manner of reconstructive surgery. I am afraid I did not think much about it then.

> February 2 2012: Ground Hog Day /
> Feast of the Presentation

Victor, Gracia, Jim, and I made small talk, told each other it was going to be "fine." "O.K." "These are good doctors."

Granny Pearl is with "my babies," Jim reminded himself, and, I guess, us several times. She has moved in for the duration.

I left the waiting room and took a walk on a remarkably balmy afternoon in sunny Southern California. When I returned Victor asked us to come with him to the hospital chapel to pray with him. I said I would wait in case the surgeon came to talk with us. It seemed we had been waiting an overly long time.

Dr. Marianne Nufield first told us that Gabriella "is just fine. She came through the surgery beautifully. You will be able to see her in an hour or so." She introduced herself, and we told her who we were and our relationship. Victor said, "Thank God. Thank you, Doctor."

Dr. Nufield looked at Jim as she continued, "We did do a double mastectomy. But this is good news. There will need to be some follow-up radiation, but there is every reason to hope that she will be free of any malignancy for the rest of her life. Do you have any questions?"

I certainly did: like why should we only be hoping? Why the radiation? But I tried just to make a brave face.

Instead Jim asked, "When will she be able to come home?"

Dr. Nufield smiled. "Probably in another three or four days, assuming there are no complications and she feels up to it. You will be having someone at home for her, won't you? She shouldn't be lifting things for at least several weeks."

Sunday February 5 2012

I went to see Gabriella this afternoon—prepared to tell her that everything was fine at Zito and Sons and anything else positive she wanted to hear. Granny Pearl was standing at the foot of the bed, smiling. Probably she had been telling her about the children. Gabriella was half-propped up in her hospital bed. There were still a couple of lines running out of her—one to a monitor flickering numbers and running a wavy green line. But she looked . . . perky—her short hair washed and pinned back and with a little lipstick.

She gave me a quirky smile and rolled her eyes to the other side of the bed.

"Hello, Marc."

"Carol. I…"

"I thought I might see you here."

"But I had no idea. We haven't seen each other in . . . what is it?"

"A long time."

"Gosh, you look good."

"So do you. I like your white hair."

"Silver. I'm afraid it looks old."

"Distinguished."

"Well, pardon me," Gabriella broke in. "I thought you two had come to admire me."

There are only two or three things I learned today, but I am having a hard time staying put to write them down. Minnie senses my agitation or whatever it is . . . following me wherever I go: out in back to see if the flowers need watering. I sit down. I stare at the wall. Then to the kitchen to pour some coffee. Sit down. Back to the kitchen to put some milk in the coffee. I recall the agony of that weekend with Carol, but also winning the tennis tournament and our kiss. Then back to the kitchen to heat up the coffee. Look for a different pen.

1. Gabriella says she feels as good as she looks. She has medication for the pain and plans to be home by Tuesday at the latest. And "No. None of you can see me boobless. No one can. In a few months I'm going to have cosmetic surgery. Jim has his prosthesis and I'll have mine, thank you very much. Tee, hee. I can't laugh yet."

2. Gabriella and Carol have managed to stay at least in touch all these years. "We've stayed good friends."

"But I had no idea."

"You weren't supposed to."

3. Carol has two children—a boy eight and a girl five—nearly the same ages as the twins and Pearl.

4. Carol does look good...more mature, of course, but just . . . very nice.

February 20 2012 Presidents' Day

Gabriella is doing "as well as can be expected," which I suppose is O.K. She tires easily. I brought the kids over to play here yesterday afternoon, but I also got in some good tennis on Saturday. I need to get my game back in shape.

Who will be the next president of these United States? Obama, of course, has the nomination locked up and, a few rumors to the contrary, will probably keep Biden on the ticket.

It is almost comical to watch the Republicans with nearly a new front runner of the week, pushing Romney further to the right than he wants to be, and then trying to like Mitt again as their man.

Which he almost surely will be. They have no other viable candidate. And, who knows? He may do very well in this neatly divided country of ours—especially if the jobless rate continues to be so high. This, the Republicans seem determined to make sure of until they can get reelected. In their defense, they are confident that only less government and lower taxes can make the economy grow. And they want to prove that nothing else works.

Under what I considered artful questioning, Gabriella has revealed the following: Carol is living in Canoga Park, having moved back to the area almost a year ago to take a job in Macy's billing department. "It was the only job she could get. And she wanted to be at least nearer to her parents. Darin..."

"You mean Darin from Dana Point"

"Gabriella scowled. "Darin, I guess you could say, didn't turn out that well. They were fine for a while, but he kept losing his job and was abusive—drinking, I know."

"Darn."

"For sure."

"Divorced?"

"Not yet. Her father helped her get a good lawyer. Complicated by the fact that Darin has disappeared."

"Do you think she still plays tennis?"

"Marc! How should I know? Probably not, with everything that has happened. Why don't you ask her?"

"Maybe . . . sometime."

"On second thought, maybe not. She is still pretty burned and says she's had it with men. And she doesn't exactly remember with fondness the way you treated her."

Wednesday March 28 2012

Good news, Dodgers fans. The sorry saga of Frank McCourt's divorce and ownership of the Dodgers is apparently over with a sale to a group that includes no less than Magic Johnson. Maybe even I am ready to come back and see how "dem bums" will do under new ownership.

The media keeps talking about how bad the management was under McCourt. Actually, if you like a financial success story, see this guy who borrows a ton of money for the purchase, carves the entity up into separate divisions for tax and money-making purposes, and finally must have hired a crew of clever lawyers. McCourt made out like a bandit. The total sale price is supposed to be plus two billion dollars and change. A huge chunk of that will come from the TV rights, though one can imagine the good old loyal fans will again end up paying part of the freight. Too bad that more sports teams are not owned by the fans like the Green Bay Packers.

Easter April 8 2012

There was certainly something to celebrate this morning. Gabriella looked beautiful: too skinny if anything in a kind of shimmering dress. Her hair is coming back. The "mop-up radiation treatments" are over.

She is ready to return to work. We are arguing about that. I remind her that she can work from home. We have settled on two days a week at the office and working from home.

After Mass we repaired to Marcello's for Easter brunch. I did not know that old Marcello, Victor's friend over the years, had died. But his son greeted us—yet another Mark: having shortened Marcello and spelling it with a 'k'. So that made three of us with nephew Mark: "I use a 'k' too." He then had a fist bump with Marcello Mark.

I wondered aloud to Gabriella whether we might have invited Carol to church with us.

"She's not Catholic, Marc. You know that."

"I don't remember that part. But we could call it evangelism." I tried giving Victor a wink.

"I think she's taken the kids and gone to be with her parents and maybe her brothers and their families. Her dad hasn't been doing too well."

"How many brothers does she have?"

"Two. You remember that, don't you? That's what she said made her such a tomboy."

"I did not think of her like that."

"How did you think of her?"

How indeed? The real question is why am I thinking of her so often now. Her life sounds tough; a working mother with two kids. Money has to be a problem. Maybe I just want to help . . . to see what I can do to help. With money? Be a rescuer? A father figure to the rescue?

Maybe. Who knows all one's motives? The more I think of it, I think I want to take off my clothes and feel her bodily warmth and make love to her. And I fear that is a fantasy. I had no idea that it might be a possibility again. And now I want it and I do not know how to begin. Maybe Gabriella can ask her for me. I mean maybe she could ask Carol if I could ask her to possibly have lunch or dinner or coffee or play tennis or something with me.

Steve and I played tennis yesterday. We were not great, but now I do want to work on my game again. He and Bryan have been with me since Thursday. They are over at Shelley's now, mostly so Steve can be with his mother.

Yesterday afternoon the five of us sat on the deck in the spring sunshine. Bryan told Steve he was tired of chilly, foggy San Francisco and ready to move to So Cal.

It was mostly a pleasant, family-like conversation. Susan could not join in but she called Shelley and Stephen by name and seemed content to regard Bryan and me as friends. I could overhear snippets of Steve trying to be helpful with Shelley about "Mom's future. If it gets to be too much for you, Shelley, you know I can help at least with money."

"It's not money, Steve. We've got that. She's got that. I just don't want her to be alone in some place with people in the same condition or worse."

"There are some good places."

"Reasonable, maybe. When we have to. I'm not trying to be stubborn. I love her."

"So do I."

And Steve also loves Bryan. One can tell it by the way they argue without hurting. They might as well be married. And that is what they want to do, "as soon as they get this damn hold on overturning Proposition 8 out of the way." I gather it could go all the way to the Supreme Court. I should try to follow the ins and out more closely. I told them, "I shall be glad to be there when you tie the knot." They laughed, "We're kind of knotted up already." Bryan put Steve in a full nelson.

I thought of trying to tell them how I feel about Carol, but did not know how to give it words and felt too self-conscious even to try.

Friday April 20 2012

In today's mail I received a handsomely engraved invitation to the May 14 graduation from the University of California at Berkeley—to be held at the Edwards Track Stadium—of one Nathan Provezano, He is to become a Bachelor of Science in Computer Science and Engineering. An added note card indicates that the speaker at the graduation will be Google's Eric Schmidt. I should go and tell Mr. Schmidt to hire Nathan on the spot. Nate and I have had practically no communication since he went to Berkeley, but I feel proud of him and touched that he would send me the invitation. I will tell him that in a note and maybe include a little graduation present.

George graduates with high honors from Wesleyan sometime later in May. I have no invitation, but he is my boy, too.

Sunday April 22 2012

I should be putting all my attention and energy into the business. There is enough going on as the housing market has clearly bottomed out and, with lower inventories, the price of single-family houses is ticking up. Later rather than sooner, this may have effects on apartment leases, but our vacancies are under five percent. I do not know what I would do without Robert's steady hand. I talked myself into worrying that someone could poach him, but in a lengthy conversation, he convinced me that he continues to like working with the Zitos, as he sometimes calls us. Such loyalty deserves another raise before long.

Or I could worry more about some of the skullduggery, machinations, and even atrocities that our military, the C.I.A., and diplomats have been involved in as revealed by all the Wikileaks leaks. Meanwhile pilotless drones seem a cost-free way in American lives to deal with our enemies and/or the enemies of governments we are trying desperately to prop up in the Middle East. Ongoing is the atom bomb-making in Iran, civil war in Syria, troubles in Yemen, Somalia, Libya, Iraq, Afghanistan, and with our Pakistani "allies," and, behind it all, the seemingly never ending enmity between Sunnis and Shiites. It is enough to want to make sane persons throw up their hands in disgust and give up. But we cannot, even while little we try or do seems to help. Maybe Egypt is on the track to some greater stability. That could make a difference for the whole region.

But instead my emotional energy has gone mostly into thinking about Carol and practically begging Gabriella to ask Carol if it would be all right to phone her or even email her or something. "I don't want to be a bother. I would like to help her if I could. I don't know, Gabriella. I am sure she is a different person and probably does not even want to see me. But would it not be nice if we could maybe be friends again?"

I was afraid my good sister might make more fun of me. I think instead she felt sorry for me. "You have to know, Marc, her main concern now is with those two children. You can imagine they have problems of their own too. She may not have time or personal energy for much else. But I'll ask."

Thursday April 26 2012

There is an email from Carol Dunning <carold3@yahoo.com> which I have not yet opened. I know. I should check my personal email during the day. I should be more active on LinkedIn, etc., etc. I should even "twitter."

Instead I took Minnie out and talked to her. It turned out Minnie did not understand about email and may have been jealous of Carol anyway. But I fed her and she seems fine now. I opened some boxed soup from Trader Joe's, poured it into a pan, and put two slices of bread in the toaster. But I stopped and opened a beer and am now sitting at my computer almost ready to check on the email.

I could see it was relatively short. It began "Dear Marcus." That looked nice. "Dear" is a standardized form of greeting, but it still has some tenor to it.

"Dear Marcus: Gabriella said you were kind enough to ask about me. That is good of you. A lot of my life is centered on these two beautiful children. Have a look. Carol."

One of the pictures is of the three of them and then one of each child. The captions tell their names: Dana and Danielle, which sounds to me like Darin's doing. Dana looks like an earnest eight year-old, smiling a little too hard for the camera, and though her hair is dark, Danielle makes me think of a little Carol.

Surely this is some kind of invitation to respond. But I want to say more than the children are cute. How do I tell her I would love to see her? or at least stay in touch? Should my message be short like hers or can I tell her about myself? Should I wait for a day or two? though I do not want her to think I was not glad to hear from her. I think another beer is in order.

Sunday May 6 2012

I still have not heard back from Carol. After several drafts, I thought the email I sent her was nicely low key: friendly, with a few items about how the company was doing and about young Mark, Mary and Pearl. I wrote that her children were darling and that I especially liked the picture of the three of them—omitting that I had printed it out and taped it to a cabinet in my kitchen. I concluded simply enough: "It would be great if we could see each other again sometime."

Signing it was the harder part. I typed "love, Marc" or "love, Marcus" two or three times. After all, 'love" does not have to mean that much, and we have really cared for each other. But she might have thought I was trying to get her to sign "love" back. I settled for "Your friend, Marcus." But maybe now something has put her off or she thought it did not need a response. But she ought to say something.

I have learned that she has brought Dana and Danielle up once or twice to play with Mark, Mary and Pearl. Maybe one day I could just be strolling by when they were all there.

At my computer yesterday evening I came across an article about the Encyclopedia Britannica halting its print publication after 244 years. After I thought about it, I must say I was not surprised. Even I have not consulted it in . . . I do not know how long. It is the triumph of the digital age and Wikipedia.

I imagine Wikipedia is the first place many students go now. How many trips to the library did young Harold Barnes make—sometimes to help write a school paper—sometimes just to finish reading an article I had found on the solar system or China or, indeed, the history of printing and books.

We bought (I think it was) the 11th edition for Steve and Shelley. It was expensive to us then. I loved having it—handsome in some twenty plus brown volumes in our den. I wonder what happened to them. I hope Steve has them somewhere. I cannot believe anyone would throw them away.

Sunday May 13 2012

So. O.K. I emailed Carol again: still friendly, newsy. I construed Marcus' childhood memories of the Encyclopedia Britannica and asked her if she had any. I asked her if Dana and Danielle used a computer yet. *Hi, I am here*, is what I was trying to say.

Shelley called me. They were having a mini-crisis with her mother, which is apparently coming more often. Some of it is physical—with the tremors—and I guess other issues. *Dear, dear Susan.*

She is also more often agitated and, perhaps oddly (perhaps understandably) gabbles more, if incoherently. "Among the people she goes on about is my father, Marcus. Somehow you seem to be able to calm her down."

Our favorite song now seems to be "Sentimental Journey," though I can only recall some of the lyrics. "Going to take a sentimental journey / gonna set my heart at ease / gonna make a sentimental journey / to renew old memories...I long to hear that 'all aboard'...counting every mile of track—that takes me back." But then I found myself singing, "Where are all the flowers gone? / long time passing / Where are all the flowers gone?"

"Do you remember, Susan? The protests against the Vietnam war?"

I studied her face and thought maybe she was studying mine. "When will they ever learn? / Oh, when will they ever learn?"

Monday May 14 2012

A nice email from Carol today. It was longer. She told me about her father's heart problems, her job at Macy's. She apparently likes the people but not the work that much. There is little challenge to it, though she does not need to bring the job home with her. Dana is doing O.K. in 3rd grade but his teacher suggested that Carol might have him tested for ADHD. "Dana can have trouble sitting still and paying attention to things, but I don't know that a 3rd grade teacher (maybe particularly this one) should be telling me this. And I'm not sure my health insurance would cover it anyway or our pediatrician would agree."

I had to look up ADHD: Attention Deficit Hyperactive Disorder. I am no doctor either, but I wonder too. They could have said I had it when I was eight. Probably Steve, too. Maybe half the boys in America. I will bet they do not often diagnose it in girls.

I probably will not say any of that when I write her back, but I do want to be sympathetic. I am thinking of signing it "with love" this time. That would just be honest, but maybe not yet.

May 28 2012 Memorial Day

I have not heard from Carol in nearly two weeks. I reread the message I sent her to see if it could be anything I wrote.

"I have no idea, Marc." Gabriella responded. "You know she really has her hands full. I haven't heard from her in a while either."

Gabriella is back in the office now three days a week, working usually Tuesdays and Thursdays from home. I find that I do not mind—in fact rather like it. She and I with Robert can often make a good team batting about ideas and personnel decisions, and I had just as soon feel I do not need to shoulder the full responsibility for the company.

She had a "good checkup with Dr. Nufield and Dr. Sprague. He does not need to see me again until the fall. I'm thinking of joining a breast cancer survivors' group that he told me about."

I googled "breast cancer survival rate" and found the statistics and information confusing and not presented well. I understand it has to do with age and "stage" of the cancer. I imagine that is what Gabriella and Jim have to live with—checkup-by-checkup, four to six months at a time. If one can get to five years, the odds seem a lot better. So we shall pray for five years and perhaps try myself to live better one day at a time.

I also realized I have not heard anything about the cost of the operation and all. Maybe that is good news and we can thank the doctors, nurses, hospital, health insurers, and all that this patient's share is small. Or maybe all the bills are not in yet. Or maybe it is so bad they do not want to talk about it. I am prepared to help shovel money to the health care industry if I have to. No doubt Victor is too. Or maybe we should try to hire one of Frank McCourt's lawyers.

I have found a photo of Carol and me, smiling away after we won the tennis tournament. (Truth is: I knew where it was.) If I figure out how to have it scanned into my computer, I might send it to her—maybe just by itself. Or maybe I will try to include a clever hint that we might play tennis again sometime.

Sunday June 10 2012

This is the email I received back from Carol: "Dear Marcus - I laughed to see that picture of the two champions. Goodness, I look so young. I'm afraid I haven't played tennis in years.

My big concern now is what to do with Dana and Danielle once school is out. I have some money from my parents. There must be day camps or such. I'll ask Gabriella what she does. Do you have any ideas? Carol."

So maybe the tennis gambit will not work, but here is another way to a mother's heart. I will talk to Gabriella. She has to be thinking about it, too, for her kids. There ought to be a plethora of opportunities if one has the money for it. And I'll ask Shelley. She is the gal with contacts.

Sunday June 17 2012

You cannot say that I don't do my part. I talked to Gabriella. I talked to Shelley. I called a couple of working women mothers I know through Rotary. It turns out that there are any number of school-run, park-run, church and synagogue-sponsored summer opportunities for learning, arts and crafts, sports— one that takes kids up to Ojai. I sent Carol the list and added: "If there is any way I can be of further help, please let me know." And I gave her my phone number.

Two days later I received a seven-word reply: "Thanks a whole lovely bunch, Marcus. Carol."

What am I to make of that? Perhaps what I should do is play hard-to-reach for a while, but I cannot imagine that will get me anywhere.

Monday June 18th

Today I received my first electronic birthday card by email. When I clicked on the colorful minivan at least a half-dozen clowns emerged and danced and sang Happy Birthday. The message line was "Happy Birthday, Marcus. Love, Carol."

1. How did she know it was my birthday?
2. When is her birthday? Maybe I recently missed it.
3. Is "Love, Carol" just convention on a birthday card?
4. Why clowns? Is there some message in that?
5. Why is a 44 year-old guy mooning around like this?

Sunday July 7 2012

I actually saw Carol a week ago and met Dana and Danielle. We can call it an "accident." I just "happened to be out with Minnie and came by to see if my favorite nieces and nephew were home."

Fact of the matter, whether on purpose or not, Gabriella had mentioned that "Carol and Danielle and Dana might be coming up on Saturday to play and maybe have a little picnic."

It turned out to be an easy family-like couple of hours. "Uncle Marcus" spent most of his time thinking up games and responding to the interests of five lively kids. It helped that Dana and Danielle quickly picked up from the others that "Uncle Marcus" was somebody special and "fun" and soon they were calling me "Uncle Marcus" too. Pearl and Danielle had games of their own invention and Danielle especially took to Minnie, which, after a while, was too much for Minnie, who retreated to a corner and looked at me balefully.

I agreed I could stay long enough "for a quick bite" and Carol, Gabriella, and I talked—mostly about the children and how well they played together until Mark and Dana got into some kind of a shoving match.

If I do say so myself, I was a remarkably cool, fun-loving Uncle Marcus. I left thanking Carol again for my birthday card, telling her "you have great kids. Let's get together again sometime."

To which her reply was "Sure, Marcus. Maybe next time we're up here."

I came home and fretted: How do you say "great kids, Carol, but I would like to see you without the children." "How about just coffee, just to talk." Or even a whole lunch. If we played tennis you wouldn't even need to talk with me.

And so that evening I rather blew my cool and emailed her about "just a quick game of tennis again. Or we could just hit some balls. I could sure use the exercise." After sending it, I fretted some more—this time about how lame the last line was. At least I had not said, "I'll bet you could too."

I did, however, call Gabriella and suggest we invite Carol and her kids to the Folly. "I don't think so, Marcus. I don't think she would want to come anyway," was her reply.

Otherwise the Fourth Folly seemed to be a great success. Gabriella insisted on having it at their house again, but yielded to my insistence that I hire the couple who catered for me two years earlier.

Victor was there in great form. Whatever medicine he was taking seemed to work well that day. For some reason he had decided to be General MacArthur this year. The hat was good and his aviator glasses helped; he knew how to repeat "I shall return." But otherwise I did not find him much of a facsimile.

The General did, however, quiet everyone down and announce that this was the 20th anniversary of Zito and Sons Fourth Folly. Gabriella shouted "Hurray" soon joined by the children

"Right, Marcus?" Victor looked at me. I quickly calculated that I had been to 15 or so of them. "Right, General MacArthur," I saluted. "We are free. We are independent now." Adults and children just stared at me until I added "Hooray," clapping my hands as the kind children joined in.

As I later sat out in the quiet of the distant fireworks with Shelley and Rob, George and Katie and Susan, I knew in my heart that this was the last Fourth of July my grandchildren would be together like this with their grandmother. She kept smiling pleasantly enough and once said George and Katie's names, but there is just not much of her left—so frail.

There was again conversation about moving her to a place where she could get better care. If I knew how to do it, I would have volunteered "across the street." Instead I sipped on my Scotch and used the cover of darkness to occasionally dab at my eyes.

George has signed up for a stint in a program called "Teach for America," which is sending him to San Francisco "where I'll be teaching in an inner-city high school and be able to see Uncle Steve." I had the impression Rob was acquiescing in this with the understanding that George would take a couple of pre-med courses along the way and stay committed to going to medical school.

Sunday July 15 2012

Robert tells me that we have been getting letters of inquiry from a REIT, which is a Real Estate Investment Trust. They want to know whether Zito and Sons would be interested in selling its apartment buildings, possibly even the whole company. "They could be willing to buy everything primarily to get hold of the buildings," Robert surmised. "The rental demand continues to shoot up as do leases and prices. I could see if they want to name a figure. I've done a bit of checking. Best I can tell, they're largely owned by a couple of hedge funds. Probably plenty of money there."

Gabriella's response was "No way, José. Not as long as Daddy is alive. I suppose we could find out if it's some fabulous figure, but I would much rather grow what we have here. Only other thing to do would be to take the money and start over again."

We told Robert to wait and see how interested they are.

Maybe that is what Carol is doing with me. If so, I am passing beyond frustration. I try to understand her situation, but she must be somewhat lonely too. I guess I will either have to give up for a while or at least give up on the tennis and try something else. We have now exchanged five emails on the subject on which she replies, "You don't really want to play tennis with me."

I even tried to reinvigorate her competitive spirit, to which her response was, "I'm more afraid of losing my balance than losing to you."

Saturday July 21 2012

In a movie theater in Colorado a deranged young man shot and killed 12 people and wounded over 70. "Guns don't kill people; people do." Correct: Another lonely, warped, young, white man with access to an arsenal of weapons and ammunition, killed lots of people.

Tuesday July 24

Would you believe it? Persistence—or whatever it is—gets somewhere. Carol and I have a tennis date: Saturday morning. She has someone to sit with the children. "But not for long, Marcus. For one thing I don't want them watching too much Saturday morning television." "It will be fun, but remember. It's been a long time."

Sunday July 29 2012

Out of practice maybe, but she still has a strong game. We mostly rallied from the baseline where she more than held her own.

Nor did she lose her balance much less her figure. Sure: some older, some fuller perhaps, but a very nice looking woman and just plain nice.

"That was fun, Marcus. Look at me; my face is all red."

"Me too. I mean fun"

"Thank you." She gave me a peck on the cheek. "I need to get home."

"Of course. Want to try again?"

She set her tongue between her teeth and arched an eyebrow. "We're going to see my parents next weekend. Maybe Saturday after that."

"It's a deal."

Saturday August 11

I almost do not know what to write. This hand is not fully steady. I take a sip of Scotch. I rest my chin in my hand. I smile at Minnie sleeping—her hind legs now and then quivering.

It was my suggestion that she drop off Dana and Danielle with Gabriella and Jim. I could pick her up there. I think I wanted Gabriella to know that we were at least playing tennis—and maybe Carol to be aware that Gabriella knew. It somehow would confirm that we were seeing each other. Of course, maybe Gabriella already knew.

The tennis was good. We rallied and then played several games—one going to deuce a half-dozen times. We fought over it. I won. She aced me on her next serve and waved her racquet in triumph.

I drove us back—both mopping our sweating faces.

"So maybe we should go for the mixed doubles crown again," I smiled at her.

"Don't press your luck, fella. And watch where you're going."

"That's my house," I pointed out as we drove near.

"Looks nice."

"Want to see it?"

"Why not?"

Minnie greeted her and checked her out. I showed her the kitchen (where if she saw the taped-up picture of her with Dana and Danielle, she did not say anything), living room, den, and the loggia out back and my flowers. We came back inside. "Want to see the rest?"

"Is it clean?"

"I am Mr. Neat. It's pretty big, just for me. There are two bedrooms and a sort of a study bedroom down the hall. This is the master bedroom—or at least it is my bedroom."

As I turned to let her look in, our bodies came near—our faces close.

I heard a double intake of breath. The first kiss was tentative, then more testing as our bodies came together.

By some unspoken agreement we ended up in my shower, touching, soaping one another, laughing, then drying each other—and scampering to the bed.

Afterward, we propped ourselves up. In days gone by, the man—or both of them—would now smoke a cigarette.

"You're staring at my breasts, sir."

"I am not."

"Yes. You are. They're not what they used to be. Somewhat used."

"They are gorgeous. Both of them. You are beautiful. How about my hair?"

"It's handsome. You're handsome." She was silent. She drew in and blew out a deep breath. "Well, we did it."

"I loved it."

"No problem this time." And she began to cry.

I held her until she stopped. She looked up at me and gave me the sweetest of kisses and jumped out of bed. "We can talk some other time. We'd better get up there. What are they going to think of us?"

"We could tell them we had a long match."

"Gabriella will be able to tell just by looking at me."

Labor Day 2012

Obama is out campaigning on his way to the Democratic Convention. Romney, for whatever reasons, has decided to stay home today and issue a message extolling the American "work ethic." Meanwhile, the unemployment rate is stuck at nearly 8% and a lot of Americans wish they could exercise their work ethic.

Jim tells me that the unemployment rate for veterans is closer to 6%, and he feels there is progress. "But that is still a ton of vets without work, and it's and much worse among those with PTSD. What really busts me up are the twenty-plus suicides a day—a day."

Some days I am surprised he still has his job with Walmart. He is an agitator about race and gender discrimination and says he has even spoken up in favor of some form of unions. Yet they still have promoted him twice and sent him to other parts of the country to advise. "But no Uncle Tom here," he laughs.

Actually, he does look more and more like someone's uncle. More crinkles around his eyes, and his close-cropped hair, though not white like mine, is graying. He looks like a young Nelson Mandela. He is also a good father and husband and my brother-in-law and friend.

Steve flew down yesterday—mostly to see his mother. He is staying over tomorrow to go with Shelley to check out a place called Belmont Village and at least one other further away in Santa Monica. "Shelley wants to keep mom as close as she can, to be able to visit her and keep tabs."

Steve shed a few tears last night. I wanted to put my arm around him. We had at least a couple of beers.

I told him about my new tennis partner. I told him about Carol and Dana and Danielle and that I was in love. He clanked his beer bottle on mine and informed me that "Shelley knew that something was up. She has seen a woman go into your house a couple of times—once, she said, with a couple of kids."

"Well, that old snoop."

"She always was," Steve snickered. We clanked bottles again.

Sunday September 15 2012

Cardinals 5—Dodgers 2. The Cards scored 3 in the 9th to beat the new-look and big spending Blue Crew. It was the first time Dana and Danielle had seen a big league game. They did not seem to know much about baseball, and Uncle Marcus explained a few of the intricacies of the game as well as providing them with hot dogs, popcorn, and a cotton candy for Danielle, to which Carol tried to object.

They, of course, fell asleep on the way home, and I told Carol how fond I was of them.

"I worry about them, Marcus." She fell silent. "I love them. They are my reason for living now. Whatever else, I got them from my marriage."

"That is a lot," I told her, followed by more silence.

"Maybe I could help," I tried.

After what seemed a full minute, Carol responded, "I don't know. Maybe we'd better slow down. These kids have been through a lot. I've been through a lot. You don't know what you'd be getting into."

"No. But who does? The point is that I would do it with you."

"That's sweet. But what do you know about raising children?"

"You would be surprised."

"You are full of surprises, aren't you, sweetheart?"

Sunday October 14 2012

Gabriella (with four members of her support and survivors' group), Carol, Jim and the five kids and I went on a Making Strides Against Breast Cancer walk this morning during the Breast Cancer Awareness month. The walk began and ended in Balboa Park. "I would often get my run in here," I boasted, and enjoyed describing the whole area to them. "We could go boating on the lake, kids, and look at the new children's park."

"Tennis courts," Carol noted and swung a pretend racquet in invitation in my direction.

"That, too," I swung back.

Jim needed to rest his leg after a bit, and little Pearl sweetly offered, "I'll rest with you, Daddy." The other seven of us finished the walk, and we all then drove back to Gabriella and Jim's house where Gabriella suggested Carol and I might go and have a quick lunch just by ourselves.

Instead we drove quickly back here and then took our sweet time making love. I feel like a twenty-year old in love. "I have a hard time believing you've been a virgin all these years. You don't make love to me like some beginner," Carol whispered, then sticking her tongue in my ear.

"Thank you," was my self-satisfied reply.

Sunday November 11 2012 Veterans' Day

I went with Jim to a Veterans' Day ceremony in Granada Hills this afternoon—sponsored by the local Rotary Club and the Veterans of Foreign Wars outpost. There was a color guard and a little speech, but otherwise a rather low-key event. Part of the reason Jim wanted to go had to do with the financial support the event was giving to the Wounded Warriors Project, which I had never heard of before. Zito and Sons wrote them a check as did the local Walmart.

Jim holds out little hope that Obama's reelection will benefit veterans. He thinks Congress will stay too divided and divisive.

Obama's victory surprised me in some ways. The amount of money spent on the whole election cycle was mind-boggling, the Republicans made some clever attacks, and there is still enough *sub rosa* racism in America to take parts of the country out-of-play entirely. Yet thanks to women, 'minorities'—including a lot of Asians—and young people, he pulled it off. It should settle some things—particularly about the Affordable Care Act, which one can at least hope will do something to control health care costs for a smallish company like ours. Robert tells me that we are already spending close to 20% of our compensation packages on health insurance and that the projections could soon take it up another 10%, which is unsustainable. Our only answer has been to make our employees pay more of the premiums and, in most cases, choose plans with higher deductibles, but that cannot go on forever either. I would be glad to listen if someone had other plans based on something beyond their economic theories. Pragmatism seems to be in short supply.

Monday November 12

This morning I went with Shelley "to see mother in her new digs." I found the facility clean, with a seemingly caring and even friendly staff. I can also imagine it is quite expensive and can only hope that Susan ended up with enough money to pay for it—depending on how long she lasts. "Rob," Shelley told me, "says that, although her mind and many of her motor skills have deteriorated, her heart and other organs aren't all that bad."

Susan was in a wheelchair with a group of other "residents" watching television—except that most of them, including Susan, were not. They either slept or were staring elsewhere. God, that part was depressing. We wheeled her to another area where Shelley talked with her, and I was allowed to hold her hand for a while. We then took her back to her bedroom.

On the wall over a blue upholstered chair that came from our old home was her chalk and watercolor of Hal Barnes. I must have stared. "That is my father," Shelley explained. "Mother painted it a few years before he died. Nice, isn't it?"

I cleared my throat. "Yes. Very. Would you mind if I come to see her from time to time?"

"Mind? Not at all. That's very sweet. I think she came to be rather fond of you. But I'm afraid now she may not know who you are."

On the way home I decided to tell Shelley about Carol—at first mostly so she would know that I knew she knew, but then realized I could use her advice.

"Oh, Marc," she exclaimed, "how wonderful for you." She stopped before saying "at your age." "It sounds a little complicated, but it must be so nice for her too. I had no idea."

I let her play dumb, but then added, "You might have seen her two children out in front at times last weekend. We walked Minnie, too."

"I thought I saw a couple of kids. I wasn't sure. I thought maybe they were relatives of yours or someone's."

"What I do not want to do is to offend any of our neighbors."

"Oh, poof. Not in this day and age. Anyway, it's none of their business."

"What I am hoping—not that we're sure—I am hoping that maybe they will move in with me after the New Year. I'd like to get them into the school here, too. It is . . . well, the divorce is not final yet."

"Marcus, I think that is wonderful. I can't wait to meet her. I'll bet she's really nice. With George and Katie having flown the coop, we can use some new kids on our block."

December 9 2012

I was privileged to be the driver as the four of us went to Lompoc this weekend to visit Carol's parents in their retirement home. It was a tight fit, and I thought it best to stay in a Motel 8 nearby. Nadine Campbell (also Granny Naddie) hugged me at first meeting. I can imagine something of what she has been through with Carol these past years. Grandfather Ralph, who had a career as a cardiologist, appeared younger than I thought he might and healthier for a man who is supposed to have a serious heart condition. Each night we had a Scotch together and agreed that our economy needed a lot of fixing and that most politicians were more interested in getting reelected than voting for the common good. We also agreed that the Dodgers looked set for a good season come 2013.

On the way home I taught Dana and Danielle how to make up limericks.

"We drove all the way to Lompoc
To see grans Naddie and Doc,
We had lots of fun
We got nothing done
But still we made Lompoc to rock."

That was our best one until kill-joy Mommy insisted that other people pronounced Lompoc with a long 'o'. So:

"We drove late at night to Lompoc
And early next morning awoke,
To have lots of fun
And get nothing done,
And, believe us, that is no joke."

December 12 2012

Yesterday in an elementary school in Connecticut a deranged young man—hardly more than a boy—with access to an arsenal of weapons and ammunition—shot and killed 6 staff members and 20 first graders. Those sweet little tykes. Those forever grieving moms and dads and grannys. Rips your heart out.

December 18 2012

Six health care workers dispensing polio vaccines in Pakistan were killed by terrorist assassins—probably in the name of their sect. The headline jumped out at me, along with the news that there are new cases of children's polio amid the Syrian tragedy. It had been so close to eradication worldwide. We Rotarians and others must not give up. I think we have the Gates Foundation with us now too.

20

Saturday January 5 2013

Dana, Danielle and I decided to call New Year's Day our first official day, even though they all moved in two days before. Mark, Mary, and Pearl then came over to inspect Dana's and Danielle's new rooms and to play. Gabriella and Jim approved of the rest of the house, and Shelley, Rob, and Katie joined us for a few minutes to toast the New Year and house and family.

We brought the kids' toys and Danielle's stuffed animals and their beds up from Canoga Park. Carol's china and silverware, every day flatware, and kitchen things are a welcome addition. A few items of hers and mine went into storage, and we picked out our new king size bed and linens together. And here we are.

Congress barely managed to keep us from falling off the "fiscal cliff," and Wisconsin lost again in the Rose Bowl. I guess they like the nice weather this time of year, but one would think they might give up.

On Monday Dana and Danielle begin their new school "where Mary and Pearl go, and Mark, too." They have been given the option of calling me "Uncle Marcus" still or "Mr.

Dad." "Mr. Dad has won out and, if a bit tentatively, the "Mr."
is sometimes dropped.

"The only one of us who may be a bit uncertain is you,
isn't it, Minnie?" We have had this place pretty much to ourselves for a long time. You like them, though, don't you?
There are more people to pat you and to beg from, even
if you might like to sleep more." Minnie lifts her head and
yawns at me.

Minnie and I are home alone for maybe a couple of
hours this morning as the rest have gone over to play at
"Aunt Gabriella's." It only dawned on me on New Year's Day
that keeping this journal has become a problem. I can imagine a time might come when I would try to share my history
with Carol, but I cannot conceive of it now. That day would
need to be some years away and even then I would fear she
might be hurt that I had never shared my whole self with her.

Yet, I try to convince myself this is my whole self now.
If there is another me—that me is also who I am. If every
person has another side to them, I may be better aware of my
whole self than most.

If we are our memories—in the stories of our lives that we
tell ourselves, I now have so many memories as Marcus. And
those further back have become part of all that I remember.
Personality is always changing as one grows and alters. And,
in any case, one changes personality almost daily as one plays
the roles of father, teacher, husband, brother, grandfather,
tennis player, business man, carpenter, sleeper, lover—sometimes changing clothes or doing without to do so.

All my musing and rationalizations aside, I would not
know what to say should Carol ask me, "What is that you're

writing, darling?" Or perhaps she would come across these pages in a bottom drawer—perhaps even after something had happened to me.

It may be that I no longer need a journal. I have someone with whom to share my stories, share at least many of my thoughts. I no longer need a journal to try to remember what is happening to me and sort out my feelings. Perhaps it could be destroyed, burned as all must be by time. This could be my New Year's resolution for the sake of my new family.

Yet I am not sure. This has been a kind of security blanket for me—my link to the past and what is becoming past. Perhaps I will take it to work and hide it there. What? In some brown paper bag in a desk drawer?

Wednesday March 20 2013

I feel like a sneak. I am also a bit of a liar. Having told Robert that I wanted to inspect our Sherman Oaks building, I took a quick look as I drove past and am now sitting in the branch public library where I had not been in some 15 years.

The journal notebook is in the back of the bottom drawer of an old desk in the office, and I am now writing whatever I am going to write on a sheet of paper I will add to it.

What makes the library look different are the computer stations, but even they appear to have been around for a while. More and more people are probably using tablets and smart phones and who knows what else? Or they are reading books on e-readers which, I gather, one can check out here. The two older gentlemen at the computers look like men who cannot afford their own computers and connections. One hopes there are still library visitors who check out old fashioned books—maybe even wander the stacks and shelves looking for something interesting. Perhaps I should take my journal and place it deep within the stacks to be discovered by some curious individual 10 or 20 years from now.

You can imagine I have not had much time to myself. I could wish work were not so demanding, but, whatever the economy, people need places to live. The rental market is still hot and another REIT has come knocking at our door— probably with a bunch of computer experts already figuring out how much they can raise rents, cut some jobs and salaries and benefits, and borrow against the buildings. I could show them how to do that with pencil and paper.

But I am not complaining. Work is good—certainly a lot better than no work.

That being said, I have talked Carol into taking some time off. That may sound sexist in this day and age, but it did not take much persuading. She has been under so much stress the last couple of years. I do not think she even realized. She cried when we talked about her having more time for the kids and my assuring her that we did not need to worry about money.

The divorce should come through soon, and we have agreed that she should now return to Campbell for her last name and have Dana and Danielle do so too—doing what we need to do legally. Last night she began crying again, confessing her worry that Darin would show up someday and want some partial custody of the children and maybe even try to get money: "He can smell money."

"Well, if he does, he will have my lawyers and me to deal with."

She began laughing through her tears: "You have lawyers?"

"Sure. Zito and Sons has two of the best when we need them."

She poked me in the ribs. "They don't do divorces and things. They do stuff with rentals and contracting."

"Well, then, let us just say that we contractors know how to use a back hoe and cement to make a body disappear. Remember what happened to Jimmy Hoffa."

"Who's Jimmy Hoffa? What happened to him?"

"The same thing that will happen to Darin if he shows his face around here."

"Oh, my Captain! I do love you."

And I love her, and I should get back to work. But I should also add that Victor is very much on board with this even though he has not met Carol and the kids yet—or at least has not seen Carol in—what? eleven or more years. We will have them up after Easter.

Easter was one reason I wanted to tell him about my new family. "And, Dad, I will be going to Easter services with them this year."

"Where's that?"

"Carol wanted a church for her and the children. Our neighbor suggested Valley Presbyterian where she goes."

"So, your Carol is Presbyterian?"

"No, not particularly, I don't think."

"Why don't you take her to a Catholic church?"

"She is Protestant. Now she likes Valley Pres."

"Do you go with her?"

"Yes. When I can. She wants me to."

"Glad to hear you're going to church."

"I could go to Mass, too—sometimes."

"Are you happy?"

"Yes, I am happy."

"That's what I want to know, and I want to see those new kids of yours."

Tuesday April 16 2013

I love the way Susan can still smile. I have no idea what is there anymore. I sing to her and she looks at me and smiles. Then she stares before her head falls. I tell her stories of Shelley and Steve, and she smiles and her head falls sideways and then down. I have fed her a half-spoonful of the custard from her bedside table. She licked her lips and smiled. I have told her about Carol, Dana, and Danielle, and she smiled.

Meanwhile Hal's picture looks down on us as she sits bundled up in her wheelchair and I in the wingchair that was once in our living room.

During the pomp and hymnody—with trumpets, no less—at the Easter service, I felt guilty about not having visited Susan more often., but I found myself also wishing she could see us: Carol and Marcus with their two children, sitting together and singing hymns with Shelley and Rob and Katie.

Carol Budde Campbell and Marcus Ditmar Zito are to be married at Valley Presbyterian Church. It will be a June wedding. We have already met once with Dr. Madsen who tells us he is "overjoyed" that we are new members of the congregation and "to preside at your nuptials." He asked me if I might be interested in teaching Sunday school in the fall.

"It will be a small wedding," I told Susan. "We want my sister Gabriella to be the maid-of-honor and my brother-in-law and best friend will be my best man. I know my Catholic Dad will come together with the lovely Mexican American woman he married a few years ago. You see, my mother died when I was in high school."

Carol's brothers and sisters-in-law will be there with at least some of their grown and nearly grown children. I do not imagine Ralph will give his daughter away a second time? I don't think you do that. But I know how pleased they are.

We are driving up to see Ralph and Nadine again this weekend where I will meet her brother Tom and his wife Laura, perhaps playing tennis with them. "We were a tennis family, Marcus. I just wish my Dad could still play."

Dana wants to learn to play tennis. He is getting a racquet for his birthday. "Kids are a handful, Susan. You remember? I had to admit that I had sort of forgotten. We worry because Danielle is so quiet and does not talk very much. On the other hand, Dana is on the aggressive side. When I try to discipline him, he punches his arms at me and has even hit me a couple of times. Carol thinks he should see a child psychologist. I am trying to see that he gets plenty of exercise."
Susan's eyes focused for a moment, and she smiled.

Monday July 8 2013
We had a good Fourth Folly—nicely catered again this year, while yours truly once more did the honors at the barbeque.
Then I drove the nine of us down to the Santa Monica pier for the fireworks. When Katie and Shelley found out the Lords and the Campbell-Zitos were all going, they piled into the van too. Do not tell anyone, but for this excursion I loaned myself the new company van.

The weekend gave me more time to read with Dana and Danielle. How I love to do that, especially in the evenings when they are in their pajamas. Dana and I, appropriately for

413

the 4th, are into a book about the young George Washington. Danielle often selects Olivia books for me to read.

Yesterday our doorbell rang. Carol answered, and, as she put it, "a very handsome and polite young man, who looked quite surprised to see me, asked 'does Mr. Zito still live here?'"

It was Nathan, come down from graduate school to see his parents. He came to thank me for the note and check I sent him "when I graduated—gosh, it was a year ago."

He told Carol and Dana the story of the bone marrow transplant. "When I was about your age, young fella." Afterward Carol half-stuck out her tongue and peered at me. "That must have been quite some bone marrow, fella."

"It is," I told her, "a gift that keeps on giving."

Friday August 30 2013

Today's handwriting could be challenging for someone to decipher one day. This is one of the bumpier flights I have had up to the Bay area—maybe due to some convection coming up from the coast range below.

It seems to be my year for weddings. Steve has asked me to be his best man. I do not know how they do these things— whether this makes me best man for Bryan, too, though I understand his sister will be standing up for him or next to him. I don't know what that makes her. I do know that I was flattered to be asked. I hoped Carol could come too.

"How did you get to know them that well, Marcus?" she asked.

I explained that Steve was Shelley's brother and the tennis and why Steve and Bryan would sometimes stay with me when they came to visit Shelley and Steve's mother. It was the best I could do.

Shelley is flying up in the morning. Maybe she will be standing with us too. The wedding is at Grace Cathedral. I understand there will be a lot of their friends there—quite a few more than at my wedding.

Today's paper—as on most days—is full of bad news from the Middle East. The hope that Egypt might become at least a reasonably democratic beacon in the region is dimming fast. Syria is one of history's great tragedies with the Iranians, Russians, and now Hezbollah continuing to prop up Assad, while Iran goes on enriching uranium and now plutonium, and Israel tries to inveigle or cajole or force us into some kind of military action. Meanwhile, Obama wants to "pivot" our major foreign policy attention to Asia. Good luck with that.

There is a party tonight. Is it a rehearsal dinner party? I have not heard anything about a rehearsal. Or maybe it is a bachelor's or bachelors' kind of party. Maybe I am supposed to say something—or at the reception afterwards.

Thursday October 17 2013

I do not know how much they paid for them, nor will they tell us how they got them, but Carol and Gabriella were proud-as-punch pleased with themselves to present Jim and me with 4 tickets to last night's playoff game between the Dodgers and the Cardinals. Mark and Dana made the foursome, much to the consternation of Danielle who fortunately took it out on her mother "for only getting four tickets."

The Dodgers actually hit four home runs and won fairly handily. Now they are headed back to St. Louis where they still have to win the last two in a row. Hope springs eternal, but it surely does not help to have Hanley Ramirez' ribs hurting him like they obviously do.

On the way home I told Jim about our latest buy-out offer: "For the whole company. You ready? Twenty-two and a half million buckaroos."

"Man," Jim said, "that's a lot of jack. Why don't they just make it 25? You can't turn that down."

"Oh, yes we can. If we are worth that much, we are the ones who can take it to the bank and do the borrowing if we want to. And we will still have a company to run and jobs for our employees."

"That's still a lot of money . . . a lot of money. But I'll bet that's what Gabriella wants too."

"She does. But it leaves us with trying to figure out health care for next year. I was hoping the Affordable Care Act was going to help. But a lot is still up in the air."

"Doesn't help that the Republicans have the government half shut down."

"That's supposed to end tonight or tomorrow, but who knows where we will go from there. It is crazy in Washington, especially if you are trying to run a business."

Friday November 29 2013

There was again much to be thankful for this Thanksgiving. Gabriella and Jim and their brood came to my 2823 White Oak. Victor and Gracia too. Carol baked a turkey and Victor insisted on bringing a smoked ham. Victor said grace. He included a thanksgiving for "our blessed Pope Francis, who is bringing so much hope to us, opening up the faith to be more loving and helping us again to see that the poor must come first in the hearts of our blessed Lord and his Mother and of the Church and each one of us." I snuck a peek at little Pearl who was wide-eyed watching her grandfather and perhaps wondering with me whether he would remember to say anything about the food.

He got that in, too, and we all ate too much, or at least I did.

What is less to be thankful for is this mess we are in with our health care program for 2014. Robert and I have been here for the last four hours with a consultant trying to figure out what will be best with so much confusion now with the rollout of the ACA or Obamacare or whatever we call it. A main problem is that we are right at the cusp of 50 employees. One thing we could do is to fudge or actually cut several employees or make them very part-time, but apparently now some of the requirements for companies with 50 or more employees are being postponed for a year anyway.

We looked at switching everyone over to Kaiser Permanente or maybe having a series of plans since almost everyone has different needs and compensation anyway. Robert suggested we think about just adding what we would pay for their health insurance to everyone's pay and letting them go and find their own plan on an insurance market. We may need another consultant to help us figure out what could be workable. One can then add that to the cost of health care!

It would be interesting to know what Rob is saying now. I doubt whether I want to know.

One does know what the Republicans are saying though it would be more helpful if they had their own ideas rather than just being glad to return us to all the problems we had before. My prediction is that at some point the country is going to have to come to something like Medicare for everyone. It would be at least a lot simpler and probably a lot cheaper by taking out, as Rob seems to argue, many of the middlemen in the system. But, of course, now the job market and the stock market are so dependent on these middlemen companies. I surely do not know.

Thursday December 12 2013

Two things worth reporting happened at the gym today. In recent months I have taken to heading out to what (after Bally's bankruptcy) is now LA Fitness by 6:30 on the mornings when I can. One certainly sees a different collection of people at that hour, many of them working out before their jobs, and bringing their work clothes with them. Back to that in a moment.

1. On my iPod I listened to an NPR program about Nelson Mandela and the extraordinary contribution he made, not only to the new South Africa and the end of apartheid, but to the world and the human adventure. One of the commentators asked a confidant of his why he had not been bitter and angry after 27 years of imprisonment. The confidant responded that personally Mandela was bitter, but had concluded that he could not carry that over into his public life and service. That is what I found most extraordinary.

2. I was fairly sure I recognized an older gentleman who comes to the gym at this hour—balder and, no doubt, moving more slowly than in the past. I thought he could have been a friend of the Barnes.

I may have glanced at him too often, trying to remember, for this morning he began a conversation by asking me if I came to the gym frequently. We ended up introducing ourselves. When I asked what he did, he told me he was retired but still doing some writing.

"What kind of writing do you do?" I asked.

"Oh, various. It used to be mainly history and theology. Now more poetry and possibly a novel."

"Really. That's interesting. I used to read novels, even to teach . . . or at least want to teach. Maybe we could talk sometime."

"Sure."

"Coffee?"

"I'll do you one better. How about breakfast. I'll even buy. And I have the time."

"That's good of you. When?"

"Today? I like my breakfast—my favorite meal."

And he did: a bowl of fruit, a poached egg, bacon, and rye toast with some marmalade he had brought in his own jar. "Ones they have in restaurants are too sweet. You do any writing?"

"Some," I answered.

"I was guessing that is one of the reasons you wanted to talk with me. What kind of writing do you do?"

"Mostly a kind of journal."

"Good for you. I tried to keep a diary for a while. Never could stay with it."

"Actually, in a way it is someone else's diary."

"Now that has to be odd. You must be a writer with a lot of imagination."

I took in and blew out my breath and tried to sound confidential. "Did you know Harold Barnes?"

"Indeed. He was my neighbor for several years. Then his wife lived there for quite a time after he died. Nice people. How in the world did you know that?"

"I was pretty sure I remembered seeing you talking with him once."

"You a relative?"

"Not a blood relative, but in a way, and I came to know him fairly well. It is his diary or journal I took on. And my own too."

"Barnes died right in the very gym where we were."

"I was there when it happened."

"Really? That's remarkable. You were the young guy who threw up?"

"You were there too?"

"Poor guy. He was only in his sixties and had just retired. So then you tried taking over something of his journaling. I'm not sure how you would do that. Maybe, for whatever reasons of yours, assuming aspects of his perspective on life and what do we say? His personality or mindset? And living and writing as though you were him. I'm just guessing here."

"Well, I . . . he . . . what happened is actually hard to tell. So I have a rather odd favor to ask you—sort of one writer to another."

"Try me."

"Let me explain. I would like to ask you to keep the journal for me. My problem is that I got married recently. That's not the problem, but there are things in the diary about my past life I think might be difficult for her. I don't mean anything salacious or…"

"Too bad," he broke in.

I laughed back, too, trying to lighten the mood. "Since then I have been storing it in an office drawer, occasionally adding to it or sticking in pieces of paper I have been writing on."

"How big is it?"

"It is getting up there. I'm not sure. It is almost twenty years of . . . memories, reflections. What I would like to ask you is to keep it for me. I am worried, for one thing, that something might happen to me."

"At my age it is more like something will happen to me."

"I have tried to think about what should be done with it. In a sense, it may have served its purpose. Then you could just burn it."

"I'm not a book burner. But tell me more. Sounds like it is hand-written? That might be tough for these eyes."

"I'm afraid so, but, except maybe for a few places, I believe my hand-writing is fairly legible."

"Both, you mean? I thought you said some of this was from a journal of Barnes."

"That is why you should read it."

"I'll be inclined to apply Occam's razor and assume you are the one who is quite the story-teller, Marcus. You would have to persuade me that you didn't imagine the whole of it."

"Do this, if you will. Put a big note on it with my name and address, indicating that if something happens to you, it is to be returned to me. Maybe it should never see the light of day. But, if you will help me in this way, you can read it. Then maybe we can talk about what, if anything, to do with it. I would probably like to add a few more pages. I could bring those to you at some point."

"Tell me. Is it mostly real or at least a good bit of it made up?"

"You are a writer. A lot of it is what happened, but you know, however real things seem to us, we still have to shape them into some kind of a story."

"All right. You have this reader hooked. And I may see you again from time to time in the gym. I ought to be careful who I talk with there."

3. I should add a third item: Christmas presents? I do not know what to give Carol. I have two children to delight on Christmas morning. And Carol says she wants to send out at

least a few Christmas cards. I have not done Christmas cards in years and years.

And I feel a need to give something to Susan. I guess Christmas will mean nothing to her now. Rob does not think she can last that much longer. However good much of her life has been, this last stretch now seems so cruel. I may bring her some flowers. She loved flowers.

21

Friday January 3rd 2014

Our Christmas tree is still up. Dana and I have promised to have it down by the weekend. Carol had a few ornaments but we needed to buy others. When Hal Barnes left us, he and Susan had a surfeit of ornaments. Some of them went to Shelley, I know. I can wonder what happened to the others.

It was a festive season. My first with a family in our home. Healing is taking place with all four of us. I am in love with them all. Danielle and I—with some help from Carol—watched most of the 125th Rose Parade on our big screen television. One of the biggest hits for me were the several Beatles' songs. Indeed, the media in general could give the impression that the biggest event of 2014 will be the remembering of the Beatles invasion of America 50 years ago.

When Jim came over with the kids and Gabriella to watch the 100th Rose Bowl game, it became my duty during the half-time ceremonies to explain the phenomenon of the Beatles to the young ones. I amazed them and all the adults by being able to remember some of the lyrics to the "Yellow Submarine":

"In the town where I was born / lived a man who sailed the sea / and he told us of his life / so we sailed on to the sun." I then taught the kids to sing with me: "We all live in a yellow submarine / yellow submarine / yellow submarine."

Somehow this led to an argument among the adults as to who remembered the Beatles better, which I attempted to trump by reminding them that "none of you were even born when the Beatles first came and were on the Ed Sullivan Show and all that." This earned me a stare-down from my sister and, "so I suppose you were."

Carol brought us back to a happier mood by looking up on her phone the words to "All you need is love" and singing to us in her sweet voice: "There's nothing you can make that can't be made / No one you can save that can't be saved / Nothing you can do but you can learn / how to be you in time / It's easy," and then we joined in: "All you need is love / All you need is love / All you need is love, love / Love is all you need," To this I added a "Yeah, yeah, yeah" and Danielle, followed by Pearl, clapped their hands.

On this note of "how to be you in time" I have made a New Year's resolution to bring this journal to some manner of conclusion. I do not want to continue to write what I cannot share with Carol. Who knows what the year 2014 will bring? It looks like severe drought for one thing. Great weather, while California desperately needs rain. And surely there will be some surprises.

Friday January 31 2014

"When will they ever learn? Oh, when will they ever learn?"

"You're singing, Marcus. What are you singing?" Carol startled me last night as I was watching a documentary about Pete Seeger.

"He died a couple days ago. He loved it when he could get people to sing along." I wanted to tell her more, but she sat down and we watched together: his support of workers and unions, his refusal to share his political views with the House Un-American Activities Committee on the grounds that this was forcing him to do something un-American, his gift of "We Shall Overcome" to the civil rights movement, "If I had a hammer" and his opposition to the Vietnam War ("Where have all the soldiers gone? / Gone to graveyards everyone"), the cleaning up of the Hudson River, and his singing with children—never giving up hope for them.

I turned the TV off as the last notes died, although we could almost hear him still singing.

"I recorded it," I told her.

"What a voice," Carol said, "and could he play that banjo, and the guitar too. I can see why Joan Baez worshipped him. I barely remember any of that."

"But it does make you want to sing, doesn't it?" I replied. "I loved our watching it together."

Monday March 3 2014

Jim came over early last evening, telling me he had "what I think is a classy idea I want to try out on you." He turned down my offer of a beer as we caught the last minutes of the news before I clicked off the TV.

"Now I guess it's Ukrania or the Ukraine or whatever we're supposed to call it. One thing after another," Jim muttered dolefully.

"No war or at least no big war," I told him. "Let's hope Putin and Obama and the others are too smart for that. That country is poor enough anyway."

"They still could be playing with matches. History is full of smart people making mistakes when they feel their country's pride or honor is at stake."

"Your right about history, Jim. The danger for Obama is that some of the politicos and pundits will try to make hay by telling the country he is not strong enough—not tough enough. The fear of that helped get poor Lyndon Johnson deeper and deeper into Vietnam and pushed George W. into Iraq. It takes a really strong president to push back and avoid war: Eisenhower for one, and even Reagan when the chips were down, maybe because of his tough sounding rhetoric."

"I suppose," Jim responded. "Maybe. We still gotta stand up for something."

"Exactly. But I'm sorry. Tell me about your classy idea."

"Well," he began tentatively, "I think you may like it. Actually you're one of the guys who will get it. I don't know what to call it yet, but it's vets as personal trainers—even some of the amputees, maybe especially some of them. They could be really good at it."

Although he twice interrupted to remind himself that he wanted to get home and help put the children to bed, he spun the project out. "I've been thinking about it for longer that I want to admit. It won't let me go, and I'd love your help. Just like the old days."

"You would not give up your job with Walmart?"

"No. No. Couldn't afford that, and we're making some progress. They like me or at least put up with me. This would be more like a sidebar for a while. I've even got the start of a possible first group lined up. Our job would be to help them get the training and education and use some old contacts to find them work. Like you remember Randy?"

"Unforgettable."

"Then we would keep them together for a while and sort of be a support group and maybe help recruit some new ones. We could put together an advisory board to guide them and raise money to help with the education part and to keep going at first . . . maybe from Rotary; maybe Dad could help us from Catholic Charities. Maybe the company? Maybe we might even get some government money. I could try for a grant from Walmart."

"It's quite an idea, Jim."

"I'm sort of hoping that several of them might get further education and become physical therapists too."

"Does begin to sound something like that onetime business idea of ours, except that your veterans will be doing the actual work."

"That's it. They would have jobs and even a kind of profession."

"I like it and your enthusiasm."

"Yeh, I got that. I also need my old buddy to help a bit."

"I don't like the 'old' part. Let's say 'veteran' since I am one too. The rest of it sounds like an idea worth chasing. We had better stay small to begin with. Maybe keep it small to make it work."

"You'll help?"

"I will, veteran buddy."

Monday April 28 2014

Susan slipped away on the day after Easter. There is hardly any other word for it; mentally and physically there seemed to be so little of her left. I believe—and I guess I pray—she was pretty much pain-free in her last days.

With sun streaming through the stained glass in the nave of Valley Presbyterian her memorial service took place on Saturday morning. George read well the passage about love never ending and being the greatest gift from the Corinthians letter. Katie read a poem which ended "I'd like to leave an echo whispering softly down the ways / of happy times and laughing times and bright and sunny days / I'd like the tears of those who grieve, to dry before the sun / of happy memories that I leave when day is done." She had trouble getting through the last lines, which, of course, caused her relatives to dab at our eyes before the tears would dry. Dr. Madsen extolled "this lovely and devoted member of our congregation—for nearly 44 years, whose husband was also commended to God in this very sanctuary some years ago." I may have recognized several of our former neighbors in the little congregation—one with a walker.

Perhaps others might have come had they learned about it. Or they may have moved too far away or been too infirm to come. That's the problem with dying old: too few left to mourn.

At the end, and perhaps because it was near to Easter, we sang, "The strife is o'er, the battle done / the victory of life is won / the song of triumph has begun," which, for whatever reason, did not help my mood, as looking about I realized that "some years" hence those sitting about me— maybe Shelley or Steve, Rob or Bryan—or even I could have another memorial service at Valley Presbyterian. Or, pray God, it would not be Carol, sitting next to me and sometimes glancing toward me perhaps to wonder what I was thinking, sometimes holding my hand.

Yet at the close of the service as we all hugged—I even with Rob, and shook hands with acquaintances, including the man to whom I had entrusted the journal, I found a sense of . . . I am not sure: of serenity with all this mortality and the passing of time, of having come together . . . of home.

Saturday May 24 2014

Just up the 101 in Isla Vista a lonely 22 year old, blaming his unhappiness and sexual frustration on women who rejected him and writing that having a gun made him feel important, killed several innocent young people and randomly wounded a bunch more. Another school related slaughter, but we may otherwise have been lucky. Even with California's somewhat better controls, he had two additional semiautomatic handguns and 400 lethal rounds of ammunition with him when he died. Maybe someday we could be like Canada with many guns, but sensible laws and far fewer per capita gun deaths. That is a hope for our children.

Thursday June 19 2014

At my birthday party last evening, we told Dana and Danielle that they were going to have a baby brother or sister. It was more Carol's idea than mine, although I will say that I happily did my small part.

Carol already knows if it is a boy or girl, but I have told her I am old fashioned and want a surprise. It is surprise enough that I will be a father at the age of 46, to which Carol kindly responded, "There are a lot of older fathers these days." I am looking forward to telling Grandfather Victor and Aunt Gabriella: "I did it."

Danielle says that "if it's a boy we should name him after Prince Harry. I think he is a lot of fun...and he is a prince." I told them that I never thought I would see the day when "Harry" could be a popular boy's name again. Carol explained to us that "Prince Harry's real first name is Henry."

"Then we could call him after Harry Potter," Dana chimed in.

"Harry is also a nickname for Harold," I informed them. Wouldn't that be something? But who knows what will happen in this life of ours?

Editor's Note

I imagine it is because I may be the only one who has come to know both Harold and Marcus that I was asked to do my best in transcribing the journal. The single request was that I alter several surnames and settings to protect loved ones. Otherwise I was free to present these reflections much as they came to me and to publish if and when it seemed good to do so.

Frederick Borsch
Los Angeles
August 2014

Made in the USA
Charleston, SC
08 September 2014